TO STEAL A THRONE

GABI BURTON

A Rock the Boat Book

First published in the United Kingdom, Republic of Ireland and Australia by Rock the Boat, an imprint of Oneworld Publications Ltd, 2026

Published by arrangement with Bloomsbury YA, an imprint of Bloomsbury Publishing Inc

Text copyright © Gabi Burton, 2026
Cover art copyright © Elena Masci, 2026
Map art copyright © Sara Corbett, 2026

The moral right of Gabi Burton to be identified as the Author of this work has been asserted by her in accordance with the Copyright, Designs, and Patents Act 1988

All rights reserved
Copyright under Berne Convention
A CIP record for this title is available from the British Library

ISBN 978-1-83643-237-1
eISBN 978-1-83643-238-8

Book design by Jeanette Levy
Printed and bound in Great Britain by Clays Ltd, Elcograf S.p.A

This book is a work of fiction. Names, characters, businesses, organisations, places and events are either the product of the author's imagination or are used fictitiously. Any resemblance to actual persons, living or dead, events or locales is entirely coincidental.

No part of this publication may be reproduced, stored in a retrieval system, or transmitted, in any form or by any means, electronic, mechanical, photocopying, recording of otherwise, or used in any manner for the purpose of training artificial intelligence technologies or systems, without the prior permission of the publishers.

The authorised representative in the EEA is eucomply OÜ,
Pärnu mnt 139b–14, 11317 Tallinn, Estonia
(email: hello@eucompliancepartner.com / phone: +33757690241)

Oneworld Publications Ltd
10 Bloomsbury Street
London WC1B 3SR
England

Stay up to date with the latest books, special offers, and exclusive content from Rock the Boat with our newsletter

Sign up on our website
rocktheboatbooks.com

Praise for *To Steal a Throne*

'Packed full of lies, schemes and betrayals, this fast-paced, twisty story will keep readers guessing until the last page. I love the characters Gabi Burton has crafted – sharp, ambitious and deliciously flawed, each one hiding secrets as deadly as blades and willing to risk everything for power.'
Kika Hatzopoulou, bestselling author of *Threads That Bind*

'Burton has done it again! *To Steal a Throne* is the perfect mix of politics, magic, and romance, with a ruthless heroine at its core... A thrilling start to what promises to be a captivating fantasy duology.'
Kate Dylan, *Sunday Times* bestselling author of *Until We Shatter*

'A deliciously heart-pounding cocktail of deceit, ambition, and magic with the most tantalising enemies-to-lovers slow, simmering burn. Unputdownable!'
A.Y. Chao, #1 *Sunday Times* bestselling author of *Shanghai Immortal*

'With a propulsive plot, astounding twists, and the most delectable tension between rivals to lovers, *To Steal a Throne* left me completely enraptured.'
Pascale Lacelle, *New York Times* bestselling author of *Curious Tides*

'A clever, compulsive read full of twists and compelling characters. Perfect for fans of YA, you won't want to put it down.'
Rachel Greenlaw, author of *Compass and Blade*

'With political intrigue and worldbuilding as alluring as the slow burn romance, this book is effortlessly entertaining and full to the brim of earned female rage.'
Hayley Dennings, *New York Times* bestselling author of *This Ravenous Fate*

'An immediately immersive story entwined with an addictive, steamy romance.'
Terry J. Benton-Walker, bestselling and award-winning author of *Blood Debts*

'Gabi Burton is the queen of dark fantasy.'
Kamilah Cole, bestselling author of the Divine Traitors duology

'*To Steal a Throne* is my favorite fantasy read of all time!'
N.E. Davenport, *USA Today* bestselling author

'Smart, well-paced, and expertly crafted.'
Rena Barron, author of the Kingdom of Souls series

'Clever, conniving, and deadly.' AM Kvita, author of *An Unlikely Coven*

ALSO BY GABI BURTON

Sing Me to Sleep
Drown Me with Dreams

*For Black girls who smile
when they want to scream*

N

QUETLANA

MOUNTAIN CREST

HAVELLEN

THE COLLAR

WIDOW'S HALL

MOUNT SAIDU

OPHERA

VIRDEI

TSHIRA MINES

IVENNA
CAPITAL

PETRUVIA

- FARVELLE
- ALOCETTE
- ISKADA *CAPITAL*
- SYLBAR
- SAFELL
- LEONI
- TWILROQUE

SUTORIAN SEA

CHAPTER ONE

THRONE OF LIES

When we couldn't afford wood for the hearth, my mother's lies warmed our home.

She lied constantly, about everything: promised we had enough coin to survive the long, cruel dark seasons at the base of the mountain; swore to the stars we weren't slowly starving to our deaths; insisted a better life awaited us, just around the corner . . .

My mother was a liar. Fortunately for me, so is everybody else.

In this tiny room, I keep one hand pressed to a wall of tshira. It's black like pitch, streaked with bands of red and bronze, and so maddeningly cold, it sets my teeth on edge. My free hand curls around the sparrow-shaped tshira talisman dangling from my wrist. It emanates faint warmth into my hand—there's a lie trapped inside.

At my coaxing, the heat of the lie flows from the trinket and into my palm. Magic hums through me.

I bask in the sensation, like one of those rare moments of sunlight we get in the dark season. The warm, buzzing feeling starts in my fingertips—where my skin touches the talisman—works its way up my arm, and pulses from my other hand, still pressed to the wall.

Magic smooths out a panel in the rough surface. It lightens

to a translucent white, frosted over like a screen of ice that peers into the adjoining room, where two people sit on opposite ends of a long table. The window is one-way, so neither of them can see me, and only one of them knows I'm here.

"You haven't answered my question, Ms. Harcot." Luc faces the door, arms folded to appear stern. Even while sitting, he's tall enough to look imposing. He has thick, black coils of hair, skin dark like ochre, and deep-set brown eyes identical to my own. "What is your relationship with Honorate Jasper Nox?"

His chair is high-backed and packed with royal-blue cushions that make it almost comfortable, if not for the spine. It was hand selected (by me, of course) because it's rigid like a steel rod. Sure, it makes the chair a wreck on the back, but it also makes it impossible to slouch. Lucien Kyler might be Praeceptor of the Republic of Virdei, but he has the posture of a dying blytheweed flower.

"I beg your pardon, sir." Pelene Harcot sits on a three-legged stool at the other end of the table. She's tiny, and her voice is even smaller than she is. Her skin is light like sand, eyes dark like tar, and hair thick and auburn hued like sagegrass. "I'm not sure I understand the question. I used to work for him. That's all."

Heat.

Magic, fresh from its source, is hot. When it courses through me, its intensity is like a flare set alight in my belly. The flames of Pelene's lie flood my veins, hot, sudden, and fervent.

"I see," says Luc. "So, you claim you're *not* having an affair with him?"

Panic flashes over Pelene's narrow face. Seconds flit away as she scrambles for a believable answer.

Her silence grates my restless nerves.

I have many skills. Patience isn't one of them. Especially not now, the day before the most important vote of my life.

Finally, she says, "No." Her trembling voice gives her away, even before the heat of magic gathers in the pit of my stomach. "There's no affair."

Stars in hell, she's an awful liar.

I shove the magic from Pelene's poor attempt at deception out, to the torch over her shoulder.

It shudders and, for a flicker, glows brighter.

Luc glances at it, nods, and looks back to Pelene. "Ms. Harcot, do you think it's wise to lie to your Praeceptor?" His words are firm, just as I taught him. But his tone is feather soft.

I make a mental note to scold him for it later.

Not that it matters. Luc's tone must be convincing enough for Pelene, because her body wracks with shivers. She strokes the glimmer of gold on the inside of her right wrist in the shape of a crescent moon. A tattoo by name, brand by function. A bright and permanent warning to all that she's not from here. That she doesn't belong, and she never will. "I-I'm not lying."

More heat roars through me. I make the torch leap higher, nearly singeing the ceiling.

Luc's eyes follow the flame. "Think carefully about your next words," he says. "If they are untrue, swallow them and try again."

"I—" Her throat bobs. "Yes. We had an affair. It was brief."

The flame rises with the heat of more lies.

Luc sighs. "Ms. Harcot . . ."

Her sallow cheeks flush. "I'm sorry, sir. We've been seeing each other for the past four years."

"His wife doesn't know?"

"No, sir."

There's no heat this time. She's telling the truth.

A slow smirk settles over my face. If Nox's wife doesn't know, then we have leverage.

Pelene's shivering intensifies. Her dirty nails are chewed to the beds, and her clothes are dotted with patches. Worse, they're *thin*—practically a death sentence this high up in the mountains. "I'm not a bad person, sir. When I met Jasper, I was a servant in his home. He was sweet to me. He promised me he'd leave his wife. But as time went on . . ."

"He didn't," Luc finishes for her, eyes soft with sympathy he should know by now to disguise.

Pelene looks sheepish. "I'm not proud of it, but I promise our relationship never affected his work, sir. Or his votes."

No flare of magic accompanies her words.

It's disappointing. A girl who seduces an Honorate to sway his power in her favor is clever. Rare. A girl who falls for a sleazy Honorate's false promises is as starheaded as my mother. Worse, she's common as snowfall.

The Republic of Virdei is ruled by a council of twenty men called the Honorate. Leading them and all of Virdei is the Praeceptor. Once his five-year reign ends, he's meant to step down, making way for his successor, never allowed to try for the throne again.

At least, until tomorrow, when the Honorate cast their ballots to decide if the Praeceptor can vie for the throne as often as he pleases. I've secured nearly all the votes I need to ensure the end result is yes.

Luc *will* be Praeceptor again. I can't afford any other outcome.

Luc pushes back his chair. "You're free to leave, Ms. Harcot. Thank you for your time."

Pelene stares at him in shock for a few moments before

scooping up her jaw and scrambling to her feet. "Th-thank you, sir." She starts for the door.

Perfect.

Close enough, anyway. Luc performed well. As always, I have a few notes for improvement, but overall—

"Pelene," says Luc suddenly.

Stars in hell.

Pelene stops, looking petrified. "Sir?"

"He's never going to leave his wife. You know that, don't you?"

Her fear flees, and her shoulders sag. "Sometimes."

The resignation in her tone makes my heart twitch. Her words are as familiar as they are unremarkable. Deluding herself just as my liar of a mother used to.

I shake myself, discarding the thought along with the flicker of sympathy that rears its head in my heart.

Well, I try. I'm not wholly successful. I never am when it comes to memories of my mother.

Pelene should leave now, but she wavers. "Sir? May I ask you something?"

Say no, I mentally chant. I know he won't.

Luc nods. "Ask."

"How did you learn of my relationship with Jasper?"

"The Shadow Queen."

Pelene's dark eyes widen. "We were discreet. How did she—" She swallows nervously. "You don't think she's going to write about this, do you?"

"I have no idea, Ms. Harcot. I don't control the Shadow Queen. Nobody does. You know that."

She shudders. "Of course. Thank you, sir." She's shaking harder than ever as she rushes from the room.

The Shadow Queen of Widow's Hall is as infamous as

she is legendary. She lurks in the shadows, collecting secrets of the powerful men who rule Virdei. Anyone curious about the lives of the elite can find the sordid details in her column. For many, the Shadow Queen is a champion of virtue, holding the Honorate accountable. She publicizes the wicked deceptions of those in power and exposes the truth, no matter how scandalous.

But those whose secrets she gathers like roses for a crown of thorns know the truth: the Shadow Queen does not work for the people. She does not care about justice or truth. She operates for herself. She is more than willing to keep anyone's secrets out of the public eye—for a price.

No one knows who the Shadow Queen is. She first surfaced three years ago and swiftly rose to infamy.

Some believe she's the bitter wife of an Honorate; others that she's a scorned lover, hungry for revenge; still others believe she's a servant in Widow's Hall, spying on her employers.

They're all wrong. The Shadow Queen is me, and I am none of the above.

Widow's Hall is about as high up as you can climb without freezing your nose off. The view from up here, from the stone balcony hanging off Luc's private study, is the most breathtaking in the Republic.

The top of the mountain is illuminated by three beacons—massive torches that rise from the roof of Widow's Hall, magicked to burn year-round. Below me are dense trees lining the stone roads paved into the ice of Mount Saidu. It's midday, but it's the dark season, so the sky is the color of midnight and blanketed with thick gray clouds that drop snow lazily through the air.

I tilt my head back, enjoying the soothing sensation of snow melting against my cheeks, when the balcony door whines open behind me. Luc has joined me.

With a parting look over the mountain, I turn, half smiling—

My movements falter.

It's not Luc standing behind me. It's a tall, stern-looking man and a short, smug-looking woman. Both familiar, both unwelcome.

My stomach drops into my feet. My eyes dart around, searching for an escape. Nothing. Not unless I want to take my chances and hurl myself over the side of the balcony.

It's tempting, but I straighten my spine and fix my expression. "Mathson, Yelina." I try for a polite smile. "I didn't realize we were expecting you. Luc isn't here."

"We know. We're here for *you*," says Mathson.

Few things scare me. My father and stepmother wanting a private word makes fear cling to the back of my throat like a dry biscuit soaked in honey. I try to swallow it—it sticks the whole way down. "Oh?"

"The time is coming for you to prove I wasn't wrong to open my home to you, Remira."

It's an impressive rewrite of history. After I lost my mother, Mathson didn't let me come live with him out of the goodness of his heart. At ten years old, I arrived on his doorstep alone and starving, with no home or mother to return to. I begged him to take me in—after all, he was my father.

"You're either useful to me, or you're nothing," he'd said, before slamming the door in my face.

So, I made myself useful. Stole a secret of an Honorate for Mathson to use as blackmail. I proved my worth, and he let me stay. I've been proving it ever since.

My thumb traces the golden tattoo on my inner wrist. "If this is about tomorrow's vote—"

"Of course it's about the vote." Yelina cuts me off with a stern glare. "I expect my son to be the longest-reigning Praeceptor in history."

"He will be."

"For your sake, I hope so." There's a dark gleam in her eyes. She's a petite force of a woman. Shorter than me by a head, and skinny, yet still terrifying. "The decurio are always looking for new soldiers. I'm sure they'd be interested to learn you've kept your gifts hidden all these years."

My breath mists from the freezing air, and my fingertips lose sensation from her chilling threat. The decurio, the Republic of Virdei's military force, entirely comprises those of us with magic. All magic users are required to report themselves. Failure to comply can result in anything from imprisonment to forced service.

Some dream of joining the decurio. I know better. Opheran soldiers are expendable. It's no secret we receive the least training and most dangerous assignments compared to those born in Virdei.

My mother knew a man who turned himself over to the decurio. They trained him for a week and sent him off to die just two days later. There was no announcement or service following his death. The only person who mourned him was my mother.

My tattoo marks me as Opheran. It doesn't matter that I'm the Praeceptor's sister—an assignment in the decurio would be my death sentence.

"The order will pass," I say. "I guarantee it."

There's a rattle from inside as Luc enters his study. Mathson and Yelina linger just long enough to give me one last withering scowl, before stalking inside to greet him.

I take a moment. Breathe deeply, steep myself in the freezing air, allow it to cool my temper and settle my dread, before following them inside.

"Lucien." All the animosity of our exchange is melted away as Yelina stretches up on tiptoe to embrace her son. "We came by to extend a personal invitation to you and Remira for dinner the day after tomorrow. To celebrate your victory."

Luc chuckles. "The order hasn't passed, Mom."

"*Yet.*" Yelina backs away from Luc and slings a casual arm over my shoulder. Still smiling, she gives a squeeze. Not hard enough to bruise, but enough to remind me that she could. "You'll remember what we discussed, won't you, Remira?"

The feeling of her hand on me makes my body itchy and tight, as if I no longer fit in my skin. I want to wriggle out of it, burn it off—anything to get her to stop touching me.

I force a smile. "Couldn't forget if I tried."

I don't breathe until she and Mathson say their goodbyes and finally leave.

Luc settles into the seat behind his desk, looking at me expectantly. "I assume you have notes?"

I always do. I write his speeches, arrange his haircuts, and spend all my time coaching him for this position I stole for him. "You went soft toward the end." I slide into my role as though tugging on an oversized sweater. "Your tone was too kind, and you used her first name."

Luc groans. "It slipped out. I felt bad for her. What was I supposed to do? Be rude?"

"We've talked about this." I keep my voice even. "When you interrogate someone, you're not Luc, you're—"

"I know, I know. I'm Praeceptor Lucien Kyler. But that isn't what I asked."

"Yes," I say flatly. "Be rude."

"It's not easy for me, the way it is for you." He runs a hand tiredly down his face. "She was so young. She reminded me of Aja."

My chest burns, not from magic. Ajalique Selane. My mother.

Like Pelene, Aja was a liar. She lied constantly, but rarely alone. There were dozens of men swooping in and out of our lives and her bed, spewing lies of their own: that they loved her, that they wanted to build a better life for her—*with* her.

I saw through them like glass. Aja scarfed them down like warm bread.

Maybe I should be grateful for the lies. After all, they'd fueled my magic, and magic was the only thing keeping us warm in Ophera. Growing up, I'd stare at the icy peaks, begging the stars for *that* life, in one of the hulking houses built into the mountain.

I guess the stars were listening. And I guess the stars are assholes, because they shoved me into the mountainside Republic of Virdei, right into the arms of that new life my mother was always promising.

All it cost me was her.

At the sound of her name, faded memories flicker to life in my mind's eye: Aja holding my hand and squeezing tight as my tattoo was inked into my skin; me, curled into her side, stumbling over words as she taught me to read.

Seven years later, and I still miss her every day.

"Aja is dead." I say it harshly, but I feel myself softening.

"I know," Luc says gently. "I'm sorry. But don't you wish someone had been kind to her?"

More memories whirl like snowflakes in a blizzard. Aja smiling at some wide-mouthed man who talked too fast and made too many promises he never intended to keep, Aja sobbing her broken heart out in front of our empty fireplace, Aja promising me she wasn't shattered when they left. And they *always* left.

She was the only person who loved me with no agenda, and my clearest memories of her are of a heartbroken liar.

"I don't wish more people were kind to her." I fold my arms and jut out my chin. "I wish someone were *honest*."

Luc flinches. "You're right. I'm sorry. I shouldn't have used Ms. Harcot's first name. Next time, I'll do better." He risks a peek at my face. "Are you mad?"

Yes. I force the tension from my body. "No."

He accepts this lie with no resistance. "I'm nervous about tomorrow."

"Don't be. Everything is under control," I say. "Tonight, Nox will receive a letter from the Shadow Queen. If he doesn't want his private affair made public, he'll vote the way we tell him, and we'll have the majority."

"What if he refuses?"

"He won't. Luc, look at me." I wait until his worried eyes meet mine. "*Relax*. After tomorrow, it's over. Only Honorate and their sons can try for the throne. We have secrets on all of them. When you announce you intend to rule again, you'll run unopposed."

Luc still looks anxious.

I hold in a sigh. Time for my secret weapon. "Do you trust me?"

"With every lie I'll ever tell."

I take all my fears and doubts and tuck them away behind a wide smile. "Then we're golden."

It's our code and, as always, it works. His tension eases, and he wraps me in a warm hug. "Thanks, Mira. I don't know what I'd do without you."

With my face safely hidden in his shoulder, my fake smile is free of its audience, free to fade away. I've salved his worry and quieted his fears, but I still carry mine.

By all counts, I've made it. I live in Widow's Hall; I have a breathtaking view of the entire mountain and the affection of the most powerful man in the Republic.

From below, this life was all I wanted. Now that I'm here, I wish someone had told me that the shadows of Widow's Hall are just as cold as our empty fireplace in Ophera.

If I'm being honest, there's not a day that goes by that I don't miss shivering and starving at the base of the mountain with my mother who was incapable of telling the truth. Except when she, without asking for anything in return, told me she loved me.

Turns out, the breathtaking view from the top isn't a reminder of how far I've come—it's a constant threat of how far I'll fall if I ever make a mistake.

CHAPTER TWO

HER SLEIGHT OF HAND

This greyhorn is punishing me. It's the only explanation I can come up with for why this smelly ox keeps flicking its tail, scattering its putrid scent everywhere.

When I secreted this ox away from the stables at Widow's Hall, I'd hoped that if the cold robbed my nose of feeling (it did, ten minutes ago), it would also spare me my sense of smell.

No such luck.

Two greyhorns drag their shaggy legs through the trails in the icy mountain roads with obvious reluctance. Despite their thick, gray wool, they look about as frozen pulling the sledge as I feel steering it.

I'm covered, head to toe, in a combination of wool, fur, and leather. Feet tucked into fur-lined boots, shoulders and neck wrapped in a thick wool sjaal, face hidden behind a goats-hide and leather mask with mesh over my eyes. I'm still shivering.

The mountains are always brutal, but at night, they're unbearable.

It's not snowing, but wind swirls ice crystals from the ground, narrowing visibility so much, I almost miss our destination until it's right in front of us.

I yank the reins, tugging the oxen to a halt.

They snort in irritation but stop, stomping their hooves in

place to keep warm. Reaching back, I rap on the black coach of the sledge to capture Sef's attention.

I pat one of the oxen on the flank as I slip off the bench and waddle over to tug open the coach door.

Sef descends from the sledge, somehow bearing more of a resemblance to a goddess than an icicle despite the frigid air. We're both in disguise tonight. I'm dressed as a stablehand, and she's dressed as me. Well, as the Shadow Queen. Sef wears a black dress and overdress, bloodred sjaal, black velvet mask that covers her entire face, and black lace gloves.

Sef and I rarely deliver blackmail notes to Honorate doorsteps like this, but when we do, it's always in costume. We want the select few who catch glimpses of her to describe someone ethereal, mysterious, and with*out* that telltale golden tattoo on the inside of her wrist.

Sef holds an envelope with Honorate Jasper Nox's name scrawled on the front. Tomorrow morning, he'll find it tucked under his doorway and know instantly it's from the Shadow Queen. At tomorrow's council meeting, Nox will arrive ready to do as I say and vote in favor of the proposed order.

He and the rest of the Honorate have already been warned against competing for the throne. In Virdei, power is a prize to be earned. If there's more than one candidate for Praeceptor, they face off in the Tournament of Thrones—a series of deadly competitions designed to test a candidate's cunning and prowess. First to win two of the three trials wins the throne.

It's the Republic's favorite tradition. I intend to snuff it.

Luc barely has the stomach to deliver harsh words to sweet strangers, let alone the cruel streak necessary to win a Tournament of Thrones. If my brother is to reign again—and he will—then he must run unopposed.

"You ready?" I ask Sef, voice muffled beneath my mask.

"Always." She tips up her chin and glides from the sledge as though skating on ice. She reaches the front door of Nox's manor and raps on the dark wood. Like most Virdeian manors, Nox's house is large, not tall. Mount Saidu is pelted with unforgiving winds and heavy snow most of the year, so there aren't many tall structures. Most manors have one or two aboveground stories of tshira and mortar, and the bulk of the house is carved into the mountain.

Sef slips the envelope under the door and turns back, making her way across the stone-lined walkway to the sledge.

She's halfway back when someone cries out.

I straighten to attention. A servant races out from the side of Nox's house, headed for Sef.

The man calls out again. Sef runs faster, but she's not quick enough. Her pursuer's legs are longer and not tangled up in a skirt.

My heartbeat quickens. Time to show off my magic.

If you believe Virdeian legend (I don't), magic was gifted to us hundreds of years ago by a lonely god. He sprinkled it like sugar into the streams that flow through the mountains, infecting the people who drink it and the tshira deposits throughout the mountain with its power.

Even magic has limits. The few of us with magic, the aikkari, need a source to fuel it. An aikkari's source can be anything. Something tangible, like the red-brown sagegrass that grows in patches on the mountainside; something intangible, like a particular shade of yellow; or something invisible, like an emotion.

We're taught from an early age: *magic must be fed*. Mine feeds on lies.

Alongside the aikkari are the isha (another gift from the alleged lonely god). With a single touch, they can sense an aikkari's source. They're useful, but rare. There hasn't been an isha reported in Virdei for decades.

I yank open the coach door for Sef, before hauling myself onto the bench behind the greyhorns. They huff and stomp their legs faster, eager to get moving and return to the warmth of their stables.

The servant is gaining on Sef. He'll be upon her in a matter of seconds.

I peel off one glove and slide the other down, exposing my wrist. Icy wind nips at the sliver of bare skin. My teeth grind against the cold as I touch my palm to the tshira pendant on my bracelet. The magic stored within fills me with familiar, comforting warmth.

Sef is almost to the sledge. The servant chasing her is just a few paces behind.

In a practiced motion, she flicks a hand over her shoulder.

I send a wave of heat at the ground behind her.

Snow melts into icy, slippery sludge. The servant chasing Sef isn't expecting it. His next racing step sends his feet skidding. With a shout of surprise, he splashes to the ground.

Sef darts through the open coach door.

I tug the reins, urging the greyhorns to move. The sledge's runners are oiled up every night, so they glide smoothly over the ice as we rush away.

I glance behind me. The melted snow at the man's feet is already freezing again, making it difficult for him to rise.

He opens his mouth and cries out, but the sound is lost to the wind.

In a few seconds, silver snow clouds my vision, and I can see him no longer.

I'm shivering and exhausted by the time the oxen trot through the stable entrance at Widow's Hall. A ramp leads from the blistering wind outside to the tunnels running underneath that contain the stables and dungeons. The sledge glides down the incline, deeper into the mountain, until we reach the animal stalls.

My body is ready to collapse, but there's no time for that. I shove aside fatigue, discard my mask, and unhook the greyhorns from the sledge.

The stable walls are lined with tshira. Perfect for the decurio and their magic to keep the walls nice and warm so the animals don't freeze. I fight a yawn as I brush snow and mud from the greyhorns' thick coats.

Sef removes her mask next to me. "Want help?"

I give her a small smile. "Have you forgotten how you're dressed?" I wave a hand over the thin Shadow Queen costume. Sef must be freezing. "Go to bed. Thanks for tonight."

She rolls her eyes. "You know you don't have to thank me, Mira."

"And *you* don't have to help me."

"It's my job."

I pick up a handful of straw and throw it playfully at her. "You're meant to be a personal maid. This is far beyond your job requirements."

Sef's laugh is her only acknowledgment that she knows I'm right. "I think he was faster than the others."

I smirk. "I fear you're getting slower. Must be your old age."

Sef is barely twenty, but she gasps as though offended. "Just for that, I *will* go to bed now." She stretches her arms above her head. "Good night, Mira. See you tomorrow."

She turns to leave—and stops. A stablehand idles in the

stall doorway. He's so shocked to see us, he hasn't sounded an alarm yet. Now that we've spotted him, he finds his voice. "A-are you meant to be here?"

Seeing as it's the middle of the night, and Sef and I are clearly not stablehands, the answer is obviously no.

I reach for the tshira pendant at my wrist. Cold. *Damn.* I used magic at Nox's manor, and then again on our way back to warm the coach for Sef. My trinket is useful, but small—it can only store so much magic at once.

Fortunately, lies are rarely hard to come by.

I nudge my shoulder into Sef's, and an unspoken understanding passes between us.

Without missing a beat, Sef smiles at the stablehand. "Yes. Of course we are."

Heat from her lie spreads through me like ink. I don't take the time to savor the feeling. I rush forward and press a hand to the man's forehead.

He doesn't speak. As my magic pierces his mind, his expression drips like melting candle wax. His eyelids droop, body slumps, and anything he might've been preparing to say wisps into nothingness. When I'm sure the magic has done its job, I lower my hand.

The stablehand sways on his feet, eyes half lidded and dazed, as though waking from a nap with no idea how much time has passed.

Sef and I slip away while he's still disoriented.

He won't remember this interaction. In a few months, echoes of recollection will likely come back to him in his sleep. Since the memory was brief, he'll probably dismiss it as a strange dream. Longer memories are harder to erase. They require more magic, and even still, over time, stolen memories start to trickle back in.

All aikkari can manipulate heat, tshira, and their magic's source. For me, that source is deception. In practice, that means I can alter a person's *perception* of the truth—their memories.

When the smoke clears and the stablehand comes to, he'll find himself alone in the stables, dizzy and muddled, unsure of what's just happened. And Sef and I will be long gone.

CHAPTER THREE

GODS AMONG MEN

The Honorate are revered as gods. As such, they must be perfect. Their rules of conduct are practically carved into the mountain. Any missteps—a whisper that they're not the gods the Republic demands—is a breach of decorum tantamount to treason.

I watch our supposed gods from the rafters. The chamber is only open to the Honorate and their sons, so I observe from the narrow space between the ceiling of the council chamber and the sloping roof of Widow's Hall. Luc and I discovered this place. We pulled up the wood in the center of the floor and replaced it with a thin layer of tshira. Now, with a touch of my finger and a hint of magic, my floor (the Honorates' ceiling) becomes translucent as frosted one-way glass.

I painted the walls deep green and the ceiling a midnight blue flecked with golden yellow stars. The floor is littered with glass jars fitted with tshira lids. Half of them are empty, ready to be filled, and the rest are already swirling with red smoke. *Magic.*

The chamber below my feet is a wide, echoey room with gray stone walls and a deep blue carpet. Pillars of marble line the perimeter, and the dais at the front looms above the twenty wooden benches, one for each of the Honorate. They're seated and dressed for council in robes of emerald green wool, heavily embroidered with glittering gold thread. Luc sits at the dais, decked in the Praeceptor's formal golden robes, reciting the speech I wrote for him.

I wear Honorate robes of my own, spinning around the floor. It's my favorite part of chamber: dancing on a sheet of ice, dressed in the trappings of power. Here, I can play pretend. That I'm not stewing in anxiety, that I'm untouchable, that my future doesn't depend on this vote.

I don't stop spinning until Luc reaches the final paragraph. The fear I've been pretending away creeps up my back, and my fingers pluck nervously at a loose thread dangling from my sleeve.

Two aikkari selectmen raise their arms. Trays of tshira rise and swoop, delivering parchment to the Honorate for them to mark "yes" or "no."

My fingers pluck the thread faster, keeping pace with my heartbeat.

There are twenty rostered Honorate, but only nineteen who matter. For the past two years, Honorate Arliss Vale has been too sickly and bedridden to come to council, let alone vote. With his absence, all we need are ten votes for a majority.

The air is tense as selectmen retrieve the ballots and present them to Luc. I hold my breath as he sorts them into two piles.

A draft blows through my attic, cool enough to make me shiver, but I burn with trepidation, and my palms are sticky with sweat.

Luc clears his throat. "The votes have been counted. There are nine opposed . . ."

Relief is a splash of cool water. My racing heart slows. Luc will be Praeceptor again.

He keeps going. ". . . and ten in favor. With that—"

Thud.

Luc's words lurch to a halt.

Everyone whips around to face the source of the disturbance—the chamber's double doors slamming open.

That brief rush of relief abates into confusion. An unknown figure marches into my field of view. He strides confidently down the center aisle, as if he's done it a thousand times before.

Except he hasn't. I watch every single council meeting, and I've never seen him before.

I eye the selectmen, waiting for the guards to tackle the intruder and haul him from chamber.

No one moves.

Their inaction stings. More than it should. If *I* stepped foot in chamber—if I so much as lingered in the open doorway a beat too long—Luc's guards would waste no time in shoving me aside and slamming the door in my face.

Doesn't matter they've known me for years; they never miss a chance to remind me just how unwanted I am. Yet they let this stranger stroll in without question.

Luc is the first to speak. "Excuse me, but these are private proceedings. Open only to—"

"The Honorate and their sons," the stranger interrupts smoothly. "I'm aware."

The chamber rumbles with whispers. Whoever this interloper is, he just spoke over the Honored Praeceptor. A flagrant breach of decorum, and still, the selectmen do nothing.

The stranger reaches the front of the chamber and turns. Dismissively gives his back to the Praeceptor in a move that can't be anything but intentional. The council is buzzing. Luc should call him out for this slight, but I'm not there to tell him what to do, so he says nothing.

My glare roves over the intruder. He's young (around my

age) and tall (even taller than Luc). Dressed in a green wool sweater and thick pants made for snow. Through his heavy layers, I see his build. The way his clothes mold perfectly to his body. He's broad in the shoulders, muscular in the arms, and his skin is dark, rich, and smooth, like mahogany. His black hair is a bit too long for my tastes, but the rest of his face more than makes up for it.

A jawline that could mine tshira. Cheekbones that appear carved from ice. His mouth is wide and lips are full, as though made for laughter, and his brows are arched with good humor.

My throat dries as I stare.

"My name is Kaidren Vale." The intruder has a deep, husky voice filled with warmth, like being wrapped in a wool cloak. "I am the only son of Honorate Arliss Vale. And before we continue . . ." His lips curve up, into the tiniest of smirks. "I have a vote to cast."

He must be lying. Arliss Vale never married and has no children. I tense, bracing for the soothing heat of a lie—

—except I'm ice cold.

Stars in hell, he's telling the truth.

The debate chamber erupts. Honorate leap to their feet, shouting their disbelief and demanding he leave. Selectmen finally move to escort him out.

As for me, I do nothing. I can't. My entire world is shifting, like I'm trying to balance on a sphere rolling downhill.

He's telling the truth, he's telling the truth, he's telling the truth . . .

No matter how many times I turn those words over in my mind, I can't believe them. I've made it my job to know everything so I'm prepared for anything. I wasn't prepared for this.

"I assure you," Kaidren says, raising his voice to be heard over the din. "I speak the truth. Arliss Vale is my father. As of six months ago, I am eighteen years old. Therefore, I have the right to vote in my father's absence. I can prove it." He shoves a hand into his pocket and procures a sheet of parchment.

Selectmen—the only people who are *actually* allowed to approach Luc while he's on the dais—snatch the parchment and hand it to Luc on Kaidren's behalf.

The chamber waits, breaths bated, as Luc reads. "This is a signed statement from Arliss Vale," he says slowly, "attesting he's your father." His words shrink in volume as the sentence reaches its end.

Whispers twist through chamber like a mountain stream winding downhill.

For several seconds, Luc stares at the parchment; then his gaze shoots to the rafters. He can't see me, but he instinctively seeks my presence for guidance. A crutch we can't afford, but I haven't been able to shake him of it. "We'll need to corroborate this further," he says.

"Of course," Kaidren agrees smoothly. *Too* smoothly. I don't like anyone who has an easy answer for everything. "But while we're here, I would like to cast my vote."

I hate the way he speaks. Hate that he's already acting as if he's one of the most powerful men in the Republic. Hate that he thinks he has any authority here.

More than anything, I hate that he's right.

"I know what order is on the agenda," Kaidren says. "I vote in opposition."

It's as if the sheet of tshira beneath me splinters.

Ten in favor, ten opposed. This smooth-talking stranger just deadlocked the votes.

CHAPTER FOUR

ILLUSIONS OF POWER

I am so angry, my vision tints red and my throat burns from the effort it takes to hold in expletives as I march through the halls.

Months of planning and sleepless nights. Set alight by an arrogant stranger who's never stepped foot in Widow's Hall before today. And I know nothing about him. Secrets are power. The most effective weapons in my arsenal are all the things powerful men do in the dark. Without them, I'm defenseless.

I take a deep breath. *Steel and ice.* I'm made of steel and ice.

At least, that's what I tell myself as I rap on the door to Luc's study behind the dais.

My brother sits at his vanity, head thrust into his palms, shoulders hunched. Selectmen swarm him like flies around rotting meat, buzzing uselessly.

I clear my throat.

Luc raises his head and meets my gaze in the mirror above his desk. His shoulders loosen with relief. "Everybody out."

The selectmen frown in confusion until they see me. Their expressions collectively curdle like milk left out in the sun.

"Sir," one of them starts.

"*Out.*" For once, Luc is firm without me having to remind him.

His guards grumble, but obey. It doesn't stop them from

giving me their usual glares soaked in resentment, or from shoving their shoulders against mine as they pass.

I stay stoic and say nothing until they're gone. "This was my fault." I place a gentle hand on Luc's back. "I should've reserved more votes."

A lie. I make the votes as close as I do because winning requires a delicate balance of give and take. It's why I do favors for *all* the Honorate, not just Luc. Why I ensure not every order Luc proposes passes. Why the orders the Shadow Queen nudges along always win by near ties.

People need to believe either side has a chance of winning. Otherwise, brows would rise and revolutions would stir. Important votes are always split down the middle, to create the illusion of choice. Give people the illusion of power.

Luc pushes back his chair to pace. He's quiet, which means he needs more cajoling. "There's no need to worry." I keep my voice soft. "Sef and I are going to dig. By this time tomorrow, we'll know everything about Kaidren Vale. Every lie, mistake, and mess he thought he'd swept clean."

"What if there isn't anything?"

"Everyone has secrets."

Luc stops pacing. He squints at me, analyzing my carefully neutral expression. "You're truly not stressed about this?"

Of course I am. "No."

"You're *sure* everything will work out?"

No. "Absolutely."

He shakes his head, looking a combination of bewildered and awed. "I don't know how you do it, Mira."

There's a knock on the door before I can reply. Luc looks startled, but I roll my eyes. "Probably one of your guards come back to be useless some more. I'll get rid of him."

I fling open the office door, intending to tell the selectmen to leave us alone. My eyeline is fixed where I expect the guard's to be, but I find myself staring at someone's chest. A broad chest that's straining the confines of its emerald sweater.

Slowly, my eyes trail up, over the toned contours of his torso, muscles of his shoulders, and chiseled jaw, until I'm staring into the deepest brown eyes I've ever seen.

Kaidren Vale.

He's looking me over, eyes widened, head tilted with curiosity, as though I'm the most fascinating creature he's ever seen.

After years of hovering in shadows, being looked at so thoroughly stirs something in my gut. "Can I help you?"

His assessing eyes finish their perusal and meet mine. His gaze is bright, eager, and friendly. "Pleasure to meet you." He holds out a hand for me to shake. "I wanted to—" Kaidren's words falter as he catches sight of Luc behind me.

His demeanor shifts.

That relaxed, curious light in his eyes extinguishes like candlelight in the rain. He's no longer looking at me like I'm interesting—he's not looking at me at all. He's stiff as a plank, flashing Luc a broad, perfect smile that's completely devoid of life. He lowers his hand. "Is there water?"

I blink, startled by the sudden change. "What?"

"Water?" He's still not looking at me. "I'm thirsty. Fetch me some?" He sidesteps me before I can tell him I don't *fetch* things, and makes his way to Luc without sparing me another glance.

Whatever warmth flickered within me when he first appeared in the doorway is stone cold. Destroying my carefully laid plans in chamber wasn't enough—no, Kaidren Vale has to be a dismissive asshole just like everyone else.

I glower at no one and slam the door.

"Pleasure to meet you, sir." Kaidren thrusts out a hand to Luc. "My sincerest apologies for interrupting you earlier. I meant no disrespect." His words are smooth and practiced. I get the feeling he stared in the mirror for hours, rehearsing those lines again and again, to make them believable.

He's successful. Taken at face value, he sounds convincing. Except for the sudden flare in my gut.

It's chilling. Not the fact that he's lying—I'm used to liars—but because of how good he is at it. If I didn't feel the rush of magic, I might have missed the way his wide, near-perfect grin is the *slightest* bit uneven, tipping it over the edge from genuine to taunting.

It's subtle. Subtle enough Luc doesn't notice and shakes Kaidren's hand with a smile of his own. "The pleasure is mine. I still have to confirm—"

"Of course." Kaidren cuts him off again.

My teeth grind together.

"I'm just so excited to meet you," Kaidren continues. "I have so much respect for you. I've never been one to listen to rumors, and I *certainly* don't think your reign is tainted by the fact that you didn't compete in the Tournament."

With every word, the searing sensation of my magic intensifies. The Republic spends years looking forward to the Tournament of Thrones. People from all over Virdei travel up the mountain to the arena to watch. We even invite guests from Petruvia, a nearby coastal kingdom, to stay in Widow's Hall during Tournament season.

Virdei is all about illusions and projection. The Praeceptor is expected to do more than win—he must prove to the world that he's *earned* his power. Luc took the throne without competing, and there have been rumors swirling ever since that he's unfit to rule. And here Kaidren is, rubbing Luc's nose in it.

Another day, I might've been willing to let the snide comment slide, but Kaidren wrecked my plans, snubbed Luc, and tried to order me around like I'm worthless. Which means I have the right to ruin him and enjoy every second of it. "Should His Honored Praeceptor expect to see you at tomorrow's council meeting?"

Kaidren's smug smile slips. "What?" He whirls to face me. "There's another meeting tomorrow?"

"Of course." It takes all of my willpower not to smirk. "To vote on the order from today."

"That order failed."

I smile sweetly. "Forgive me. I know little about Honorate meetings, but I was under the impression that today's vote was a draw. Which—I *think*—means the Honored Praeceptor can call a revote whenever he so chooses." I channel all the innocence I can muster into widening my eyes. "He chooses tomorrow."

Kaidren's face is pinched, as though he just smelled something foul. "If that's so, I'll be there. And, once again, I'll cast my vote in opposition." He turns to Luc, looking more irked than before. "Again, a pleasure to meet you, sir. I look forward to seeing you tomorrow."

My insides are on fire as he gives a parting lie and leaves without so much as glancing in my direction.

He'll pay for that later. He'll pay for *all* of it. Kaidren thinks he's playing a game and that he's winning. He thinks he'll win again tomorrow. And he thinks his opponent is Luc.

Kaidren is wrong. About all of it.

His true opponent is me. And I don't play games.

I win.

CHAPTER FIVE

THE FALSE QUEEN

Servants talk. They see and hear all the tawdry things their employers whisper to each other when they don't think anyone is watching. It's part of why Sef and I make such a great pair. She hunts for rumors while I parse out the lies from the truth.

"What did you find?" I call out to Sef (she's sitting on the edge of my bed) from my place on the floor of my vault, rooting through my notes on the Honorate. My vault is the size of a small closet, walls lined end to end with chest-high shelves stacked with leather-bound volumes full of information. They range from the commonplace, like family history, to the arcane, like an Honorate's darkest secrets.

"Not much. At least, not yet." I've known Sefina Ceraway since I first moved to Widow's Hall when Luc became Praeceptor. Everyone resented that he brought me, Opheran street scum, to live with him. I was supposed to be assigned a team of aikkari selectmen for protection, same as Luc (and every other live-in family member of the Praeceptor in the history of the Republic). Instead, they assigned me Sef, a maid with no defense training at all.

I never complained. Both because I refused to give anyone the satisfaction, and because, within days of meeting her, I knew they had drastically underestimated her. Sure, Sef is young, has no magic, and would sooner sprout wings than fend off an attacker. But she's also crafty, loyal, and quick to laugh—an invaluable combination I wouldn't trade for a slew of selectmen. Widow's Hall is dreary and lonely. Her friendship is the only bright spot that makes it bearable.

I wedge a book under my arm and emerge from the vault, locking it after me. It's tucked behind a hidden door in the back of my closet. There's no visible handle; it's just a crack in the wall that, when peeled back, reveals the tshira-lined door. A necessary precaution. I safeguard too many secrets to remember them all, and I know better than to keep my arsenal lying around for anyone to find.

My room is so tiny, I take two steps outside my closet and I'm standing in front of Sef, a half pace from my bed. Another thing I never complain about.

I quirk an expectant brow at Sef. "Well?"

"Kaidren's mother is dead. And you'll never believe this—" She drops her voice and chin. "She was *Opheran*."

The book under my arm tumbles to the floor. "Kaidren's Opheran?" Impossible. He doesn't have a tattoo. I'd have noticed. *Everyone* would've noticed. Opheran children undergo a ceremony on our fifth birthday. We're marked in golden ink with a symbol of our birth season. The majority of the year, we suffer the dark season, so most Opherans have tattoos of crescent moons. I was born in the brief glimmer of the light season, so mine is of a sun.

It's beautiful. I used to love it. I used to admire the way the golden ink looked against my brown skin. Then I came here, and they looked at it—at *me*—like I was less than trash. I struggle to see the beauty now.

"He doesn't look Opheran," is all I say. "He didn't sound Opheran either." Virdeians and Opherans have similar accents, but Opherans linger on their vowels, and their sentences tend to drop at the end. I've lived here for seven years, and I still sound Opheran when I'm not careful.

"I know it's not much to go on," Sef says, "but I'll keep digging."

This is much less than what she usually finds, but it's still early in the investigation process. "Thank you. I'll see what I can find on my end as well, and we can compare notes." I move to my desk that doubles as a vanity with the leather book from my vault. It's full of everything I've collected about Honorate Rishelvu over the years. I snag a pen and a sheet of parchment.

> Honorate Rishelvu,
>
> There exists such a special bond between father and son. Almost as special as the bond between a firstborn and his inheritance.
>
> On my honor, I will not direct anyone to search for what you so carelessly gambled away. Provided, of course, that you change your vote in favor of the proposed order on the agenda tomorrow.
>
> Fondly,
> Shadow Queen

I sheathe the letter in an envelope and press the Shadow Queen's seal to it with a smirk.

There's nothing the Honorate fear more than a scandal. A position in the Honorate is for life and inheritable by their oldest son—so long as they stay godlike. Any Honorate who fails to uphold the veil of perfection is in danger. People have the right to challenge an Honorate if he breaches decorum, and an ousted Honorate can't transfer his position to a son.

I hand the sealed envelope to Sef. "Can you deliver this tonight? No need for theatrics."

"Of course." She reaches into her pocket and pulls out a stack of envelopes—missives for the Shadow Queen. "Trade?"

"Thank you." I take the stack of letters, and Sef takes the note for Honorate Rishelvu. I flip open a second book, where I keep track of unsubstantiated rumors. My pen taps idly against the desk as I read.

> Shadow Queen,
> I've heard rumors Honorate Portannis is engaged in an affair with a married Petruvian. I can give you a name if you can ensure the order he is drafting fails.

It isn't signed. They often aren't. I jot down the potential affair to look into later, even though I doubt its validity.

Virdei and Petruvia have a strained relationship, to put it mildly. Virdei controls Mount Saidu and more than half of Ophera. Petruvia controls the coast and the rest of Ophera. The feud started around two hundred years ago, when both countries raced to take over the coastline. Petruvia won.

As Virdei licked their wounds, they moved farther up the mountain, where they realized it was full of resources even more valuable than the ocean: tshira and, most important, *magic*.

Before that, there were a few aikkari scattered throughout the two kingdoms, but there weren't a lot until Virdei climbed higher up Mount Saidu.

War started again. This time, Virdei had an undeniable advantage and won. To this day, Petruvia claims Virdei cheated. According to them, the Republic resorted to cutting off the water supply to everyone below the mountain to ensure their victory. The details are unclear, but in the end, all that matters is Virdei won the mountain, the tshira, and an army of aikkari soldiers no one else can compete with.

I open the next envelope.

Shadow Queen,

I have a maid who is Opheran. She claims she's spotted Petruvian soldiers on her land with no consequence. If this is true, can you ensure the order to send more funding to Holsbane Academy passes?

I raise my brows at Sef, who reads over my shoulder. "Any chance this is true?"

"I haven't heard anything," Sef says. "But then again, my friends here are Virdeian. The only Opheran I know is, well, you."

A fair point. Opherans aren't meant to reside in these hallowed halls. I write down the tip before moving on to the next.

Shadow Queen,

Two days ago, I received a disturbing letter from someone purporting to be you. It seems you have a rival looking to replace you. Please advise.

I frown, more confused than wary. There's a second scrap of parchment in the envelope, crumpled and creased as though it's been unfolded and refolded multiple times. The second note is addressed to Honorate Selva Sixmen and scrawled in deep indigo ink.

Honorate Sixmen,

I wonder how much longer that title will apply? An Honorate with no Honor is no longer deserving of his position. The stars see all, as do I. You and I both know there's not enough snow on this mountain to wash your hands clean of the blood that stains them.

Fondly,
Shadow Queen

My breath catches in my throat.

I read the letter again. And again.

Over the years, I've written dozens of similar notes.

This one is signed by the Shadow Queen—by *me*—but I didn't write it. It seems there's a second queen of shadows roaming these halls.

CHAPTER SIX

VACANT SMILES

The Praeceptor's personal dining room drips opulence. Walls made of tshira, streaked with bands of red, green, and gold, lined with black pillars. A six-tiered chandelier hangs over the dining table and its twenty-one seats. Only one head of the table gets a chair, because only one person is above the rest. It's made of dark wood and cushioned with soft maroon velvet that I sink into. During the day, it belongs to Luc. This time of night, with no one around to see, it's mine.

It's my favorite place to work. I feel powerful here. Everything—and every*one*—feels small.

Tonight, I work on an order that will send more soldiers to the Opheran border. The Honorate has already rejected previous versions of this order twice, which means I'll need to slip it into something unrelated if I want it to pass without interference from the Shadow Queen.

I've only just unpacked my bag when the door rattles.

My head jerks up. It's nearing ten in the evening—no reason for anyone else to be here.

The double doors swing open, and Kaidren Vale's deep brown eyes find me, curious and intent.

My heartbeat accelerates. I hate being caught off guard, and this is the second time he's done so in a single day. I struggle to keep my face still as I stand to greet him.

"Hello there," he says with a smile that's as oily and fake as my stepmother's hair. "I thought I saw you come in here."

"You were looking for me?" I surreptitiously flip my notes over. Kaidren isn't close enough to read them, but his stance is leaned forward as though he intends to narrow the space between us.

His stare is unwavering as he closes the gilded door and rests his back against it. On the surface, it's a casual move, but I want to flee, and he's blocking my only exit.

"I was hoping to catch a word," he says. "I've seen you. Skulking around in the shadows."

Does he mean *before* today?

I fight a frown. "You've seen me before?" I sidle around the table. Not because I want to be any closer to him, but to place myself nearer to the door. "Where?"

"Around Widow's Hall. Hovering near the Praeceptor. And I'm not sure if you'll remember, but we actually met briefly earlier today."

Around Widow's Hall.

Those words echo around my mind, dulling the rest of his sentence. I was certain today was his first time here, but if he's seen me before, he must've walked these halls.

He saw me, but I didn't see him. I couldn't have—with a face like his, I'd remember.

My gut stirs with unease. I quiet it. "I *think* I might remember you. You're . . ." I pretend to be deep in thought. "*Oh!* You're that new Honorate, aren't you?"

He grins. "Yes. Good memory. You're welcome to call me 'New Honorate,' but most people just call me Kaidren." He pauses, giving me time to chuckle.

I don't.

He continues. "As you said, I'm new here. This place is overwhelming."

"Yes." My thumb traces the tattoo on my wrist. "Widow's Hall can be unforgiving to strangers."

His easygoing smile pairs with a few steps in my direction. Combined with the intensity of his stare, it feels more menacing than friendly. "Then let's not be strangers."

Kaidren has such a blithe, familiar way of speaking, as though we've known each other for years. He probably thinks he's being charming, but he's not subtle, and I'm not a fool.

He saw me with Luc and now he's seeking me out in the middle of the night. It isn't hard to guess what he's after: information on the Praeceptor, hidden behind a guise of kindness.

I have no desire to make friends with this slimy creature, but in a game of who can fake the sweetest smiles, I'll win.

I tilt my head to the side and grin. "I'd like that."

He moves even closer. Close enough I have to tilt my head—just a bit—to maintain eye contact. "In that case, it's lovely to meet you. I'm Kaidren Vale. Do you have a name, shadow skulker?"

"Remira."

"Remira what?"

Interesting. He's seen me around but doesn't know I share a surname with the Praeceptor. Either that, or he's pretending. "Just Remira."

"Well, Just Remira." When he smiles, his teeth are perfectly straight. It irks me. "I'd like to get to know you better."

I'm flooded with heat. Kaidren thinks I'll lower my guard because he has a handsome face, eerily perfect smile, and eyes that look like laughter.

He expects I'll be a fool. I expect he'll be sorely disappointed.

"How perfect." I keep up my fake smile. "I think I'd like to get to know you too."

"You *think*?" His words are light and teasing.

"We've only just met." I match his tone. "How should I know if you're worth it?"

He throws his head back and laughs. "It's a relief to finally meet someone so . . . *friendly* here."

No one in their right mind has ever called me friendly. I keep smiling.

"I haven't quite found my footing. I feel like I'm doing everything wrong." His head lowers with his voice, as though we're conspirators in some joint scheme. "What I really want, more than anything, is a friend."

Another rush of heat with another obvious lie. No one comes to Widow's Hall looking for friendship.

I keep on smiling.

"Especially a friend who knows how this place operates." There's a huskiness coloring his tone. "I fear I blundered today. Apparently, I accidentally breached a rule of decorum."

Actually, he broke three.

I keep smiling.

"Perhaps we could help each other? I need help navigating these halls and its rules, and you—well, this doesn't seem like the sort of place that's kind to the help."

The help?

My false smile slips. There he goes, dismissing me again. "Is that what I am?"

"Aren't you?" Kaidren's eyes drop to my wrist.

Instinctively, I tug down my sleeve, hiding the sun tattoo. The most rancid kind of bitterness settles within me.

Of course.

We're both Opheran, but *he* gets to be an Honorate, and *I* must be the help. If he knew anything about Widow's Hall, he'd know that Opherans don't work here. The Honorate often hire them to work in their private homes, but here, in the center of

Virdeian politics, I am one of a kind. I'm not here as *the help*. I'm here as the Praeceptor's sister. Kaidren Vale sees none of that. He just sees the tattoo.

Kaidren's smile softens. He can sense he's offended me, but grossly misreads how. He bends, so that I can more clearly read his pity, and more easily picture what it would feel like to throttle him. "Would you like to know something?" he says. "I'm Opheran too. I never got a tattoo, though. Wish I had. Yours is stunning."

Heat. He's lying again. Either about wishing he got a tattoo or about liking mine. Probably both.

He means to position himself as my ally. Align himself with me, the poor little Opheran girl, against the rest of Widow's Hall.

Anger swirls painfully within me, but I don't have the luxury of unleashing it. I paint my smile back on. It feels sloppy. More obviously fake. Not that he notices. His eyes are fixed on my face, but he's not seeing me. All he sees is a means to an end. "You're Opheran?" I will myself to sound shocked, not hollow. "Wow. And now you're an Honorate."

"I hope my new position is a win for people like us."

What a fascinating and meaningless phrase. There is no "us." We have nothing in common.

Kaidren's father claimed him willingly. My father reluctantly took me in as an irksome pet. Kaidren gets to sit on the council of the most powerful men in the Republic. I will never have any more power than I do now as Luc's shadow—barely seen, never heard.

Kaidren doesn't even have a damned tattoo. He can float through life pretending to be whatever he wants. He can toss around that part of himself when it suits him—like when he's making the acquaintance of pitiful Opheran girls skulking in the shadows of Widow's Hall.

"What do you plan to do for"—I have to pause, swallowing my indignation, before choking the words out—"people like us?"

"Use my position in the Honorate to make Ophera better. More funding, for a start."

I'm used to lies, and I'm growing ever used to Kaidren's. Usually, they don't make me so incensed, but listening to this, my hands round into fists.

Growing up in Ophera, I found it easy to learn my source. My mother was a compulsive liar, and my magic flared just about every time she spoke.

I let them glide off me. Because no matter how often she lied, those rare moments she told the truth—"*I love you, Mira*"—made up for it.

We barely had food, our house was drafty, and my clothes were thin as parchment, but it was enough for me. Close enough, anyway. At the time, close to enough was all I needed.

I never told her what fueled my magic. She knew I was aik-kari, but it seemed cruel to call my own mother a liar—so I didn't. I told her I didn't know my source, and she believed me. She always did. Together, Aja and I dreamed of our grand escape from Ophera. *"You're going to get out of here, Mira. That house on the mountain, more food than you know what to do with . . . you're going to have it all,"* she used to say. For eight years, she meant it, and it was almost enough for me.

When I was nine, she told me again of the grand life I was going to live someday, and for the first time, her words filled me with fire. Her expression was the same as always. She was smiling and hugging me and she loved me, she loved me, she loved me—

But she didn't believe anymore.

Losing her broke my heart. When I left Ophera and arrived at the Kylers', I swore to myself and the stars that I'd do whatever I could for people like Aja. Opheran dreamers who deserved better. I think of her when I write orders for the Honorate. When I look in a mirror and see her features reflected in my own. When I hug my brother and remember what it felt like to be loved without conditions. Aja and Ophera are forever tucked in a corner of my heart.

Kaidren might be from Ophera, but he doesn't give a damn about the people who live there. He has no intention of doing as he says. It isn't surprising, but for him to dangle my home over my head like this . . .

I hate him so much right now, it burns. "It's nice to finally have someone in the Honorate who wants to improve things." The smile I'm faking strains my cheeks and my self-control.

"I hope they accept me enough I can actually make a difference." Kaidren clears his throat. "*You* seem to have done well, winning the Praeceptor's favor. Any advice how I can do the same?"

Here come the questions about Luc now that he thinks he's softened me up. "Just be yourself. People respect sincerity." I back away and begin gathering my things. "Is that why you came to Widow's Hall? To endear yourself to the Praeceptor?"

"I'm here to improve the Honorate."

"Interesting." I sling my bag over my shoulder. "I've never heard of someone coming here without a hidden agenda."

He chuckles. "Guess I'm the first."

It's rare I meet as skilled a liar as myself, but Kaidren lies without so much as a twitch of the eye. If I didn't hate him, I might be impressed.

"What about you?" he says with a teasing grin. "Do *you* have a hidden agenda?"

"Me?" I smile sweetly. "I'm just the help. What you see is what you get."

CHAPTER SEVEN

TOUCH OF RUIN

Kaidren Vale doesn't know where to sit. While the other Honorate stream into the chamber and flock to their assigned benches, Kaidren hovers in the back, awkward and small.

No one spares him a glance, let alone offers to guide him to his father's bench (now Kaidren's). It's only after the final Honorate takes his seat that Kaidren rushes for the only remaining bench in chamber. He reeks of embarrassment as he tumbles haphazardly into the seat.

A few Honorate snicker, loud enough to echo mockingly.

If they resented him yesterday—and they did—it's nothing compared to now. The Shadow Queen's latest column, released early this morning, announced to the world that Kaidren Vale is Opheran. An unforgivable offense.

Tension crackles as Luc enters the dais, and the meeting begins. There's only one item on today's agenda.

The spiteful whispers have dried up by the time ballots are collected. Luc doesn't even try to mask his pleased smile when he's finished counting. "There are nine opposed and eleven in favor. The order passes." He beams as he repeats the words I practically carved into his memory: "I would like to take this time to formally announce my bid for candidacy for Praeceptor once again."

I curve my lips in an expectant smirk, waiting for the warmth of happiness to sink in.

It doesn't.

I'm not happy—I'm only relieved. Relieved that Luc will be Praeceptor for a second term, relieved I won't have to endure threats from his parents for at least another five years.

Five more years of glares and disdain from Luc's guards and everyone else in Widow's Hall; forgoing sleep so Luc can be well rested; spending hours writing orders only for Luc to sign his name to them, because he might be hopeless without me, but I'm nothing without him.

Lost in bitter thoughts and a heavy heart, I don't notice Kaidren rising from his seat until he's at the front of the chamber, overlooking the Honorate.

Another breach of decorum. Honorate are meant to stand at their benches and face the Praeceptor as they speak, but Kaidren clearly hasn't learned his lesson since yesterday.

"Fellow members of the Honorate." He no longer looks nervous. He stands tall, words bold and self-assured. "I know I'm new and still have much to learn. Which is why I'd like to offer my services to the Republic as an isha. Together, we will find more aikkari and expand the decurio."

I send up a prayer to every star in the sky that he's lying—but I'm frozen solid.

We have an isha in Widow's Hall.

Horror pits in my stomach.

If Kaidren touches me—if his skin so much as brushes mine in passing—he'll know I'm aikkari. He'll know I never reported myself to the decurio. He'll have all he needs to get me thrown in prison or forced to enlist. From there, it will only take a bit of digging for him to learn my greatest secret: that I am the Shadow Queen.

With one touch, Kaidren Vale could ruin me.

Once again, Kaidren has set my world alight—and he's

not even finished speaking. "I'd also like to take this time to announce my own intentions for the throne."

My knees are weak.

He wouldn't dare . . .

Kaidren gives an unmistakable smirk as he turns to face Luc on the dais. He bends into an exaggerated bow, more mocking than respectful. "I look forward to competing against you in the Tournament of Thrones, Honored Praeceptor." I can no longer see his face, but I imagine that smug little grin widening before he says, "May the best man win."

CHAPTER EIGHT

KEPT THREATS & BROKEN PROMISES

The thing about dinner with Luc's parents is that it's never *just* dinner and never *just* with his parents (which, in and of itself, would be torture).

If this dinner were anything but mandatory, I wouldn't be climbing into the sledge waiting for me and Luc outside. I wouldn't be bundled up in a dress Yelina will no doubt find an excuse to mock, and enough layers of wool to keep me warm for the journey to the Kyler home.

"You look lovely," Luc says as I settle into the coach across from him. He means it, but I know him well enough to see through his attempt to soften me up before I have to endure his parents.

"Thank you." Tense and full of unease as I am, I appreciate the compliment. I despise Yelina Kyler almost as much as she despises me, but I still spent hours on my hair (with Sef's help) and painstakingly selected what I hoped was the perfect dress for the occasion.

In the few minutes it takes for us to travel from Widow's Hall to the Kylers' manor, Luc and I fall into our usual bickering. He tries to convince me to call his parents *my* parents; I remind him that Mathson Kyler would sooner wander into a blizzard fully nude than treat me like a daughter, and Yelina would've stabbed me in my sleep as a child if she thought she'd get away with it; and Luc denies it even though we both know I'm right.

"I promise, Mira, it won't be as bad as you think," he says.

"No. It'll be much, much worse." Foreboding forms a bottomless cavern, making me feel ill. "They're going to be furious about the Tournament."

"That wasn't your fault. I won't let them blame you for it." Luc knocks his knee into mine, enticing me to look at him. "They'll behave tonight. If they so much as scowl at you, give me a look and I'll shut them up."

Warm hope relieves some of the pressure on my chest. "You mean it?"

"Of course. I know they're worse when I'm not there. I won't leave your side all night. Promise." He gives my hand a squeeze, and for a moment, I feel lighter. Moments like this—moments in between—are rare. Between eavesdropping and plotting, when he's not the Honored Praeceptor and I'm not a tool he uses to collect secrets; when he actually feels like my brother, and I actually feel like his sister.

Our conversation is cheery for the rest of our short trip. To live above the Collar of the mountain is to be an elite. The homes here, closest to Widow's Hall, are some of the only aboveground structures on Mount Saidu, aside from the temples. Everything about the Kylers' manor—from the stone exterior to the intricately decorated interior—is splendid. The floor in the entryway is swirling tiles of alternating black and green marble like a chess board. Household servants move around in green uniforms, carrying trays of food and drink for guests.

Luc and I hand our outer layers to an attendant in the foyer and make our way through the lounge in search of his parents. The ground floor is crowded with the wealthiest members of Virdeian society, and just about all of them greet Luc as we pass:

"Honored Praeceptor, we are so looking forward to the Tournament this year."

"Pleasure to see you tonight, sir."

"Good luck in the Tournament, sir."

Everywhere we turn are warm smiles for Luc that freeze over at the sight of me. I surreptitiously drag my sleeve over the flicker of gold.

It's only supposed to be dinner, but all the guests are dressed extravagantly, in embroidered dresses and overdresses, tapered pants and wool coats, and pearls far as the eye can see. Petruvia blocks Virdei's access to the ocean, so the few Virdeians who can afford pearls, shells, and sea crystals love to show them off.

We're a few steps into the dining room when Luc is enveloped by bony arms. "Lucien!" Yelina trills, tugging his elbow from my grip. "You're finally here." Tonight, her hair falls to her rib cage in dark, glossy ringlets, secured with pearl pins. Her natural hair is short, kinky, and almost all gray now. I haven't seen it in years.

"Of course." Luc smiles. "Mira and I wouldn't miss this for anything."

Yelina's sharp brown eyes find me and narrow frostily, searching for a fault to attack.

I've never confessed to Sef how much seeing Yelina gnaws at my nerves and fills me with dread. But she knows. She always does her best work on days when I'm to see my stepmother. Tonight, she oiled my roots with rosemary oil and twisted my thick, dark hair into a series of braids pulled tight from my face and held in place against my scalp with thin golden hair cuffs. It's braided to the crown, where it flares in a pouf of springy curls. I'm dressed in a gray gown and golden yellow overdress, laced up the middle with silk ribbon. I'm not dripping in jewelry, but I look the part of an aristocrat's daughter.

Coming up empty, Yelina bares her teeth at me. "Remira. You're here."

My grin is as thin and unpleasant as she is. "Yelina. You're as delightfully observant as ever."

Her eyes narrow in warning, but we're in public, so we keep up our scowls, thinly veiled by fake smiles, as Yelina guides Luc and me through a stone archway carved with roses, leading into the ballroom. At the front, a twosome of fiddlers play upbeat music on a small stage. Some guests mill about in the corners, while others fill the center of the room, twirling in dance.

As soon as we enter, Mathson approaches with a wide, cheery smile. "I'm so glad you could make it. I've been looking forward to dancing with my daughter all night."

It takes me four beats of fiddle music to realize he means me.

I mean, I *am* his daughter, but only in a literal sense. Mathson has despised me from the moment I appeared sobbing and starving on his doorstep. At the time, he was still an Honorate. He stepped down and passed the position to Luc shortly after my arrival. He never said why, but I knew. The scandal of my existence was evidence he'd violated the rules of decorum by having an affair with my mother—an Opheran woman who used to work in his home.

His "early retirement," however unconvincing, was preferable to a public and forced resignation. He managed to keep the Honorate position in the family, but he couldn't keep the scandal of his bastard Opheran child from spreading through the mountain.

He's been punishing me for it ever since.

Mathson seizes me by the elbow. Outwardly, he's all smiles as he begins dragging me to the dance floor, away from Yelina and Luc. His tight grip is the only indication he's not as pleased as his expression suggests.

Frantic, I twist my head, trying to make eye contact with Luc. He promised he wouldn't leave my side, promised he wouldn't abandon me to the wrath of his parents.

His mother clutches his arm as though she has talons, smirking as Mathson hauls me away, and Luc stares at the floor, avoiding my gaze, saying nothing.

Perhaps I shouldn't be surprised. I am. Perhaps silence shouldn't have claws that tear me open. His guts me like a fish.

I choke down how much it hurts along with how foolish I feel for actually believing he'd do as he promised and stay by my side. At the time, he meant it, but it's easy to mean things before they happen. Just as it's easy to be a coward when it counts.

My heart stammers a sharp, terrified rhythm. "Mathson—" I try to speak, but the glare he shoots over his shoulder could melt steel. "*Don't.*" A single word. Dripping so much venom, I purse my lips and say nothing.

He waits until we're a safe distance from being overheard to start in. "A Tournament of Thrones was *not* the plan."

My throat is dry. "I know. But—"

"But nothing." Spit flies from his mouth as he affixes a broad and obviously fake smile to his face, settling his hands into position so we can begin this sham of a dance. "You swore Lucien would rule another term."

"He will. I made sure the vote passed, didn't I? I'll do the same to ensure he wins the Tournament."

"Your assurances mean nothing." Mathson spins us deeper into seclusion as another pair dances too close. "This is a Tournament of Thrones. You are out of your depth. The Honorate is child's play compared to this."

I already know this. It's all Sef and I have been working on since Kaidren dropped the life-shattering news that he's competing against Luc for the throne.

The Tournament is overseen by a private committee that organizes each event and coordinates with the decurio to ensure everything goes seamlessly. Getting Sef on that committee is our top priority. Then we'll shift our focus to preparation for the three trials.

The first trial is always the same; the second, always a surprise. Both of these are judged solely on the skills of the candidates, but if there isn't a winner by then, Widow's Hall hosts a masquerade ball before the third. It's a chance for candidates to consort with Virdei's elite and garner whatever support they can before the final trial, where they are allowed to use supplies (usually weapons) bought for them by constituents.

Each trial is dangerous, violent, and highly anticipated. Until now, I've dealt in secrets, not blood. To win, I'll have to adjust my skill set.

Mathson isn't finished. "There will be more eyes on you and Lucien than ever before. If anyone learns there is interference in the Tournament . . ." His dark eyes are identical to mine, but there's a cruelty in them that sharpens as he lowers his voice. "You're going to wish being enlisted in the decurio was your biggest problem."

The Tournament is more than a competition—it's a show, and all of Virdei and our Petruvian guests are the audience. At the end of the Tournament, the new Praeceptor sits down with the Petruvian visitors to make revisions to the flimsy treaty and maintain their tentative peace. Petruvia will be watching the Tournament closely, seeking flaws and weaknesses they can exploit. They'll pounce on any excuse to revise the terms of the treaty in their favor. Ten years ago, the Honorate who won the throne performed poorly and was forced to cede more land to Petruvia than Virdei was willing to part with. The Republic was displeased. Luc can't afford a poor showing.

"I'll be discreet. I always am." I pause as we dance past a group of people who watch us curiously. I stay quiet until we sway out of earshot. "As for everything else, I'll learn. I'm a quick study."

"These will be physical challenges. Lucien studied swordplay and combat at the finest academy in Virdei. I assume Arliss ensured the Vale boy did as well. *You* have no physical skills to speak of. You will be outmatched in every trial."

I bite the inside of my cheek against the urge to spill my thoughts. Yes, Luc attended Holsbane Academy, and yes, he studied warfare as well as academics, but he was a below-average student. The only reason he graduated was because if he ever fell behind in a course, all it took was a firm word from Mathson Kyler for the problem to miraculously disappear.

"I am warning you, Remira, if you lose—" His words stall as he glances over my shoulder.

It's my only warning before someone jostles me from behind.

"My apologies." I half turn to address the person at my back, even though *they* bumped into me. "I wasn't watching where I was . . ." I stop speaking.

Kaidren Vale stands behind me, annoyingly handsome, impeccably dressed, and *very* uninvited.

Words fail me as his mouth stretches into a broad grin. "Remira. What a surprise." He says that, but he doesn't look surprised to see me. He looks like a wolf that just cornered a sheep. Meanwhile, I'm so startled by his sudden appearance, I say nothing.

Kaidren mistakes my shock for confusion. "Kaidren Vale. The new Honorate. We met yesterday, remember?"

"Oh." I swallow, trying to hide how flustered I am. *Why* do I keep letting him catch me off guard? "Of course. Lovely to see you again."

Kaidren turns his disarming smile to Mathson. "Sir, can I steal her for a dance?" His voice is smooth and charming, but I catch a taunting glint in those deep brown eyes. Kaidren publicly challenged Mathson's son to a Tournament of Thrones, showed up uninvited to a private event at his home, and is asking to dance with his daughter. It's a move so bold, I'd take notes if I wasn't panicking.

A dance with Kaidren is dangerous. For him, because bad things happen to people I despise. For me, because one touch from him and my world crumbles.

I look pleadingly at Mathson, trying to convey with my eyes that he has to refuse, for both our sakes. But we're drawing curious looks, and the last thing Mathson Kyler wants is a scene.

"Of course. So long as you promise to bring her back in one piece." Mathson releases my arm and, without looking at me, walks away.

Kaidren extends a hand to me, brows raised expectantly. "Shall we?"

Neither of us is wearing gloves. My throat feels tight and itchy. "Actually, I'm . . ." I scramble for an excuse. "Hungry."

Kaidren doesn't miss a beat. He lowers his hand and holds out the crook of his elbow instead. "Then let's get food."

This is safer, but I tug my sleeves over my hands, still tense as I loop my arm through his. I lean my body away from his as we walk.

Kaidren smiles as he guides me through dancing guests toward a table along the back wall filled with food. "It's lovely to see you again, Remira *Kyler*." He emphasizes my surname with a smirk. "You failed to mention you're the Praeceptor's sister." The good humor in his expression makes it clear he's teasing, not genuinely upset I didn't tell him.

"You didn't ask for a family history." I mimic his playful tone.

"I asked for your surname."

We reach the table, and I immediately drop his arm and step back. "Most people here already know who I am. I enjoyed the anonymity." I draw in my brows pleadingly. "I hope you're not upset with me?"

"Not at all." Without asking, he begins preparing a plate for me.

I watch over his shoulder, pleasantly surprised when he puts a generous heaping of goat stew on the porcelain plate—my favorite. "I didn't realize my father included the new Honorate on the guest list."

Kaidren moves on to the next dish (roasted potatoes) and drops his voice. "Can you keep a secret?"

"Depends how scandalous it is."

He chuckles. With a quick glance around to ensure there's no one near us, he leans in, breath ghosting my ear. "I wasn't invited."

I pretend to be shocked as I draw back. "Really? Then why are you here?"

His grin softens. "To see you again, of course."

A blatant lie. Kaidren always has an ulterior motive, and judging by the way he's shamelessly flirting with me, he's willing to toy with my emotions to get what he wants.

He could just treat me like the rest of the Honorate and pretend I don't exist. This is crueler. I'd rather a man ignore me than play me for a fool.

Still, I flutter my lashes and duck my head with a shy grin like I don't see him for what he is. "Really?"

He chuckles. "You sound surprised, but I told you I want us to be friends."

"I thought you were just being kind."

"I wasn't." His gaze is bright and earnest. "I couldn't help but notice you and your father seemed to be having an intense conversation."

Right on cue. His seamless transition from friend to snoop. "You overheard us?"

"No, but it looked serious. Is everything all right?" He hands me my finished plate.

"Thank you." I'm not actually hungry, so I pick at it idly and keep my focus on him. "We were talking about the Tournament and how thrilling it's going to be. You must be excited."

Kaidren's usual confidence sputters. It's subtle, but for a moment he looks nervous, before that carefully crafted smile returns. "I saw the last Tournament. Just a glimpse. My aunt took me up the mountain to watch. We sat in the very back of the arena, but I could see everything."

"What was it like?"

He hesitates for a few moments, considering. "It was exhilarating. One of the most exciting things I'd ever seen."

Heat. I trail my eyes over his face, searching the nuances of his expression, trying to guess what he doesn't say. "You must've been young. You weren't scared?"

He seems surprised by the question. "I—well, maybe a little."

I raise an eyebrow, waiting.

He wavers a bit longer before releasing a sigh and a rueful grin. "Fine. You caught me. I was terrified. I still have nightmares from that day."

"Nightmares about what?"

He shudders. "Watching someone die."

His voice is raw—*real*. It terrifies me.

The last Tournament was ten years ago. News of its brutality reached my mother and me in Ophera. That year, there were four candidates. Two of them nearly died, and at least seven aikkari soldiers *did* die.

At the time, I didn't care. Powerful men are violent and irrational. If they wanted to kill each other, so be it. Now . . . the powerful man in question is Luc, and the person responsible for keeping him alive is me.

"But you don't need to worry." My words are directed at Kaidren, but I'm trying to reassure the both of us. "Honorate don't die in the Tournament."

"No, but soldiers do."

"You'll protect them. I was just telling my father how I was nervous for my brother. He reminded me that Luc received all the training he needs at Holsbane. I'm sure whatever academy you attended prepared you just as well."

"Um—" Kaidren's smooth surface cracks as he clears his throat, looking uncomfortable. "Yes. You're probably right. Is your brother nervous?"

"No, he couldn't be more excited." I speak absently, hardly paying attention to my own lie. I'm distracted by the sudden heat coursing through me. Kaidren didn't attend an academy. An Honorate who didn't study in Virdei is unheard of. When the rest of the mountain hears about this . . .

Kaidren's eyes fall to something over my shoulder. He chuckles. "Your mother is glaring like she wants to murder me. Does she—"

It takes me a beat too long to realize he means Yelina. I'm snarling before I remember myself. "That woman is *not* my mother."

Kaidren blinks at me, startled by the outburst.

My eyes widen and I duck my head, shamefaced. "I-I'm so sorry." I can't believe I just did that.

"I should be the one apologizing," Kaidren says. "I didn't mean to offend you."

"You didn't." Any fool can see that's not true. I clear my throat. "That's Luc's mother. My stepmother. I should—uh—probably go see what she wants." I set my mostly untouched plate on the table. "Good luck in the Tournament."

The smile he gives me is broad and teeming with misplaced confidence. "Thank you. But I won't need it."

I smile back as though he's right.

Cutting through the crowd, I pretend to make my way to Yelina, but once I'm out of Kaidren's eyeline, I shift direction to search for Luc instead. I find him on the edge of the dance floor. His eyes widen with guilt when he sees me. "I'm sorry," are the first words out of his mouth.

I fold my arms derisively. "You promised you'd be by my side all night."

"I know, and I'm sorry, but I was watching you the whole time."

If anything, that makes it worse. "Your father left me with *Kaidren Vale*." I lower my voice, but frustration sharpens my tone. "He's an isha. If he had touched me—"

"He didn't."

My nostrils flare. "You didn't know he wouldn't."

"I know *you*. You'd never let that happen."

I want to scream. "What if he had? Would you have bothered to step in?"

I watch him process the question. See more guilt flicker over his expression.

I'm *more* than angry. I've been angry my whole life—she is my close and personal friend. I know how to handle rage, how to trap it within me and frost it with ice and a smile. This is deeper than that. This is a visceral kind of betrayal that follows going unseen by someone you were foolish enough to trust.

I wish I was only angry. My heart is sturdy. Rage alone can't melt it. It's a lethal combination of fury and sorrow that causes me to falter—heartbreak.

Heavy, racing footsteps approach from behind. I know even before I turn who it is. Mathson and Yelina are bright and cheery to the casual observer, but I know them. I see the tension they carry in their shoulders, the way their grins are more eerie than kind. They are hungry for blood—mine.

Yelina takes my arm, fingers digging in hard enough to bruise. "Why did I see you speaking with Kaidren Vale?" That narrow, vicious snarl she calls a smile doesn't slip as she speaks through her teeth.

"Ask your husband. He's the one who left me with him."

Yelina doesn't shift her gaze from me. "I'm not a fool. I saw the way you were looking at each other."

I force my eyes not to roll out of my head. Kaidren's act to flirt his way into my confidence had no effect on me, but clearly, it was convincing enough for Yelina. "The only thing I want from Kaidren is for him to drop dead. I assure you, the stars will freeze in hell before I allow myself to be charmed by someone like Kaidren Vale."

My conversation with Kaidren wasn't a total waste. He's an isha desperate to prove himself, and now I know what bait to dangle before him.

Luc will win the first trial. I'll make sure of it. The world will watch as he earns the throne for a second term. And then, I'm going to use Kaidren's pride against him and trick him into quitting the Tournament altogether.

Win Luc the throne, and get rid of the only person in Widow's Hall with the power to destroy me, in one fell swoop.

CHAPTER NINE

HOW TO STEAL A THRONE

First step to stealing a throne: get rid of the competition.

I wait around the corner of the Vale manor, watching his front door. It's early morning, and gray clouds blanket the mountainside with snow. I'm wrapped up in a dress, overdress, coat, gloves, and sjaal, but I leave my face uncovered and recognizable.

I'm in the middle of a full-body shiver when the Vale door ekes open, and a figure steps out. Tall, broad, and muscular. His face is covered by a thick sjaal, but I recognize his build. Kaidren strides in my direction, boots crunching in the snow.

When he's just a few paces away, I slip around the corner, gaze fixed on the toes of my shoes.

Two paces later, I collide into something sturdy.

I release a startled shriek and skid back. My arms flail as I fall.

Large hands band my waist, trying to keep me upright.

Honorable, but pointless. We're on an inclined road slicked with ice and coated with snow. Together, Kaidren and I tumble to the ground, icy powder spraying around us.

His back slams into the ground and I land on top of him, cheek pressed to his chest.

The impact of the fall leaves us both winded. I'm on his chest, recovering my breath, feeling the scattered rhythm of his heartbeat as the warmth of his short, surprised exhales crests my cheek.

With a groan, I brace myself against his torso and push up. His arm is still around me, and I only manage to pull back enough to hover my face over his.

Kaidren looks dazed as he brushes snow from where it sticks to his scarf. "I'm so sorry—" He stops, recognizing me. "Remira?" He tugs at the scarf, revealing the lower half of his face.

"Stars in hell. I'm mortified." I slide off him, pretending to be embarrassed as I bat snow from my clothing to avoid looking at him. "I can't believe I stumbled into you *again*."

Kaidren laughs. "I'm sure it was my fault. Both times." He gets to his feet and holds out a hand for me.

The gloves we're both wearing are the main reason I orchestrated this coincidental run-in outdoors. I let him help me up with a grateful smile. "Thank you."

One hand pulls me to my feet, the other rests against my waist, steadying me. I make the mistake of looking up.

He's closer than I realized. Wind whips his scarf around, framing his face against the white of the mountain, making his eyes look deeper than ever. He's gazing at me intently. Not smirking or flashing a fake smile, just studying me with concern that appears genuine.

My spine crawls with a shudder, and I remember myself.

I pull away from him. The hand at my waist falls to his side. "Sorry," I mumble.

"Don't be. I like running into you." I'm startled when he takes my hand and drags me to stand in an alley between two buildings. Snow still falls around us, but we're more sheltered from the winds.

"That's better. I can actually see you now." Before I can reply, he surprises me again. This time, by swiping at the loose snow on my collar. It's a familiar action—something I'd expect from Sef, or someone who knows me—not from a near stranger. When he's satisfied, he keeps talking as though nothing happened. "You always seem to be hiding. It's a shame. I like looking at you. You're just about the only thing in Virdei I actually like."

His stare is so intense, I almost believe he means it. I'm grateful for the rush of heat accompanying his words. A reminder that everything he does is a manipulation. "My brother thinks it's best I avoid notice."

Kaidren's eyes drop to my wrist. "Because you're Opheran?" He scoffs. "Why should that matter? I would never hide you."

A bold claim followed by yet more heat.

Kaidren's gaze drifts lazily toward my lips. He stares at them with . . . *stars in hell*—is that *longing* I detect?

Kaidren doesn't want to kiss me any more than I want to bathe in greyhorn manure, but he thinks charming me is the way to get what he wants.

I force a smile. "Thank you."

He grins and I find myself counting the reasons I despise his smile. Too wide, too many teeth, too strained at the cheeks. To the untrained eye, it's perfect, and I suspect it's served him well. It will get him nowhere with me. "I can't imagine what it's like to be Opheran in a place like this," he murmurs. "Surrounded by Honorate who lie constantly, and seeing the truth of it in the Shadow Queen's column. I want you to know, I'm nothing like them. A man is only as good as his word. When I say something, I mean it."

Lie after lie after lie. "I didn't know they still made honorable men. Not here, anyway."

"I intend to bring honor back into the Honorate. So, what do you say?" His deep brown gaze flits back to my lips, lingers for a moment, and then it's fixed on my eyes again, and he's smiling a perfect, secret smile. "Can I see you again tomorrow? On purpose, this time?"

He thinks I'm as starheaded as my mother. I'm itching to prove him wrong—and I will—but in the meantime, I have to pretend to trip and fall into his amateurish trap. "I can't tomorrow. But another time."

Kaidren slumps in disappointment. "I'm holding you to that."

"I hope you do, because I really admire you."

"Truly?" He perks up, looks pleasantly surprised. "Why?"

"You're tenacious. Even when the rest of the Honorate are reluctant to accept you." I drizzle honey into my tone, willing him to latch on to my baited hook. "I think it's admirable that you don't let petty rumors bother you." *This* is the reason for our contrived collision this morning.

Kaidren's brow furrows. "What rumors?"

"About you being an isha." I speak slowly, as though this is something I assumed was common knowledge.

There's no trace of his perfect smile anymore. "What do you mean?"

"I've just heard whispers of—" I stop myself. "Never mind. I'm sure it's just gossip."

He looks irritated, but quickly clears his expression with a neutral yet strained smile. "What are people saying about me being an isha?"

"Nothing. Only that it's convenient. That perhaps you invented it to draw notice."

"What people?" Kaidren's tone is sharp. "People in the Honorate? Your brother?" His lips twist into a sneer. "Does the Honored Praeceptor not believe me?"

"I shouldn't have said anything." I press my hands to my

face as though it's flushing. "I assumed you'd heard. Ignore me. It's just talk." I lay a comforting hand on his arm. "*I* believe you. Besides, it's impossible to prove to everyone that you're an isha. Short of a spectacle like Eteria." I fake a laugh.

Kaidren is hanging on to my every word. "What's Eteria?"

To anyone raised in Virdei, the question is absurd. But Kaidren grew up in Ophera and, clearly, hasn't done his research.

I swallow a smirk. "A public demonstration of an isha's abilities. A chance for isha to show off their skills and aikkari to show off their magic." Eteria used to be a major event. A few aikkari and civilians were chosen at random. The isha would reveal the aikkari and their sources to a roaring crowd, and the aikkari would in turn show off their magic to the world.

"People used to love it," I say. "But we haven't seen an isha for decades, so there hasn't been Eteria in years."

I watch Kaidren carefully as I speak. The subtle twitch of his brows, the ticking muscle in his jaw . . . He's aching to prove himself. And I've just dangled the perfect opportunity in front of him.

There's a deep hunger in his eyes that's familiar to me. The all-consuming, ravenous urge to prove to the world that you're more than they expect. Everyone has a weakness. A loose thread I can pull and pull until they unravel. I know Kaidren's thirst for validation like I know myself. It will be his undoing.

"I appreciate you telling me this, Remira," he says stiffly.

"Of course."

"I have to get going, but I'll see you soon." He starts to leave but stops. His eyes fixate on my neck. "That isn't all you're wearing, is it?"

I glance over my outfit. "Is there something wrong?"

"There's nothing covering your face."

I wave him off. "Oh. I'm fine."

"Absolutely not. It's snowing."

"It's always snowing."

"I didn't realize more snow makes you less likely to freeze to death," he says dryly. "How much farther are you walking?"

In truth, I have no destination. I'm only here to trip him into this conversation. I start to feed him my prepared lie, but he's already unwinding his own scarf from around his throat.

I frown. "What are you doing?"

"I just told you I'm a man of honor." Kaidren smirks. "I can't make that claim and leave you to freeze your face off." Holding either end of the scarf, he loops it around my neck. With a tiny grin and a tug, he pulls me toward him.

I gasp, stumbling, hands braced on his chest. "I—" My breath catches as our eyes meet. I swallow. "I can't take your scarf."

"You're not." His eyes dance with amusement. "I'm giving it to you." Kaidren's fingers tuck the wool around me, carefully draping my neck and shoulders in warmth, eyes fixed steadily on mine.

I try to bat his hands away. "I can do—"

Smirking, he tugs the scarf over my mouth and nose, muffling my objections. When he's finished, his gloved hands linger just above my collarbone.

I want to push him back, but my pulse is racing and loud, drowning out rational thought.

Kaidren ducks. Warm breath skates over the shell of my ear as he whispers, "If you want to give it back, you'll have to come find me. I look forward to our next meeting, Remira Kyler."

He's turned on his heel and disappeared into the snow before I can uncover my mouth and reply.

CHAPTER TEN

BEHIND ENEMY LINES

The walls in the entryway of Widow's Hall are crafted from tshira. It's good, in the sense that I can use magic to watch Petruvia's arrival from an adjoining room. Bad, in the sense that I can make out each anxious bead of sweat dripping down Luc's forehead.

I don't fare much better. My stomach's been a churning mess of apprehension since I opened my eyes this morning. Once the Petruvians are here, I'll have to begin the performance of a lifetime to keep Luc afloat and myself alive.

Although Virdei defeated Petruvia in their battle for control of the mountain, the true loser wasn't Petruvia—it was Ophera, caught in the middle of a war between two more powerful enemies.

The fragile peace between Virdei and Petruvia depends on the ever-changing treaty. With each revision, they slice control of Ophera differently. Some years, Virdei comes out with more; other years, it's Petruvia.

Ophera never wins much of anything.

It feels as if all of Widow's Hall is holding its breath, waiting, when at long last, the front doors open. A member of the decurio enters, guiding a procession of underdressed Petruvians. They wear indigo cloaks of an expensive-looking velvet, but no sweaters, overdresses, or sjaals. They've only just arrived, and already their teeth are chattering.

"Honored Praeceptor." The decurio leading their group bows. "May I present the Petruvian court."

Luc smiles warmly as the first guest comes forward. He is tall, shaped like a barrel, and shakes Luc's hand with a stiff smile. "I'm Taelon Night, adviser to King Pendrix. This is my wife." He gestures to a spindly-looking woman standing just behind him. "Lorwen."

"Pleasure to meet you both," Luc says.

Taelon's smile sharpens into a smirk. "Yes. How nice to finally meet the new Praeceptor of Virdei."

Luc's pleasant expression slips slightly with his confusion. "New? This is my fifth year on the throne."

"I've been King Pendrix's adviser for over twenty years, and I've never seen you before," says Taelon snidely. "Sounds new to me."

The decurio all stiffen at the blatant disrespect.

None of the Petruvians react. They're practically icicles in our court—cold, sharp, and pointed, and they each sport nearly identical smirks.

Luc bristles and draws his hand back. "There wasn't a Tournament of Thrones when I took over."

"So we've heard. Unsurprising to hear a Virdeian feels entitled to something they never earned." Taelon wraps an arm around his wife's waist, and together they stride farther into the entry hall, dismissing Luc altogether.

Luc is visibly shaken. A few decurio reach for their swords, but no one draws.

After a long silence, Luc puts on a strained smile and greets the next Petruvian, a short woman in a long, dark wig. "Amber Sansem, sir. Cousin to His Majesty King Pendrix."

As each person introduces themselves, I write down their name and title. In addition to the ambassador and the King's cousin, there's a commander in the Petruvian army responsible for transporting correspondence between Virdei and Petruvia; a noble who owns a large plot of land that produces most of Petruvia's crops; and an adviser to the youngest Petruvian prince, Prince Raevin.

When the introductions are finished, Luc frowns. "I was under the impression we would be receiving a member of the royal family? Will they be arriving later?"

They're all smirking again. It makes my skin crawl.

"Unfortunately, none of the princes could attend this year. Nor the princess. Nor any royal," Taelon says smugly. "Perhaps they'll attend the next Tournament, if your successor invites them."

Successor?

Taelon is implying either that Luc will lose this Tournament or that Petruvia won't send one of their own until he's no longer Praeceptor.

It's a clear slap in the face. Both Taelon's words and the absence of any member of their royal family. The Tournament ends with treaty negotiations—at least one of the royals should be here to facilitate that. It's not as if Petruvia doesn't have plenty to choose from. Four princes and a princess, and not a single one is here.

Luc looks as unsteady as I feel. I have to force air into my lungs. Force myself to remember that everything is under control. Sef already secured herself a spot on the Tournament planning committee. After this, I will do my part to physically prepare for the first trial. Between the two of us, we are impervious to surprise. Luc won't lose. I won't allow it.

As though sensing my thoughts, Luc's eyes shoot to the wall where I'm watching. He can't see me, but knowing I'm here calms him. Clumsily, he looks back to the Petruvians. "Well, then.

You'll be shown to your rooms. The opening ceremony of the Tournament is tomorrow morning. Soldiers will direct you to—"

"The arena," Taelon finishes Luc's sentence, looking bored. "I'm aware. I've been to several Tournaments. I've shaken the hands of many Praeceptors before you, and I am sure I will shake the hands of many after. I know how a Tournament is meant to work."

He doesn't say it out loud, but his smug expression speaks volumes: *I know how a Tournament works. And you don't.*

It's snowing (*again*), the air is freezing (as always), but my palms puddle with sweat as I enter the arena.

The domed tshira roof is drawn today, as the field is being used for decurio training. Although the arena is open to viewing, the stands are empty. Virdeian soldiers dot the field, all casting me lingering, confused looks as I pass.

I keep my head high and pretend I don't notice.

My roving gaze scans the soldiers, stopping when I catch sight of one in particular. Flynn Sixmen. A decurio I know by reputation but have never formally met. Nothing about his appearance is bold, but the way he carries himself makes him impossible to miss. At just twenty years old, Flynn isn't much older than me, but he's already made a name for himself. He's only decent-looking, but he has the confidence that comes with being the son of an Honorate, and one of the decurio's rising heroes.

Flynn is taller than me but not tall. Broader than average but not stocky. Close-cropped hair (all men in the decurio have the same haircut), eyes that are light and brown like amber, and a tiny mole above his upper lip. He's in the middle of a tense conversation with a fellow soldier. I move closer.

"The General isn't willing to risk war," Flynn is saying.

"Petruvia is growing restless. We can't—" He stops mid-sentence when he notices me. He mumbles something I can't hear to the soldier before dismissing him.

He raises his eyebrows expectantly as he approaches me. "Remira Kyler. To what do I owe this pleasure?"

I wasn't expecting him to know who I am. Everyone knows him, of course, but I usually spend as little time around the decurio as possible. A small, silly part of me fears proximity is enough for them to figure out I'm one of them. "Hello, sir. Your reputation precedes you."

"Are you here on behalf of His Honored Praeceptor for the opening ceremony tomorrow?" he asks.

"I'm actually here for more personal reasons," I say. "I'd like to learn how to fight."

I've always done my best work in the shadows. Eavesdropping and manipulating and pulling strings from the safety of obscurity. It won't be enough. Not for the Tournament.

Tomorrow is the opening ceremony. One week later is the first trial. In it, Luc and Kaidren will lead a team of aikkari, each fighting to put the other candidate in a death position. They can't actually kill the candidates, but there are no rules against killing other soldiers.

It will be dangerous. Deadly. If I'm to cheat Luc's way to victory, I'll have to step out of the shadows and onto the battlefield myself. To win—to survive—I must expand my skills to physical combat.

Flynn looks bewildered by the request. "I can't teach someone who's not aikkari how to wield magic. You know that."

Magic is a birthright. It can't be taught. Still, there are charlatans who peddle baubles and contraband they swear to the stars can give its users magic. They're overpriced, useless, and *very* illegal.

"I have no interest in magic, sir. I want to learn basic combat." I prepared a sob story to tug at his heart. "My brother has a team of selectmen for his protection. I don't." I relax my face, drooping the corners of my mouth into a frown. "There are so many newcomers at court. Luc has more guards than ever, just in case any of our guests wish him ill. Everyone looks at me as if *I'm* a threat somehow." I trace my tattoo, trying to make the motion look absent. "There are eyes on me at all times, and I feel their disdain. If one of them were to attack, I would have no means of defending myself. I only want to feel safe in my own home."

The wariness in Flynn's eyes subsides as he regards my tattoo with thinly veiled pity. "First of all, call me Flynn. Second of all, if you want to learn to fight, Miss Kyler, I will happily instruct you."

Relief floods my chest. Of all the soldiers in the decurio, I specifically chose Flynn Sixmen for a reason. His father, Selva Sixmen, received a letter from the imposter Shadow Queen. I can use our time together to prod Flynn about his father and prepare myself for the first trial in one fell swoop. "Truly? Thank you, sir."

He gives me a sharp look. It takes a moment for me to interpret its meaning. "I mean, thank you, Flynn." For once, my smile is genuine. "And please, call me Mira."

"I can't promise to make you an expert, but I can teach you the basics of self-defense. It's the most personal kind of attack. You use your specific set of skills to your advantage. Take yourself, for instance. You're not very tall, and you don't have much muscle." He pauses. "No offense."

I don't fight a grin. "None taken."

"Which means you need to focus on exploiting weakness. If you aim for the groin or eyes, you can disorient an attacker and escape."

I nod along. "Or distract them long enough to knock them out."

Flynn blinks a few times, frowning. "Well—sure. You could do that. Another approach is to aim for the joints. Get their knees to buckle, you can knock them off-balance and give yourself enough time to run away."

"Or attack," I say.

Flynn's brows shoot up, and he laughs. "You're very enthusiastic about violence."

I smile as innocently as I can. "Just an eager student."

"Yes, I can see that." He's still chuckling. "I have the opening ceremony to prepare for, so why don't you come back in a few days and I'll get you a uniform. I'm very curious to see if you're as violent in action as you are with your words."

CHAPTER ELEVEN

PHANTOM PAIN

The corridors of Widow's Hall are bustling with our newest arrivals from Petruvia's shores. The chambers of Ambassador Taelon and Lorwen Night, however, are exceptionally quiet.

Why? Perhaps because Taelon Night spends his alone, while his wife lies with a member of Virdeian court. Someone should have warned the Nights that the corridors of Widow's Hall have eyes—and they see all. As do I.

These halls are awhisper: the Nights have strange new bedfellows. Lorwen has taken up with a Virdeian lover, while Taelon has fallen out of bed and out of favor with King Pendrix.

Why? Well, whatever the reason, believe you me, if anyone is to find the truth, it's a woman who lives enshadowed.

Fondly,
Shadow Queen

I spend my night listening in on our Petruvian guests so I can rattle them the way they did Luc. Even made sure to slip a copy of the Shadow Queen's column under each of their doors this morning, so they can't miss it.

The arena at Widow's Hall is a dark gray-stoned structure formed into an elongated ring. The center is a large grassy field, its perimeter lined with wooden tiered benches. Since this space is mostly used for decurio training, there are rooms built into the base of the arena for equipment storage.

Usually, the arena is covered by a domed ceiling made of tshira. For today's event, the roof has been retracted with magic, allowing the light from the beacons atop Widow's Hall to illuminate the stage.

I sit on the edge of the same row as Mathson and Yelina, trying not to squirm. There's no reason to be this nervous. The opening ceremony is painless. The decurio will perform a demonstration, Luc and Kaidren will each give a speech, and then we all go home. Easy.

Why, then, is my stomach so knotted?

Sef sits with me, looking far more at ease than I feel. I'm so busy watching the field, tensely awaiting the start of the ceremony, I don't notice the approaching Petruvians until Yelina says loudly, "Why don't you join us?"

I look up, startled.

It's Taelon and his wife, Lorwen, in their indigo cloaks. Their heads are high and haughty, as though they don't notice the reproachful looks they're getting from the rest of the stands. Most people have already read the Shadow Queen's column this morning.

"Sit with us." Yelina pats the space around her. "My son is the Praeceptor. It would be an honor." Her Petruvian accent slips out—her lips curl on her *s*'s, her *t*'s are sharpened, and her *o*'s are elongated.

Lorwen's face lights up. "You sound Petruvian."

"I am." Mathson and Yelina Kyler's marriage was never one of love, but rather one of political advantage. Decades ago, Honorate Mathson Kyler was sent to one of Petruvia's tournaments. Yelina, the daughter of a high-ranked member of

Petruvian court, was promised to him in marriage as one of the terms of the treaty.

Treaties are tenuous and can change depending on the regime—the whim of a fickle Petruvian king, or the shifting priorities of the ever-changing Virdeian Praeceptor—but a marriage treaty is permanently binding.

At Yelina's invitation, Lorwen Night becomes a completely different person. Her frosty demeanor melts as she sits beside my stepmother. Taelon stands next to her, saying nothing. There isn't room for him.

My stomach drops. I see what's about to happen.

"Remira, you don't mind giving up your seat for our guests, do you, dear?" Yelina asks me, voice dripping with false sweetness. "She's Opheran," she adds in an exaggerated whisper to the Petruvians. "She probably prefers standing anyway."

I picture ripping her hair from her scalp. Then I force a smile. "Not at all." I take a quick look around. I don't see any open seats nearby.

Sef takes my hand and gently squeezes my fingers. "Don't worry. I have a better spot in mind." Without another word, we descend the bench steps to stand beneath them, watching between the legs of the rest of the audience.

Relegated to the shadows. As always.

At least this time I have Sef with me. Yelina chatters away above us. She takes quickly to Lorwen, who launches into a long-winded rant about the cold. Yelina offers her sympathies, sounding more genuinely sincere than I've ever heard her.

I scowl. "I could hardly stand Yelina before. What are we supposed to do now that there's two of them?"

"We could always murder one and trade them between Virdei and Petruvia every few months. If we keep their faces covered, who would even notice the difference?" Sef muses.

I whack her on the arm, laughing. "You're horrible."

"You laughed."

"Then we're both horrible."

We stop talking as the benches break out into cheers. Luc and Kaidren enter the arena together. Excited watchers stomp their feet, rattling the wooden stands and filling the air with shrill whistles.

Well, everyone except the Petruvians directly over us. They seem determined to appear as miserable as possible as the candidates for this year's Tournament take their places on the stage at the edge of the field.

Footsteps pound from outside the metal gates that serve as entrance to the arena. The gate bursts open and Flynn strides in, followed by ten rows of soldiers marching in neat lines.

Acclaim surrounds Flynn like dense fog. The entire Republic went giddy when he revealed that the source of his magic is snow, one of the most readily available resources in Virdei. He quickly rose to prominence in the decurio, and now he is known for his quick wit and skills with magic—a winning combination.

Snow swirls around Flynn as he glides toward the center of the arena. Flurries dance in thick spirals, first circling his head, then over the crowd, drawing incredulous gasps.

A plume of snow congeals, shaping into a large white butterfly. It flaps its massive wings and flies above the stands.

Heads crane to watch. Even the Petruvians can't help but look awed by the display.

This level of control over one's magic is practically unheard of—especially with a source like snow.

Flynn stops in the dead center of the field. He crouches, touching snow piled on the ground with bare hands.

When he rises, he extends his arms. Snow explodes into the air, forming more winged creatures that flutter over the shocked audience.

The soldiers marching behind him stop as one. In a practiced move, they each drop something dark to the ground. Tshira, leveled into flat boards.

The soldiers step onto the planes of tshira and draw up their arms in unison. Slowly, the tshira begins to rise, carrying the decurio with it.

The soldiers aren't exactly floating—their movements are too jerky for that—but they rise to join the butterflies of snow in the air. They're *flying*.

I've never seen anything like it. The crowd's screeches of excitement reach a fever pitch.

Magic is almost always used for its utility. To see it create something beautiful is enough to make spectators lose their heads, myself included.

When it's finished, Flynn takes a bow with a wide smile.

After magic, tshira is the most valuable resource in Virdei. The Tournament of Thrones is about more than selecting the next Praeceptor; it's about reminding our enemies how powerful we are and how foolish they would be to cross us. Our Petruvian guests still aren't smiling, but they look sufficiently impressed.

Flynn Sixmen takes his place on the stage. "Thank you all for that warm reception, and thank you to this great Republic."

More cheers and whistles. Flynn waits patiently for the uproar to die down before he continues. "I have been graced with the honor of introducing our candidates for this year's Tournament of Thrones. Please join me in welcoming Honorate Kaidren Vale and reigning Praeceptor Lucien Kyler."

Kaidren gives his speech first, followed by Luc. My brother recites the words I wrote for him calmly. His delivery is a bit wooden (I make a mental note to coach him on this later), but all things considered, it's a good performance.

Flynn claps with everyone else as Luc finishes speaking. "Let the Tournament of Thrones begin! We will commence with an opening challenge. The winning candidate will have an advantage in the first trial next week."

Luc and Kaidren go rigid with shock. Gasps erupt throughout the stands. Sef and I look at each other, eyes wide.

I didn't know this was coming. If the surprised excitement that fills the arena is any indication, *no one* did.

Sef looks stunned. "This can't be right. The Tournament committee didn't plan it."

I'm annoyed, but not with her. I thought we were prepared. We got her a spot on the Tournament planning committee. She learned all about how the Tournament works—or so we thought. Clearly, there are still a few surprises awaiting us. I do *not* like surprises.

Flynn keeps going. "The opening challenge is quick. Each candidate will select one member of the decurio to represent them. Their soldiers will fight—to the death."

The crowd rumbles as decurio spill into the arena. I squint, assessing them. There aren't as many soldiers to choose from as I anticipated—just a few rows—and these soldiers are smaller and less physically impressive than those who just performed in the opening ceremony.

Luc chooses first. He points to the largest soldier. A good, safe choice named Erik. Kaidren's pick is a spry-looking young man called Vellen.

Luc selects a sword for his soldier; Kaidren selects a long knife for his.

The two decurio stand in the center of the arena field, circling each other. I'm tense, clutching Sef's sleeve for comfort.

Erik—Luc's soldier—makes the first move. He brandishes his sword. Vellen lurches out of the way, but he's a bit too slow. His thigh is caught by the blade. Red blooms on his uniform. A shallow cut, but it looks painful.

Watching them fight, I frown. They each lumber more than they lunge. Their reflexes are off, and they look more awkward with their weapons than they should. They're slower than I thought decurio would be. Slower than the soldiers from the opening ceremony.

Vellen rushes forward, moves around Erik, and tries to stab him from behind.

Erik doesn't turn quickly enough; the dagger lodges in his shoulder. He reaches to yank it out, and I see it—a flash of gold on his wrist.

He wrenches the knife from his back and throws it at Vellen. It misses, skidding over the ground behind them.

Vellen is now unarmed. This should be an easy win for Luc's soldier. But he's too slow, giving Vellen time to sprint for his knife.

Erik hacks at his opponent with his sword, trying to stop him. He misses. By a lot.

Why are they so *slow*?

As Vellen reaches for the knife in the ground, I see another glimpse of gold.

I frown. They're *both* Opheran?

What are the odds of that? The decurio recruit from Virdei and Ophera alike, but far more aikkari are born in the Republic. Opherans comprise a very small portion of our soldiers. The likelihood of two Opheran soldiers being selected at random for this challenge are slim. Practically impossible.

As I watch Vellen seize the knife and hurl it at Erik, I'm left with the horrifying realization that there's a reason these two appear poorly trained compared to the other soldiers: because they are.

The knife sinks into Erik's chest. He stumbles before falling over, dead.

There's a reason the pool of soldiers for this so-called game was noticeably small: They drew competitors from a selection of Opheran soldiers. *Only* Opheran soldiers.

After all, Opherans are expendable. They're poorly trained, underprepared, and who cares if they fight each other to the death?

Erik is still. He lies in the snow, blood seeping from the wound in his chest. All the while, the audience is cheering, and Flynn is congratulating Kaidren on his victory. As if he did anything more than watch two insignificant Opherans try and kill each other.

I can't look away from Erik's body.

I recall Kaidren's words, that he still has nightmares of his first Tournament. Of the first person he watched die.

The sight of the unsung soldier lying in the snow, dead and ignored, is seared into my brain. I fear Kaidren was right: I'll never get the image out of my mind, not even in sleep.

CHAPTER TWELVE

THE ART OF GOSSIP

I don't have to fake my shivers as I knock on the front door of the Vale manor. I'm dressed plainly in a gray dress and overdress made of thin, scratchy wool; patchy cloak with a frayed hem; tattered scarf; and a pair of worn leather gloves.

It's too cold for so few layers, but I convincingly look the part of a servant girl who can't afford anything warmer.

Kaidren is currently at Widow's Hall, entertaining Petruvian guests with Luc. No idea how long it'll take, but I don't plan on staying for more than an hour.

A woman opens the door. Her face is pinched in irritation, but it softens when she sees my trembling figure. "Stars in hell, girl. Come in, come in." She shuffles me inside without a second thought.

I stumble over the threshold with a nervous smile. "I'm so sorry to intrude, ma'am."

"You're not intruding, dear. The lord of the house won't know, and his son is out. Give me your cloak. It's drenched."

Now that I'm inside, the snow that gathered on my cloak is melting, soaking through to my skin. It's a relief to peel it off. I take care to twist my wrist as I remove my gloves, so there's no way to miss my golden sun tattoo. Most days, it causes me less trouble to hide it. Today, I want her to know: I'm not just a poor servant. I'm Opheran. Infinitely more pitiable, and infinitely more trustworthy.

I'm in need of gossip. No one in Widow's Hall seems to know anything about Kaidren, so I'm seeking it from the source. Who better for the Vale servants to gossip with than one of their own?

The woman sucks her teeth when she sees my tattoo but doesn't comment. "My name's Frida, dear. I'm the head housekeeper. What brings you here in this weather?"

I take a heavy breath and with my exhale release the story I've formulated. "I'm sorry to bother you, ma'am. I'm a new cook for Honorate Ruick. He made a request for dinner, but we don't have all the ingredients and he hasn't given me money to buy anything, so I've been asking around and everyone's turning me away, and I fear he's going to fire me—"

"Slow down, and calm down." Frida puts her hands on my shoulders in a soothing gesture. "No one's getting fired. Tell me what you need, and I'll see if we have any to spare."

"Leek leaves."

"Is that all?" Frida smiles kindly. "I'm sure we've got some. Let me ask the cook. In the meantime, why don't you rest up in the sitting room, dear? We've got a fireplace. You walked all the way here from the Ruicks'?"

Honorate homes are all above the Collar. They're near enough to each other and Widow's Hall by sledge, but on foot, a trek from the Ruick manor to here would be torture. "Yes, ma'am."

"You must be freezing." She leads me into the Vales' sitting room. "Take a seat. I'll fetch some tea to warm you up." She motions for me to sit before the fireplace and scurries off.

The sitting room is curved into a half circle, with the

fireplace on the rounded side. Oddly shaped rooms are common in Virdeian manors. They're built into the mountain, so they're often constructed to accommodate the mountain's whims rather than their owners'.

A mint-green and silver patterned rug covers the dark wooden floor. The fireplace is wider than my arms can stretch, and as tall as my hips. A few paintings of landscapes hang over the mantle, but not a single portrait of a person or family.

Frida returns, balancing a tray of tea. I fake a shiver and take a cup. I've mostly warmed up by now—I wasn't outside in my thin clothes for as long as I've led her to believe—but I need an excuse to stay and keep her talking. "You're sure your employer won't mind?"

"I swear. He's practically dead to the world. Barely left his room in years."

I blink rapidly, as though coming to a startling revelation. "This is Honorate Vale's home?"

"Yes."

"Wow. I've heard whispers about him."

Frida chuckles. "I can imagine. The Vales are the talk of the mountain. Especially now."

She means because of Kaidren. I try not to appear too eager as I take a sip of tea. Scalding hot, just the way I like it. "You said Mister Vale is bedridden, but are you certain his new son won't find me here?"

"You don't have to worry about him. He just left."

"What's he like?" I lean toward her, keeping my eyes round, curious, and clueless as a newborn calf.

"He's kind. Which is rare here. Do you read the Shadow Queen?"

"Her column doesn't usually make it to Ophera."

"I thought as much." Frida nods to my wrist. "He's like you."

"He's Opheran?" I touch a finger to the golden sun. "I hadn't heard."

"The Shadow Queen just wrote about it. It caused quite a stir. He doesn't even have a tattoo."

"Really?" I shake my head as though awed. "I've never met an Opheran over five years old without one. When did Honorate Vale learn he had an Opheran son?"

"Just a few weeks ago," Frida says.

My stomach ignites as she lies to me for the first time.

Casually, I drink my tea, musing over a way to coax out the truth without accusing her of lying.

I incline my head with a sly flick of my brow, alerting her I'm about to share something shocking. "Don't tell anyone, but I overheard my employer saying he was surprised Honorate Vale doesn't have *more* bastard children."

Frida laughs. "That's hardly a secret, dear. Honorate Vale has had many . . . indulgences."

An understatement. Arliss Vale is one of the few Honorate over the age of forty to never marry. Before he fell ill, he was known for taking many, many women to bed.

I pretend I don't already know this, pressing my hands to my face as though I've been scandalized. "I didn't realize." I hush my voice. "*Does* he have other children?"

"I doubt he would know, even if he did."

I scrunch my brows together and purse my lips, as if I'm trying to solve a particularly challenging arithmetic problem. "But if his son's mother is Opheran, how did they meet? I didn't think the Honorate spent much time with Opherans."

"She used to work here. She . . . left her employment shortly after Honorate Vale learned he had a son."

The pause before "left" doesn't escape my notice. Frida

hasn't said as much, but I'm willing to bet Arliss fired Kaidren's mother once he learned she had his child.

Just as Mathson fired my mother when he learned about me.

I suppress a scowl and focus instead on the opening Frida has inadvertently given me. "I didn't realize she worked here so recently."

Frida looks confused. "What?"

I warm my hands around the teapot. "You mentioned earlier that Mr. Vale only learned he had a son a few weeks ago. I assume that means his mother left employment here only recently as well?"

Frida's brows draw in as she realizes her mistake.

If my eyes were any wider, they'd roll right out of my head. *Innocence.* Hopefully, if I chant it in my mind enough times, I'll make myself look it.

"I misspoke," Frida says after a long pause. "Honorate Vale first learned he had a son years ago, when the boy was still a child. But Honorate Vale didn't claim him until last year. After he fell ill."

"Poor boy," I say with as much false sympathy as I can manage. "Do you know why?" Kaidren came to Virdei earlier than I thought. I assumed he'd arrived shortly before I first saw him in Widow's Hall, but apparently, he's been living with his father in Virdei since last year.

"Honorate Vale is an honorable man," says Frida. "I have no doubt he was merely doing what he thought best."

The fever of her lie is so sudden, so unexpected, I accidentally heat the teacup in my hands. Clearly, Frida disapproves of her employer's actions but doesn't want to admit it, not even as gossip.

"If she used to work here, you must know her?" I say.

Frida smiles sadly. "I *knew* her. Zara was a seamstress. She passed away almost eleven years ago. The boy was raised by her sister, Julissa."

Just a few years before I lost my own mother. Unbidden, I feel my expression soften. "Mr. Vale didn't send for his son after his mother passed?"

Frida sucks her teeth. When she replies, her words are measured. "As I said, I'm sure Honorate Vale did what he thought best."

Another lie. She doesn't like the way her employer handled this but doesn't want to speak ill of him. I need to tread carefully if I don't want her to shut down completely. "Honorate Vale seems like such a gracious, benevolent employer."

Frida's brow clears with relief. "Yes. He's a kind—"

Her words are slashed by a piercing shriek down the hall, followed by a crash.

My heart stutters as I leap to my feet. I hardly notice that the sudden motion knocks over the tea tray, spilling it onto the carpet. "What was that?"

Frida is frozen. Her head is swiveled toward the doorway, but she doesn't reply. I'm not even sure she heard me.

Another shriek—same voice, but louder, more anguished.

Fear clogs my throat and chases my heart into a sprint. My feet carry me racing from the room, around the corner, searching for the source of the crash. I slow when an open door catches my eye in the hall ahead of me.

I pause, just outside, listening. All I hear are harsh, shallow breaths.

Slowly, I step through the open door—

And stop.

I'm in someone's bedchambers. A maid stands alongside the bed, remnants of a dropped breakfast tray scattered around her feet.

Lying in the bed is a man I know, but hardly recognize.

I last saw Arliss Vale over two years ago, before he was too sick to leave his home. He looks like a completely different person now. Tall and skinny, with yellow-tinted, sagging skin. His once dark hair is faded to white and thinning.

He's aged decades over the course of just two years. Despite how old and frail he looks, the most concerning aspect of his appearance are his eyes: brown, glassy, and wide open; and his chest: perfectly still.

He's dead.

CHAPTER THIRTEEN

A VICIOUS GIRL

The once great, now late Arliss Vale is among the stars. Or burning in hell.

The entire mountain knows Arliss has been slowly sinking toward death for years. What they don't know: someone helped drag him under. With poison.

The decurio have their theories, but my eyes are firmly fixed on his son—Opheran bastard Kaidren Vale.

Where did Bastard Vale learn the skills of leadership? According to my sources, it wasn't at a Virdeian academy.

What makes him a man of honor? Certainly not hiding his status as an isha until it suited him.

Did Bastard Vale murder his father? Did he lie to us all about being an isha? Let's just say, you can change your name and don Honorate robes, but once a bastard, always a bastard.

Fondly,
Shadow Queen

A gloved hand clamps over my mouth. His arm curls around my waist, yanking me against the heat of his body.

I shriek. It's muffled, and all I've accomplished is tasting the leather of his gloves.

His arm slides up until his fingers curl around my throat and squeeze.

My legs flail as I scramble to recall his instructions.

First, I need him to release me.

I claw, raking the hand at my throat with my nails. His gloves absorb most of the impact, and his grip remains as firm as ever.

Next plan. I drive my elbow back, into the soft spot on his side.

He doesn't release me, but he grunts. Good. It hurt. So, I do it again. And again. Enough that he switches tactics, grabbing for my swinging arm and unlatching his hold around my waist.

I stomp my foot on his, hard as I can. It draws a hiss. The fingers locked around my throat loosen.

I scramble free, taking deep gasps of air. He's taller than me. Faster than me. I have no weapons. To escape, I need to incapacitate him.

My foot kicks out, slamming into his knee. It buckles, and I kick him again, this time right in the groin.

Flynn falls to his knees. I rear back to strike him across the face, but he snatches my wrist. "I think that was more than enough, Mira." His voice is strained, but he gives me a small grin. "Good job."

I'm out of breath, and my heart is still racing. "Thanks." I hold out a hand.

"You have good instincts." Flynn takes my hand and rises gingerly to his feet. "I didn't think you'd be so . . ." He trails, searching for a specific word. "Ruthless. Most people are afraid to hurt a pretend assailant, so they hold back. You didn't. You fought as if your life were truly at stake."

"Oh." I frown, not sure what to make of this. "I'm sorry."

"Don't be. You did well. It's better to practice as though it's real."

"You think I'd stand a chance if you were actually trying?"

"Against a trained decurio soldier? Probably not. But give it time. Victory favors the vicious, and something tells me you are as vicious as they come."

Hearing his praise makes me smile. The light, pleasant sensation doesn't last for long. It's drowned by the prickling feeling of eyes boring into me.

I don't have to turn to know what it is. The Petruvians are here to observe training. They're supposed to be watching the decurio, but I keep feeling their probing stares on me.

Taelon and Lorwen Night are eerily stoic. They sit in the stands, silent and expressionless.

I glance in their direction to find them already staring back. I shudder and look away.

Flynn gazes at me knowingly. "Just ignore them."

"They bother you too?"

He scowls. "Let's just say I'll be happy when this Tournament is finally over and we can get back to training in peace."

"Can't the General kick them out? Or you?"

"Petruvia has a Tournament of their own, to decide how land is allocated. When they compete, we watch. Fair is fair."

"More like fair is creepy," I mutter with a dark look at the Nights, who are still staring at me.

Flynn chuckles and doesn't correct me.

We continue sparring under the watchful eyes of the Nights while I try to figure out a way to broach the subject of his father.

As we break for water, I say, "Doesn't this business with Arliss Vale bother you?"

Flynn frowns, looking wary. "I barely knew the man."

"It doesn't bother you that there might be someone murdering the Honorate?"

Flynn doesn't answer right away. He takes a long drink of water, not looking at me. "No."

I figured someone of his stature would be better at lying. "That wasn't convincing. Come on. Your father is an Honorate. You must be worried whoever killed Arliss is going to strike again."

He lowers his voice. "Mira, we're not allowed to discuss ongoing investigations with civilians. I could get in trouble."

Interesting. His objection to talking about the case is that he's not allowed to—not that he's *unwilling* to. I can work with that. "What if I fight you for it?"

Flynn sputters a laugh. "What?"

"A fight. I manage to pin you to the ground, you answer my questions. You win, I'll drop it forever."

"It's not a fair fight. I'm going to win."

"Then I guess you have nothing to lose."

He wavers, looking more amused than conflicted. "What are your terms?"

"Well, obviously you're not allowed to use magic, and you have to keep one arm behind your back. You know, to keep it fair."

"Mira, I'm a trained soldier." I can feel the strain in his voice not to sound condescending. "Nothing will make this fair."

"Does that mean you agree?"

His eyes are narrowed, but the corners of his mouth twitch. "Fine." He tucks one hand behind his back. "You ready?"

I widen my stance into a crouch. "Ready."

He lurches toward me, clearly wanting to end this quickly. I skirt to the side, eyeing the ground as he turns back again, facing me.

He leans on the balls of his feet, preparing for another lunge.

According to the rules we set, Flynn isn't allowed to use magic. I never said anything about me.

I can't use magic in an obvious way, but Flynn just made the fatal error of lying to me. He claimed he wasn't worried about someone killing the Honorate, and the magic of that lie is still warming my belly.

As he springs forward, I send heat—just a bit—to the frost-tipped grass in front of him, melting it. Not enough for him to notice, just enough to make it slippery.

His foot lands on the slicked grass and skids forward.

For a split second, he's surprised and off-balance.

In that moment, I dart forward, throw my arms around his waist, and tackle him to the ground.

We go sprawling. He crashes onto his back, and I land on top of him.

Flynn gawks at me as I stand. "I'm impressed."

"Don't be. I cheated." I'm telling the truth, but he laughs, thinking I'm joking. "You didn't let me win, did you?" I ask, eyes narrowed as though suspicious.

"No." He sounds bemused as he pushes to his feet. "You won."

"Good. I believe this means you owe me answers."

With a sigh, Flynn puts a hand on my back and guides me closer to the stands, opposite the Petruvians and away from the other soldiers. "What do you want to know?"

"Who do you think killed Arliss Vale? Do you think someone's targeting the Honorate?"

"I think . . ." He hesitates. "Well, there's a reason the Shadow Queen is as terrifying as she is. All the Honorate have something to hide."

"Something worth killing for?"

He hesitates for several seconds. "Maybe. Probably."

I take a breath. Now for the question I *really* need answers to. "Including your father?"

Flynn recoils. "You can't expect me to answer that."

"I won, didn't I?"

He groans. "Of course including my father. He gets letters from the Shadow Queen, same as anyone else. And he's been paranoid for months."

Months? Selva Sixmen got a letter from the imposter Shadow Queen two weeks ago—why has he been acting strange for months? "You don't know why?"

"He never said, and I never asked. Why are you so interested in this?"

"I'm worried about my brother. What if he's the next target?"

"Mira, one person died. That doesn't mean there's a conspiracy against the Honorate."

"What does the decurio think?"

He looks over my shoulder. I follow his line of vision, and my eyebrows shoot up. "The Nights?"

"Not them specifically. But the arrival of Petruvia is too suspicious to ignore. Arliss died right after they got here. Can that truly be a coincidence?"

I study the Nights for a few moments until they look at me, yet again, and I swiftly turn my gaze elsewhere. It's true that Petruvia arrived right before Arliss's murder and the timing is suspicious . . .

But there's someone else who arrived in Widow's Hall around that same time. Someone else with a clear motive I can't ignore. Kaidren Vale.

CHAPTER FOURTEEN

ARTIFICE AND CHARM

There's someone at my bedroom door. Which by itself isn't odd. But they don't use Sef's signature knock or call out to me the way Luc does. Which *is* odd. Plenty of people live in Widow's Hall. Only two of them ever visit me.

I'm tense as I creep to stand behind the door. "Who is it?"

"It's Kaidren."

He's the last person I was expecting.

Swiftly, I survey my room, making sure there's nothing suspicious lying around before opening the door.

For the first time since we met, Kaidren looks messy. Patchy stubble grows around his chin, dark circles hang beneath his eyes, and his shoulders are heavy. He is still undeniably and frustratingly good-looking, but there's an air of defeat about him.

"Kaidren?" I don't hide the incredulity from my voice. "What are you doing here?"

He drags a hand tiredly over his face. "I'm sorry for disturbing you. I—" He stops, frowning as he catches sight of my room. "These are your chambers?"

"Yes." I slide over to block more of the open doorway. It's a useless move. I'm not short, but Kaidren is tall enough to easily peer over my head. "Is something wrong?"

"Your room is smaller than I expected." He scrunches his brow. "Your brother hasn't demanded a larger room for you?"

I can't imagine why he's so concerned with my sleeping arrangements. I fold my arms, trying not to look as annoyed as I feel. "I don't mean to be rude, but what are you doing here?"

"Sorry." His left leg bounces with nerves. "The first trial's tomorrow, and I was hoping you might help me with something."

And *I* was hoping to get some sleep the night before the most important event of my life, instead of fanning the flames of this fake friendship. Apparently, I'm not so fortunate. "What do you need?"

"Um—" He looks over my head at my room again. "Maybe we can discuss this in the Praeceptor's dining room?"

I'm exhausted, and I want to refuse, but I haven't seen him since the death of Arliss Vale, and the obvious question echoes in the recesses of my mind: *Did* he murder his father?

Curiosity gets the best of me. "Of course."

A few minutes later, we're in Luc's dining room, and Kaidren looks more nervous than before. "Why don't you sit?"

I take one of the side chairs instead of the head of the table as I usually do. Kaidren stands in front of me. "You know of the Shadow Queen, don't you?"

I keep my face carefully blank. "Doesn't everyone?"

His expression sours. "Probably. I take it you read her most recent column?"

"Yes . . ."

He rummages in his bag and tosses the Shadow Queen's column on the table, followed by a stack of crumpled parchment.

My eyebrows rise. "What is all this?"

"Letters. They've been arriving at my father's house. You know what they all have in common? They accuse *me* of murdering my dad. All because of what the Shadow Queen wrote. The entire mountain thinks I'm a murderer."

Myself included. "I'm sure that's not true," I say. "*I* certainly don't."

He gives me a small smile that doesn't reach his eyes. "Thank you. I wasn't expecting this from the Shadow Queen. I've read every column she's ever written. I used to admire her. I never realized how careless she is with her pen."

He looks so forlorn and miserable, I'm almost moved.

Until I remember: Kaidren Vale is a liar. He lied about why he came to Widow's Hall, lied about wanting to be my friend, he even went so far as to pretend he wanted *more* than friendship, all so he could manipulate me into talking about my brother.

As soon as he realized I'm Opheran, he saw me as nothing other than a means to his ends. He doesn't deserve my sympathy.

Does that make me cruel? Maybe. But I make no apologies for it.

"I'm sorry." I soften my voice until it's gentle and soothing. "That sounds like a lot to deal with. Especially so soon after your father's death. Have you thought about dropping out of the Tournament?"

He sighs. "I don't want to quit. But thank you. You don't have to worry about me. My father and I weren't exactly close."

"Even still, losing a parent is never easy."

Kaidren studies my expression. "You sound as if you speak from personal experience."

I hesitate. I didn't plan on divulging anything about myself—at least, not anything *true*—but this is what friends do, and that's what he thinks we are. "Yes," I say after a pause. "My mother died when I was young."

"I'm sorry." He looks like he means it.

"Thank you." I sound stiff. Which isn't the plan. I'm meant to sound warm and inviting to keep his guard lowered, but I struggle to keep calm and collected where my mother is concerned.

"What happened to her? If you don't mind me asking."

I *do* mind. I'm already sitting on the edge of tears, and thinking about what happened to Aja doesn't help. She fought as best she could to take care of us. No matter how bad things were, she always promised me we'd survive. Toward the end, she could no longer afford to feed the both of us. Everything she had, she gave to me. All her love, all the blankets when the nights got cold, and what little food she could afford.

It was her undoing.

Food was scarce, so she stopped eating. She fed me but never herself. She didn't complain, just slowly wasted away.

"Don't worry about me, Mira. I'm going to be fine."

That was Aja. A liar to the end.

"She starved." My voice sounds as hollow as I feel. I clear my throat. I need to get us back on track—shift the conversation before I burst into tears. "It was a long time ago. And as I said, it's never easy. Your father's death was so sudden. Did you have any idea it was coming?"

Kaidren doesn't pause. "No. I was just as surprised as anyone."

Heat sweeps through me, but nothing in Kaidren's demeanor changes. It's almost scary how good of a liar this boy is. It's easy to believe someone so manipulative is capable of murdering his own father. "I'm sorry for your loss," I say.

"Thank you." He reaches for my hands.

My heart careens into a flutter. Neither of us is wearing gloves.

I jerk to my feet. The move is sharp and sudden. To disguise it, I start to pace. "Let's say you're right. That the entire mountain thinks you're a murderer. What are you going to do? And why come to me?"

My pacing halts when Kaidren steps into my path, placing his hands on my shoulders to keep me still. We're standing close—*too* close. I am acutely aware of each of his fingers where they dig into my gown. Of the warmth of his skin radiating into my shoulders.

I stroke the tattoo on my inner wrist as I try to get my frantic pulse under control.

Intense brown eyes bore into mine. "Something sinister is afoot, and I think your family is squarely in the middle of it." The severity softens. "You are nothing like them. You're nothing like anyone on this damned mountain. You've been nothing but kind to me."

His thumbs rub soothing patterns into my shoulders. My gown is loose. All I can think about is what would happen if he nudged my sleeve. If the dress slipped from my shoulder—dipped the smallest fraction down my arm—his thumb would graze my skin.

"Of course," I say softly. "We're friends."

I'm surprised to see something like guilt flicker in his eyes.

Stars in hell, is Kaidren starting to feel shame for manipulating his gullible, trusting friend?

The flash of empathy is gone before I have time to question it further.

Kaidren leans toward me. "I need a favor. Your brother works closely with the decurio, and I was hoping you might keep me apprised of their investigation into my father's death."

"You want me to tell you what the decurio find?"

"Yes. Anything that will help me clear my name. I intend

to win the Tournament and rule the Republic—I can't have the people thinking I'm a murderer. Someone is spreading lies to the Shadow Queen." Kaidren casts a nervous look around the room, as though we might be overheard by the chandelier. "How close are you with your brother?"

Realization hits me, and I feel foolish for not seeing it sooner. *This* is why he's here. He wants to know if Luc is the one accusing him of killing Arliss.

I hush my tone in a mimic of his. "You don't think Luc had anything to do with this, do you?"

"Who else would benefit?" Kaidren's chest expands with a heavy breath. "First, there was the rumor that I lied about being an isha. Now I'm accused of murder. I'm not saying it was definitely your brother, but someone wants to ruin my reputation. Do you think Lucien is capable of something so heinous?"

"I—I'm not sure."

Kaidren's eyes blaze. It wasn't a direct confirmation, but it was close enough. "Remira, someone is spreading lies about me. I'm going to find them and prove it to the world."

I'm scrambling for a response, but I must take too long, because he drops his voice even further. "I appreciate you." His eyes are surprisingly gentle. "More than you'll ever know. You are kind and funny and brave—"

"I'm hardly brave."

"Kindness in a place like this *is* brave. I've never met anyone as sweet as you. No matter what happens with the Tournament and your brother, I hope there are no hard feelings between us."

I'm floored with the realization that he means it. He's been lying to me from the moment he arrived, but somehow, in spite of all that, he genuinely thinks he likes me. He thinks I'm *sweet*.

I've never been called sweet before. I can't say I like it, but he's offering me his version of a meaningful compliment and I'm meant to be grateful, so I smile. "Thank you."

His thumbs slow, and his expression is thoughtful as he takes me in. He raises a hand—I think to brush hair back from my face—and all I see is that he isn't wearing gloves. All I think is how easy it would be for him to ruin me.

I hurl words to stop him from making contact. "I've been so lonely here. I'm glad we found each other."

As I hoped, the hand stops its approach. That glimmer of guilt returns.

I take advantage of his stillness to back away. I rest against the table, relieved at the newfound distance between us.

Kaidren's eyes track me. "As a friend, can you do something for me?"

"What do you need?"

"Tell your brother my suspicions. And when you do . . ." He speaks slowly, advancing deliberately with each step. "Give him a message from me. Tell him I know what he's doing, and it won't work. He can throw all the accusations at me he wants—I'm not backing down. If he wants war, I will gladly give it to him."

His every step is heavy with meaning, until I'm trapped against the table, his stare boring into mine. In the depths of his gaze is a fierceness that wasn't there before. Or perhaps it was, but it was hiding behind a veil of pretense.

I've always known Kaidren is attractive. He is sculpted perfection who draws appreciative looks wherever he goes—it's impossible to miss. Until now, he was crafted from fake smiles and feigned charm. Now he appears born from fury. His eyes reflect a desperate kind of rage that is as raw as it is familiar.

It transforms his face. He's no longer merely good-looking in the obvious way, dripping with the shallow ornaments of charisma. In this moment, he is truly magnetic. His brown eyes are intent and harsh and filled with malice.

I can't look away.

Fury shouldn't call to me. His sings my name. Spite shouldn't entice me. His draws me in like a pulled sledge.

With the varnished, waxy shell of his exterior melted away, I finally see him. This isn't a charming, polite boy. This is a boy of simmering ire, moments away from boiling over. Infinitely more dangerous. Infinitely more alluring.

My heartbeat picks up speed and volume the longer we stare. My throat is parched, and my hands clench the sides of the table, steadying myself.

I have no idea how long we stare and no idea what expression I'm making, or whether Kaidren sees a glimpse of himself lurking in my eyes, as I do his.

He's the first to look away. He inhales and rises, blinking rapidly, looking dazed.

There are several beats of silence, and then that refined, straight-toothed smile is back, perfect and lifeless as ever. "Can I trust you to deliver my message to your brother?"

My hands unclench as I catch my breath and fix my lips into a fake smile of my own. "Of course," I say. "What are friends for?"

CHAPTER FIFTEEN

THESE DEADLY GAMES

There isn't a single empty seat in the arena. So many people. So many opportunities for this to fail spectacularly.

The domed roof is open for the first trial. Light from the beacons illuminates the wide field. Flynn Sixmen stands on a raised platform, flanked by Luc and Kaidren. Before them is a sea of soldiers filling the field. There are far more decurio here than there were for the opening ceremony. I can't see their wrists, but I know—these aren't just the Opheran soldiers.

It makes my insides riot with fury, but rather than freeze it, I lean into that feeling. I have a Tournament to fix.

Luc stands with his feet apart, head high. He looks as bold and regal as I reminded him to be, over and over. His only flaw is his left boot. It taps nervously against the stage in a quick, irregular beat. I doubt anyone else notices, but I can't look away from the crack in his facade.

Kaidren is on Flynn's left. Like Luc, Kaidren's head is high. Unlike Luc, I can't find any indicator that he's anything less than wholly calm. It bothers me that I can't tell if it's real. Is his self-assurance as manufactured as his smile? It must be. He came to me devastated just last night, but there's no hint of that now.

The cheering crowd quiets as Flynn announces the rules of the first trial. On the stage before him is a large marble bowl full of slips of parchment, each with a name of an aikkari soldier.

When Flynn's introduction ends, it's Luc's turn to select his team. His boot finally stops tapping as he reaches into the bowl.

Luc unfurls the first slip of parchment. "Dhavik Chambliss." His voice is smooth and steady.

Dhavik shoves his way through the decurio. The audience twist in their seats and crane their heads, trying to get a better look at the first competitor. He's tall and thick shouldered, with close-cropped hair, same as all the men in the decurio.

The first of ten. My fingers drum restlessly against my thigh. Luc draws more names. I examine each soldier called and their build, searching . . .

Luc calls the name of his seventh soldier, "Esi Dreylock," and a girl approaches.

Her appearance is unremarkable and, under normal circumstances, wouldn't draw the eye. Except for her build. Out of everyone Luc's called, hers most closely resembles my own. She's taller than me by a few hairs, and her arms have more muscle, but from a distance, covered in armor, I doubt anyone would notice.

I nudge Sef, but she's already looking at me. "Her?"

"Unless you disagree?"

"No, she's perfect," Sef says. "I'll take care of it."

"Thank you." I give her hand a firm squeeze and slip out of the arena benches. In a few minutes, Sef will inconspicuously follow. In the meantime, no one notices me duck into one of the rooms built into the base of the stands. The wooden walls are bare, the only furniture is a small table, and there's no floor—just grass.

Sef and I prepared this room ahead of time. My aikkari armor (a gift from Flynn during training) waits for me, neatly folded on the table.

Virdeian armor is a combination of leather, wool, and fur. White wool shirts with flexible tan leather stitched along the sides and elbows for padding, leather caps covered in fur to protect the head, tan wool pants with leather at the kneecaps, and fur-lined boots. They're heavy enough to be protective and warm and are breathable enough to move in. Over the face, soldiers wear cloth masks with mesh eyeholes to protect their vision from snowfall and keep them warm.

Practical, but a pain to put on. There's no insulation in this room, so I'm freezing as I strip off my regular clothes. I've just finished putting on my uniform (leaving off the fur-lined gloves) when the door opens and Sef enters with Esi.

Esi is already wearing her armor, with her mask tucked under her arm. She frowns when she sees me. "What's going on?"

I touch the tshira trinket at my bracelet and soak up the comforting warmth of the magic stored within. "Sorry about this," I say. Before Esi can question my meaning, I press a hand to her forehead.

Heated magic releases, and I channel it into her mind, specifically her memories of the past fifteen minutes.

The confused furrow in her brow smoothens. Her eyelids droop with sudden exhaustion as her recent memories are wiped clean, and she slumps over.

I catch her before she falls. Sef and I brace our hands under her arms and guide her to lean against the wall. Dizziness is a common side effect of this brand of memory magic, but most only fall over if the memories affected are longer than a few minutes.

Esi will be fine, but by then, I'll be gone, and she'll have no recollection of being chosen to serve in the Praeceptor's army for the first trial of the Tournament.

I tug on my gloves and mask, obscuring my face as I head off to find Luc. He and Kaidren have fifteen minutes before the event to meet and strategize with their teams. If Luc is following my instructions, his first move was to ask each member of his team about their source, and by now, he's moved on to recounting the details of the rest of my strategy.

We have ten soldiers at our disposal, and Kaidren has eleven. We need to split ours up to be as efficient as possible. Six soldiers on the front lines, forming a wall of protection. Two will hover back, myself and another. We'll serve as Luc's personal guards. If anyone manages to get past the screen of soldiers, we're at his side to keep them from getting Luc into a death position. The final two soldiers are attackers. Their job is to fight on the front lines when necessary, and to search for a breach in enemy lines to reach and defeat Kaidren.

Luc and the rest of the team are in one of the larger private rooms at the base of the stands. His foot is tapping again. There's a table scattered with weapons, some crafted from tshira, some stone. Luc's soldiers surround the table, picking through the weapons.

I sidle to my brother's side. "What's going on?" I ask lowly. If I can avoid it, I want to keep the other soldiers from hearing my voice, just in case any of them know Esi well enough to recognize the differences in the way we speak.

Luc brightens when he sees me. "Mira—I mean—" He darts a glance around, ensuring no one heard his blunder. *"Esi."*

Stars in hell, he's awful at this. "What did I miss?"

"We were given a choice between tshira and stone weapons. We chose tshira."

Each soldier is allowed one weapon for the game. Luc's team is arming themselves with tshira-hilted swords and daggers and weapons with blades crafted from the dark, banded material.

My pulse gathers speed. "You chose wrong." I hold in a curse of frustration. If I'd known this was coming, I'd have prepared him for it.

"What do you mean? Tshira weapons are sharper, lighter, and easier to wield. They survive better in the cold, and they're best for aikkari."

He sounds like he's reciting words from a damned course book. My eyes are hidden by my mask, so I let them roll. "Yes, but every single person on the other team is aikkari. If we use tshira, they'll be able to manipulate all of our weapons. It'll give them an advantage over us."

Tshira weapons are great for enemies outside of Virdei. Petruvia's military is twice our size, but every member of our army has magic, while only a fraction of theirs does. What we don't have in numbers, we make up for in magic. Using tshira weapons with enemy kingdoms gives us an advantage. In this arena, however, Kaidren's team has just as much magic as we do. Tshira weapons are *awful* for dealing with other aikkari.

Luc's foot taps faster. "Are you sure about this?"

"Positive. Kaidren's going to select tshira for his team. Right as the game starts, we can disarm as many of his soldiers as possible. He has an extra team member; we need every bit of leverage we can get."

Luc can't see my face, but I read the uncertainty in his. We're running out of time. He needs to make a decision *now*. I nudge my shoulder against him. "You trust me, don't you?"

"With every lie I'll ever tell." Luc still doubts this will work—I can see it in his brow—but his faith in me outweighs his misgivings. He raises his voice to address the rest of the team. "Change of plans. We're using the stone, not the tshira."

I catch a few confused glances exchanged between soldiers, but they don't argue. This challenge isn't about aikkari thinking for themselves. It's about which candidate has the winning strategy.

Five minutes later, there's a rap on the door. The time for strategizing is over. The trial is starting.

CHAPTER SIXTEEN

AT ALL COSTS

Fear stews me alive. I'm drenched in sweat from my frazzled nerves, and the heat of it all is ensnared by the fur and leather of my armor.

We eleven soldiers stand in a row on one side of the arena.

Well—nine soldiers, one Praeceptor, and one fraud.

Kaidren's team stands at the opposite end. There are twelve of them. Eleven soldiers with Kaidren proudly in the middle. He's the only one not wearing a mask.

Terror's hooks dig so deeply into me, I don't even feel a rush of vindication at the sight of Kaidren's team clutching tshira weapons, exactly as I predicted.

Flynn begins the countdown. "Four . . . three . . ."

The energy in the arena somehow doubles. They pick up the chant with him. "Two . . . one!"

Kaidren's team races forward. Our team is still. We raise our hands, focusing magic on our opponents' tshira weapons.

My target is at the end of the row of soldiers. His sword has a wooden hilt wrapped in leather and a blade of sharpened tshira. Magic rushes from my outstretched hand. At my command, his blade liquefies. It drips to the ground in black rivulets, settling against the stark white snow like tar.

I smirk. On to the next.

I channel magic into a second soldier's weapon—a tshira-hilted dagger in a holster around his hip.

My entire body jolts, from my toes to my rattling teeth, and the dagger remains whole.

I mutter a curse under my breath. The soldier used his own magic to hold the tshira in shape. He must've seen the melting weapons around him and reacted accordingly.

The soldier next to me wears a chain of woven leather around his neck twisted with strands of ivy. He touches the sliver of skin between his glove and sleeve to the ivy, siphoning his source and pushing it toward another soldier on Kaidren's team.

The dark blade of their tshira battle-ax puddles to the ground.

The first wave of our attack is over. I count six disarmed soldiers. In a matter of seconds, we've rendered more than half the opposing team all but defenseless.

Because of me.

I feel a swell of pride. It's just for a flicker, but in that moment, it's deep enough to bury my dread.

Luc motions our team into action. The six soldiers designated to rush the front lines swoop, spreading out across the width of the arena, forming a human wall.

Kaidren's team is ducked around him—he must be hastily doling out new instructions, since half his team have lost their weapons.

Dhavik and I, the two soldiers assigned to flank Luc's side, press in closer. Dhavik grips a sword, while I have a knife tucked into a pocket on my thigh. In my short time with Flynn, I learned basic self-defense, not swordplay, so I selected a weapon I might actually be able to use.

Kaidren's group disbands. I take a quick survey of their

revised strategy. It appears Kaidren gave up his own sword to one of his disarmed soldiers. Like Luc's team, Kaidren's soldiers form a wall. Unlike us, there are eight of them. With an extra team member, he still has three soldiers who remain by his side, guarding him more closely.

Six of Luc's soldiers clash against eight of Kaidren's in the center of the arena.

The crowd roars at the first clang of weapons slamming into each other.

It takes only seconds for one of Luc's soldiers—a short man called Pol—to drive a sword into the stomach of one of Kaidren's unarmed soldiers.

I don't know him, but my throat tightens as he tumbles over.

The wound in his gut is deep, spilling blood over the snow. No one pauses. Not even his own team.

Pol steps casually over the body and begins hacking at a second decurio like it's nothing.

The fallen soldier is still alive, but fading quickly. He'll be dead soon without medical attention, but he just lies on the ground, ignored by the war around him.

I have to look away. No one is going to save him, and I don't want to watch him slowly die.

Pol clashes with another soldier. There's a brutality to his movements that's unsettling. He's battling another member of the decurio of his *own* army, yet he fights with the same ruthless intensity I'd expect from someone attacking an enemy.

Flynn was surprised how viciously I fought him. He'd noted how rare it is to see in untrained soldiers. I wonder if the decurio are instructed to be violent, with no regard for their opponent. If cruelty against their own is encouraged, even in training.

With a screech, Pol uses his blade to sweep his opponent's legs out from under him. He falls to the ground, and Pol raises his sword. All he has to do is swing down, and his opponent is dead.

Luc takes a small step forward, as though to call out to him—to tell Pol there's no need to kill.

I catch his arm and shake my head, as subtly as I can.

Pol plunges the blade through the other soldier's chest, killing him instantly.

Within the first three minutes, Luc has all ten members of his team still standing. Kaidren has lost two.

The wall of soldiers is a blur of swishing weapons and violence. I can't decide where to focus, until a third one of Kaidren's soldiers drops to the ground in a spray of blood and frost, either dead or injured enough they can no longer fight. Both teams now have six soldiers fighting in the middle of the arena.

"*Go*," says Luc urgently. He has two team members hanging back. Their job is to try and skirt past the wall and get to Kaidren. Hopefully, the battle in the center is enough of a distraction they can get through to the other side, put Kaidren in a death position, and finish this.

They're halfway to the center of the arena when the snow beneath them melts. The soldier on the right slips and falls.

My eyes snap to Kaidren's team. Someone used magic to heat the ground beneath them. One of Kaidren's soldiers breaks away, running toward the fallen decurio. He pushes to his knees, trying to rise, but before he can, Kaidren's soldier swings a sword at his legs.

He screeches as his left leg is sliced. He can't fight back before he's cut again, this time on his torso.

Blood streaks the snow as he collapses. He isn't dead, but he won't walk for the rest of the trial. Maybe ever.

Kaidren's soldier doesn't take so much as a second to pause

before turning to Luc's second flier, Aleta, and stabbing her in the stomach.

Aleta doesn't make a sound. The soldier twists the sword in her gut, and she collapses like a stone.

To my horror, the blade is still in her. As she falls, it keeps slicing.

I cover my mouth to muffle a shriek. My knotted stomach drops to my feet as Kaidren's soldier draws back his sword. Aleta is dead.

One of Luc's team members pounces on Kaidren's soldier, and they begin a dance of darting limbs and clanging weapons. All the while, Dhavik and I keep tight to Luc's side. Part of me feels guilty we don't move to help, even as I know there's nothing I could do to stop this.

There are casualties on both sides now. The sounds of battle heighten. The screeching of the crowd grows louder. Each team fights harder now that they've lost someone. More bodies drop as both sides attempt to force the other back, closer to the opposing team's candidate. Neither is gaining ground.

My hopes of this being over quickly are slashed when I see Pol—Luc's most vicious warrior—plummet in a shower of red blood and white snow.

By this point, Kaidren has five soldiers left. We have seven.

Except two of Luc's soldiers—me and Dhavik—aren't actually fighting. We stay back with Luc to protect him.

My heart pounds, and I'm burning up under this armor.

All five of Kaidren's remaining warriors are at the battle in the center of the arena, fighting against five of Luc's. Kaidren is alone on the other side of the wall of war. The three soldiers initially designated to guard him have been drawn into the bloodbath. He no longer has a direct guard—he's practically an open target.

We need one person to get across the field and fight him into a death position.

Just one.

The blood pulsing in my ears quiets as I force myself to think. Now is the perfect opportunity to send one of us to attack Kaidren, but someone has to stay behind and defend Luc.

Which is more important: defeating Kaidren or protecting the Praeceptor?

The answer is obvious. Defending Luc is the most important thing. Crossing the arena will mean nothing if, in the process, someone gets to Luc and we lose before we have a chance to win.

I can't risk leaving Luc with the only soldier on this field with no training—me. The *real* decurio must stay and defend him, while the fraud should go after Kaidren.

My only weapon is the knife tucked into the pocket at my thigh. All I have to do is press the blade against Kaidren's throat, and this is over. Luc wins. *We* win.

I turn to my brother. "I'm ending this."

His head jerks to me. "What are you talking about?" His eyes widen as he glances across the arena to Kaidren, answering his own question. "No. Absolutely not. Have you lost your mind? You'll have to run through the battlefield."

"It's our best option."

I've never seen him look more panicked. "There are at least three people already dead. Do you understand me? You could die."

"Or we could *win*."

Luc stares at me like he's never seen me before. He shakes his head emphatically. "Mira, *no*. I forbid—"

I don't let him finish. If I do, I might let him talk me out of this.

Instead, I let my terror drown in his words. Before he can stop me, I take off in a sprint across the arena, gaze fixed on Kaidren Vale.

CHAPTER SEVENTEEN

THE TRUE QUEEN OF WIDOW'S HALL

I'm winded within seconds. It's embarrassing, but in my defense the length of the arena looks smaller from the end than it feels when actually running it.

My path to Kaidren is curved. I sprint around the wall of soldiers slamming into each other and cling to the perimeter, closer to the stands of onlookers.

I ignore them, forcing everything into the background except for my opponent on the other side of the wide, snowy field.

From the corner of my eye, I see another one of Kaidren's soldiers drop to the ground. It's a good sign, but I don't look to see if he gets back up, or react as the crowd roars in response. I tune it out and run faster.

Kaidren stands behind the wall of soldiers, as Luc does, watching it all unfold. He's so rapt by the violence, he doesn't notice my approach. Not until I'm close enough that my footsteps capture his attention.

His head snaps in my direction.

I'm wearing a mask, and he isn't. I read his fear in the whites of his eyes and scrunch of his brow. He's weaponless, with no formal training, and he thinks I'm an experienced soldier.

I scan his imposing figure, assessing for his weakest points.

Eyes, knees, groin, feet, sides. I chant Flynn's advice to myself.

Kaidren is tall, and he gave his sword to a disarmed soldier. My most effective tool—magic—has already been drained from the tshira I carry with me, so my only weapon is the small knife in my pocket. I intend to use it to get him in the death position, but first, I need to bring him to his knees. Get his throat within easy striking distance.

Kaidren raises his hands to block himself at my approach. It leaves his sides unguarded, so I swing a fist at his left flank.

My hope is to exploit the small advantage that I've had at least some training with—

Kaidren captures my fist, and with it, my brief hope that this will be easy.

My throat dries and I jab with my other hand, striking him on his unguarded side.

Kaidren doesn't even blink.

The decurio uniforms have flexible leather stitched around the ribs, which, unfortunately, provides enough padding to block the sensation of my feeble punches.

Dammit.

New strategy—exploit his only weakness: he can't multitask. He was too focused on capturing one hand to deflect the other.

I kick him in the shin.

That gets a flinch out of him, sharp enough I can tug my wrist out of his hold and jerk back.

We circle each other, silent and wary.

I lunge first, aiming a punch at his gut.

He clumsily bats my hand away, but as he does, I kick his shin again.

That earns me another flinch, but it does little to weaken him overall.

Kaidren and I skate over snow in a jumble of uncoordinated limbs and ineffective hits.

I might be smaller and more nimble than he is, but it's only slightly helpful. After two minutes of hitting his sides and kicking his knees, I'm no closer to knocking him over than I was when this started. My problem isn't speed or accuracy. It's impact.

I can land a jab, but I can't hit him hard enough for it to matter.

Time to shift strategy. If I can't generate enough force with my fists and legs, I need something larger.

Kaidren tries to swipe my feet out from under me. I leap over his extended leg, pressing closer to him.

I curl a fist and thrust it at his side, slower than before.

He takes the bait. Snatches at my arm before I can strike him.

As Kaidren focuses on grabbing me—I ram my body into his.

The force of an entire person hurtling against him is enough to put him off-balance. He doesn't tip over, but in his shock, he throws out his arms for stability.

My body is still near his. I hook a leg around him and shove my heavy boot into the back of his knee.

Kaidren's leg buckles. My palms slap against his chest, sending him tumbling, flailing limbs and all.

My goal is to land on top of him, so I can press the knife hidden in my pocket to his throat.

I fail.

Well, not entirely.

I knock him over and land astride his body, as planned. He's on his back, and I'm poised over his chest, legs on either side of his wide torso.

Where I go wrong: I underestimate his reaction time. The

instant his back hits the ground, he wraps his arms around me and rolls us over.

I'm breathless as he slams me into the snow. Kaidren's body is laid out over mine. I feel each pane of him, warm and solid. His broad chest, rising and falling rapidly; the muscles of his abdomen, taut and clenched tight; the cords of his thighs, muscle bound and warm, as they dig into my hips.

Our breaths are heavy, faces a hairsbreadth away, panting white mist into the air between us.

This is the closest we've ever been. Through the mesh eyes of my mask, I see him. Every contour of his face, the light flush of his cheeks from exertion and cold, the soft lines around his mouth, the slight crookedness of his nose. From this distance, I can count his damn eyelashes.

The false kindness he dons like armor is gone. As I breathe his air and feel his heartbeat, he is all harsh lines and wild eyes.

His lips curl into a snarl as a creeping, gloved hand slides down, down, down, along my side . . .

My eyes follow its path. We've landed near a discarded blade. It used to have a tshira hilt, but that's a puddle of useless goo now.

The blade is *just* outside his arm's reach. If he shifts us over, he'll have all he needs to kill me in seconds. Worse, he could win.

Not an option.

I try and bring up my arms to shove him off me.

Before I can, he slots his free arm over my chest. His arm spans the width of my shoulders, pinning them—and me—to the ground.

I struggle ineffectually beneath him, glaring through mesh.

Ice crystals creep through the fabric of my uniform around

my neck. I shudder at the sensation of snow melting against my skin, burning and cold, all at once.

Kaidren takes a deep breath—and the hand straining for the sword wavers.

A murky emotion flickers in his deep brown eyes. They widen in something like surprise, and his slightly crooked nose scrunches in confusion.

Why? I have no idea, nor do I care. My arms are trapped, my knife is stuck in a pocket I can't reach, and I have only a moment of reprieve to get myself out of this.

Panicked, I draw up the only part of my body I have left at my disposal—my legs—and ensnare them around his waist.

Kaidren tenses. His reaching hand freezes.

I cross my ankles behind his back, drawing him even closer. Breath rushes from his lungs to fan against my mask as his chest slams into mine.

The impact makes my mask slip. The edge rides up, leaving a sliver of my jaw and lower cheek exposed.

Kaidren's halting breaths heat my bare skin. Panic clogs my throat. If he presses forward, he will touch me, and all of this will be for nothing.

My arms are still trapped, I can't fix my mask, and I'm clenched all over with the terror that he's going to make contact.

I refuse to lose like this.

I burrow my neck and head deeper into the snow. The cold is a creeping tendril that slithers down my spine, making my teeth chatter, but it puts a bit of distance between my face and Kaidren's.

The shock from his expression fades, and his attention shifts back to the blade. His arm stretches toward it again—

No.

I need to roll him over. I need to turn him in the opposite direction so he can't get hold of a weapon.

Using my thighs to tether myself to him, I drag them down his waist, until they're coiled around his hips like a belt.

I expect Kaidren to realize what I'm doing and fight back.

He doesn't. Instead, he stills. His perfect teeth grit together, eyes fluttering. He looks cold, as if he has snow melting down his neck as well. Or as if he's in pain. Or . . .

Stars in hell.

Only now do I consider our position. We're both sweaty and flushed. My legs are knotted around him like twine, my chest is flattened beneath him, and our hips are practically welded together.

What I see on his face—feel from his racing pulse—isn't pain. It's arousal.

In any other situation, I might be embarrassed. From the way I've thrown myself against him, or from the way his body reacts so readily to mine. But there's no time for shame.

Kaidren has no idea the girl beneath him is me. If the feel of a stranger's body is enough to melt him into a starheaded fool, I'll happily use it to my advantage.

I have no experience in seduction, but I artlessly rotate my hips.

Kaidren's head falls forward.

My jaw is still uncovered, so I jerk my head to the side. His forehead slams into my opposite shoulder with a tortured sound I now know is a muffled groan. "Stars in hell, what are you doing?" His voice is huskier than I've ever heard it.

My heartbeat quickens. In truth, I have no idea what I'm doing, but whatever it is appears to be working.

Maybe a little too well. His voice is roughened like this. He sounds tense and out of control. Most days, Kaidren Vale is full of a practiced charm I hate, but in this moment, in the middle of an arena, he's untamed.

The snow against my back is cold. Everything on this damned mountain turns to ice, but wherever my body touches his is scorched.

I'm scalded from within, as though flames are licking greedily at my insides. I'm horrified by the realization that I *like* the way he feels against me. He is firm, muscled, and warm.

It doesn't matter. Doesn't matter that his body responds to mine, or that my body reacts to his—I despise him. I'm plotting his ruin. And I'm going to win.

The arm banded across my chest has loosened, enough for my fingers to glide down his side.

He shudders. He's not even fighting back.

I almost can't believe how easy this is. This is a different kind of control from what I'm used to. Different from the power I've been chasing since childhood. *This* power—the kind that comes from unraveling a man with allure I didn't know I possessed, rather than with secrets and magic—is deliciously addictive.

My trailing hand reaches the knife in my pocket.

Kaidren doesn't notice. He's staring through the mesh over my eyes, attention fixated on the face he can't see, breathing deeply.

Before he can react, I twist. Clench my thighs, rotate my hips, and roll us over.

I'm poised over him, straddling his torso. My face hovers above his, a gasp of air away, both of us are out of breath—

And I've got a knife's blade pressed to his throat.

The haze of desire fades from his eyes. His mouth drops open in shock.

He can't see my face, but I smirk. I lean, masked mouth to

his ear. "I believe this means I win." I deepen my voice, so he doesn't recognize it. And just to rub it in, I add, *"Bastard Vale."*

The rest of the world comes sharply into focus.

The arena is screaming around us. Even louder than before, because there's a winner and it's *me*.

The remaining soldiers drop their weapons. A few peel off their masks, looking relieved.

I count them. We started with twenty-one. There are eight bodies scattered across the field, either dead or too injured to stand.

I scramble off Kaidren. He's still panting, looking shocked, but I ignore him. My eyes search for Luc, wishing I could remove my mask so he can see my grin.

That brief swell of pride wisps away. My heart falls.

Luc is on the other side of the arena, joined by Tarek Fain, General of the decurio. He grabs one of Luc's arms and raises it, heralding him as the winner, calling on the audience to cheer for their Praeceptor, champion of the first trial.

As the General shouts to the crowd, going on and on about Luc's impressive victory, and the audience shrieks and stomps their feet in the stands, Luc doesn't glance back at me. Not even once.

Blood and fervor pulse through me, fiery enough to burn.

I keep staring, willing my brother to look at me. Willing him to meet my gaze with a secret smile that says that he *sees* me. That he knows this moment, this victory, is because of me.

He doesn't.

Icy tears of hurt and fury sting my eyes.

The survivors of Luc's team gather around him. They jump, celebrating him, applauding him, right along with the rest of the crowd.

Luc cheers with them. Smiling wide enough to split his face open. And still, he doesn't look at me.

My heart cracks in two. Both halves shatter in the snow.

I don't move. I just watch. My throat burns with words I want to scream, but I can't, because I'm not a person with a voice. I'm a shadow in the rafters, and shadows are, above all else, silent.

I crafted him a plan for victory. *I* forced him to memorize it. *I* took the mortal risk of disguising myself as a soldier. *I* charged across a field of war and blood. *I* wrestled a man trying to kill me to win Luc this victory.

And none of it matters. He doesn't care, and when this is over, after I've won him his Tournament and stolen him his throne, nothing will have changed. Not for me, anyway.

Ice and steel. You're made of ice and steel.

Normally, if I repeat it to myself enough times, I can force myself to feel it. Freeze my heart, hide it behind a steel wall, and fake a smile.

Here, surrounded by snow and screaming spectators, my rage doesn't cool.

I am a cheat, a sneak, and a thief. All I have to show for it is a temporary place in Luc's shadow. It isn't fair. Nothing is. Fairness is the childish fantasy of a starheaded little girl who used to dream of this life I've grown to hate.

For the past five years, I've dedicated my life to being anything and everything that Luc needs me to be. Stealing power, trading secrets, all to suit him—and he can't even spare me a glance after I've risked my life so he can have it all.

"You're either useful to me, or you're nothing."

I am so, so tired of being nothing.

The crowd cheers for Luc, but *I* won this trial. Luc was born and raised in the glittering softness of Virdei. He was handed luxuries like compassion and kindness, only to waste them on everyone but me.

He has never known the heartbreak of being forgotten, cast aside, and taken for granted by those meant to love you. He will. I promise myself, I'm going to make him feel the way I do right now. Make him feel as heartbroken and powerless and *useless* as he makes me feel day after day.

And unlike Lucien Kyler, whose parents have now joined him in the center of the arena, hands raised, accepting the twin praise of Virdei and Petruvia, when I make a promise, I deliver.

I'll show him just how cruel I can be.

I've outgrown my current mask. I'll craft myself a new one made of ice and a spine of steel. I'll keep up the facade. I'll take what he asks of me. I'll win him this damned Tournament. I'll serve Lucien Kyler the Virdeian throne on a silver platter.

And then I'm going to steal it for myself.

CHAPTER EIGHTEEN

CONNIVING, VINDICTIVE, CRUEL

Revenge is a multistep process. It requires careful planning, attention to detail, and enough fury to set the world alight. I have all of the above.

Luc's parents use the Praeceptor's private dining room to celebrate his victory. I'm convinced they pick it just to spite me. To fully pound it into my skull how easily I can be discarded.

I wasn't invited. Yelina gave me a smug, simpering smile as she placed a bony hand over her chest (presumably where her heart resides; I'm unconvinced she has one), feigning devastation as she delivered the news. "Unfortunately, Remira, I think it would be best if we don't remind our guests of the scandal." (Scandal referring to the horrifying fact that I exist.) "This is an important dinner. You understand," she'd said.

Luc said nothing in my defense, and for the first time, it didn't sting, because for the first time, I knew to expect nothing.

Besides, much as I hate Yelina, I *do* understand. I'm the one who's always telling Luc to make a spectacle of his wins and obscure his shame. Sometimes, I almost let myself forget that his biggest shame is me.

With my favorite place taken, I work in the library. I set up my things at one of the tables along the windows that span the back wall. As the clock ticks closer to the start of Luc's dinner, I play pretend that I'm not seething.

I know how this night will begin. Luc will come and find me to apologize for failing to defend me. As always. I'll smile as though all is forgiven. As always.

One hour until Luc's celebratory dinner . . . thirty minutes . . .

Just ten minutes to spare when the library door finally creaks open.

I hunch farther over the table so Luc doesn't catch me watching the clock as his footsteps pad closer.

"You shouldn't be here," I say without looking up.

"That's strange. I was under the impression the library is open to all members of the Honorate," says someone who definitely is *not* Luc.

Kaidren.

I stiffen in surprise as his steps pause just behind my chair.

I fix my face into a smile and turn. In my current mood, he's the last person I want to talk to, but we're friends. Or at least, he thinks he's manipulated me into believing we are. "Kaidren. I wasn't expecting you."

"Hope you're not disappointed." He circles the table to stand across from me.

Something in the way he moves is off-putting. There's tension in how he carries himself, different from his usual laid-back demeanor. There's a table separating us, but the way he hulks over me, the way he leans forward . . . it feels almost predatory. Even that signature perfect smile of his is ever-so-slightly *off*. His eyes are tight in the corners, lips thinned, teeth looking more bared than pleasant.

"I've been searching for you," he says. "I looked first in the Praeceptor's dining room, but there's a celebration there tonight. Seems neither of us was invited." His tone lacks its usual fake warmth. Instead, his words are as frigid as lake water in the mountains.

"I wasn't expecting an invitation," I say.

He's still smiling that small, unsettling grin. "That doesn't mean much to *you*, though, does it?"

His tone sets me on blade's edge. I spoke to him just two days ago. He took great pains to coat his words in honey intended to ensnare me. Now his voice is bitter, and his stare is sharp.

I tilt my head to one side, trying to guess the reason behind this shift in him. "What do you mean?"

"This wouldn't be the first time you showed up somewhere uninvited," he says coldly.

My heartbeat quickens. His words are too delicately chosen to be anything other than an accusation. He knows about the first trial. But how?

I'm scrambling for a defense but coming up blank. I settle for playacting confused. My brows scrunch together. "I feel as if I'm missing something."

"You know exactly what I'm talking about," he snarls. "Yesterday. The arena."

My blood is ice. My throat clogs with fear. I swallow it.

I was completely covered in the arena. Kaidren didn't see my face or touch my skin. How he guessed it was me, I don't know, but so long as I deny it, he can't prove anything.

"What about the arena?" I feign confusion.

"It was *you*. You hid amid the aikkari and disguised yourself as a soldier. Don't bother denying it." There's not a trace of doubt in his tone. With the glare he's leveling at me, I can no longer convincingly play the role of his dewy-eyed, eager-to-please friend. Whatever trust he had in me is up in smoke.

That doesn't mean I can't continue to manipulate him. I'll just have to adjust my tactics for an opponent who sees me as a foe, rather than a friend.

I recall the patronizing way Yelina put a hand over her heart when she told me I wasn't invited tonight. I mimic her. Place a hand on my chest and draw my brows together in a semblance of sympathy I know he'll see right through. "Oh, I understand. You're upset you lost the first trial, and now you're lashing out."

Kaidren bends closer to the table, eyes narrowed in fury. "Stars in hell, you can drop the act. I've got you all figured out, Remira."

I doubt that. I'm enjoying myself too much to stop. Usually, I have to hide behind the Shadow Queen's name to verbally spar like this. Taunting him now, watching the way my words burrow under his skin, gives a new kind of satisfaction.

"Why are you being so mean?" I widen my eyes the way I do when I want to appear innocent, but allow the corner of my mouth to tip up in the tiniest of smirks for him to see. "I thought we were friends?"

His palms slap against the table with a glare scorching enough to raze mountains. "You know damn well we were never *friends*. You've been playing me since the day we met."

Finally, I allow the glass mask of feigned hurt to fall and shatter. My eyes harden to steel. "Now, how could I have possibly done that?" I drop the falsely sweet tone, and for the first time since we met, I address Kaidren Vale with all the derision I feel. "I thought I was just *the help*?"

Kaidren reels back as though I've struck him.

I keep going, rising to my feet as I stare him down. "And you're wrong." There's still a table between us, and he's still tall enough to tower over me, but the shock on his face makes me feel as though I'm in total control. "I haven't 'played' you—that suggests a risk of losing. We haven't been playing a game; I've been beating you. Over and over again."

Kaidren's nostrils flare. He looks as though he's seeing me for the first time and doesn't like what he sees. "Clearly, I've underestimated you."

"That's the first intelligent thing you've said since you got here."

Realization dawns in his eyes. "I told you I was Opheran when we met. The Shadow Queen mentioned it in her column, and I couldn't figure out how she knew, but you wrote to her, didn't you?"

"I did nothing of the sort. Although, I confess I've always thought 'Bastard Vale' had a nice ring to it."

"And it was *you* who accused me of murdering my father," Kaidren continues as though I haven't spoken. He slowly rounds the table, advancing on me as the revelations keep coming. "Not your brother. You must've had quite the laugh at my expense when I came to you for help."

"I admit to laughing at you. Every other accusation is absurd."

"You fought me yesterday in the Tournament." He's on my side of the table and moving steadily closer. "I'm certain of it."

I step back. He takes another one forward.

"If you're so convinced, prove it." My back hits something hard and cold—the wall of windows. I can retreat no farther. My pulse is racing. I have no idea how he worked out I was in the arena, but if there's evidence, I need to know what it is so I can destroy it.

Kaidren's slow march in my direction falters. To my

surprise, he looks almost . . . embarrassed. "Your eyes gave you away."

I'm so relieved, I chuckle. "You saw a girl with brown eyes you could barely see through a mask, and you think it was me?"

"Well, that, and . . ." He hesitates and, again, I catch a glimmer of embarrassment in his expression.

"And what?" I prompt.

"Your scent." The lightest hue of pink tints his cheeks. "It's that perfume you wear. I'd recognize it anywhere."

I wave him off dismissively. "I don't wear perfume."

"Yet you always smell of rosemary."

It takes everything in me not to flinch. I wasn't lying—I *don't* use perfume—but Sef adorns my hair with rosemary oil. I'm stunned Kaidren noticed.

I hide my surprise behind a scoff. "You saw brown eyes and smelled rosemary. That's hardly irrefutable proof."

It was the wrong thing to say. Kaidren's expression is stormy as he stalks closer and closer, until I am pressed to the window, his body fencing mine. He stoops, face a gasp away, our breaths intermingling. We're close enough our noses would brush if I inclined my head. Close enough I see a vein thrumming furiously in his forehead. Close enough my pulse races with the fear he's going to close the distance and touch me.

I flatten myself against the cold windowpanes and hold my breath, petrified my shallow inhales will be enough to bridge the narrow gap that divides us.

"Your eyes aren't just brown." His tone is harsh as his gaze flits over my face, soaking in every detail as though carving it into his memory. "They're chestnut. But that doesn't matter. You think eyes are distinguished by color? They're not. Even when I thought you were a servant, there was a fire in them I'd recognize through smoke. The girl I fought in the arena was *you*. I am certain of it."

I didn't think there was enough space for him to draw nearer still, but he does.

My breath catches. All of him surrounds all of me, trapping me in a cage of flesh and fury. My heartbeat is frantic, as though trying to flee from my chest and the threat of his skin.

I say nothing and don't move.

Kaidren's glare is unwavering in its intensity. "Your scent isn't just rosemary," he murmurs. His eyes remain harsh, but his tone has softened. "It's rosemary and dust and a faint hint of lemon. If you truly don't use perfume, then it must be your soap, because I can smell it on you, even now. You want evidence I can present to the decurio? I have none. But I don't need proof, because I *see* you. More clearly now than before."

He's certainly looking at me as though he sees me. Deep brown eyes bore into mine, and my stomach inexplicably clenches in an unfamiliar emotion that isn't fear. This close, there's no escaping him. As much as it puts me on edge, there's something mesmerizing about Kaidren when his veil of civility falls away. When he reveals the dark, desperate boy lurking under the surface.

He drags his heated stare over my face, until it rests on my lips. The gap between us crackles like a bonfire, and I find myself intensely aware of every pinprick of distance. With a twitch, I would feel his skin on mine—and hand him the power to burn me. Terrifying. *Enticing*. I never realized how closely intertwined the two are.

My ungloved hands creep up. Palms settle on his chest. His breath catches.

I shove him, hard as I can.

My mind is clouded from his proximity, but as he stumbles back, it clears. "You see nothing."

He's still only a pace away and eyeing me hungrily, as though he means to approach again.

I push from the window and duck under his arm. I won't allow him another chance to corner me.

He turns with me, stalking my movements across the room. "You deny it?"

"Obviously." I roll my eyes to hide how I'm still struggling to catch my breath. "You have nothing but baseless accusations, and you are far out of your depth. You came to Widow's Hall thirsting for power. You assumed a few simple tricks were all it would take to steal it, but you were wrong."

"Of the two of us, I'm not the one who has to steal power, Remira. I'm the son of an Honorate. The only thief here is you."

"Better a thief than a fraud." I'm near the table, facing him, back to the rest of the library, heart thudding so loud it hurts. "You claimed to be an isha to gain favor with the Republic. You claimed you came here to rid the Honorate of corruption. All the while, you're no better than the rest of them."

"I'm nothing like them."

"You know what, I think you truly believe that," I say. "As always, you're wrong. You want the throne because you want power—not because you care to improve the Republic."

His nostrils flare. "You have no idea what I want."

"Don't I?" I raise a challenging eyebrow. "How can you claim to me of all people that you're not a liar? You tried to manipulate me. You faked kindness and friendship so you could coax me into betraying my own brother."

"What do you care? You were pretending too."

"Maybe. But I knew I was conning a conman. You had no

idea I was faking anything. Tell me, Bastard Vale, what does that say about you?"

"That you clouded my judgment."

"What?" I smirk. "This sweet little Opheran girl?"

"There's nothing *sweet* about you." He spits out the word. "I didn't know you before, but I know exactly what kind of girl I'm dealing with now. Conniving, vindictive, and cruel."

I laugh mockingly. "You make those sound like insults. I'd rather be vindictive than an easy target. Since we're being honest, let me confess that pretending to be your friend was the hardest thing I've ever had to do. Now I'm finally free to tell you how much I despise you."

"The feeling is mutual." He chuckles darkly. "I can't believe I actually felt bad for toying with you. It seemed heartless to manipulate someone so . . ." He glances at my wrist, where the edge of my sun tattoo peeks out from under my sleeve. He stops himself. "Forget it."

I glare, guessing what he doesn't say. "Go ahead. What did you think of me? Did you think I was pitiable? A gullible fool?"

Kaidren meets my glare head-on. "Gullible, maybe. But more than that, I thought you were exquisite."

I flinch. It's not the word I was expecting. Worse, I'm ice-cold—he means it. He's done nothing but try to manipulate me since we met. He pretended to like me, pretended he was drawn to me, and apparently, it wasn't all fake.

The confession stirs something in me. I'm ashamed to admit it, but part of me *liked* the way his gaze used to linger. Liked watching his eyes stare into mine and soften into something bordering on affection. At the time, I assumed it was for show, but knowing a small part of that was real . . . My stomach flutters weakly.

But then I remember the way he called me "the help" and

ordered me to fetch him water. The way he fed me lies about using his newfound position to better Ophera.

I smother that foolish, needy feeling. Kaidren only thought he had feelings for me because I pretended to fall for his nonexistent charm. A girl who is easily manipulated can be exquisite. A girl who does the manipulating . . . not so much.

I scowl. "Sorry to disappoint."

"Pass a message along to your brother for me: I'm calling for Eteria. I'm no fraud, and I'm going to prove to the world that I'm *exactly* who I say I am."

It takes everything in me not to smirk. "Planning on cheating?"

"I believe cheating is your skill set, Remira." His expression darkens. "It's a shame. I felt guilty for manipulating the girl I thought you were. I will revel in destroying the girl I know you to be."

My hand curls into a fist. Once again, he's underestimating me. I might fight best from the shadows, unseen and unheard, but I'm more than prepared to battle Kaidren Vale out in the light where he can see me. "Careful. That almost sounded like a threat."

"It was. Before, I declared war on your brother. Clearly, I threatened the wrong Kyler. Something you should know about me, Remira: I never make the same mistake twice."

CHAPTER NINETEEN

WHERE THE BODIES ARE BURIED

Selva Sixmen only showed me one letter he received from the imposter Shadow Queen. He received it just before the start of the Tournament, two weeks ago, but according to Flynn, he's been acting paranoid for months.

I thought it was strange that the note Sixmen shared from the imposter was so vague. There was no mention of what secret he's being blackmailed with, and no specific demands.

Taken all together, I'm led to one conclusion: Sixmen has received more letters from the imposter than he let on. Probably because he didn't want the real Shadow Queen to know what secret her imposter is holding over his head.

In preparation for today, I reviewed all my notes on Sixmen. He has one son, Flynn; his wife, Neveah, died last year; he had a number of affairs while she was alive; he falsely testified in court to get a former friend thrown in prison for a crime he didn't commit; and he once accepted a hefty bribe to vote for an order regarding taxes.

For all the secrets I know about him, there must be another, darker one he's hiding. Something he thinks the real Shadow Queen doesn't already know.

Which is why I had Luc request a private word with Selva, why I checked on Flynn to ensure he's on guard duty at the base of the mountain right now, and why I'm currently standing outside the Sixmen residence, confident both of them are out of the house for the foreseeable future.

The outside of the Sixmen manor is gray stone. No tshira in sight, and no chance of me using magic to get inside.

I check the windows next, but unfortunately, all the ones on the ground floor are locked.

Which leaves my third strategy: knocking on the back door that leads into the kitchen.

No one answers.

After a long pause, I try again, more insistently.

An impatient-looking woman yanks the door open. She looks even more annoyed when she sees me. "Who the hell are you?"

Definitely not as friendly as Frida. Fortunately, my plan doesn't require I talk to her for too long.

"Oh, I'm sorry." Before she can stop me, I lean past her, poking my head through the kitchen door and peering around, as though looking for something. I angle my body, blocking her view of the doorframe.

As she glowers at me, the hand hidden behind my back presses a scrap of leather drenched in paste to the doorframe, right where the bolt will slide home when she no doubt slams and locks the door behind me.

Once I'm sure the leather won't slip, I pull back, twisting my expression into one of mortification. "I am so, so sorry," I say. "I think I might have the wrong house. Could you direct me to—"

She slams the door before I've finished speaking.

It doesn't matter. As soon as the kitchen is clear, I'll slip inside. In the meantime, that leaves me stuck out here, seconds away from freezing my ear off, listening to the sounds of shuffling feet and clanging pots.

My instincts tell me the imposter Shadow Queen is Kaidren. The timing can't be a coincidence. He comes to court trying to beat out Luc for the throne, and around the same time, someone *else* starts blackmailing Honorate in my name. There's a connection. There must be. I plan to destroy Kaidren in any way I can. First, by humiliating him in Eteria tomorrow. Next, by exposing him as a blackmailer as well as a fraud.

After the longest two minutes of my life, the sounds of movement in the kitchen fade.

I wait another second. It's still silent.

I inhale a lungful of wintry air, preparing. I'll need to move fast. No idea how long the kitchen will remain empty, or what will happen if anyone finds me.

Gently, I nudge open the door. The leather in the doorframe has done its job, keeping the lock from fully closing.

I peek around the door into the kitchen. Empty.

Slipping inside, I peel the leather from the frame and close the door behind me as softly as I can.

I'm not familiar with the layout of the Sixmens' house. I don't know where the bedrooms are—or even if the bedroom is where Selva would keep blackmail notes—but I figure my best bet is to move up.

There's a servants' stairwell on the other side of the kitchen. I pause here, at the base of the steps.

No creaking or voices. A good sign.

I hold my breath as I dart up the stairs. The old wood groans. I wince, moving faster before someone comes to investigate.

As soon as I'm upstairs, I fling myself through the first door I see.

"Bel?" A woman's voice echoes up the stairwell after me.

My hand claps over my mouth, holding in the sounds of my breaths, heavy from nerves and my brief sprint up the stairs.

The room is dark and silent, save for my muffled breaths. I wait, but the stairs stay mercifully quiet.

I keep my hand over my mouth as I look around. It's a dressing room, by the looks of it. Yelina has one just like it. A whole room dedicated to things like clothing, jewelry, and mirrors. This one looks as if it hasn't been touched in years.

At the other end of the room is a door. Hearing nothing on the other side, I open it to reveal a bedchamber. Selva Sixmen's, I assume.

Portraits hang around the room. One of an older man, one of a little boy, one of a woman I recognize. Selva's late wife, Neveah Sixmen. She was one of the few Honorate wives I actually met because she was good friends with Yelina. She used to hang around the Kyler house, laughing at Yelina's unfunny jokes and drinking that disgusting tea Yelina loves. I didn't know her well, but I despise her on principle. Anyone who finds my stepmother's sense of humor tolerable must be awful.

I crouch alongside Sixmen's bed and feel beneath his mattress. Nothing.

Next, I look through his drawers. I start with his bedside tables, then his dresser. In all, there's nothing of note.

I cast a long look around the rest of the room. Above the mantel hangs a family portrait. Selva, Neveah, and Flynn, all smiling. Flynn looks much younger, but I know it's him. He's got that mole above his upper lip and the signature haircut of a member of the decurio. My gaze flits lower, to the two urns sitting on the mantle.

It gives me pause. One urn makes sense, for his wife's remains. The other . . .

I open the lighter of the two. Shoved inside are crumpled sheets of parchment.

I unfurl one, and hold it up to the window to read.

Honorate Sixmen,

I am certain your behavior has Neveah rolling over in her early grave.

Let's ensure the rest of Virdei never finds out how despicable you truly are, shall we? You vote against the order that will increase the number of decurio around Ophera, and I'll keep my mouth shut.

It's signed from the Shadow Queen but, as before, I didn't write this. There are five more letters. All from my imposter, all that Selva kept from me.

Six letters total. I could stay here and read them all, but that's foolish. The longer I stall, the higher the likelihood I'll be caught. If I take them, Selva will know they're missing, but considering all the efforts he took to keep them secret, it's not like he can tell anyone they've been stolen.

Mind made, I shove the notes in my pocket and put my ear to the bedroom door, listening for approaching footsteps. Nothing.

I hold my breath as I creep out and back down the stairs. I don't risk the kitchen a second time. Instead, I steal into the empty drawing room, unlatch the window, and climb out before anyone sees me.

You've followed the rules well. If only your fellow Honorate were so obedient. There is another order on the agenda tomorrow. If it passes, there will be two dozen more soldiers sent to the Opheran border. You will ensure it never passes. Vote in opposition. Convince your fellow Honorate to follow suit.

> *If it passes, I do not care who is at fault, I will blame you. I know what happened to Neveah. If this order passes, the rest of the Republic will too.*

With each note, my heart sinks lower. They each demand Selva oppose an order, each vaguely mentions something awful he did to his wife, and each commands Selva to block an order that would provide more security to Ophera. Any attempt I've made in the past few months to send soldiers to the Opheran border, my imposter has forced Selva to oppose.

That in and of itself is concerning. But there's something else weighing on me. The imposter never explicitly states what terrible secret Selva is carrying, but they each imply that perhaps Neveah didn't simply die—perhaps she was murdered.

> *Honorate Sixmen,*
> *That title will only apply until the next council meeting. The next time the Honorate convene, you will announce your intentions to retire the position. I have decided you are no longer fit to lead.*
> *Feel free to argue, Sixmen, but we both know the consequences if you fail to do as I say.*

Stars in hell . . .

I wasn't expecting that.

Months of threatening Selva, all for the imposter to force him to resign anyway. It doesn't make sense. What's the point in gathering secrets of a man who doesn't have the power to *do* anything?

If Selva truly murdered his wife, he'll have no choice but to do it. It will cause a stir. He's only in his forties. Far too young to quit. No one is given power only to throw it away. Especially the Honorate.

I smooth out the final note.

> *Honorate Sixmen,*
>
> *Tell me, did they ever find your wife's body? A shame.*
>
> *I know they found the body of Arliss Vale. If you refuse even one of my demands, I assure you, they will find yours exactly as they did his.*
>
> *If you don't believe me, I can tell you how he died. Arliss Vale was killed by a poison called kishori. If you aren't careful, so will you.*
>
> *Tell anyone, and you are next.*

The parchment flutters to the floor.

I hardly notice, too wrapped up in my own horror.

My imposter has been busy. Blackmailing Selva Sixmen, blocking all my attempts to provide more security to Ophera, and—most terrifying of all—murdering Arliss Vale.

CHAPTER TWENTY

PULLING HIS STRINGS

The Republic of Virdei takes honor and tradition seriously. Especially when we're being observed by outsiders who hate us and want nothing more than to take our land and resources.

Which is why the General of the decurio insisted we use ceremonial robes for Eteria, to be tailor-made for Kaidren Vale by the official seamstress of Widow's Hall.

I've never met the woman, but Sef is skilled at making friends.

The hall leading to her work chambers is wide, quiet, and empty. Clearly, she doesn't get many visitors. Sef and I peer around the open door into her room.

It's huge, with jagged stone walls and clothes everywhere. Some are hanging on wooden racks, some are folded, and some are draped over wooden figurines molded into the shape of human bodies.

Kaidren's robes for Eteria are proudly displayed in the middle of the room, laid out over a stone table. They're impossible to miss. Black with shimmering gold-threaded trim, an emerald green lining, and a sash of the same color around the middle.

The seamstress flits about the room, not watching the door. She's a short and solidly built woman. Her hair is in locs that fall to her hips. The hair at the base of her skull is dark brown, and the ends are dyed silver and studded with dark blue beads.

She wears a pin cushion dotted with needles attached to a thick leather bracelet, and at least two pins stuck in her hair.

Sef enters the room with a cheery smile. "Hey, Novi."

The seamstress looks up in surprise that swiftly melts into happiness. "Sef!" She moves in for a hug, taking care to hold the arm with the pin cushion bracelet out and away. "What are you doing here? You haven't come to see me in weeks."

"I know, I know," Sef says sheepishly. "You know my mistress. She keeps me busy." She and Novi fall easily into conversation. Sef is a natural at this. Effortlessly charming, casual, and cheery.

As she and Novi talk, Sef slowly shuffles to the side. Novi turns with her, not breaking their conversation or even noticing the subtle shift. In a few moments, she's facing away from Kaidren's robe, and her back is to the door.

My eyes narrow on the robes. I rise on my tiptoes and slink across the room. Sef raises her voice, just barely, to mask any noises I hope I'm not making as I grab one of the robe's sleeves. My fingers work quickly, pinning a rectangular scrap of fabric to the inside lining. I pin it on three sides, leaving one open. The end result is a makeshift interior pocket. Into it, I slide a hollow tube made of tshira.

I lift the sleeve, ensuring the tube doesn't fall out. It stays.
Perfect.

I'm back out the door before Novi the seamstress knows I'm there.

Every single seat in the arena is filled and every single person is screaming at the top of their lungs. I feel the reverberations of their cheers and the tangible excitement of it all as I enter the spectator stands.

My eyes immediately find Luc. He's hard to miss. His seat is in the front row and it's built into a throne, complete with plush cushions and armrests. Most of the benches are already filled, but there's a gap right next to him. He saved me a spot. He said he would, but it's not until he catches my eye and waves that I believe him.

I can't help smiling. I push my way through the stands toward him. A foot slams into the bench, right where I was planning to sit.

I trace the shoe up to its owner. Yelina. She's dressed in yellow and black furs and wears a short black wig. She gives a smile, sickly sweet enough to make me ill. "Remira, dear, I am so sorry, but there isn't space for you."

My eyes narrow. I glance at Luc, but the cheerful expression he gave before has fled, and he's no longer making eye contact.

I bite the inside of my cheek to fight a scowl. "Luc saved this seat for me."

"Yes, he told me. But unfortunately, Mrs. Night needs this spot. Her husband is already seated. You wouldn't want to separate a husband and wife, would you, dear?"

Lorwen Night despises the mountain air. I've been eavesdropping on her since she first arrived, and I've heard every rant about her hatred of Virdei, listened to her complain about how she hasn't felt warm in weeks, and heard her whine endlessly that she didn't even want to come to Eteria. "I was under the impression Mrs. Night wouldn't be attending."

"She wasn't, but there's been a change in plans. I think it was her husband who changed her mind."

I'm warmed with a lie, confirmed by Yelina's tiny smirk.

Taelon didn't persuade his wife to attend—Yelina did. She

wants me to know it without her having to say it aloud in front of witnesses.

Steel and ice. I'm made of steel and ice.

I bare my teeth into a smile. "Of course. If Mrs. Night needs a seat, I'm happy to give her mine." I don't even bother glancing at Luc again. There's no point. I already know he's silently watching his feet, like always.

I keep my head high as I pick a new spot, this one close to a set of stairs that leads out from the arena.

It's better. It'll make it easier to sneak out without detection or having to come up with an excuse when the time comes. No matter how many times I remind myself of this fact, I can't settle my roiling fury.

I'm fuming up until the start of the demonstration.

The arena gate flings open, and Flynn enters to thunderous applause. It's to be expected for an aikkari whose source is snow. Most aikkari with physical sources either carry around bits of it for easy access or keep tshira stored with magic somewhere on their person. For Flynn, it isn't necessary. He's never far from his source, making him a formidable opponent. It's no secret that he's being groomed to take over as General of the decurio when General Fain retires.

Flynn raises his arms, waving at the adoring crowd. Ten contenders trail after him. Only five are decurio soldiers, but they're all dressed the part.

From my new seat, I have a perfect view of Luc and his entourage—they're the only ones in the arena not cheering. Luc smiles and claps when appropriate, but his parents are stone-faced, and the Petruvians—especially Lorwen Night—look actively bored.

The ten contenders get into place as Flynn finishes explaining the rules. They each stand behind a burlap sack. For the aikkari, the bags before them contain their sources, ready for the demonstrations. For the civilians, the bags contain a large rock for show. No one in the stands knows which—or how many—of the contenders are aikkari, and which are not.

Well, no one except for me.

The air buzzes as Flynn cues Kaidren's entrance.

Kaidren emerges from one of the rooms at the base of the stands. He struts confidently into the center of the arena, head high in his black and gold robes, shoulders back. There isn't a trace of nerves, not a hint of indecision.

He walks as though he's already won. I can't tell how much of his confidence is a screen and how much of it is real. My guess is it's mostly fake. Kaidren strikes me as the kind of person who's always acting. Always putting on a show.

Flynn motions to the first contender. "Gavin Tassim. Tell us, Honorate Vale, is this man aikkari?"

Kaidren places a hand on Gavin's forehead. His head bows, eyes slip closed. After a pause, he opens them. "He's aikkari. His source is cerulean blue."

The entire arena seems to lean forward, eager to see if he's correct.

"Step aside, Honorate Vale." Flynn guides Kaidren out of the way before pulling a cord. It runs across the arena, under the stands. There, hidden from the audience, is a massive crossbow. And Flynn just pulled the trigger.

A spear of tshira launches through the air, hurtling right toward Gavin.

The audience catches their breath.

Gavin doesn't hesitate. He reaches into his bag and pulls out a cerulean blue tile.

He throws a hand up, palm out.

The tshira spear is only a few breaths away from piercing

his stomach, but its trajectory suddenly shifts, as though met with a great burst of wind. It sails to the side, where it embeds itself harmlessly in the ground.

The audience erupts into raucous cheers. But the demonstration isn't over yet.

Three members of the decurio rush into the field from a room at the base, each carrying bows loaded with a tshira arrow. As one, they release their bowstrings.

Gavin springs into action. His dropped tile shatters against the ground, but he ignores it and raises his arms. All three arrows move together, away from him, away from danger, and land in the snow.

Even I'm impressed. I don't have nearly so much control of my magic.

The crowd screams even louder, and Kaidren's smile is wider than I've ever seen. He's correctly identified the first contender and their source.

My eyes follow the trail of the cord Flynn pulled to launch the tshira. I make a mental note of where it ends, beneath the stands on the other side of the arena.

Flynn announces the name of the next contender. "Reyna Halifore."

Kaidren lays a hand on her forehead. This time, he doesn't bother with any of his previous theatrics. He shakes his head. "She's not aikkari." He doesn't wait for a prompt from Flynn before moving aside.

Again, Flynn pulls the cord, and again, a tshira spear launches at the girl. She shrieks, hands flying to cover her face, as though expecting the spear to hit her.

Flynn swiftly holds out his arms, sending the bolt gliding off to the side.

Kaidren's grinning again. "You can look now, Reyna."

She peeks open one eye, then the other, breathing a sigh of relief when she sees she's still alive.

There are eight contenders left. Kaidren works down the line. He correctly identifies the next seven. Four are aikkari, three are not.

I slip out of my seat before the second to last participant. No one pays me any mind as I duck beneath the arena stands and make my way to the other side—to where the cord Flynn pulls to trigger the crossbow leads. I hear rather than see Kaidren's deep, confident voice proclaim the final contender isn't aikkari.

As the audience stomps their feet, I stop moving. I'm directly under a giant weapon. It looks like a crossbow, but larger than any I've ever seen, and the loading mechanism is piled high with additional bolts that slide into place when the previous one is released. The next spear is already loaded, just waiting for a trigger.

By this point, everyone is cheering, Flynn is all smiles, and Kaidren is soaking up the attention.

Flynn takes Kaidren by the wrist and holds it up. "Congratulations to Honorate Kaidren Vale . . ."

He keeps speaking, but I'm no longer listening. It's too easy to reach for the cord connected to the massive crossbow and loop it loosely around the ankle of a man seated overhead. I send a tendril of heat to his seat. Not enough to burn, just enough to startle.

He leaps with a yelp. The motion pulls the cord. The device beneath him launches, and another tshira bolt sails toward the center of the arena, right at the final contender, Rilan.

It takes people a moment to notice it. After all, the event is supposed to be over. No one is expecting *another* attack.

Then someone screams.

The decurio in the arena react quickly, but not quickly enough. As they scramble for their sources to use magic to deflect the spear, Rilan is utterly terrified and completely defenseless.

Instinct takes over. His hands shoot up to guard his face, and he cries out.

The crossbow bolt is a whisper away from him when I shift it out of the way. I'm not as practiced as the decurio, so it's not nearly as graceful as it jolts to the side. The jerky movements of the tshira only serve to better sell my lie: it *looks* as if the man the tshira was about to spear just used magic to protect himself.

The same man Kaidren Vale very clearly announced to the world *isn't* aikkari.

Rilan's scream of terror fades.

The excitement of the arena softens into confused whispers.

Kaidren's jaw slackens. He whirls to Rilan, expression flickering between shock and confusion. "What—how did you do that?"

Rilan lowers his hands. "That wasn't me." He wavers and stares at his hands in astonishment. "At least, I don't think it was."

Flynn's frown is deep, and the furrow in his brow grows more pronounced. He raises his voice. "Will the aikkari responsible for blocking the misfired bolt please come forward?"

All around, aikkari glance at one another in question, waiting for someone to claim responsibility.

No one moves.

Clearly frustrated, Flynn moves down the line of soldiers. He stops in front of each aikkari participant and directly asks them: "Did you move that crossbow bolt?"

When they each deny it, he pushes further: "Are you *certain?*"

Each aikkari confirms they are.

Confusion abounds, in the stands and the arena alike. Flynn fixes his gaze on the final participant, Rilan. "It must have been you."

Rilan stares at his hands again. "But I'm not aikkari. That's impossible."

"Just because you didn't know doesn't mean you don't have magic. It's not uncommon for someone to be aikkari and not know their source."

"I've never done anything like that before."

"You were about to be killed—you acted on instinct. Did you feel a rush of heat before the spear moved?"

"No, I—" Rilan hesitates, now doubting what he felt. "Maybe. I was panicking. I didn't even notice. But maybe I did."

If the audience was confused before, it's nothing compared to how it feels now.

Flynn snatches Kaidren's arm and pulls him to stand before Rilan. "Honorate Vale, can you tell us what this man's source is?"

Kaidren's already shaking his head. "He isn't aikkari. When I touched him, I didn't feel anything."

"Maybe you missed something. Try again."

Kaidren touches Rilan's cheek. Holds it for a few seconds. He frowns. "I'm telling you, he isn't aikkari. He doesn't have a source. I don't know what's going on, but—"

I release another surge of magic. This time, I direct it at the tshira tube I hid in Kaidren's sleeve. It falls free from Kaidren's robe and lands in the snow. I send a final wave of magic to roll it over the ground, coming to a rest at Flynn's feet. Impossible for him to miss.

Flynn looks from Kaidren to the tube and back again. "What's this?"

Kaidren frowns and shakes his sleeve to see if anything else falls out. Nothing does. "I have no idea."

Flynn casts Kaidren a doubtful look as he scoops up the tube and finds a rolled-up sheet of parchment tucked inside.

The crowd can't see what's written on it from the distance, but I already know. Because I wrote it.

Gavin Tassim: cerulean blue
Bahni Hidday: orchid

It keeps going. Five names. One for each of the aikkari who participated in Eteria along with their sources.

I wrote it yesterday, in my hidden room next to the interrogation chamber. Luc shook hands with each aikkari set to participate today. He confirmed that their source would be present in the arena. And I listened and wrote them all down.

Judging by the several seconds Flynn spends staring at it, the doubt is properly sown.

His face darkens as he finally looks to Kaidren. "Honorate Vale, can you please explain to me what this is?" His voice is tempered. Controlled. But anyone can hear the anger underlying each word.

"I have no idea what you're talking about." Kaidren reaches for the parchment, but Flynn jerks it out of reach.

"Honorate Vale, on this parchment are the names of each of the five aikkari contenders and their sources. You obviously didn't write them during Eteria, so you must have written them beforehand. You cheated."

"*What?*" Kaidren successfully snatches the parchment from Flynn as the audience sucks in a collective gasp.

Whispers intensify.

From beneath the stands, I catch a few of the accusatory whispers directed at Kaidren Vale:

"*He's a liar.*"

"He cheated?"

"The Shadow Queen was right—he made it all up."

Kaidren is shaking. "I've never seen this before in my life."

"Yet it was on your person."

"Someone must've put it there."

"That's a serious accusation. Do you have a name for me?"

"No . . ." Kaidren's frantic gaze flits around the arena. He knows I have something to do with this—he must—but he can't prove it. "But it wasn't me. I swear. I *am* an isha. I had no need to cheat."

Flynn scoffs, disbelieving. "You claim you've never seen this before, yet you were able to correctly identify each of the aikkari and their sources except for Rilan. Either you're an awful isha, or a terrible liar. Which is it?"

"I—" Kaidren's sentence falters. He has no excuses. No explanations. All he knows is that the sense of victory he felt only moments ago is gone now. "I can prove it. Give me your hand, sir. I'll tell you your source."

"Of course you will. You've clearly done your research."

"I *haven't*. Give me any aikkari and I'll prove it."

Flynn gestures toward Rilan. "*Him.* Tell me his source. He is the only aikkari here whose source I don't already know."

Kaidren doesn't have a response to that.

Scowling, Flynn raises his voice. We could all hear him before anyway, but now he addresses the crowd directly. "I apologize, everyone. Thank you for attending Eteria. Unfortunately"—here, he shoots Kaidren a sharp look, dripping fury—"it would seem we do *not* have an isha in Virdei after all."

CHAPTER TWENTY-ONE

CAPTIVE AUDIENCE

One Vale dead, one Vale a liar. I'm not sure which fate is worse. Or which Vale is more damned.

Two weeks since Arliss Vale was murdered. Five days since Bastard Vale revealed himself as a cheat in Eteria. And five days since anyone has seen or heard from the liar himself— from the shadows or otherwise.

Is Bastard Vale hiding his face because he is embarrassed? Or is he perhaps hiding a guilty conscience?

He showed the world he is eager to lie. Could he also be eager to kill? Arliss Vale was murdered, and this Queen of Shadows thinks it was Bastard Vale himself who poured the lethal dose.

He might not be set to stand trial for his crimes, but in this court of judgment, Bastard Vale is guilty on all charges. Clearly, there is no honor among thieves. Or murderers.

Fondly,
Shadow Queen

My teeth chatter as I stumble over the ice-coated roads to Mozeri Temple. I'm fighting a scowl as well as a chill.

The note Kaidren slipped under the doorway of each of our Petruvian guests' rooms sears a hole in my pocket, taunting me.

You are cordially invited to come see the future of the great Republic of Virdei in person. Come to Mozeri Temple at midday to witness your next Praeceptor, Kaidren Vale, discuss his plans for the future.

Apparently, even after his failure in Eteria, his opinion of himself hasn't dimmed at all.

I'd hoped public shame would be enough to prove to him that he is far out of his depth. No such luck. Despite the whispers, despite the Shadow Queen, despite the fact that all of Virdei thinks he's a fraud, he seems as determined to frustrate my plans as ever.

I slip into the back of the temple, relieved to be inside, away from the blistering cold.

Virdeian temples are devoted to the stars. Many believe that each star is the soul of a god, dead or alive. The lonely god who supposedly gifted us magic is said to be the brightest of them all. Some believe he's the only one still alive (hence the loneliness, hence the gifting us magic) and that he shines brighter because the other stars are the souls of gods that have long since died.

I don't believe in the gods, but I know there's magic in stars. I used to spend hours with my mother staring at the endless expanse above, feeling the weight of everything float away. She knew nothing of constellations, so she made them up. Said they were all different kinds of birds, and that one day, they'd fly us far, far away. Whenever I was sad, or scared, or angry, we'd watch the sky. It made everything better. Maybe believing in stars is just as foolish as believing in gods, but I do.

The bulk of Mozeri Temple is a wide, windowless room. Stained glass panes hang framed on the walls, but none of them actually look outside—an effort to trap in as much heat as possible. The wooden benches that typically fill the space have been pushed to the side to provide room for people to stand.

The temple is packed. My nose is buried in the wool of someone else's cloak, and all around me, people stretch on tiptoe to glimpse a peek of Kaidren. I rarely venture below the Collar. It feels different from the arena's raucous crowds. The people who fill this temple are clearly eager, but they're quiet, listening raptly.

I lean around attendees and peer over shoulders until I find Kaidren. He's in the pulpit at the front of the chamber. He isn't wearing the emerald green robes of an Honorate, or a thick cloak like someone of his status and recent inheritance can afford. Instead, he's wearing thin layers and no sjaal.

People like us. It's what he said when he tried to convince me we must be twin flames because we're both Opheran. He's doing the same thing now. Costuming himself as one of the people below the Collar so he can pretend he's one of them and gain their support.

I grit my teeth against my irritation at the transparent act and watch him. He's in the middle of a speech. It's definitely rehearsed, but he doesn't sound stilted, and there's no sign that he's reading from anything. He strikes an imposing figure, but his face is composed into an oily smile that makes him look approachable. Framed by six torches, he's surrounded by a hazy stream of golden orange light that softens his features.

"I still have every intention of defeating the Praeceptor in the Tournament of Thrones," Kaidren is saying. "I know there are people who doubt me and my word. But I am not walking away from the Tournament, or the Republic."

As I watch him, only one question plagues my mind: Did he kill his father?

I've done my research. Kishori—the poison the imposter

Shadow Queen claimed she used to kill Arliss Vale—is a thick, purple liquid that acts quickly. It's harmful in small doses, but not deadly. In large quantities, it's lethal within an hour. When I saw Arliss's body, he was already dead, and he hadn't eaten breakfast. Which means he must've received the deadly dose in his dinner the night before. Kaidren was already living in the Vale manor at the time—it would've been all too easy for him to slip poison into his father's meal.

"Lucien Kyler is unqualified for his current role," Kaidren says. "He sits on the throne and yet he's never won a Tournament himself. He hasn't had to earn his position. He's not like us—hardworking people who have had to fight to get where we are."

There's that expression again. *People like us.*

Kaidren is nothing like the Virdeians who fill this temple. He lives in a manor at the top of the mountain. He just inherited more money than any of these people will ever see in their lives. Despite that, his words strike a chord. The quiet crowd buzzes around me.

Virdei calls itself a Republic, but we rarely have elections. Unless scandal forces an Honorate out of the council, seats hardly ever open up, and the people seldom get to vote on anything. For one of the godlike beings on top of the mountain to descend from Widow's Hall to speak with them is more than a rarity—it's unheard of.

I crane my head, trying to estimate just how many people are here. It must be over fifty. Maybe even close to a hundred.

As I scan the crowd, I catch a flash of an indigo cloak. A Petruvian.

"Lucien Kyler does not care about you," Kaidren says. "He does not care about anyone but himself. He has not failed on his promises—he failed to make you any in the first place. When was the last time someone in Widow's Hall cared enough to visit? Let alone cared enough to *listen*? Never. Because everyone else at Widow's Hall is a coward. They care only for their interests and the interests of their friends. I intend to be the opposite. To usher in a new future for our Republic."

People start clapping. The energy within the temple swells with his words.

I keep an eye on the Petruvian cloak as it leans to the side. Its wearer mutters something to the person next to them, in a similar cloak. Their head turns as they speak. Lorwen Night. Whispering something to her husband, Taelon.

I push through the crowd to stand closer to them, hoping to overhear their conversation.

Kaidren is giving his signature waxy smile that shows off his perfect teeth. He doesn't cheer with the crowd. He has a calm, quiet confidence. The kind that comes with the knowledge that he already belongs here and doesn't need to shout in order to prove it.

I'm a row behind the Petruvians when the crowd has quieted enough for Kaidren to keep going. "This great Republic deserves better than what its current Praeceptor has done. When I win the Tournament, I will make it a priority to expand the academies. Right now, Virdei has two, and both are above the Collar. When I am Praeceptor, my *first* priority will be getting the Honorate to fund more schools throughout the mountain.

"Right now, the council of honor that determines which Honorate are too disgraced to carry the title is composed only of those who live above the Collar. I will expand this so all of Virdei has a say in its leaders."

Each of his pretty proclamations is met with excitement. The energy in this temple is tangible. I have to admit, in another context, I might be swayed.

The only issue: I'm on fire. Every word out of Kaidren's mouth is a lie, and I'm the only one here who knows it.

People often say things they mean in the moment, but when the time comes to follow through, they balk. Luc does it to me all the time. Kaidren is different. He's disingenuous from the start. He *knows* he won't change anything, even now, but he says it anyway.

I press forward until I'm right behind the Nights.

"Remind me why we must make a farce of negotiating with these people," Lorwen mutters. "They don't even respect their king—"

"Praeceptor," Taelon corrects her.

Lorwen brushes it off. "Same thing. Is this not treason?"

"They're a Republic, Lo." Taelon sounds bored. "They can say what they want."

Kaidren is still speaking, but I'm less interested in his platitudes than I am in the Nights.

"Well, *I* say that it's freezing," Lorwen mumbles. "When can we leave?"

"When it's over. His Majesty expects reports. It's our job to keep him apprised of the Tournament. Especially considering his upcoming plans for—" He cuts himself off and looks around, ensuring no one is nearby.

I duck my head, keeping my hood low.

Taelon continues, voice even softer than before, so much so, I have to strain to hear. "*Ophera*," he hisses.

"I don't know why His Majesty insists on playing games," Lorwen grumbles. "This bastard here has more acclaim than their king. If the people don't respect their leaders, why should we respect the treaty?"

"Because it is treason otherwise." Taelon sounds less bored

now, and more annoyed. "*These* people have no respect for their rulers. But *we* do. You'd do well to remember that."

Lorwen clearly means to argue further, but her husband nudges her to silence.

"Widow's Hall is corrupt," Kaidren says. "Full of people more concerned with protecting their family legacies than making it any better."

All true.

"As Praeceptor, I will make it my mission to weed out this rampant corruption in the Honorate."

Lie.

He is identifying real problems and offering real solutions. But he has no intention of ever implementing them.

For all the liars in Widow's Hall, Kaidren Vale is the most putrid, most vile.

Unfortunately, the best lies are the ones that align with what we *want* to hear. So, even though I burn with the force of his deception, the Virdeians below the Collar are riveted, pleased to have finally been heard.

CHAPTER TWENTY-TWO

PIECE BY PIECE

I leave the temple early. Partly because listening to Kaidren feed people lie after lie is making me ill. Mostly because I've been presented an opportunity.

The Nights are occupied, which means their rooms are not.

Sef keeps guard in the corridor outside, equipped with a feather duster in case anyone questions her presence here, while I snoop.

The Nights' room is spacious—far larger than mine. The walls are pale blue and white, hung with paintings of oceans and sand to remind them of home, and the floor is so polished, I can almost see my reflection in the wood. Such luxury is to be expected, but it still irks me that guests from a kingdom we hate get nicer chambers than I do.

Their chambers are impeccably neat. The only thing out of place is an inkwell and pen sitting on the bedside table. Curious, I open the drawer. I rustle through a few Shadow Queen pamphlets and beneath those, find blank sheets of parchment. I flip through every sheet in the stack, but there's nothing written on any of them.

I frown. There's ink on the tip of the pen. Someone's obviously been writing something. My eyes scan the room and stop on the faintly glowing fireplace.

The fire has been snuffed, but the embers burn red, and the

hearth is filled with ash and bits of something else that catch my eye.

I crouch beside the hearth. Mixed in with the ash are charred bits of parchment.

I sift delicately through the fireplace, trying to keep my fingertips from burning on any cooling embers. Most of the parchment is too burned to read more than a few words, but I find a chunk that's charred around the edges, with enough writing in the middle to make out whole sentences.

poison us, we steal from them. It is only fair. Farvelle does not belong to

The rest of that line is charred, but it picks up again in the next one.

not a treaty violation if we take what is not theirs to begin with

I'm only able to read a few sentences, but my stomach drops. Farvelle is a farm town on the outskirts of Ophera.

Just a few weeks ago, the Shadow Queen received a letter from an Honorate claiming there were Petruvian soldiers on Opheran land. Land that is supposed to be under Virdeian control. Just today, the Nights—ambassadors for the Petruvian King—exchanged whispers regarding their King's plans for Ophera. I'm not sure what they're plotting or when, but I know one thing for certain: Petruvia is looking to steal more of my home.

Luc stares at the burned scrap of letter. "Where did you get this?"

He already knows where I got it, or at least suspects. "Does it matter? This was written to Taelon Night. Petruvia is plotting to take more of Ophera." I loom over his desk, studying each twitch of his expression, trying to guess what he's thinking.

Luc massages his temples, looking far more exhausted than he did when I entered. "You don't know that. This doesn't prove—"

"It does." I speak over him, trying not to raise my voice. "I went to the library and found a copy of the treaty." Before he can ask, I set the text in front of him, dragging a finger over the line in question. "There's a loophole. This most recent version gives control of this cluster of fields on the eastern border to Praeceptor Anleck."

Luc's head jerks up, recognizing the issue. "It specifies his name?"

"Yes. Only for this land in Farvelle. This is a *massive* oversight." Praeceptor Anleck had the throne before Luc. Which means, right now, there *is* no Praeceptor Anleck, leaving a whole section of Opheran land allocated to no one. It seems Petruvia has discovered this error and intends to exploit it.

Five years ago, there was no Tournament of Thrones or treaty renegotiations when Luc ascended to power. It left one glaring issue.

Luc is silent, skimming the section of the treaty I've pointed out to him. He says nothing for several moments, then groans. "I'll meet with the decurio. Ask the General to get more soldiers in Ophera as soon as possible."

I'm shaking my head before he's finished. "He won't do it."

"Why not?"

Any other day, it would irritate me how little he knows

about the laws of the Republic he rules. "The decurio isn't allowed to send more troops to Ophera. Not without approval in the Honorate."

During our training sessions over the past couple of weeks, Flynn has been explaining Virdei's security measures. There are gateposts at intervals around the base of the mountain, each armed with members of the decurio. If there's a breach in the perimeter, they light a beacon, signaling other gateposts to react and getting the attention of sentries farther up the mountain to mobilize the rest of the army.

Virdei takes securing its borders very seriously. That same courtesy is never extended to Ophera. The placement of soldiers within Virdei and in times of war is up to the discretion of the Praeceptor and the General of the decurio. But for lands outside Virdei during peacetime, it requires the approval of the Honorate.

Normally, that wouldn't be a problem. Normally, the Shadow Queen can nudge the Honorate to do as she wishes. Except there's someone impersonating the Shadow Queen and blackmailing Honorate to block any order that would allow me to send more soldiers to protect Ophera.

My mind spins. "You don't need Honorate approval to send more soldiers in times of war."

Luc frowns. "You're not suggesting I declare war on Petruvia?"

I want to scream, but he's right. The treaty is clear. First to spill blood or violate the treaty is the first to declare war. Petruvia might be plotting against us, but they haven't spilled Virdeian blood. We can't declare war over a burned piece of parchment I stole from a diplomat's fireplace.

Knowing he's right doesn't ease my panic. Ophera is my home. I've spent years trying to protect it in secret, and now

I'm powerless to do anything. "I don't know." I throw up my hands, fighting tears of frustration.

Luc's expression softens. "I'll talk to the General. We'll discuss the loophole in the treaty and the possibility of a Petruvian attack, just as soon as the second trial is over. We'll come up with a plan then."

I try and fail to tamp down my anger. "After the second trial? That might be too late. You don't know when they're planning to attack."

"Neither do you." With an infuriatingly calm smile, Luc circles his desk and places his hands on my shoulders. "Mira, listen to me. I *will* handle this. But I can only do so much at once. There's a council meeting tomorrow, and the second trial is just a few days away. I can't deal with this right this second, but I will as soon as I can."

"Ophera is important to me, Luc."

"I know. And I'm not going to let anything happen to it. The second trial is in five days. Give me five days, and then I will sort this out."

I stare at him, doubting.

"I promise, Mira."

He means it. As he always does.

I pretend to believe him. As I always do.

CHAPTER TWENTY-THREE

SHADOW SKULKERS

Sef waits for me when I return to my room. I'm happy to see her—her company is always welcome, and my mood is especially dreary after the day I've had—but she carries news that makes my spirits sink further: "I was fired from the Tournament committee."

It takes a moment for the weight of her words to settle. "What? Why?"

"They found out that I work for you. They feel it's a conflict of interest so soon before the second trial. They don't want the appearance of an unfair advantage for either candidate."

The second trial of the Tournament is always a surprise. It's meant to test the candidates' ability to think on their feet. I was counting on Sef's access to the Tournament committee for insight. Without it, I'm as clueless as anyone else.

I collapse on my bed, trying to think through my approaching headache. "We can still make this work. Do you know when and where their next meeting is?"

"Tonight. Conference room on the ground floor." Sef tilts her head to the side. "Do you think you can find a way to eavesdrop?"

Right now, it's the only thing I'm sure of. "Definitely."

"I'll come with you."

I turn my head to glare at her. "No, you won't. What about

dinner with your parents? You've been looking forward to it for weeks."

"I know, but what if you need a lookout?" She twists her hands together fretfully.

I grin, trying to channel a false sense of calm into it. "I'll just have to be especially careful. We'll debrief tomorrow. I'll get those breakfast pastries you like and tell you all about the meeting, and you'll tell me all about dinner. Deal?"

Reluctantly, she nods. "Deal." She's still twisting her fingers, still looking nervous.

I prop myself up on my elbows, frowning. "What's wrong?"

"The committee let slip who it was that told them there was a conflict of interest." She raises both brows knowingly. "I'll give you one guess who it was."

I flop back onto my bed, burying my face in my hands with a groan. Stars in hell, I hate that boy.

Years of traversing Widow's Hall have made me adept at keeping hidden as I slink through the corridors. The halls are mostly empty, but I cling to walls and linger in shadows as I make my way to an empty, forgotten bedchamber that sits above the meeting room where the Tournament committee convenes.

I've come prepared to pick the lock, but when I turn the handle, it opens with a low whine.

I hurry inside and lock the door behind me.

For a pause, I'm still, taking inventory of my surroundings. Faint light from the beacons outside streams in through a gap in the curtains, illuminating a sliver of the floor. Most of the space is filled by a large bed against the back wall. To the left is a wardrobe, and near the windows is a desk. Everything appears coated in a thin layer of dust, making it difficult to search as my eyes skirt along the floor.

There. A hole in the floorboards. It's small, but torchlight from the conference room beneath shines through.

Dust from the floor billows into my hair and nose as I crouch to press my ear to the floor.

". . . agenda tonight is the second trial," a woman is saying.

Relief courses through me. I made it. And I can hear everything clearly.

Wood creaks from behind me.

Tension returns to my spine as I whirl.

Nothing. The room is just as still and empty as when I entered.

I turn back.

". . . last trial was a battle of strategy," the speaker is saying.

Another creak. This time, I ignore it. It's an old, abandoned room. Strange sounds are to be expected.

"Well, well. Look who's where she wasn't invited, yet again."

My heart stops.

A boy stands leaning up against the bed, watching me with a bemused smirk. He's tall and broad. Dark and handsome and familiar. Kaidren Vale.

I stagger unevenly to my feet.

Only now do I see streaks in the dusty floor leading under the bed. He must've gotten here before me and hidden when he heard me coming.

"What the hell are you doing here?" My voice is a soft hiss. Chatter from the conference room below is easily heard from these chambers. I have no idea how well sound carries in the opposite direction, but I'm not curious enough to find out.

"I was going to ask you the same thing." He chuckles.

"Probably should've guessed you'd be here. I heard your servant was forced to leave the Tournament committee. You must be getting desperate."

"The only desperate one here is you." I speak with more confidence than I have. It's my only defense against how exposed I feel. "You lost the first trial and then humiliated yourself in Eteria. How does it feel to lose, Vale? I wouldn't know."

His amused expression slips. It flickers back almost immediately, but it's more embittered than before. "If you think your stunt at Eteria changes anything, prepare to be disappointed."

"I'm well versed in disappointment. I've been pretending to be friends with *you* for weeks," I say. "Why are you here?"

"The second trial is meant to be a surprise. Since meeting you, I decided I've had enough surprises for a lifetime."

I recall the way he effortlessly commanded the crowd at Mozeri Temple. He was lying through his teeth, but he had the entire audience eating from his hand. "Surprised you didn't just charm the committee into telling you everything."

He smiles, slow and sharp, and pairs it with a few steps in my direction. "You think I'm charming, Remira?"

I roll my eyes, hoping it draws his attention from the way I retreat a few steps. "I think many people find you charming. Just as I think many people are fools."

"That wasn't an answer."

I scoff. "Of course not. I can see right through you."

"Is that so?" Kaidren quirks a brow. "Tell me, what am I thinking, right now?" He drags his lingering gaze over my body, as a slow, appreciative smirk slinks across his face. The intensity of his perusal reminds me of how he used to look at me, back when we were playing a very different kind of game.

Then, I faked smiles and pretended to be flattered. *Now*, I glare openly and hurl insults. *Now*, I wear my disdain for him proudly on my sleeve. Why, then, does his heated stare feel more real in this moment than it did before?

A shiver works down my spine. I fold my arms to disguise the involuntary response to his eyes on me. "Using shallow flirtation to try and get your way again? I thought you were finished with that game."

"I've only just started to play."

His brown eyes appear brighter in this dim lighting. I have to look away. My gaze drops to the floor, to the hole over the conference room. "You never answered me. Did the committee tell you anything about what to expect in the second trial?"

"Maybe, maybe not. Why would I tell you? Unless . . ." His expression brightens. "Are you proposing a trade? I answer a question of yours, you answer one of mine?"

We're broaching on dangerous territory. I'm about to tell him just where he can shove his "trade" when I hear the softened thuds of approaching footsteps from down the hall.

I go rigid. Kaidren frowns. "Are you ignoring—"

I rush forward to shut him up, shoving my sleeve over his mouth and muffling his words.

His brow knits in anger. I press a finger to my lips, willing him with my racing heart and frantic expression to keep quiet.

He stops fighting me, and his eyes widen—now that he's shut up, he hears the footsteps as well.

We stand in tense silence as the steps get closer and closer. They stop just outside the door.

My chest is tight, as though bound with rope. Terror crawls over my skin and into my rapidly beating heart as I peer around the room. The dust trails leading under the bed make it too obvious a hiding place.

The door rattles. It's locked, which buys us precious seconds.

The sleeves of Kaidren's sweater are rolled up, revealing his forearms. Too much exposed skin to risk grabbing them. Instead, I snatch the front of his sweater, bunching the wool over his chest.

The lock clicks—whoever is here has a key.

Without a word, I shove Kaidren back, toward the wardrobe. One hand nudges open the door, the other forces him as far inside as possible.

I tuck myself in after him, drawing the door closed behind us as softly as I can.

Kaidren's back is pressed to the rear of the wardrobe. My body is crammed against his.

The bedroom door creaks open.

I stop breathing.

Our chests are shoved together, hearts pounding one sharp, frenzied pace.

Footsteps plod into the room.

I'm holding my breath so intensely, I'm lightheaded, praying to any star in the sky the intruder leaves. Steps shuffle around the room. It's likely less than a minute, but it feels like hours drag before the steps fade and finally leave. The bedroom door clicks shut.

Still, Kaidren and I don't move. We don't speak. We don't even breathe.

I count silently to ten.

"I believe," Kaidren's low murmur caresses the shell of my ear when my mental count reaches eight, "we were in the middle of negotiating."

My chest is still constricted, and I'm battling waves of residual fear. I shove all that aside to level him with a glare. "Only in your dreams."

There's hardly any space to move, so I blindly thrust a hand behind me to open the wardrobe door.

Kaidren's arm bands my waist, stopping me.

I curl my hands between us, where they're not at risk of touching his skin.

He has one arm around me, hand flattened against my back. His eyes are steeped in determination and something softer. Something unexpected and undefinable. "I never said I'm sorry. I should have."

Of all the things I thought he'd say, this was dead last. "What are you talking about?"

"I'm sorry. For assuming you were the help. For underestimating you." His unwavering gaze is pensive as it bores into mine. "I don't know how I ever looked into those eyes and thought you were helpless."

My breath catches. There's a quiet vulnerability to his words that tugs at my heartstrings.

This is a game. He's playing you.

The reminder is a much-needed splash of cold water to the face. I push against him again. "They're gone. We can get out of here."

"Come on." His hand at my lower back brings me flush against him. "Let's make a trade. I'll tell you anything you like—all you have to do is answer something for me."

My mind staggers under the weight of a thousand questions. Did he murder his father? Why does he want to be Praeceptor? Is he the imposter Shadow Queen?

I can't ask any of this, but he's trapped me in this wardrobe and is far, far too close. I swallow. "What do you want to know?"

"Tell me about Eteria." His voice is silky smooth. "I've been going over it in my mind and I can't figure out how you pulled it off."

"Fine. I'll tell you." I lick my lips nervously and meet his eyes. There's a hunger in them. He's desperate to understand how I bested him. I can see it. How the questions have been gnawing at him, torturing him.

I open my mouth to answer. His breath catches, his grip loosens—and I shove out of the wardrobe while he's distracted.

I stumble back quickly, putting distance between us.

Kaidren and I stand on opposite ends—me alongside the bed, him near the open wardrobe—eyeing each other warily, as if we're feral silverwolves, pawing at the ground, preparing to pounce.

I force myself to smirk as if he doesn't terrify me. "Eteria? I have no idea what you're talking about."

I move to crouch near the hole in the floor, but Kaidren snatches my arm.

"What are you doing?" I scowl. "We're going to miss the meeting."

"Then I guess we miss it. Tell me about Eteria or I'll scream. Loud enough someone will come running. Whoever shows up, I'll tell them how I caught you here, spying on the Tournament committee."

My pulse jumps with his threat, but I keep my voice steady. "I'll deny it. Everyone knows you're a liar."

"Maybe. But you'd still have to explain what you're doing here."

"As would you."

"I don't know these halls. I got lost." He shrugs. "What's your excuse?"

I'm glaring so hard, I hope he bursts into flames. "You wouldn't."

His eyes are bright with the challenge. "I would."

Damn him and everything he loves, because I'm freezing. Figures this would be the only time he chooses to tell the truth.

My nails dig half circles into my palms. "I hate you."

"The feeling is mutual. Now answer me."

"It was easy. I had Luc get the name and source of the aikkari participants, and I wrote them down. All I had to do was put it in your robes."

"What about that spear? It fired at a civilian. Surely, you wouldn't risk someone getting hurt?"

I make a show of rolling my eyes. "I paid an aikkari to make sure the spear didn't hit anyone. I paid him double to keep quiet."

Kaidren blinks slowly, mulling it over. "That's it? But that was so . . . simple."

"The best schemes are. Less to go wrong."

He studies me for several seconds, before sighing and releasing me. "Fine. Your turn. What do you want to know?"

"What did they tell you about the second trial?"

He smirks. "Absolutely nothing."

I'm shocked it's the truth. "That was a wasted question."

Kaidren looks impossibly smug. "Then ask another. I've got plenty lined up for you."

I'm not playing any more of his games. Rather than answer, I shoot a scowl his way and resume my stoop to listen to the rest of the meeting.

"—handle getting someone to zone the crest of the mountain in advance. We don't have much time, so we need to work quickly."

There are murmurs of assent from the rest of the committee.

Virdei spans most of Mount Saidu, and Widow's Hall sits just below the crest—that final steep slope before the peak.

The crest is dangerous. A barren wasteland of treacherous

winds and steep drop-offs, and it's streaked with ribbons of ice. If the next trial takes place up there, Luc will be in *way* out of his depth. We both will.

I keep watch over the hole in the floor for the next several minutes, listening to every word spoken, but they don't drop any more hints. By the end, all I know is that Luc and Kaidren will be at the crest for the next trial, and I have no idea what they'll be asked to do.

I *hate* being caught unprepared. Not knowing will eat away at me, all the way up until the trial. Kaidren, on the other hand, is grinning. "I can't *wait* to watch you lose. I suppose I'll see you at the next trial. Unless . . ." He tilts his head to the side, feigning confusion. "Will I see you at tomorrow's council meeting?" Then his eyes widen, as though making a realization. "Oh. Wait. I forgot. Only Honorate allowed. What's your role here, again? Pawn for your brother? What a shame."

My eyes narrow. Is he merely taunting me, or hinting at something more? The imposter Shadow Queen ordered Sixmen to resign from the Honorate at the next council meeting—tomorrow. Is Kaidren smug because of the second trial, or smug because he knows what's to come?

There are so many things I want to ask, but with a smirk that makes my skin crawl, he leaves without answering any of them.

CHAPTER TWENTY-FOUR

SECRETS OF A POWERLESS MAN

It is so rare to see scum remove itself. Yet just today, Former Honorate Selva Sixmen formally resigned from his position, leaving one question on everyone's mind: Why?

I have heard the whispers. Some claim Selva was merely growing old. Others speculate that perhaps the former Honorate is sick. This Queen of Shadows has her ear and nose to the floor, and she smells something far more devious—a scandal. What secrets is Former Honorate Sixmen trying to hide with his abrupt exit from the council? I suspect time will reveal all. As will I.

In the meantime, congratulations are in order for all of this Great Republic. Selva Sixmen's replacement leaves nothing to be desired. Flynn Sixmen is a decurio who needs no introduction. Whatever the reason for Selva's departure, I think we can all agree his successor more than makes up for it.

Fondly,
Shadow Queen

It was Kaidren. I *know* it. He blackmailed Selva into resigning from the Honorate, he killed Arliss. If only I could prove it. The sooner I do, the sooner I can get rid of him altogether.

Sef and I meet early. We exchange gossip and theories over breakfast pastries. She tells me about dinner with her parents, and I tell her about the evening I spent with Kaidren Vale. When we part ways, Sef is off to dig up anything she can about the second trial, while I go to find Flynn in one of the rooms built into the base of the stands.

He sits at a table, cleaning equipment. He's facing away and doesn't look up when I enter. I clear my throat. "Honorate Sixmen. It's a good name. Glides off the tongue."

Flynn chuckles as he twists to face me. "That's because it's my father's name. Well, it was."

"It sounds better on you."

He's still smiling, but he shifts in his seat, looking uncomfortable. "It's good to see you, Mira, but I can't continue your training. I have new responsibilities with the Honorate now, which means I'll be spending less time with the decurio. But don't worry. I'll find someone else to work with you." His somber expression turns teasing. "Though it'll be a challenge finding someone who can handle you."

I grin back. "I figured things would change now. I actually came to thank you. For everything. I've learned a lot from working with you." I nod to the equipment. "Do you want help?" I sit and pick up a cloth before he can object.

These weapons are used for training, so they're coated in snow, sludge, and blood. Cleaning them is disgusting work, but I have one last chance to pry information about Selva from Flynn, so I need to take it. Subtly.

After a few moments of cleaning in silence, I prick my finger on the edge of a sword. "*Ouch.*"

Flynn's head jerks up. "What—" Seeing the droplet of blood on my finger, he curses. "Dammit, Mira. Be careful." He rushes to a cabinet for gauze, then kneels at my side to gently wrap my finger.

"It's just a small cut," I say defensively.

"These blades are sharp." He's finished but stays crouched beside me. "Cuts aren't always as shallow as they appear. You could've been seriously hurt."

"Sorry," I mumble. "I was distracted. I'm having a bad day."

Some of his frustration lessens with concern. "Do you want to talk about it?"

"No, it's nothing, I just—" I sigh. "Do you know Yelina? She's my stepmother."

"Of course I do."

"Oh, right. I forgot. She's close with your mom. Or—" I look down, pretending to be embarrassed. "She was. I'm sorry. I didn't mean to bring up something so . . ." I let my sentence trail. "Sorry. Yelina's been yelling at me all day. I forgot—" I swallow the rest of the sentence, hoping it's enough to get Flynn talking about his mother.

His expression darkens in agitation. "Forgot what? That my mom disappeared?"

Disappeared?

"I'm sorry," I say again.

Flynn rises and starts pacing the length of the equipment room. "Don't be. You'd think I'd be able to talk about her by now. Maybe I'll never get used to it."

I feel guilty, forcing him to speak of his mother, but if Selva killed her, I need to know. If Kaidren found out about it, I need to know how.

Before I can reply, the door to the supply room opens. General Tarek Fain pokes his head inside. He glances at me, then focuses on Flynn. "When you're finished here, there are some new recruits who need uniforms by the entry gate." He grabs at a flat metal disk hanging around his neck and holds it up. The silver winks in the torchlight.

"Understood," Flynn says. "I won't be much longer."

With another swift look at me, General Fain ducks out without a word.

I frown after him. "What was that around his neck?"

"A medallion. Decurio leadership flash them when they give orders. We spend a lot of time with our faces covered. Medallions signal to fellow soldiers that the person giving the order is who they claim to be."

I nod along. "Do you have a medallion?"

He reaches into his collar and shows me. Like the General's, it's silver. "I do."

"You're young to have so much authority in the decurio."

He shrugs it off. "It's just because of my dad."

"The General of the entire decurio turns to *you* as his right hand. That's more than your father, that's all you." I smile. "I'm sure your mother would be proud."

That sad look returns to his eyes. "She was."

"I'm sorry," I say softly. "What you said before . . . I didn't know she disappeared."

"Two years ago. They never found a body, so she was only officially declared dead last year, but I've known for a while now that she's gone. She disappeared one day, and no one ever saw her again. But I know she's dead. If she was alive, she'd have come back for me."

"Did the decurio investigate?"

"Yes, but they didn't find anything."

I feel a rush of heat. I can't exactly accuse the grieving son of lying, so I move to stand before him with a soft, coaxing smile. "You're sure? Nothing?"

"Nothing that made sense. A maid who worked in our home was arrested for stealing around the same time. My dad said it might have something to do with Mom's disappearance."

"You think she was involved somehow?"

Flynn looks as if he's about to answer, but then shakes his head. "I'm sorry, Mira, but I can't talk about this. She's gone. The investigation is over."

There's more I want to ask, but I hold my tongue. Selva Sixmen accusing a maid of theft might not sound suspicious to an outsider, but I know better. This wouldn't be his first time lying to the decurio.

Years ago, he falsely testified to keep himself out of prison for pilfering public funds. Selva pocketed the money, the man he accused went to prison in his stead, and the Republic was none the wiser. The Shadow Queen has threatened him with that secret before. And now he's accused someone else of stealing.

Is this maid truly guilty? Or just another victim of Selva Sixmen's lies?

"I'm sorry." I lay a hand over Flynn's.

He sighs sadly. "Thank you. I spent a long time obsessing over what happened to her. Sometimes, I swear I still hear her voice, telling me she loves me."

"Trust me. I know the feeling."

Flynn smiles gratefully at me, and I smile back. All the while, my suspicions are piqued. Somewhere out there is a maid who knows something Selva Sixmen fought like hell to keep buried.

CHAPTER TWENTY-FIVE

RAGE AND RUIN

The supposed thief's name is Eduma. For the past two years, she's been rotting in the prisons at the base of the mountain.

There are dungeons in Widow's Hall for holding alleged criminals awaiting trial and prisons at the base of the mountain for those found guilty. Prisoners are expected to work, often in the mines alongside desperate Opherans willing to risk cave-ins and tunnel collapses for a meal.

I take the sky cart to the base of the mountain and slip a few coins to a guard. That's all it takes to speak with a prisoner.

"Hello, Eduma," I say as a guard deposits her into a chair and leaves us for the next fifteen minutes.

Eduma is taller than I expected, and very skinny. Her dark hair is messily pulled back into a pouf, there's a gap between her two front teeth, and there's a golden sun tattooed on her inner wrist. She's inexplicably bound to her seat. There's no reason for it. She doesn't put up a fight, her arms look like they'd snap in half if she tried to throw a punch, and she's shaking like a pine needle in the wind. "W-who are you? The guards said you were family."

I never told them we were related. They probably saw my tattoo and just assumed. "I'm a friend. I work closely with the Praeceptor. I have a few questions about your former employer, Honorate Sixmen."

Eduma's eyes round with terror. "I swear I didn't steal anything." She looks like she's about to cry. "I know he said I did, but—"

I reach across the table to lay a hand over hers. "Eduma, I believe you."

Eduma's shaking subsides, but she still looks wary. "You . . . you do?"

"Yes. I wanted to ask you about something else. Do you know that around the time you were arrested, your employer's wife, Neveah, went missing?"

Tears well in her eyes. "I don't know anything about that. Please, I told all of this to Mister Sixmen and the decurio already. I was telling the truth the first time. Please, can I go home now?"

Heat swells with the force of her lie. My heart shatters for her. It's rare that I wish to be wrong, but I do now. Eduma looks to be in her thirties. Too young to no longer have the rest of her life ahead of her. I make a vow to get her out of this. She won't rot in prison for something she didn't do. "Help answer my questions truthfully, and I'll talk to the Praeceptor about pardoning you."

Eduma stares at me in shock. "Truly?"

"I swear. Now, can you tell me the last time you saw Neveah?"

Eduma swallows. "I didn't see her. I heard her and Honorate Sixmen."

"When was this?"

"Around this time two years ago." Eduma ducks her head. "She went missing later that same day."

"Where were you when you heard them?" I ask.

"The kitchen. I wasn't supposed to be there. No one was.

But I'd forgotten something, so I ran in to grab it. I heard Honorate Sixmen . . . exchanging words with his wife."

The pause before *"exchanging words"* doesn't go unnoticed. "They were arguing?" I press.

Eduma swallows before answering. "Yes."

No wonder Sixmen got rid of her. He was arguing with his wife the day she mysteriously disappeared.

"Did you hear what they were saying?"

"No," Eduma says quickly.

A rush of heat accompanies her words. I tense. I don't want to push this frail woman too hard, but I see no other choice. "Eduma." I soften my voice further. "I can't help you if you don't help me. That's not true, is it?"

"I—" Eduma's eyes dart around nervously, looking anywhere but at me. "I'm sorry. Mister Sixmen came to see me last year. I thought I was finally getting out of here." Tears well in her eyes. "But nothing happened. I don't want Mister Sixmen to know I said anything and keep me here longer."

"I promise you, you won't get in trouble. I won't repeat anything you tell me to Mister Sixmen. I just need to know the truth so I can get you out of here. Now, what did you hear the day Neveah went missing?"

She shifts in her seat, and her eyes flutter shut for just a moment. When she opens them, she seems to have decided to trust me.

"Honorate Sixmen was mad at his wife about something. She told him it was a mistake she made over twenty years ago, and he needed to get over it. He started yelling at her."

Twenty years ago . . .

I've made a life of collecting secrets. Years of operating as the Shadow Queen have made me well versed at reading between the lines of what people *do* say to hear what they *won't* say.

Someone mentions a "mistake" in a marriage, they're almost always referring to an affair.

What really snatches my attention isn't the inkling that Neveah had affairs of her own—it's the time frame. Twenty years . . . Neveah's only son, Flynn, is just over twenty years old.

Stars in hell . . .

What if Neveah was hiding more than just an affair? What if she was hiding that Flynn isn't Selva's son? The news would be catastrophic. It would mean Selva Sixmen has no children. No sons. No heir to inherit his position in the Honorate. It would be an end to the Sixmen legacy.

Right now, it's just a theory. But if it's true, it's a secret Selva would've killed to keep buried.

"What happened after that?" I ask.

"I don't know," Eduma says. "I wasn't supposed to be there, I didn't think they would like me listening, and . . . well, Honorate Sixmen was yelling so loud, he was scaring me. So, I left. When Mrs. Sixmen went missing later, I didn't know what to think. At first, I thought she took a break to clear her head. But when she didn't come back, I thought . . ." Her sentence trails. "Well, I'm not sure what I thought."

It's a lie. "Why do you think Honorate Sixmen accused you of being a thief?"

Eduma shudders. "I was foolish. He found out I overheard his argument. The next thing I knew, I was in prison." She's sobbing now. "But I'm not a thief. I swear I'm not."

"I know you're not. You didn't do anything wrong, Eduma. I'm going to make sure you get out of here. I just need you to answer one more question for me: Do you think Honorate Sixmen killed his wife?"

She shakes her head frantically. "No. No, of course not."

Another lie. Eduma very much believes her former employer is capable of murder. After hearing how he tossed an innocent woman in prison without a second thought, so do I. Selva Sixmen is a monster. And a murderer.

CHAPTER TWENTY-SIX

THROUGH SMOKE AND SNOW

The second trial of the Tournament of Thrones is sparsely attended. I can't blame anyone who opted to sit this one out. The few of us who *are* in attendance are shivering outside Widow's Hall with no view of anything but snow—let alone the actual event.

My breath mists in the air as General Fain explains the parameters of the second trial. It's a race, from the mountain's crest back down to Widow's Hall. The first candidate to make it to the finish line—here, where our small group of watchers waits—is the winner.

Luc and Kaidren will each receive a pickax, for the ice and snow, and a flare tied around their necks, for emergencies. The flare is to be used as a call for help *only*. Set it off, and the decurio will swoop in to rescue them. But doing so is an immediate forfeit.

As soon as the General is finished outlining the event, I rush inside. Already, I'm running out of time. The decurio is currently transporting Luc and Kaidren to the top of the mountain to start the trial, but I can't do anything about that until I have supplies.

First, I need to dress as warmly as possible. Then, I need magic.

Ten minutes later, I'm in my attic, wearing fur-lined pants, a wool sweater, thick coat, and a heavy sjaal, snatching jars of my swirling red smoke and shoveling them into a bag.

I don't hear Sef until she's right behind me. "Mira?"

I jump, putting a hand over my heart. "Stars in hell, Sef. When did you get so light-footed?" I flash her a grin and keep stuffing jars of magic into my bag.

She shuffles around me, brows drawn. "You're not seriously thinking of climbing to the crest by yourself?"

"I have to."

"Mira." Sef speaks sternly. "There's a reason Widow's Hall is here and not farther up the mountain. It's *dangerous*. Steep, icy, and cold. If you fall—"

"I won't."

"But *if* you do, you'll die."

"I know." Finished packing, I give her my most reassuring smile. "That won't happen. I promise."

The look she gives me is flat and unamused. "I'm not your brother. I'm not so easy to lie to." She takes a breath. "And there's something else."

I sling my bag onto my back. "What is it?"

"Ophera is under attack."

I stop breathing. For three seconds, I'm perfectly still. Then, "What did you just say?"

"Petruvia launched an attack on Farvelle on the eastern border."

The same section of land that, according to the treaty, belongs to no one. "Are there any casualties?"

"I'm not sure. I only just heard about it."

I *told* Luc to take care of this sooner rather than later, and he did *nothing*. My only consolation is that the eastern border is on the opposite side of where I used to live with my mother. It's a cold comfort. Ophera—all of it—is part of me. And now it's being taken over by Petruvia, ruled by a king who doesn't have a benevolent Opheran shadow flitting around behind the scenes. "Have the decurio responded yet?"

"I don't know. I heard it from a stablehand. He said a few soldiers took greyhorns down the mountain to assess the situation. I don't know anything else. I thought you would want to look into it."

I do. Of course I do. But the second trial is starting as we speak, and if I'm not there, Luc will lose.

Stay or go? Make sure Ophera is safe, or ensure my brother's victory in the Tournament?

I take a heavy breath. I know what I *want* to do. But rushing to see what's happening in Ophera is only a solution in the short term. "Can you please ask around for me? Find out what you can. I'll see what we can do to fix this when I get back."

Sef looks shocked. "You're still leaving?"

"Luc will fail without me. And I can't do anything for Ophera if he loses."

Sef stares at me for several seconds, looking almost . . . disappointed. She hugs me anyway. "If you die up there, I'll never forgive you," she murmurs into my ear. "Good luck, Mira. You'll need it."

Harsh winds and white snow batter me from all sides, visibility is nonexistent, and every step sends an ache through my entire body. It doesn't help that I have a bag strapped to my back stuffed with jars of magic, a tshira knife, and a pickax slotted through a loop at the top of my pack.

This high up, the mountain is impressively steep, but it's not the incline that makes my journey to the top absolute hell—it's the ice.

It's *everywhere*. Each step is a precarious struggle to move my foot from one slick pad to another. Just when I think I'm stable enough to pull myself up the mountain slope, it turns out the place I've set my foot is just more ice. The next thing I know, I'm nearly slipping to my death.

Before each step, I swing the ax, slicing through ice, snow, and rock, to give my hands something to grab on to, and my feet a space to slot into.

The trek is steep and painful, but so long as I use both hands, both legs, and my pickax, I make very, very slow progress. It feels more like crawling than climbing, but at least I'm moving.

I have no idea how much time has passed, but my fingers are numb, and I'm sure my lips are blue. Wind is so loud, it drowns out everything except my own labored breathing. The higher I climb, the thicker the ice, and the more force it requires to break through.

I swing the pickax once, twice, five times to carve out a space, then tuck it back into its loop atop my bag. My hands slip into the icy cleft, feeling until my fingers find something to grip—stone.

I've lost practically all feeling in my hand, but I hold firm. A groan falls from between my gritted teeth as my other hand grabs a large stone protruding from the snow. The muscles in my arms and back cry out in protest as I haul myself up and tumble onto the ledge above.

I'm sprawled on my back, exhausted. Snow cascades around me. My body is frozen, tired, and sore, but I force it to sit up and stand.

I'm tempted to use the magic in my bag to steal some warmth into my shivering limbs, but when I finally find Luc, I'm going to need as much of it as possible to get us down the mountain in one piece. There isn't enough to spare.

Just as I'm about to keep moving, I hear shuffling.

I twist, searching. The world is a white blur. I see nothing.

My head turns as though hinged as I stumble forward, prowling through the blinding storm.

Looming ahead is a flash of black. I drag my feet through the snow toward it, until I'm close enough to make out Luc. He's watching the ground, ambling his way down, so focused on not falling, he doesn't see me until I'm nearly right in front of him.

I'm completely covered in snow gear, but he recognizes me instantly. "Mira? What are you doing here?"

"You didn't think I was going to let you do this by yourself, did you?" I try to sound glib, but my teeth are chattering and my lips are going numb, so my attempt at humor falls flat.

"How did you even get here?"

"I climbed." I try and shrug it off. "Where's Kaidren?"

"You *climbed*? In this? Mira, you could've been killed."

"But I wasn't." This is why I didn't tell him the location of the trial ahead of time. I figured he'd try to talk me out of interfering. "Where's Kaidren?"

"I don't know. Last I saw him, he was pulling ahead. I think I'm losing."

"That's fine. I have a plan." My climb up gave me plenty of time to strategize. "I brought some magic with me. We're going to slide down the mountain." I rustle my frozen fingers through my bag until I reach the tshira knife. "On this."

Luc frowns doubtfully. "On a knife?"

In response, I channel magic into the tshira. It pools into an inky puddle at my feet. With another burst of magic, it hardens into a thin, flat sheet. It has no runners, but the tshira is smooth enough to function as a makeshift sled. "We'll slide on this. I'll melt the ice into a path as we go. *You* are going to use your pickax to veer the sled and keep us on course."

Luc looks between the sheet of tshira and me with thinly veiled trepidation. "This sounds dangerous."

It is. "It's the fastest way down the mountain. When we get closer to Widow's Hall, we'll stop. You'll make it the rest of the way on foot, and I'll slip away without anyone knowing I was here."

Before he can object, I crouch over the tshira, sitting on top of it.

Luc doesn't move.

"We don't have time for this," I say impatiently. "If we don't do this, we'll lose."

Luc is silent for a count of five. I'm tempted to find a rock, knock him over the head, and haul him to the finish line myself, but he finally climbs onto the tshira behind me. His legs are longer than mine and scrunched up next to me so his feet don't drag through the snow.

My heart drums into my stomach, churning all my fears and anxieties as I shove a wave of heat ahead of us, melting the snow.

I press my feet to the ground and push off, sliding the tshira onto the narrow, icy path.

My belly drops with the sensation. It's steeper than I'd anticipated, and I'm grateful I didn't have time for breakfast this morning.

I lean to the side, and the tshira slides with me. Up ahead, the mountain drops off suddenly.

"Pickax to the left," I call back to Luc.

He swings the ax into the ice behind us, and I plant my feet in the snow. We slide to a halt.

I focus magic to our right, melting us another path. We pivot and continue sliding.

We careen down the mountain, and I shout out to Luc each

time we need to stop and turn. Our trail is shaky and we stop frequently, but progress is much faster than it would be if Luc was on his own, or if either of us was on foot.

Up ahead, a jagged rock juts out from the ground.

"Right!" I call to Luc.

Nothing happens.

I rock my body to the side. The tshira sled tilts, but not enough. We're hurtling toward the rock, and Luc isn't doing anything to slow us down.

"Luc, we need to stop."

"I-I can't. I dropped the ax."

"You *what?*"

He mumbles something in response, but I can't hear him over my own terror. The rock looms closer. Panicked, I shove magic at the sled, trying to force it to stop.

The tshira shudders, but there are two of us on here, and we're flying at full speed.

The sled slows but doesn't stop.

I grunt, forcing all of my magic, every scrap of my fading energy, into the tshira.

We jolt. The sled pivots ever so slightly to the left.

It's not enough.

The edge of the sled slams into the side of the rock as we barrel past it.

I open my mouth in a scream that's lost to the howling wind as we're thrown into the air.

The sled flies out from beneath me. It falls one way, I fall another.

Air rushes by, and then I slam into the ground.

Groaning, I sit up, one hand pressed to my throbbing head.

I'm dizzy, trying to gather my bearings. All I see is snow, snow, and more snow. No Luc, no sled, no bag full of magic.

Panic is a vise around my lungs.

"Luc!" I scream his name, the sound so frantic and terrified, I don't recognize my own voice.

"Mira? Where are you?"

Never in my life have I been so grateful to hear my brother speak.

A relieved sigh shudders out of me. I brace my hands against the snow to push to my feet. "I'm over—"

Something *cracks*.

I screech as the world drops out from beneath me.

CHAPTER TWENTY-SEVEN

TEARS OF GLASS

A mound of snow cushions my fall. Which is fortunate.

The snow cushion in question is at the bottom of a pit. Which is *un*fortunate.

My head is spinning, ears ringing, and I'm winded from the crash.

It takes me several seconds to rise to my feet. The snow protected me from splattering to my death, but it's powdery and slippery, making my quivering legs as unsteady as a newborn calf's once I'm standing.

"Mira? *Mira?*" Luc's distraught, disembodied voice comes from overhead. He sounds as if he's on the verge of tears.

"I'm in here!" I try to shout, but it comes out as a low croak. I think I ripped my throat raw.

Footsteps crunch closer, until Luc's head appears over the edge of this ice cave. His eyes are wild, but when he sees me, alive and upright, his shoulders loosen. "Mira. Stars in hell. I thought—" He shudders and stops himself. "Are you all right?"

"I'm fine." I peer around my surroundings. The cave I've fallen into is carved from jagged stone and coated in a thick layer of silvery-blue ice. It leaves the surface vertical and smooth. I'm not a skilled climber on the best of days, but even an expert would struggle to find any grip to pull themselves out.

I'm freezing. Even colder in this pit than when I was hurtling down the mountain on a sled. I reach within me, hoping to feel a glimmer of residual magic, but there's none left.

My teeth are already starting to chatter. And my ass is sore from crashing into the ground.

"We're not far from Widow's Hall." I choke back my fear and try to sound more assured than I feel. "You can make it the rest of the way. You'll win and come back for me. Or you can send Sef."

It's a bad plan, and I know it. Even if everything goes perfectly with no delays, I'll be trapped in here for at least another hour. With no magic or additional heat, I doubt I'd last that long, exposed like this.

Luc doesn't respond right away. He studies me, gnawing the inside of his cheek, lost in thought. Finally, he brightens and blurts, "I have orange hair." His tone is aggravatingly hopeful.

I'm so annoyed I temporarily forget my fear. I glower frostily up at him. "You know that isn't how this works." I cross my arms, both because I'm annoyed, and because it's cold and I need to preserve what little warmth I have left. "Saying nonsense we both know is untrue won't fuel my magic. Unless there's something you've been keeping from me, this is a waste of time. You have to go. *Now*." Simply speaking an untruth isn't enough to stoke the flames of my magic. It requires deception—*secrets*. Unfortunately, Luc and I tell each other everything.

Well, at least he does.

Luc stares at me as though I've suggested he douse my body in alcohol and set me on fire. "I'm not leaving you here. Not only would you freeze to death, but I'd never be able to find this place again."

Fair points. This high up, our only surroundings are snow and ice. There are no landmarks he could use to find me if he ventured too far away. And it's snowing. If it starts to pile up, I could be buried by the time anyone comes back for me.

My eyes well, but I blink rapidly to ward off tears. I'm not going to cry. Everything is going to be fine. It has to be. Doesn't matter that I'm halfway frozen already. I'll find a way out of this. I always do.

Luc lies on his stomach and leans over the mouth of the pit. He stretches an arm down as far as he can. "Can you reach?"

I already know I can't, but I try anyway. I strain my arm, stretching as far up as I can. Stand on my tiptoes, even jump a bit—nothing helps. The pit is too deep.

He lowers his sjaal to me. I grab hold of one end while he pulls the other. I try to brace my feet against the sheer sides of the pit, but they're too smooth, too icy. All my feet do is slide, and after a few seconds of pulling, there's a horrifying ripping sound. The sjaal can't support me.

Hopelessness claws at me. I'm not getting out of here. "Luc . . ." My voice quivers. I swallow and try again. "You're going to have to leave." Now I sound as if I'm being strangled.

"*Never.*" Luc sounds as close to tears as I feel.

I'm going to die out here. Sef warned me, but I never actually let myself believe it would happen.

"There's an obvious solution," Luc says slowly.

My teary eyes snap to him with a glower. "Don't you dare."

"They gave us a flare for a reason. If I set it off, someone will come and get you out."

"They'll lock me up. You'll be disqualified from the Tournament for using outside help. We'll *lose*."

"There are worse things than losing."

A stubborn tear drips down my cheek. Well, it tries. It freezes too quickly to finish falling. I might be completely powerless right now, but I refuse to forfeit this Tournament. "If you set off that flare, I'll never forgive you."

Luc looks as if he means to scream at me. "Mira—"

"'*Mira*'?" This is a different voice.

My pulse hums with rising dread.

The rest of the world fades away. I hear nothing but approaching footsteps. See nothing but his head joining Luc's leaning over the edge of the pit.

Kaidren and I stare at each other. There's a tear frozen to my cheek, my heartbeat is a whir of helplessness, and all he does is stare at me. A myriad of emotions dance across his face, too quick for me to pick out any one of them.

Finally, his expression settles into its usual smug mask. "I didn't realize this event extended to family members, Remira."

Kaidren Vale has me exactly where he wants me. He's been seeking proof that I'm a cheat, and here it is. Irrefutable and conveniently trapped in a pit of ice.

My eyes sting, eager to give into hopelessness and release the floodgates, but I jut out my chin. I refuse to let him see me sob. I'll save that for later, when there's no one around to watch. Probably in a jail cell, judging by how things are going.

"What?" Kaidren lifts an eyebrow. "Nothing to say?"

I smile sweetly. "Burn in hell."

"Only if you come with me." He thrusts his pickax into Luc's hands.

I'm a tangled mess of startled and confused. So much so, I hardly register his next move: leaping into the pit to join me.

I'm frozen as he lands practically on top of me, before I realize what's just happened—Kaidren gave his only tool for survival to Luc and followed me into my ice prison. Willingly.

He lands less than a shiver away, smirking as my eyes widen

at his sudden nearness. "You know," he says, tone conversational, "the polite thing to do would've been to move out of the way."

"Why did you do that?" Belatedly, I stumble away from him. My back slams into the wall, shaking snow flurries loose from the mouth of the pit.

Kaidren turns his back to me. I don't move. Just watch him, trying to figure out what the hell is going through his head. He bends at the knees and looks at me over his shoulder. "Well?"

"What are you—" I'm so confused, I forget to be wary.

"I've never seen you at a loss for words before." He sounds amused. "Climb onto my back."

This is a trick. It has to be. "Why?"

Kaidren makes a noise of exasperation. He straightens and faces me again, moving closer so we share breath. "So I can get you out of here. I don't know about you, but I'm freezing."

My eyes narrow. "What are you going to do?"

"Carry you."

"And then what? Climb out? Don't know if you noticed, but the walls are ice."

"Don't know if *you* noticed, but I have a pickax. Your brother is going to hand it back to me, and then I'm going to use it to get out of here. Whether or not you're on my back when that happens is up to you."

I fold my arms. "If you think I'm touching you, you're delusional. You're tall. You can just boost me up; then Luc can pull you out after."

Kaidren laughs in my face. "I'm not half the fool you take me for. Look me in the eyes and tell me you wouldn't leave me here the moment I helped you get out."

That's exactly what I was planning.

I round my eyes. "I would *never*."

He shakes his head, looking amused. "I told you, Remira, I'm not going to make the mistake of underestimating you. Not again. Either we get out of here at the same time, or we stay trapped here forever." His gloved hand cups my face so suddenly, I don't have a chance to jerk away. His eyes are startlingly soft as he swipes a thumb over my cheek, wiping away the lingering frozen tears. "What do you say, shadow skulker? Are you on or off?"

My eyes search his. "Why are you doing this?"

"Because we're friends, of course."

He's clearly teasing me, and clearly has no intention of answering me seriously. I take a breath. "Fine. Turn around."

His gaze trails over my face for another moment before he turns and bends. Hesitantly, I place my hands on his shoulders. I'm wearing gloves and he's bundled up, but there's a sliver of skin peeking through at the base of his neck that's making me nervous.

I'm still eyeing the exposed skin when Kaidren grabs me by the backs of my thighs. I yelp as he tugs them up, hitching my legs around his hips. "This feels familiar," he murmurs. I can hear the smirk in his voice.

I ignore him and wrap my arms around his chest, tethering myself to him.

Kaidren reaches up. "Honored Praeceptor, can you hand me the pickax?"

Luc tosses the pickax into the pit. Kaidren catches it. He rears it back before swinging it into the ice.

The force of it makes me jump. I'm clinging to his back like a child, arms wrapped around his torso, legs coiled around his waist. Touching him like this is disorienting, but I force my brain to stutter back to life. There's no need for me to stay on his back while he carves grooves into the ice. I try and unlatch my legs, but Kaidren gives my thigh a squeeze. "You're not going anywhere. For all I know, if I let you down, you'll take the ax, knock me over the head, and use it to escape without me."

I roll my eyes but don't let go of him. "I'm very violent in your imagination."

"I'm not taking any risks with you. I want your hands on me at all times. Where they can't get up to mischief." He lowers his voice, so only I can hear. "Besides, I like your warmth."

I don't fight him. For reasons I can't comprehend, he dropped into a frozen cave to rescue me. Even though I'm sure he has an ulterior motive, it doesn't cool the warm glow of gratitude in my chest.

I hang on to Kaidren as he swings the pickax, carving jagged holes up the wall in uneven intervals. When he's finished, he passes it back to Luc. "You ready?" he says to me.

I tighten my arms and legs around him. "Ready."

As I speak, my breath skims the back of Kaidren's neck. He shudders and adjusts his grip on me, shifting his hands beneath my thighs and tightening. Kaidren shoves a boot into the lowest foothold and reaches out to Luc.

My brother takes his arm and, with a grunt, tugs.

With the foothold, Kaidren has the leverage to push himself up, and Luc only has to pull him to the next one.

Kaidren places his foot into the second groove and pauses for Luc to pull him again.

They continue. It's a conjoined effort. Luc pulls, Kaidren pushes. We keep going, slowly but steadily, one foothold at a time, until Kaidren reaches the top.

With a final grunt of effort, Luc yanks us over the lip of the pit. We collapse into the snow.

Kaidren's out of breath, lying on his back and staring at the cloudy sky. "Remira," he pants out my name in between gasps for air. "Are you all right?"

"I'm fine." I stand over him, and I can't help the small smile that creeps over my face. "Thank you."

For several seconds, he stares at me. Doesn't say anything, just stares. His eyes are softened into an emotion I can't decipher. "You're sure? No injuries?"

My heart flutters at his concern. "I'm completely fine."

"Good. You need to hide."

I frown, tilting my head to one side. "What?"

"Hide," he says again.

"Why would—"

Without warning, Kaidren leaps to his feet and seizes Luc's flare from where it hangs around his neck. Neither of us has time to react before he sets it off and holds it up high with his signature smirk. "Because the decurio will be here any moment to save him. And you can't risk them seeing you."

No.

With that flare, Kaidren just won the second trial.

Worse—I *lost*.

CHAPTER TWENTY-EIGHT

WHEN THE SMOKE CLEARS

The glare I direct at the floor is withering. Footsteps scuttle out of my way, clearing a path for me as I stomp the halls, back to the tiny room I'm forced to call mine.

I slam my door behind me. Bang my head against the solid wood with a groan and slump to the floor. The tears I've been keeping at bay release.

Sobs shake my body so violently, I don't realize I'm not alone.

"You're *alive*." Sef stumbles out of my bed and throws her arms around me. Never mind that I'm still on the floor. She joins me. "Don't do that to me again. I was so worried about you." Her relieved expression sobers as she pulls back and really takes me in. "Oh. You already heard?"

I swipe tears from my face, sniffling. "Heard what?"

"Those fields in Ophera. We lost them. Petruvia formed a barricade around Farvelle, and now Virdei can't get through. If we try to strike back, we'll start a war."

The tears I just wiped away threaten to come back. I want to curl into a ball and weep away the next five years. I want to find Luc and scream at him for not listening to me. But as furious as I am with him, I'm more upset with myself. "Did anyone die?"

Sef shakes her head. "Not as far as I know."

"I should've stayed."

"You couldn't have changed this. You saw that letter. Petruvia was planning this for months. Nothing you did would've stopped this." Sef settles next to me, resting her head on my shoulder. "Maybe it won't be so bad."

"Petruvia treats Opherans like dirt."

"So does Virdei."

"At least when it's Virdei, I can do something." I slam my head against the wall angrily. Thanks to me, the Honorate have passed orders that ended the extortion of landlords in Ophera who would lure in renters with low rates and then raise prices after the first month; there is more funding for things like public bonfires; and resources have been allocated for schools to teach trades and crafts. Ophera is still far from perfect, but I've done what I can.

Widow's Hall is named for the first—and only—Queen to rule Virdei by herself. This was shortly after Virdei began building up the mountain, back when it was still a monarchy. The Queen's husband died before they conceived, leaving her a childless widow.

Widow's Hall is named for her. It started as a mean-spirited nickname coined by the men who resented her rule to demean her. She embraced the title to spite them and officially renamed the mountainside fortress Widow's Hall herself, so no one could call it so behind her back.

In the end, the men who despised her got the last laugh. In retaliation, they formed the Honorate. They claimed it was to "advise" the ill-prepared Queen, but considering only men were allowed to serve, its true intention was clear.

Toward the end of her life, the Queen's mind started to slip. It was around the same time that Petruvia made its attempt to seize the mountain and its resources. On the brink of war, the Widow Queen selected a member of the Honorate and temporarily ceded her authority to him to manage the crisis. She died before he handed power back to her, making him Virdei's first Praeceptor. Shortly after, the rules for succession were written to include only men, sending a clear message in the wake of her death: never again will a woman hold as much power as the Widow Queen.

That was their intention, but it's no longer a reality I'm willing to accept. When the Tournament is over, when I steal the throne from my brother, I am going to ensure nothing like this ever happens again. If I can't protect Ophera as Luc's shadow, then I'll do so as Virdei's Queen.

Sef pulls her head from my shoulder. "If you hadn't heard about Ophera, why were you so upset when you came in?"

"We lost."

Sef looks relieved. "That's it?" She wraps me in a tight hug. "I thought you were hurt. Or worse."

After a pause, I hug her back. I didn't mean to make her worry, but it feels nice to know someone cares. Nice to be held by someone trying to comfort me, and not the other way around. "Thank you," I murmur. "For worrying."

She helps me to my feet. "Don't take it too personally. I'm just afraid that if you die, they'll assign me to someone else. I doubt my next mistress will let me wear costumes."

I laugh. "Maybe they'd even ask you to clean something."

Sef fakes a shudder. "Don't joke about that."

I'm still chuckling as she guides me to sit on the bed. We lean back, shoulders against the headboard. "So, what happened?"

I tell her everything, from my journey up the mountain, to the crash, to Kaidren saving my life, then turning on me.

When I'm finished, she's shaking her head. "You almost died."

"But I didn't. Told you I'd come back."

Sef doesn't look amused. "You take too many risks."

"Only for now. Things will be different when I've taken the throne. For both of us."

"I don't need things to be different. I like this life. *This*—working for someone like you—was always my dream."

"You dreamed of being a servant?"

"What's wrong with being a servant?" She shrugs, then smiles. "All I ever wanted was to work for someone kind."

"Instead you got stuck with me," I say.

My tone is teasing, but Sef frowns. "Don't do that. I'm glad I was assigned to you. Hate to break it to you, Mira, but you're stuck with me."

It flatters me more than I care to admit. Sef is so easy to love. She's charismatic and funny and *everyone* adores her. Making friends is effortless for her in a way it's never been for me. "I'm glad you were assigned to me too."

"Working for you has gotten me everything I ever wanted," she says. "It's fun. I get to gossip, wear costumes, and call it work. Maybe I'm just a servant, but I'm happy. Happier than most people ever are, and *definitely* happier than you. You hate it here."

I can't argue, so I don't. I stare at my tattoo, tracing it with my finger. There was a time when the sight of it filled me with wonder. A time when it made me feel connected to my home and my mother, and I thought it was the most beautiful thing in the world. That feeling died a long time ago.

"When I was a kid, I thought the mountain was everything I ever wanted," I say softly. "I was wrong. Before, I had nothing, but here, I'm invisible. When I'm not invisible, I'm scorned. And I'm tired. All the time. I have to think for Luc, for Ophera, for the Honorate, for myself. I'm shredding myself into a million pieces, and still, no one sees me."

"You could stop."

My eyes flash to Sef, angry. "You mean give up?"

"Maybe."

Mathson took everything from my mother, and she never fought back. He got the house on the mountain, the position in the Honorate, the perfect life. She got nothing.

"You're either useful to me, or you're nothing."

I've spent five years being useful. Being Luc's brain so he never has to think, and I'm *still* nothing. "I want to feel like I matter. I've earned the right to matter. Men with power take and take, and they give nothing back. I want to be so powerful that no one can take it from me, no one can threaten me, or ignore me, or discard me. People like Luc have unassailable power. Is it so wrong for me to want the same?"

This world never made space for me. So, I carved room for myself into the mountain. Shoved myself into the narrow opening. And I've been clinging on ever since.

My arms are tired. I want enough power to feel stable. Enough that no one can yank it all away from me at a moment's notice.

"Maybe it's not wrong," Sef says. "But if you're not careful, it's going to get you killed."

To hell with caution. The original Honorate weren't cautious when they took the throne from the Widow Queen and never gave it back.

That's exactly how I intend to steal the throne from Luc.

No one gives up power willingly. Selva Sixmen resigned from the Honorate because he was forced. The Widow Queen ceded power to an Honorate because she was sick, they were on the brink of war, and she had no other options.

If I manufacture a crisis, I can force Luc's hand. Create a catastrophe so urgent, he'll need me—as he always does. Then all I have to do is incapacitate him so he has no choice but to temporarily cede power to me. He trusts me. With a crisis on his hands, with no other options and no one else around, he would do it. He'd never suspect me, his sister, of keeping the power he entrusted her with. Never suspect me of using the Shadow Queen to force the rest of the Honorate into line.

By the time he realizes what's happening, it will be too late.

It will break his heart. But he's broken mine so many times, I no longer know guilt. She's a distant memory.

CHAPTER TWENTY-NINE

LOSING GRACELESSLY

Kaidren's victory speech is as smooth and polished as one of Yelina's pearls—and just as conceited and rage inducing as she is.

We're gathered in the ballroom. The walls are a deep shade of blue that's striking against the gold columns around the perimeter. All of Widow's Hall is built around this central chamber. From here, you can see the railing and ledge of each floor above us, and the high, domed ceiling. It's blue like the sky in the light season, painted with wispy clouds and streaks of yellow. A pale imitation of sunny days we rarely see.

Kaidren stands onstage in front of the room, crowing over his success. He rattles on about how excited he is for the masquerade ball next week, for a chance to garner final support before the third and final trial.

I stand in the back, half-hidden behind a column, trying not to look as furious as I am.

"I am so honored to be here, before you all," Kaidren says. "I would like to extend a special thank-you to someone without whom this victory would not be possible." That smug, self-satisfied smile that makes my insides riot stretches wider. "Everyone please join me in thanking *Remira Kyler*."

The ballroom had been silent through his speech, but at that name—*my* name—whispers sweep through the hall like a current. Even for people who don't know who I am, no one can miss that the person he mentioned shares a surname with the Praeceptor.

All around, heads twist, searching for me. From his place onstage behind Kaidren, Luc gives an undignified gasp as he hears my name. He looks so stunned, the audience can't fail to notice.

I stay hidden behind my column, jaw unhinged as I choke on fury.

"Remira." Despite the fact that I'm in the very back of the ballroom, despite the fact that I'm hiding behind a golden pillar, Kaidren's eyes pick me out of the crowd instantly. As if he already knew where I was. "Why don't you join me up here? I never would have made it this far without you. Thank you for being such a great friend." Each word drips venom. His smile is a bloodcurdling snarl.

I loathe him so much, I could scream. I could wrap my hands around his throat and squeeze until he turns blue. Heads are still twisting, still looking for me. I duck out of the ballroom before they find me.

I only manage to get two corridors away before pounding footsteps echo behind me and Yelina's voice calls out, "What was he talking about?"

My steps falter. I instantly regret it and want to keep walking, but I've already slowed my pace. Too late to flee now. "Nothing."

"I find that hard to believe." Yelina circles around me to glare. "I told you when I first saw you together there was something going on. Have you been conspiring with him this whole time? Plotting Lucien's downfall?"

"Lina . . ." Mathson comes to her side, arm around her waist. "Lower your voice. Sound carries in these halls."

Yelina moves closer to me, steps slow and calculated, eyes sparking with malice. "He *thanked* you."

"He was mocking me," I say.

"I've seen the looks you two exchange. If you are secretly working against us . . ."

"I'm not. Today, I nearly died so Luc could win this."

"Yet you still lost," she says.

The wound of defeat is still fresh. "That wasn't my fault."

"Let me guess," says Mathson. "The Vale boy promised that if you helped him, when he's Praeceptor, he'll alter the law so that aikkari don't have to report themselves."

"No," I say furiously. "He has no idea I'm aikkari and I'd be a fool to confide in him."

"Then what did he promise you?"

"*Nothing.* We're not allies."

Mathson doesn't believe me. He squints, analyzing my every move for a sign of deceit. "Let me be clear, Remira. If Lucien loses, I don't care what the Vale boy said to you. I will make sure the decurio knows the truth about you. I'll make sure *everyone* knows about you."

My teeth grind together. I'm sure to Mathson and Yelina it looks as though I'm angry—and I am—but in truth, it's all I can do to keep myself from sobbing. "Then it's a good thing he won't lose."

I don't say anything else. Partly because I'm so livid, my throat feels raw. Partly because I'm worried if I speak, they'll hear how choked up I am from suppressing tears.

Mathson and Yelina have always been awful. They've yelled at and threatened me plenty of times before, but everything feels different now. We're nearing the end of the Tournament, and I feel like I'm balancing on the point of a needle, seconds away from slipping into failure.

It's as if I'm observing my body from a distance as I shuffle through the motions. I watch myself go to my room. Watch myself root through my things and pull out a coat, sjaal, and gloves. Watch as I hurry through the halls and tumble outside.

It's freezing, and harsh winds pelt me with snow, but here in the cold night air, I can finally breathe. I press my back to the stone exterior of Widow's Hall. My knees buckle and I let myself fall.

Away from prying eyes, conniving Opheran bastards, and parents who despise me, I cry.

Snow batters me, and I welcome it. It feels a whole lot better than being kicked around indoors.

I close my eyes, allowing my tears to freeze and my mind to lose itself in the labyrinth of time.

Minutes pass. I keep my eyes closed.

"Remira." It's Kaidren's voice, shouting to be heard over the roaring wind.

Internally, I groan. He's the last person I want to see right now.

I peel open my eyes. "What do you want?"

"How long have you been out here? You're frozen solid." He ignores my protests as he takes me by the sleeve and drags me inside. I bat at his arm the whole way, until he finally releases me. "It seems a waste to save you from exposure only for you to die of it later the same day."

My outer garments are dripping wet from the snow. Melted slush puddles in the hall. I purse my lips as my eyes sting yet again. *What's wrong with me today?* I hardly ever cry. Tonight, I'm a damn rainstorm. "I was just getting some air."

"You look as if you were crying."

"Sorry to disappoint, but I wasn't."

He frowns. "I'm not disappointed. I don't want you to cry."

"Then what the hell was that speech?" I shake myself, regretting the words as soon as they're out. I don't want him to see he's managed to get under my skin. "Never mind. Don't answer that."

He's studying my face, noting the redness around my nose and eyes and the dried tear trails on my cheeks. His expression is soft with pity and something deeper. Something I can't name, nor do I want to.

Fed up with his scrutiny and the force of my own tangled emotions, I breeze past him, headed for my bedroom.

Of course, stubborn ox that he is, he trails after me.

"Leave me alone, Vale."

"Why are you so angry?"

"Because you're following me, and I hate you." My words hold none of their usual bite. They ring as hollow as I feel.

I don't know when I stopped hating Kaidren, but even now, while I'm seething and sad and overwhelmed, I don't. Sure, he makes my blood boil—that stunt he pulled in his speech made me want to throttle him—and he has a talent for rankling me, but I can't bring myself to hate him.

He's still walking briskly after me. "You're upset about something, and it's not me. Was it your parents? I had a feeling when they left just after you during my speech."

We reach the top of the stairs. "So, you came looking for me?"

"I wanted to make sure you were all right."

"Why?" I finally stop walking and throw up my hands. "Why do you even care?"

"Do you know your posture changes when you're around them? Or even when you mention them. You've got this unparalleled, unshakable confidence. But when you're with them, you wilt." He takes another step toward me, and I take one back. "It's a shame. I think you're brilliant."

Oddly enough, it's not a lie. My forehead creases in confusion. I expect his manipulation. I have no idea how to deal with a Kaidren who's honest. I feel we've started a new game, but I don't know the rules. "That's why you're following me?"

"I see how your family treats you. They're wasting you."

I frown. "I'm not a tool collecting rust, or a jar of milk left to curdle. I can't be wasted."

"That's not what I meant. Lucien can't win this Tournament without you. You know him better than anyone, and you know I'm right. But *we* would make an unbeatable team. If we worked together for the final trial, we could help each other."

I'm so startled, I almost laugh. "You mean so I can help *you* win."

"When I'm on the throne, I would make you my right hand, not my lackey."

Much as Kaidren likes to pretend otherwise, he's no better than Luc. He calls me brilliant and expects me to fawn. He tosses around compliments only when he wants something. He offers me a place beside his throne, when what I really want is to wrest it out from under him. He's just as unimaginative as my brother and the rest of this mountain, thinking I'll settle for favor when what I crave is power. "I'm not interested."

He looks incredulous. "Lucien is going to lose. I don't want to see you get dragged down with him. I'm offering you a trade."

"Shame you don't have anything I want." I shove past him and open my chamber door.

"You're being stubborn," he says.

"It took you this long to realize that? Looks like beating you is going to be easier than I thought." I give a mocking grin. "I look forward to watching you lose the third trial."

I slam the door in his face.

CHAPTER THIRTY

ONE TRUE THING

The mountain air is at its most violent in the sky cart. No matter how many layers I wrap myself in, I can't help the shivers that wrack my body.

The cart attendant watches me warily from the other side of the small wooden box we share. The journey from the top of the mountain to the base always feels long. Especially since cart attendants rarely speak to me. The trip itself is only a little more than an hour, but silence stretches longer than words.

When we reach our destination, the attendant opens the door, as he always does.

"Thank you, Tallus," I say as I exit into the evening.

He looks at me in surprise—he doesn't expect me to know his name. I leave before he can question it.

The cloak I wear to Ophera is thinner than what I'm used to, in order to draw less attention. My boots are cheaper as well, and my toes grow numb as I trudge through the dirty, gray-tinted snow piled in the streets, making my way to the childhood home of Kaidren Vale.

There are bars fitted over the windows and ratty curtains inside. I peer into each room until I find one that looks as if it belongs to Kaidren.

Well, used to. Like me, he traded in this shack at the base of the mountain for a manor at the top.

The bars over his window are steel. With a bit of magic, I heat them enough to soften and bend them out. I wedge between the bars and climb through.

I try to land softly but slip at the last moment.

I go still, waiting. No startled shrieks or panicked cries.

Relieved, I rise. I brought a small lamp with me. Dim enough it won't be spotted from outside, yet bright enough to illuminate my search as I tiptoe around the room. Kaidren's walls are heavily decorated. Not with paintings, but with words. Quotes from speeches written in perfect, elegant script; news clippings; notes to himself, asking questions.

Some of the words he's collected are familiar. Speeches I've studied in preparation for writing Luc's, and some of them are words I penned for my brother to speak. Just about all the news clippings he saved are about Widow's Hall. News on the Praeceptor, the Honorate, and *me*. Well, the Shadow Queen. I remember, not without some satisfaction, that Kaidren was a fan of mine before he came to Widow's Hall and I (she) accused him of murdering his father.

He's underlined a few passages on his wall in emerald green ink.

Honorate Arliss Vale opposed the order . . .

Honorate Arliss Vale remains the only member of the Honorate who is unmarried . . .

They're about his father, from before he fell ill.

There are a few handwritten notes tacked to the wall, overlapping the news. Over an article about Luc, he's pinned a note:

Who is the girl standing beside him?

I frown. The girl in question is obviously me. But the news clipping he pinned it to is merely a summarization of a speech he gave. It makes no mention of a sister, or anybody, accompanying him. I remember this speech well. When Luc delivered it, I stood offstage behind him, watching from the shadows as always. The only way for Kaidren to comment on my presence is if he was *there*, in person, and saw me.

His words from our first conversation float back. *"I've seen you. Skulking around in the shadows . . . Around Widow's Hall. Hovering near the Praeceptor."*

Just how many of Luc's public appearances had Kaidren attended before we met? How often was he in the audience, watching me, while I had no idea he existed? I hate the thought of him knowing something I don't. Hate the idea that he was studying me before I knew to study him.

As I look further, I find more mentions of me from Luc's public appearances over the past few years.

The girl is back
W~~ho~~ is she?

And, from a note that's more recent than the rest:

~~Just Remira~~
~~Remira Kyler~~
Mira

I stare at that final line for longer than I should. Kaidren only ever calls me Remira, yet he made a point of writing "Mira," as though we're close enough to use nicknames with each other.

I shake myself. I'm lingering, and I shouldn't be. I need to search quickly and get the hell out of here. I'm looking for anything I can find to use against him. The rest of the Honorate are easy. I've spent years collecting their darkest secrets. For Kaidren, I have next to nothing.

Something under the bed catches my eye. The corner of a flat black box.

I drop to my knees, setting the lamp next to me. I slide the box from beneath the bed and remove the lid. Emerald green fabric laced with gold winks back at me.

Honorate robes. Same as the ones I wear in my attic, watching council meetings. These are worn and fraying at the edges. From a time before Kaidren was given a fresh set of robes to call his own.

A cracked mirror leans against the wall opposite the bed. I wonder how often Little Kaidren stared into it. Wonder if he, like me, donned his father's robes and danced around, dreaming of one day being someone who matters.

I lower the robes back into the box. As I push it beneath the bed, something else glitters in the low lamplight.

My fingers close around a glass vial, so cold it's frosted over with a layer of white, obscuring its contents.

I've just shoved the vial into my pocket when something creaks behind me. I whirl to face the door.

There's nothing there.

"Find what you're looking for, shadow skulker?"

I go rigid and twist around again. A tall figure leans against the window I climbed through. He's too far for the lamp's light to reach his face, but I recognize his form, and judging from the shape of his words, he's smirking at me.

Swallowing, I stand, trying to hide my unease. "What are you doing here?" My voice is even, a stark contrast to the cantering pace of my heart.

Something hisses as Kaidren ignites a lamp on his desk, surrounding him in soft, misty light.

"I live here," he drawls. "I think my presence is more reasonable than yours."

"Did you climb through the window?"

"No, I used the door like a normal person." He tilts his head jeeringly. "Why? Did *you* use the window?"

I don't bother responding. I'm too busy plotting my escape. Where he's standing blocks the window, so it's not a viable option. That leaves the bedroom door. I wonder if I could run fast enough before he catches me.

Kaidren's chuckle interrupts my thoughts. "Don't bother. My aunt Jules locked us in. We only leave when I say."

I glare to disguise my mounting panic. "What do you want?"

"To talk." He takes a seat on the edge of the bed. His room is small enough and his legs long enough that all he has to do is stretch them out, and my path to the window is obstructed.

Kaidren grins pleasantly, as if that wasn't a calculated move, and motions for me to sit beside him.

I scoff and cross my arms. "I have nothing to talk to you about."

"The fact that you just climbed through my bedroom window suggests you might have some questions."

"I wasn't expecting to see you."

"It's my home. I come here all the time. But tonight, I confess, I followed you."

My eyes narrow and he shrugs unabashedly. "I saw you get in a sky cart and took the next one down. Figured you'd be coming to my home, because, as far as I can tell, you haven't been to Ophera since your mother died."

I can't stop myself from flinching. Thinking about Aja always gets a reaction. Emotion bubbles within me like boiling water, eager to steam out, either in tears or screams.

Kaidren watches me, and his face softens with pity. "What was her name?"

I hate that I can't hide how much the mention of her hurts. "It doesn't matter."

"Fine. We won't talk about your mother. Instead, you can tell me what you're doing here. My guess is you're looking for some way to sabotage me before the ball. Am I close?"

"You can't expect me to answer that."

Kaidren makes a show of stretching out his legs, emphasizing the way they stymie my path to freedom. "There's no need to snoop, Remira. I'll happily tell you whatever you want to know. Things you won't find from sneaking around my room. In return, all you have to do is tell me something about you. I won't even ask you to tell me anything you don't want to."

He's playing a game and I know it, but he's also not lying, and I have to admit I'm tempted. "Then what do you want to know?"

"Something about you that's real. One true thing."

"That's it?"

"That's it. I won't confess to anything that might get me into trouble, but ask something *fair*, and I'll answer truthfully. All I ask is that you tell me something. Anything—so long as it's true. It's a good trade. Completely unfair and wholly in your favor. Just the way you like it."

"Why would you agree to something like that?"

Kaidren gestures around his walls. "For years, I've seen you near the Praeceptor. I've wondered about you. Then I met you. I thought I got to know you, but it turns out it was all a lie. It's been weeks, and I feel I know less about you than I did before. I've been spinning stories and making guesses, and every time I think I'm close to knowing you, you remind me just how wrong I am."

"All this because you're curious?" I say dubiously.

He flashes that polished, charming smile. "Curiosity is a strong motivator when one's subject is as captivating as you."

My nerves are alight with suspicion, but everything he's said is the truth, and regardless, I have a clear edge. If he lies, I'll be able to tell. He'll have no way of knowing if what I reveal to him is the truth. "All right . . ." I agree warily. "But I get to ask my question first."

Kaidren laughs. "I figured you would. Ask away."

I can't exactly ask him if there's some massive scandal in his life I can use to blackmail him. But there's one question that's been running through my mind, over and over. "Why didn't you turn me in on the mountain?"

It's been haunting me. There must be some larger plan at play. Some reason he thought it better strategically to keep my interference in the second trial a secret. But I can't think of a tactical advantage for not seizing a permanent victory.

Kaidren cocks his head to one side, bemused. "Praeceptor Kyler would have been eliminated, but *you* would have gone to prison."

I pause, waiting for him to continue. He doesn't. I frown. "So?"

"So, I don't want to ruin your life, Remira."

I can't help scoffing. "Since when?"

"I recently went to the library and looked into some of the orders your brother has written since taking the throne. I hadn't read them before, so I didn't know all the details, but imagine my shock when I saw that most of them mentioned Ophera. Someone wrote provisions to fund resources and schools. That same someone snuck them into orders that were completely unrelated so they'd pass. Any idea who that might be?"

I'm even more confused than I was before I asked. "That's why you didn't turn me in?"

"I realized that my fight isn't with you. It's with your brother. You fight Lucien's battles, and you take on all the risk. You bear the brunt of the penalty and receive none of the reward."

"I know that. What does that have to do with the Tournament?"

Kaidren's eyes drop briefly to my wrist, and I realize the direction of his thoughts. I yank down my sleeve with a glare. "You spared me because you *pity* me?"

"No, I don't," he says quickly.

The heat that rushes through me burns, more than anything else. After everything, he still doesn't see me as an opponent, just some fragile, pathetic creature that needs protection.

Kaidren must read the fury in my eyes because he stands from the bed and reaches for me—I think to comfort me—but I jump back. "Don't touch me."

"I'm sorry." He holds up his hands in a placating gesture. "I feel for you. Not pity you."

"I don't care if you feel for me."

"How would you like me to feel about you, Remira?"

I speak before I've thought through my answer. "I want you to respect me. See me as an opponent so formidable, you want to destroy me."

"I have limits. Is there no line you wouldn't cross? If our roles were reversed, surely you wouldn't ruin my life to win."

"I'd ruin your life for free."

"These games we play are one thing. But to destroy a person . . ." Kaidren's eyes search mine intently. "I don't believe you'd do that."

Maybe he's right and there is a difference. What I've done

so far—soiling Kaidren's name and reputation, defaming him in Eteria, defeating him in the first trial—hasn't ruined him. At the end of it all, Kaidren is still an Honorate.

That's the difference between us: in this race for power, we are starting from two different places. At his core, Kaidren is an Honorate. I have to earn the right to matter, even if it's just a fraction as much as he does. Every scrap of authority I have was fought for and won.

If Kaidren loses, he'll still have his title. If I lose, I have nothing. *Less* than nothing. The difference between me and Kaidren Vale is I can't ruin him. Not really.

I step away from his intensity and drop my gaze to the floor. "Maybe I would, maybe I wouldn't. Guess you'll find out."

His hand twitches at his side, but he doesn't move it. "Fine. Then it's your turn. One true thing."

He mentioned my mother, and she's always fresh on my mind, so I say, "My mother named me after her favorite star."

He smiles softly. Not that over-wide, overused smile. A small, genuine one that warms his gaze and my heart. "I didn't know there was a star called Remira."

"There isn't." My tone is lighter now, and I catch myself smiling back. Because when Kaidren Vale is a real person, he is devastatingly handsome. Because I remember Aja telling me the origins of my name as though it was yesterday. "She didn't know anything about the names of stars, but when she was lonely, she'd make them up. She named the brightest star in the sky Remira. When I was born, she gave me its name."

Aja told me it was so I'd never be lonely. As always, she was lying. In truth, it was so *she* never would be. So she could look up at the sky and always have me with her.

"That's sweet," Kaidren says.

That was Aja. Sweet to a fault. Generous and trusting to

her own detriment. She gave too much of herself. She lost her parents when she was young, and loneliness was a void she was constantly trying to fill. All she ever did was give more and more of herself away. It cost her everything. Cost *both* of us everything.

My smile fades.

Kaidren is still watching me. "Where did you go just now?"

I shake off the memories. "Nowhere. But I am now. Leaving, that is." I turn for the door—planning to kick the damn thing down if it means getting out of here.

"Wait." Kaidren hurries to stand beside me. "How would you feel about having dinner with me and my aunt?"

I'm surprised by the invitation and even more surprised by how naturally he extends it. "You still eat here?"

"Virdei is lonely. I like it here. And my aunt is good company."

"You could just invite her to Virdei."

"She hates it there."

His aunt has excellent taste.

"Care to join us?" he says.

"No."

Kaidren's sweet smile turns oily, and his warm tone chills with civility. "You know, I've been really kind about the fact that you snuck in here up until now. I'm an Honorate. I imagine the decurio would be *very* interested to learn someone broke into my home."

My eyes narrow. "Is that a threat?"

"No." His smile stretches wide. "It's an observation accompanying an invitation you can't decline."

CHAPTER THIRTY-ONE

VIEW FROM BELOW

Of course, I resolutely refuse to join Kaidren and his aunt for dinner. And of course, he resolutely refuses to let me anywhere near the window to escape.

In the end, I agree, if only so I don't end up spending the night stuck in a stalemate in Kaidren's childhood bedroom.

His aunt Julissa is all smiles when we finally leave his room. If she finds my presence here strange, she doesn't let on as she leads me to a round table where dinner is being served.

She's beautiful. Kaidren is good-looking, so it's not a surprise, but I don't see a family resemblance between them. She has the kind of beauty that comes from effortless grace and wisdom. Her hair is short, dark, and thick, with some coils of gray mixed in. Her round face has a few shallow creases, her skin is the hue of pine bark, and she has the longest eyelashes I've ever seen. Like Kaidren, her teeth are perfect. Unlike Kaidren, she doesn't show each of them off as she smiles at me. "Hello, Kaidren's friend."

I almost laugh, but she doesn't appear to be joking. She must know Kaidren and I aren't anything close to friends, but it feels rude to say that when she's being kind. "Hello. Apologies for breaking into your home."

She chuckles. It's a smoky, comforting sound. "If I had anything worth stealing, I might be upset."

Her house is small, as expected, but she's draped scraps of fabric over walls and surfaces to add warmth, creating a mishmash of colors and patterns. Chaotic, but inviting.

The main room is the kitchen, dining room, and living space. There's a patchy sofa, scuffed wooden table, and a side table I'm pretty sure is just a trash bin turned over and covered with a thin sheet. Resting on the side table is a compass that, unfortunately, I recognize. It's silver and rusted and nothing special—except for a shimmer at the end of the needle. It's one of those "magic hunting" compasses. Total junk—not to mention illegal.

I look away from the compass and force my face to remain impassive as Julissa pulls out a chair at the table for me. "We're having potatoes tonight." She twists her fingers fretfully. "We don't have any meat. I'm sure it's not what you're used to."

"I love potatoes." I smile gently. "They're Luc's favorite."

Her soft brown eyes widen, and her fingers stop fiddling. "'Luc,'" she repeats in an awed whisper. "You call the Praeceptor 'Luc.'" She still looks amazed as she piles food onto my plate, giving me far more than herself or Kaidren.

"Oh, please." I shove it back to her. "I don't need this much."

"It's no trouble."

Warmth floods me as she lies. Food is expensive, and she's giving me more than my fair share even though I just broke into her house. I glare and swap my plate for hers.

Julissa makes a move to switch them back, but I raise my fork threateningly. "Try it, and I'll stab you."

Kaidren smirks. "Don't test her, Jules. She means it."

I tip up my chin in silent, stubborn confirmation of his words. I don't lower my defenses—or my fork—until she takes her first bite and I'm certain she won't try to swap our plates again.

For a few awkward minutes, we eat in silence. Kaidren must have some hidden motive for insisting I join them, but I can't work out what he has to gain from making me eat dinner with him and his aunt.

"Kaidren's told me a bit about you." Jules breaks the stillness. "You're just as pretty as he described."

I'm surprised by the lack of heat with her words. Even more surprised by the light pink that flushes Kaidren's cheeks and the glower he gives his aunt. "He told you I was *pretty*?"

"I might have mentioned something to that effect," he grumbles, not looking at me.

"Well, thank you," I say to Jules. "Can you also tell me what I'm doing here?"

Jules chuckles. "You're just as impatient as he described as well." She takes her time answering me. Spears a potato. Dunks it in the sauce she's prepared. Takes a bite, chews thoroughly, before finally responding. "I've heard a lot about you. I wanted to meet you for myself."

"What else have you heard?"

She glances at her nephew. "Kaidren mentioned that you're a difficult person to know," she says carefully.

I can't help a disbelieving laugh. "You're sure that's all he said? He didn't call me a conniving bitch?"

Jules tosses her head back and laughs.

"I've never called you a bitch," Kaidren objects.

"Just conniving, then," I say.

"Well, you are. Should I have lied?"

"Why not?" I challenge. "You're exceptionally skilled in that department."

"Yet not half so skilled as you."

"How big of you to acknowledge your shortcomings." I take a sip of water and focus my attention on Julissa, who's glancing between the two of us, looking amused. "Maybe you can answer a question for me. I've been asking Kaidren, but he's yet to give me a straight answer."

She looks intrigued. "What?"

"Why did he come to Widow's Hall?"

Kaidren groans. "I've answered this already. To improve the Honorate."

I roll my eyes, not even dignifying his lie with a response as I look back to Jules. "Well? Do you know?"

"I have no idea. You'll be amazed to hear my nephew doesn't listen to me, or anybody," Jules says wryly. "I've never understood the pull of that mountain. I told Kaidren a thousand times he was a fool for wanting to go to Virdei. Everyone I know is desperate to find a way there. No idea why. We all know the tattoo paints a target on your back, but—"

Kaidren loudly clears his throat and slams a glass on the table, making it rattle on its slightly uneven legs.

Jules's eyes widen. She presses her lips together, falling silent.

I frown suspiciously between the two of them. "Why should that matter? Kaidren doesn't have a tattoo."

There's a long, awkward pause.

"Yes, I know." Jules breaches the tension with a breathy chuckle. "I meant for other Opherans. Not Kaidren."

She's an awful liar. The flare of magic in my gut only confirms what I can already see with my own eyes. She's lying about Kaidren's tattoo.

Jules rushes on, clearly hoping to distract me. "I'll never understand wanting to leave Ophera. Everyone who travels up the mountain ends up a worse person." She blinks, realizing who she's talking to. "No offense."

"None taken. You think life is better here?"

"I think here will never improve if everyone abandons it. It's better to elevate where you are, rather than to look down your nose from the top. Virdei told us there were gods in the sky and built their way into the clouds, all so they could claim their kingdom on the mountain makes them godlike. I read the Shadow Queen's columns. The Honorate are far from gods. They are liars and cheats. Why should I want to be anything like them?"

My fork idles over my next bite. I wasn't expecting to like Kaidren's aunt.

She's still speaking. "If you ask me, they're going to get what's coming to them. They poisoned our water so we could never compete—"

"Wait." I stop her. "What did you say?"

"They poisoned our water," she repeats.

Kaidren sighs. "That's just a myth, Jules."

Jules ignores him and addresses me. "You never heard?"

"I heard that Petruvia always claimed Virdei cut off their access to drinking water," I say.

Jules scoffs. "That's a mild way of putting it. They poisoned it. When Virdei built their kingdom in the mountains, they had more magic than neighboring nations. There were more aikkari born in Virdei than anywhere else, but forming a military takes time, and they weren't making theirs fast enough to stave off invaders. So, they poisoned the stream at the base of the mountain. Ophera and Petruvia's drinking supply was sullied. It killed thousands, left Virdei with more aikkari than the rest, and gave them enough time to build up their army."

Silence reigns around the dinner table.

In all my years of listening through walls, I've never heard of such an awful rumor. "What did Virdei use to poison them?"

"Something called kishori."

The same poison that killed Arliss Vale. "I don't know if that's true," I say after a pause. "But I hate Virdei too."

Jules looks surprised. "Truly?"

"What's to like? It's cold and gray, and the people are cruel."

Julissa and Kaidren have both stopped eating. Kaidren looks the most shocked by my words. "You almost sound sincere."

"Maybe I am. Maybe I'm not." I stab another potato with my fork to give my hands something to do. "Guess you'll never know."

There's a few more seconds of terse silence before we resume dinner.

I don't know if I'll ever figure out whether Kaidren has an ulterior motive for making me eat with them. The three of us talk and laugh and tease each other for over an hour. Even though there isn't enough for a second helping, even though I don't trust Kaidren and he doesn't trust me, it's the first meal I've had in years I actually enjoy.

CHAPTER THIRTY-TWO

STARHEADED FOOL

Kaidren sits next to me in the sky cart as we journey back up the mountain. Neither of us speaks for so long, I think we're going to pass the entire hour without exchanging a word.

Finally, he turns toward me. Our knees are so close, they brush. I feel the heat of him through layers of wool. It travels up my leg and spreads through me like a furnace. "Was this your first time in Ophera since your mother?"

I jerk my knee away. Instantly, I'm cold, but I prefer it. I miss Ophera, but I hate coming back. It makes me feel nostalgic and guilty and sad. "I'm not discussing this with you."

"You really hate talking about her," Kaidren notes.

"How perceptive." I don't look at him.

Silence, for four seconds, before he sighs. "My mother was a seamstress. It's how I got those robes I saw you looking at earlier."

I glance at him from the corner of my eye, cautious but curious. "I assumed those were from your father."

He laughs, but it lacks humor. "A gift from my father was about as likely as a snowstorm in hell. He wouldn't even acknowledge my presence until he was sick. I got those robes because my mother was a seamstress for a few of the Honorate."

I can't tell if he's trying to convey without words that he isn't going to push on the subject of my mother, or if he thinks discussing his own will soften me so he can pry later. "Why are you telling me this?"

"I figured we could call a truce. If only for a while." He keeps going. "I've always known who my father is. He knew about me too, but he ignored me. My mom took those robes from one of her other clients. She brought them home and patched them up for me. Said I should practice for the real thing someday."

He pauses, lost in memories. Keeping my guard up around Kaidren is easy—except for when he discards the mask. When he's vulnerable and genuine like this, I can't help myself. "What happened to her?"

"After dear old Dad saw me for the first time, he fired her." His wistful tone sours. "I'll never forget the way he looked at me. Like I was a phantom. He knew I existed, but until he saw me in person, I don't think he realized how much we looked alike. He fired her that same day."

He falls quiet. Sad memories flick through his eyes like snowflakes. He hasn't finished his story; he's collecting himself. "He spread word, far and wide, that no one in Virdei should hire her. He didn't say why, of course, but she was ruined just the same. She was desperate for work, so she took a job in the mines."

My breath catches. The tshira mines are notoriously dangerous. He doesn't need to finish this story for me to know its end, but I don't interrupt.

"She survived six months before she went missing. It was another five days before they found her body and confirmed what we already knew—she was dead."

An awful way to lose a parent. My skin is safe inside gloves, and my heart is sad, so I lay a hand over his and squeeze. "I'm sorry."

He flips his hand over, intertwining our fingers. "So am I."

Any other day, I'd pull away. But I can read how much he misses her in the mist in his eyes, in the tone of his voice, in the stillness of his chest. I keep my hand where it is.

"I never forgave him." Bitterness douses each word. "Even when he finally deigned to acknowledge me and told me I'd inherit his title."

"He sounds like an ass," I say.

"He is. Was." It's not hard to imagine Kaidren killing his own father—to avenge his mother, to take his place in the Honorate, to punish him, or all of the above.

Neither of us speaks, and in that companionable silence, I realize why he told me his mother's story. It wasn't a trick. It was to let me know he understands what it is to be so sad, the only way to cope is to be furious. My chest is tight, and I find myself speaking to relieve the pressure. "My father is a lot like yours."

Kaidren's hand squeezes mine in reassurance. He doesn't interrupt.

"I didn't know it was possible to hate someone as much as I do him. He discarded my mother like trash. She was . . ." I blink rapidly, holding in tears of rage and heartache. "She was everything I'm not. She was kind. And she was loving and sweet and patient. And she was a fool."

Kaidren flinches. "You don't mean that."

"I do. I loved her more than anything, but she was foolish. She actually believed he loved her."

"Maybe he did, in his own way."

"He didn't. I asked him."

"You think he lied?"

"No." My throat burns as I recall the cold, irritated way he answered the question I was pathetic enough to ask. "No, he didn't even bother."

Kaidren doesn't fight me as I tug my hand away, but his eyes linger, like he wants to snatch it back. "I'm sorry," he says. "After my mom died, Jules was the only thing that made it bearable. I'm sorry your second home was somewhere you were unwanted."

"Ophera is my home," I say fiercely. "Always will be." He has more questions. I can read the curiosity in his too-earnest gaze. Time to steer this conversation to safer waters. "Speaking of Ophera." I clear my throat. "Your aunt Jules made an interesting comment about your tattoo. Which is odd, because I didn't think you had one."

"I knew you weren't going to let that go." He sighs, but doesn't look upset that I've asked. "One true thing?"

I don't hesitate. "Deal."

"I got a tattoo when I was five. Same as anyone else."

My eyes fall to his wrist, but it's covered. Without asking, I take his arm. He doesn't object as I gently peel off a glove and slide up the sleeve. My gloved fingers skirt over the bare skin on the underside of his wrist.

He shudders at my touch, but doesn't pull away.

I meet his eyes. "You don't have it anymore."

"That's true. And also untrue."

I pull his wrist up to my eyeline so I can inspect it more closely.

Squinting, I see something I didn't before. The skin of his arm is the same shade of brown, but there's a patch at his wrist that's ever so slightly discolored. "What is that? Powder?"

"Ink. I tried using powder, but it melted under fabric. So, I got a second tattoo with dark brown ink to cover the gold. It hurt like hell."

Seeing my confused expression, he answers the question I don't ask. "When my father summoned me for the first time, he didn't even look at my face. He just stared at my tattoo. He was sickly and dying, but he looked at me like, between the two of us, *I* was the revolting one. I never felt so small. I've been covering it ever since."

His gloveless hand flips my arm over. Realizing his intent but fearing his touch, I pull up my own sleeve, baring my tattoo for his perusal.

"It's beautiful," he breathes. "When I found out you were the Praeceptor's sister and you still keep yours displayed, I thought you were the bravest person I'd ever met. You're here every day, enduring their glares, and you never so much as flinch. I don't know how you don't let it get to you." He reaches out to run a hand over the golden sun, but I yank down my sleeve before he makes contact.

He doesn't seem surprised or upset by the rejection. "You made me regret hiding mine. Compared to you, I'm a coward. It's ridiculous, isn't it? So much hatred over something so beautiful."

Everything he says is the truth. Which is odd, because when we first met, he told me he liked my tattoo, but it was a lie.

Wasn't it?

I recall the moment. What he actually said was: "*I never got a tattoo, though. Wish I had. Yours is stunning.*"

At the time, I felt the heat of magic and assumed he was lying about wishing he'd gotten a tattoo, or admiring mine. But he wasn't. The lie was in the first part of the sentence, where he claimed to have never gotten one at all.

Kaidren thinks I'm brave. He thinks the stares don't crawl under my skin and make me want to scream. The truth is, if someone had given me the option to hide my tattoo when I first arrived, or even a few weeks ago . . . I'm not sure I'd have been brave enough to decline.

"Your turn," he says gently.

It takes me a moment to realize he means it's my turn to share a truth about myself.

I'm speaking before I've ironed out the emotion from my voice. "I had Honorate robes too. Luc brought me and my mom a few of his father's old ones before I lived with them. They were soft and warm, and he figured we'd use them as blankets, but I liked to put them on. Look at myself in the mirror and imagine what it would feel like to walk into a room and command respect."

What it would be like to have everything and fear nothing.

By the time we reach the top of the mountain, it's late and I'm exhausted.

We're right outside Widow's Hall. Kaidren still has a short trek from here to the Vale manor, but he doesn't make to leave. Instead, he stands before me, shuffling his feet the way greyhorns do to keep warm.

It's not snowing tonight, but it's cold enough to freeze flames solid, and loose snow piled on the ground drifts in the night breeze.

I don't know why Kaidren is still standing here, watching me like he expects me to do something, so after a few moments, I turn to leave.

"My aunt really likes you," he blurts, stopping me.

Confused, I face him again. "I liked her too."

His lips part to say something; then he closes them and clears his throat. "Probably because she doesn't know you like I do." His words are teasing, but his gaze is startlingly intense.

I raise a brow. "You think you know me?"

"Maybe not." He drags his feet through the snow, closer.

"But I'm starting to. I'd like to." His tone is soothing and warm, and it curls around me like a sjaal. The composed mask he wears like armor is gone now. He watches me with that darkness he usually hides. I can't look away.

"Don't bother," I say. "You'd be disappointed."

"I doubt that." His gaze drops, and for a moment, I could swear he's looking at my lips. "You haven't disappointed me yet."

"Really? I thought I was conniving, spiteful, and cruel?"

"You are. Doesn't mean I'm disappointed."

I'm sure of it now: his eyes fall to my lips.

Run. A little, rational voice whispers to me. Kaidren looks ravenous. Dangerous.

I don't move.

"I made a lot of assumptions when I met you. I thought you were gullible. I thought you were sweet. I thought I *liked* sweet." Kaidren continues his slow approach until the toes of our boots graze, and I feel the cloudy warmth of his exhales on my cheeks. "Now I don't think I like sweet at all."

This time, when his gaze lowers to my lips, it doesn't waver. It darkens with determination. He sucks in a breath and leans forward.

For a moment frozen in time, I stay perfectly still. His brown eyes are hauntingly deep, the kind you can drown in; his voice is smooth as churned butter; he lies as easy as he breathes; and some days I'm certain I despise him.

But there's a rage inside him I recognize. A hunger for power, a willingness to do whatever it takes to get it. It should scare me. Sometimes it *does* scare me. But with the danger he poses comes a desire I can't deny. I feel as if I know him, and I think he might be the first person who's ever seen me clearly.

Kaidren Vale is annoyingly attractive. Less so when he's flashing that fake smile I hate. More so when he's glaring in earnest. Or when he's looking at me like I'm the most fascinating thing he's ever seen. I've never been kissed before, and as his lips descend upon mine, they look so, so soft . . .

One touch and you're ruined.

The voice of reason is small, but it's enough—I pull away.

I'm dazed, and my heart flutters a combination of panic and lingering anticipation.

Kaidren's eyes fly open. He looks startled. "I'm sorry. I—"

"It's fine," I say quickly.

It's anything but fine. I can't believe how foolish I almost was. He's an isha. I wasn't seriously considering letting him kiss me, was I?

I turn to flee, but in all my fluster, I slip on ice.

I fall back, gracelessly and embarrassingly.

Kaidren catches me. His eyes are gentle as he turns me to face him, hands warm around my waist. "Mira—"

I shove him back. Even though I've been sitting still for over an hour, I'm breathless. "Don't."

He raises his hands, palms out. "I don't want you to think I was—" He releases a frustrated groan. "That wasn't a game. I swear to you, that was real."

He's not lying. Dammit, he *means* that. I can't tell which thought is more terrifying: Kaidren trying to kiss me because he *wanted* to or Kaidren playing a cruel game with my heart.

"Good night." I rush away for the safety of Widow's Hall.

If Kaidren calls after me, I don't hear it. Or maybe I just don't want to.

"You're back." Sef lounges on my bed, waiting for me. She sets aside the book she was reading as I burst through the door. "Did you find anything?"

Not really. The only thing I uncovered was that his aunt Jules collects illegal magical goods. Is it enough to blackmail him? I'm not sure, but admittedly, thinking is a bit difficult when the only thing on my mind is how close I let Kaidren's lips get to mine.

I sit on the corner of the bed, trying to churn through my thoughts. "Maybe. I'm not sure."

She waits for me to continue. When I don't, she nudges me. "What's wrong? You look . . . frazzled."

"It's nothing. Kaidren was there. He almost touched me." *Almost kissed me.* I keep that part to myself.

"But he didn't." Sef looks confused. "So, there's no problem."

"Like I said, it was nothing." Except that I almost let him. Worse, I think I wanted him to.

"I don't think I like sweet at all."

What am I supposed to do with that?

I can't think about this anymore. I begin shucking layers of warmth to pile into my closet, when I feel something heavy in my coat pocket.

Frowning, I reach for it. It's smooth and cylindrical. The vial I took from under Kaidren's bed. The frost that obscured its contents has melted. It's full of a thick, lilac-colored liquid.

My heart freezes.

Arliss Vale was killed with kishori—a purple liquid.

Sef gasps. "That isn't . . . ?"

"Poison." I sound faint, even to myself.

For months, I've hunted for anything I can use against Kaidren. At long last, I've found it, the kindling I need to burn his world down. Proof he murdered his own father.

CHAPTER THIRTY-THREE

TRAPPINGS OF POWER

Tonight is the masquerade. One week from now is the third and final trial. Except, if all goes according to plan, there won't be another trial.

I dress quickly. First, I need to find Sef, then Luc, and make sure both of them are prepared. Today is the day I finally ruin Kaidren Vale, force him out of the Tournament, and secure the throne for Luc. And, eventually, myself.

I open my bedroom door—and halt.

A white box tied with scarlet ribbon rests against the wall. There's no one nearby. Someone delivered this, clearly, but they didn't knock to make sure I got it.

Frowning, I carry it inside and set it on my bed. There's a note attached to the top, written in neat green ink.

Shadow Skulker,
  I used to put these on and dream of being the most powerful person in the room too.
  Kaidren
  P.S. Hope you'll save me a dance tonight.

I've been avoiding him. It's for the best and I know it, but that doesn't stop my stomach from fluttering as I remove the box's lid to reveal the gift inside. Honorate robes.

At first glance, I think they're the same ones I found beneath his bed. The old, worn ones he must keep for sentimental reasons. They're not. On these robes, the golden thread hasn't lost its shimmer and there are no frays. These are brand-new.

They're even nicer than the ones Luc gifted me, that I wear for chamber in my attic. He claimed it was the best he could do, and I was grateful for the gesture. *This* . . .

My heart softens. Cracks fissure the walls I've built around myself.

Steel and ice, I sternly remind myself. I can't let this small act of kindness affect me.

Tonight will go as planned. Kaidren will receive a threat from the Shadow Queen. His aunt harbors illegal magic. On its own, it's not much, but last night served as confirmation: he loves Jules. Hopefully, it will be enough to coerce him to drop out of the Tournament. So long as he does as he's told, I won't have to mention the discovery that he murdered his father.

I'll use it if I have to, but I'd rather save it for later. After all, Kaidren Vale has a long career ahead of him as an Honorate. I'll need all the secrets I can find to keep him in line.

There's no room for error, no space to get emotionally involved. Too much hinges on this dance going smoothly for me to risk it for a boy I was certain I hated just a few weeks ago.

Selva Sixmen ruined Eduma and had her thrown in prison. Arliss Vale ruined Kaidren's mother and cost her a job and, ultimately, her life. Mathson Kyler ruined Aja and cost her everything. It's the same story, over and over. Powerful men taking advantage and ruining lives because they can. They have no limits. Why should I?

I climbed the mountain, right to the crest. I'm so close to the top, I can taste it. If I fall, I fall *all* the way down. If Kaidren falls, he stays exactly where he is.

I seal the lid back over the box and shove the gift under my bed, where I can't see it. Where it can't distract me from the only goal that matters.

The ballroom is beautiful tonight. The dance floor is illuminated by a crystal chandelier hanging from the high, domed ceiling. The usually clear shards have been replaced at intervals with sky blue and white. Candlelight casts wintry light around the ceiling, walls, and floor.

A maid was supposed to replace those crystal shards, but I did it myself. I painstakingly fiddled with the chandelier until it was perfect for my plans, yet beautiful enough for no one else to notice.

The ballroom floor is tiled with squares of dusty pink and banded tshira, polished to shine. Tall glass windows of pale blue quartz line the back wall, bringing in light from the beacons outside. The golden columns are tied with silk ribbons in large bows.

Everything is perfect, down to the last detail. Sef did my hair, and she outdid herself. My thick, coily curls have never been bigger. They're displayed in a combination of tight braids, two-strand twists, and free hair. Two sections twisted in the front frame my face. Thin braids trail from my forehead to the crown of my head, where the rest of my hair is free and loose. And all throughout my curls are glittering crystal sparrow clips that match the tshira trinket on my bracelet. My dress is rich black velvet embroidered with gold along the bodice and inlaid with stars that wink within the folds of my skirt as I move. My gloves and mask are matching red lace.

Tonight, I feel beautiful. It's a rarity for me, but despite that warm feeling of confidence, I hug the back wall, watching Luc dance.

We spent hours ahead of time going over the best ways to make a good impression. He's naturally personable, but tonight, I need him to be more than nice if he's to charm donors.

So far, it looks like it paid off. Luc holds himself with poise and dignity. We're not a monarchy, but in his splendid golden robes, he looks the part of a king.

I should feel proud. Instead, I resent it and him.

I wish Sef were here. She would stand in the back and gossip with me. Give me her opinions on everyone's outfits, crack jokes, and make me feel less lonely. But she's completing a more important task right now, involving an illicit magical object and a vial of poison.

Footsteps plod in my direction as Kaidren approaches. "Remira." He speaks my name softly, as though awed.

He wears dove gray. A stunning shade against the warm tones of his skin. The small black mask around his eyes does nothing to hide who he is. Or disguise the way his gaze shamelessly rakes me up and down. His lips stretch into a smile that shows off all his teeth. Except it doesn't look like his usual campaign smile. There's a brightness to his eyes and an awkwardness to the slant of his mouth that makes this one feel genuine.

"You're exquisite," he says.

I fight a shudder. There's that word again. He said it to me before, in the library after the first trial. There's something different in the way he says it now. His tone is heavier, more reverent. He holds the word in his mouth, savoring it, before releasing it in a near whisper, for my ears only.

"Thank you." I stop myself before I say anything more and reveal how breathless I am from that single compliment.

"Did you get my present?"

"I did." I no longer sound breathy, but my throat is dry

from the way he stares at me, and my words sound more like a croak.

"And?" he presses.

I frown. "And what?"

Kaidren grins and extends a hand toward me. "Dance with me?"

I study his hand for longer than I should. We've been at each other's throats for weeks. I'm planning on blackmailing him later this very night. I shouldn't *want* to dance with him.

But I do.

I thought I despised the way his unpredictability has rattled my world; I thought I hated his ambition and the tricks he plays to get what he wants.

As it turns out, I *like* his games. I like taunting and plotting and tossing barbs back and forth until one of us slips. I like knowing that beneath his cool exterior lies a vicious, ruthless creature. I've craved power my whole life. Kaidren aims to strip me of mine and take it for himself. For some reason, that struggle—his thirst for the one thing I want above all else—is more alluring than pretty smiles and sweet words.

"I don't think I like sweet at all."

I'm starting to realize I don't either.

When I don't move, Kaidren arches an eyebrow, never lowering his hand, nor his intense gaze.

My hands might be covered, but gloves will do nothing to guard me from his lips, which are too tempting for their own good, and just as conniving as the rest of him.

I break eye contact. "I don't dance."

Kaidren's forehead furrows, and he lowers his hand. "We don't have to talk about the Tournament."

"I can't think of anything else we have to talk about."

"Remira—"

Flynn Sixmen approaches before he can finish the thought. "Mira, you're looking especially lovely tonight. Dance with me?"

"Don't waste your time, Sixmen," says Kaidren. "Mira doesn't dance."

Flynn's just given me the escape I need. From Kaidren and the way he holds my stare, calls me "exquisite," and, worst of all, means it.

I shoot Kaidren a saccharine smile over Flynn's shoulder. "With you."

Confusion clouds his expression. "What?"

"I left off the end of that sentence. I don't dance . . . with you." I turn my undivided attention to Flynn and take his arm. "I'd love to dance with *you*, Honorate Sixmen."

Flynn looks surprised but pleased as he guides me onto the dance floor. He places his hands in the correct position and smiles. "You seem nervous."

Do I? I was hoping I was hiding it. "I don't dance very often."

He chuckles. "That's not true. Your mother is always hosting parties."

"She's not my mother," I say frostily.

"Of course. Sorry." We fall into tense silence for a few beats. "So . . ." Flynn drags out the word with a sly grin. "What's going on between you and Vale?"

"What do you mean?"

"Ah. I see we're pretending neither of us noticed the way he was looking at you. Sorry. It would help if you told me in advance that we're playing make-believe."

"There's nothing going on, and he wasn't looking at me any sort of way."

"Sure, Mira. Whatever you say."

I purse my lips, hoping it'll mask my embarrassment. From the corner of my eye, I see another girl approach Kaidren.

There are nerves rolling off her, leaving little doubt she intends to ask him to dance.

Kaidren looks visibly uncomfortable. So much so, I expect he's going to refuse. But with a swift glance in my direction (I turn my head as if I'm not looking), a smile stretches across his face and he holds out an arm for the girl.

I wonder if anyone else can see how distinctly fake it is.

I try to ignore them as they dance and focus my attention on Flynn. He's always been easy to talk to and kind to me. He's the only member of the Honorate who's ever treated me with any sort of respect.

Except Kaidren...

I shoo that annoying voice away.

My eyes won't stop wandering over Flynn's shoulder to watch Kaidren. It doesn't help that each time I look, I find his probing stare already fixed on me.

I decide it's safer to look at my shoes.

"You're doing great, Mira," Flynn says encouragingly.

I can't help laughing. "You're being polite."

"No, I—" He stops. "*Dammit.*"

"What?" I look up from my feet.

A figure stumbles through the crowded ballroom. His hair has gotten longer since I last saw him. He's always been well groomed, but today, his gray-specked beard is overgrown and unkempt, and the hair on his head is greasy and knotted. His walk is a stagger, and he shoves anyone who doesn't move out of his way fast enough. He's not even dressed for the occasion. If you told me he stumbled out of bed, fell into a vat of ale, and then made his way here immediately after, I'd believe it.

Selva Sixmen.

An Honorate approaches him. "Selva, what are you doing here?"

A circle clears around Selva. No one wants to get too close.

"What am *I* doing?" Sixmen slurs his words so much, it sounds as though he's trying to speak while drowning. "What are *you* doing? Where were you when I left the Honorate? Where were any of you?" His voice rises to a gruff roar. "You're a coward—a puppet for the Shadow Queen, just like everyone else."

Flynn groans. Since the rest of the ballroom has fallen quiet with discomfort, the sound carries.

Selva's dulled eyes find us. His countenance shifts. His jaw tightens, and he lurches. Partygoers flee, clearing out a path for him to stumble through. "Flynn." Selva points a shaky finger at his son. "My own flesh and blood did this to me."

Flynn sighs. "Dad, I told you to stay home."

"You don't tell me what to do." Spit flies from Selva's mouth and lands on me. "You did this. You conspired with the Shadow Bitch to take my place."

Flynn gawks at his father. "You sound insane."

Selva finally notices me. His wild eyes flash with fury. "Everyone let me get thrown out of the Honorate, but they're fine with an *Opheran* being here?"

Flynn pushes me gently behind him, placing himself between me and his father. "Leave her out of this. You stepped down voluntarily. You need to go home and calm down. Sleep it off."

Selva lunges around Flynn and snatches my arm.

I shriek and try to wrench myself away. Even with alcohol dulling his senses, Selva's grip is strong. "Get your hands off me." My tone is frosty in an attempt to mask how much he's scaring me.

Selva ignores me. His other hand grabs my chin and twists, forcing me to look into his bloodshot, hazy eyes. "If I have to leave, I'm taking her with me. Opherans have no more of a right to be here than I do." His breath is hot and rank. I almost gag from the stench of it.

"Let go of her." This voice is eerily calm. Kaidren steps from the crowd around us, expression darker than I've ever seen it. He's teeming with a quiet, controlled rage.

Selva scowls and doesn't release me. "More Opherans. They're taking over."

"Does the fact that I'm Opheran scare you, Selva?" Kaidren calmly enters the circle, until he's right next to Selva, towering over him. "If you don't take your hands off her, I will show you firsthand that you're right to fear me."

"You shouldn't even be here. You, an Honorate, and I'm not? Absurd."

"Remove your hand." Kaidren doesn't respond to anything Selva says.

With a drunken roar, Selva rears back to punch Kaidren.

Kaidren steps aside, but Selva doesn't let up. He releases me, trying to hit Kaidren again. This time, when he snaps back his arm, his elbow strikes me. It slams into my nose, knocking the wind from my lungs.

I teeter in place, stars dancing in my mind's eye. The last thing I see before I crash to the floor is Kaidren punching Selva Sixmen right in the jaw.

CHAPTER THIRTY-FOUR

SWEET AFTER ALL

My vision blurs. My hands cup my aching nose. Red lace gloves instantly become sticky, coated in blood, as scarlet as my mask.

"Mira."

Everything is hazy. Flynn is shoving his father back and calling my name.

I see it happen, but it's as though everyone around me is moving through honey.

"*Remira.*" Through the fog of my mind, Kaidren kneels before me. "Are you all right?"

"I'm fine." Blood spurts from my nose, making speaking difficult.

"Let me—" Kaidren reaches to touch me, and the world sharpens.

His hands are bare.

Panicked, I jerk back. "I'm fine." My addled brain is working now. I'm in the middle of the dance floor, surrounded by people who are all staring at me. Flynn has shoved his father away, and a few other Honorate are guiding him out as he flails belligerently.

Flynn comes to my side, hand outstretched. "Mira, are you—"

"I'm *fine*," I repeat for a third time. I seize his hand and haul myself up. Keeping my hands pressed to my face, I rush out of the room. Whispers follow me. Someone calls my name. I don't turn to see who.

I flee into the nearest washroom, breaths shallow as I slam the door behind me. My bloody gloves stain the wood red, so I peel them off.

Before I can bolt the door, it crashes open. I stagger back as Kaidren swoops into the room. His deep eyes are agitated as they look me over. "That's a lot of blood."

Did he come here to check on me?

I'm surprised and more flattered than I should be. My gloves are already ruined, so I use them as handkerchiefs and pack them against my bleeding nose. "It looks worse than it is." My words are muffled and nasally. "Go back to the ball."

He acts as though I haven't spoken. "Tilt your head back."

I'm confused, until I reluctantly do as he says—just to shut him up—and feel immediate release. My nose is still throbbing, but with less burning pressure, it's easier to breathe.

"Better?" he murmurs.

"You don't have to stay."

"If you think for one second I'm going to leave you here, you've lost your mind. Now, stop trying to get rid of me and tell me if you're feeling better."

"Much." I cast a glance around the washroom. "Can you bolt the door?" I doubt anyone will enter, but it will at least put some distance between us.

It works for about two seconds. He locks the door and immediately returns to my side. I keep my head tilted but press as far away from him as I can in this small space.

"This might work better than your gloves." Kaidren raises a wad of gray fabric to my face.

"I can do it." Clumsily, I snatch it and hold it to my nose myself. It's only after the light gray material is drenched in my blood that I realize he's given me his shirt, and is now wearing his jacket over his bare torso.

"I'm sorry," I mumble. "It's ruined."

He chuckles. "It's a shirt. I'll live. How are you?"

"Fine." I close my eyes, head still tipped back. "I just need a minute."

"Of course."

For two minutes, we don't speak. I lower the shirt and cautiously tip my head to its normal position. There's a faint dribble of red that I wipe away, but for the most part, the bleeding's stopped.

"Thank you." I ball up the bloody shirt and do my best to look anywhere but at him. With his unbuttoned jacket, bare chest, and bloodied knuckles, he looks a bit wild. And undeniably attractive.

My throat is dry as I force my gaze away from his exposed torso. "Why are you here?"

He looks confused. "You were bleeding."

"So?"

"*So?*" he repeats incredulously. "So, I was worried about you. So, I wanted to make sure you were all right. You think I want to see you hurt?"

I use his shirt to wipe off the excess traces of blood around my nose. And to cling to an excuse to look away from him. "I think up until a few days ago, I was pretty sure you hated me."

Kaidren chuckles lowly. He ducks his head to catch my eyeline with his. "I still might. I'm not sure I know what hatred means anymore." He takes a small step forward, lowers his voice. "I've come to hate a lot of things since I met you." Another step. "I hate your brother because, somehow, he doesn't see you. I hate your father, because you are the most formidable person I've ever known, but he makes you feel small. I hate Selva Sixmen for putting his hands on you. And I *hate* that you danced with Flynn and not me."

Kaidren advances steadily. Each declaration narrows the distance between us until I'm trapped against the basin and he's standing between my knees. "I hate myself, because I can't get you out of my head." He rests one hand on the basin behind me. The other on my waist. "And *you* . . ." The thumb on my side draws slow circles in the velvet. "Maybe I hate you too. You are *infuriating*. You are vicious, remorseless, and maddeningly stubborn. You make me feel as if I'm losing my mind. If I could think clearly, I might hate you for it, but now—now I don't know why I'd want to be sane if it meant I couldn't have you."

My heart hammers away as though it's being chased. Maybe it is. Maybe it's trying to flee from Kaidren, who means to capture it as his own.

My body is frozen still. Held captive by the searing heat and raw honesty of his brown eyes.

Kaidren stares at me like he's searching for something. I have no idea what for, but he must find it, because the next instant, his lips are soft on mine.

I've never been kissed. I immediately see the appeal. At least, when the person kissing you is Kaidren Vale. His lips are gentle, yet urgent. They move against mine with a slow tenderness that makes my toes curl.

My hands move of their own accord, grabbing hold of the front of his unbuttoned jacket and drawing him closer.

Warmth pools in my stomach and seeps through the rest of me, thawing a secret place in my chest I tried like hell to keep frozen.

Magic. A different kind of magic than what I'm used to. Magic . . .

Too late, I remember myself. Too late, I yank away.

The warm glow of the kiss is gone, replaced with horror. Kaiden's eyes open, dazed. Then they widen with shock.

Fear and panic fuse together, twisting my insides. From the moment we met, I've avoided Kaidren's touch. I've pulled away, worn gloves, and evaded him like a coward.

Months of caution, rendered useless in a matter of seconds.

Kaidren finds his voice first. "You're—" He flits through a thousand revelations, each plainly visible on his face. "Stars in hell, Remira. You're the Shadow Queen."

CHAPTER THIRTY-FIVE

GIRL OF NO REGRETS

I stumble into the ballroom, dazed.

I'm ruined.

With one kiss, Kaidren wrecked my plans and gained all the ammunition he needs to destroy me.

I feel as if I'm spinning on a sheet of ice. Before, it made me feel powerful. I spun on a screen of tshira, above the most powerful men in the Republic. I was in control. Spinning above it all.

Now I'm frantic. My house of lies, five years in the making, teeters on a pane of glass. And it's cracking. I'm spinning like always, but it no longer makes me feel in control. It only makes me dizzy.

"Remira." Kaidren catches my arm, out of breath. "Please. Let's talk."

I rip my arm free and keep walking. "If you tell anyone, I'll deny it. Everyone already knows you're a liar."

"Would you stop moving and *listen* to me?" He sounds exasperated. "I'm not going to tell anyone. I swear. And you know I mean that."

He's right. I'm still burning, both from fear and from the memory of his lips on mine, but that magical part of my soul remains cold.

I keep walking, refusing to look at him. "Walk away, Vale."

He doesn't. Instead, he takes me by the hand and drags me behind a column, hidden from the rest of the ballroom. He spins me to face him, one hand on my lower back to keep me in place. "Mira, listen: I am not going to breathe a word. To anyone. I'm telling the truth, aren't I?"

I was already struggling to catch my breath, but it's even harder now that he's so close and his fingertips are a hairsbreadth away from the bare skin at my back. I clear my throat. "Yes."

Kaidren breathes a relieved sigh. "Then there's no problem." He tucks a braid that's fallen loose behind my ear, smiling softly. "I believe we were in the middle of a conversation."

"We weren't talking."

"Then let's not talk." His head ducks and for a moment, I think he's going to kiss me again. Instead, he places his lips near my neck. "Dance with me. Please. I've been wanting to dance with you all night."

I'd be lying if I said I wasn't tempted. Part of me yearns for what he's offering. *That* Mira wants to lean into his touch, smile, and allow herself to be swept away by the first boy who's made her feel like she matters.

But there's another Mira. The reasonable skeptic who has watched this exact scene play out more than once. How many times did I witness my mother do this? Give up what little authority she had in exchange for a charming smile and false promises.

She was the only person who mattered to me, but Aja was pathetic. She threw her heart around. Let herself fall for the wrong person, again and again. She never learned. The same mistake a thousand times over, and all she had to show for it was me. A kid she never asked for, a mouth she couldn't feed.

Kaidren says he won't tell anyone, and right now, he means it. But people change their minds every day.

I think about Luc. All the promises he's made me. He told me he loved me, and he meant it. He swore to keep me safe, and he meant it. Whenever the time came to deliver on his promises, he failed. Every. Single. Time.

I think about my mother.

"This one's different, Mira. He's going to change everything for us. You'll see."

She really believed them. No matter how often she was cast aside and forgotten. No matter how many times she knelt in front of our empty fireplace, sobbing.

Aja was my whole world, but I've always known if I want to survive—if I want more for myself—I can't afford to be anything like her.

I fix my hardened gaze on Kaidren and push his hand aside. "I don't want to dance. I don't want to talk. I want you to leave me alone."

It's a good thing he can't tell when I'm lying. At least, that's what I tell myself as I keep my head high and march away. This time, he doesn't follow.

Steel and ice. There's a wall around my frozen heart, and I know what I have to do.

It takes me a few minutes to find Sef, but the moment she sees me, she rushes to my side. "I've been looking everywhere for you. Where have you been?" Her worried eyes stop on my swollen nose. "Are you all right? What happened to your face?"

"Selva Sixmen. It was an accident, and it doesn't matter. Did you do what we discussed?"

Sef is still staring at my nose. "Yes."

"Good, because our 'just in case' plan is now the *only* plan."

Sef finally meets my eyes, startled. "You mean you want me to . . . ?"

"Yes."

She nods, but her expression is wary. "All right . . . but I thought you wanted to try blackmail first before going to extremes?"

"Things changed." I want to tell her why. But admitting that Kaidren kissed me means confessing to the way he's been making me feel, and I can't do that without feeling like a star-headed fool. "Convincing him is going to be more complicated than I thought. We'll have to force his hand. If everything's ready, do it. Now."

As a child, I promised myself I'd make it out of Ophera. More recently, I made myself another promise: to steal the throne I win for Luc.

Unlike every other liar in my life, I refuse to revert on my word. People like me aren't given what we want. We have to steal it.

CHAPTER THIRTY-SIX

SNOWFALL

My face is a bloody mess and my nose is swollen, but I put my mask back on anyway and return to my hiding spot on the edge of the ballroom.

The chandelier above the dance floor is anchored to the ceiling with a series of cables bracketed to the wall on the second floor. Ordinarily, there are five cables holding up the chandelier. Tonight, there are six. The sixth isn't to keep it up, but to support a small addition I made while decorating earlier this evening.

The band pauses in between songs. When they start up again, the melody is softer. Perfect for slow dancing.

Couples flock to the center of the room. Unbidden, my eyes find Kaidren in the crowd. He stands alone in a sea of pairs. He's buttoned up his suit jacket. There's a sliver of bare chest still visible, but he looks covered unless you're looking intently—which I am. His head is twisting, craning, looking for— He stops as our eyes meet.

He was looking for me.

My heartbeat picks up as he stalks purposely across the dance floor in my direction.

I know the exact moment Sef cuts the cord.

It starts snowing, right here in the ballroom of Widow's

Hall. Sheets of parchment, dyed pale blue and white to match the colored glass in the chandelier, drift through the air.

Dancing stops. Kaidren stops. His head tilts up as the parchment flutters down, down, down. The entire ballroom appears frozen, staring at the snowfall, transfixed.

As for me, I watch Kaidren. A sense of foreboding and possibly regret pools in my stomach.

As soon as the slowly sinking parchment is within arm's reach, party attendees swoop, snatching them up.

Over the years, I've penned many columns for the Shadow Queen. This one was simple in nature. Scathing, biting, cruel—designed to wreck the reputation of its subject.

I watch as Kaidren plucks one from the air. Watch as his eyes scan the parchment.

His entire body tenses. It looks as though he stops breathing.

Almost as one, all eyes in the ballroom snap to Kaidren. They latch on to him, staring in a combination of confusion, doubt, and horror.

Kaidren ignores them. His head jerks up, and he stares directly at me. The shock of his expression is to be expected. The *hurt* marring his features . . . it affects me more than it should.

I agonized over writing this most recent column for so long, I don't need to reach for a sheet of parchment to know what it says.

> People of the glorious Republic of Virdei,
> There's a villain among you tonight. A silverwolf wearing the mask of a lamb. Someone who has spent years collecting trinkets in a vain attempt to force extraordinary magic into an ordinary man.

> *When that did not work, he made false claims of being an isha.*
>
> *The thief in question is, of course, Bastard Kaidren Vale.*
>
> *Unfortunately, Bastard Vale is not merely a thief and a fraud. He is also a killer.*
>
> *With no acclaim of his own, Bastard Vale stole that of his father's—by murdering him.*
>
> *He wanted magic, so he tried to force it.*
>
> *He wanted power, so he killed to steal it.*
>
> *Doubt me? Check his room in the Vale household. He is indeed so arrogant, he did not even bother to dispose of the very poison he slipped into his father's final meal.*
>
> *Fondly,*
> *Shadow Queen*

The silence in the ballroom is chilling. Everyone stares at Kaidren, who stares at me.

He could hurl accusations now. Announce to the world that I'm the Shadow Queen herself. But no one would believe him. I've just ensured that.

The crowd parts as the General of the decurio makes his way to Kaidren. It's only when General Fain is directly in front of him that Kaidren finally looks away from me. His expression is angry, sad, and resigned, all at once.

"These are serious charges, Honorate Vale. I take them seriously."

"I understand," Kaidren says softly.

"We will need to search your home at once. You can give your consent and make this simple. Or you can fight us and make it difficult. Either way, we *will* search. Whether we use a key or tear down the front door is entirely up to you."

"Do what you must." Kaidren's eyes shift around General

Fain to find mine again. He raises his voice. He wants to be sure I hear his next words: "Let me be clear, however. Whatever you find—I didn't kill my father."

I'm frozen solid.

Guilt sinks through my chest. I framed the wrong person.

CHAPTER THIRTY-SEVEN

INK-STAINED LIES

The Vale household is in shambles. Decurio peel through furniture, flip over tables, and rip paintings from walls.

This is my fault, so part of me wants to tell them they don't have to destroy the house; they just need to look under the bed in Kaidren's room. Of course, I can't tell them this, because then I'd have to explain that I planted it for them to find. Or rather, that I had Sef do it, right at the start of the ball, so we could be certain Kaidren wouldn't find and dispose of the evidence ahead of time.

So, I say nothing. Just keep my head down and wait with Luc in the entryway.

"Sir." A decurio rushes down the stairs. "We found something in Honorate Vale's room." He holds two things: a vial of poison and a rusted silver compass.

Kaidren's eyes shoot to me. He knew to expect the poison, but I think he's surprised by the compass. He must recognize it—it's identical to his aunt Jules's. So similar, he likely assumes it's the same one.

Kaidren might've planned to deny the poison was his, but he'll be reluctant to contest the compass—he won't want them to dig into his aunt and cause any penalty to her.

Luc catches the look Kaidren sends my way. His brows draw. "What did you do, Mira?" he murmurs lowly, so no one overhears.

"What I promised your parents." I can't keep the venom from lacing my words. "I ensured your victory. Congratulations on a second term, Praeceptor Kyler."

Luc's eyes widen, and he looks at me as though he's never seen me before.

"I hate your brother because he doesn't see you."

Maybe Luc never has.

General Fain is clearly agitated. "You claim you're innocent, Honorate Vale, but this is kishori—the same poison used to kill your father. And this false magical object is outlawed. If you're innocent, how did these come to be in your possession? And how—"

"I'm not denying it." Kaidren speaks woodenly as he interrupts the General. "Those are mine."

"You admit to poisoning your own father?"

Kaidren wavers. "I admit the poison and contraband are mine. Do with that information whatever you will."

The General motions to the decurio around him. "Then, Honorate Vale, I have no choice but to put you under arrest for the murder of your father."

I thought this would make me feel in control again, but by the time I return to my chamber, all I am is tired and consumed by prickly, persistent guilt.

Why the hell did he have kishori hidden under his bed if he didn't poison his father? I don't know. Guess I never will. Can't imagine he'll be inclined to explain himself to me after this.

I kick off my shoes with a groan. All I want is to fall into bed and hunt for sleep, but I'm laced into a ball gown and my hair is extravagantly done. I should at the very least wrap up my hair for the night.

I sit at my vanity and start to remove the sparrow hair clips when I'm interrupted by a sharp knock.

I thought I was done being shocked tonight, but when I open the door, General Fain, four members of the decurio, and Luc stand before me.

"Remira Kyler," General Fain says sternly.

My eyes flit over his shoulder, meeting Luc's gaze. *What the hell is going on?* I try to silently communicate my question with my eyes, but all I get from him is blind panic. Which isn't helpful.

I force a smile at General Fain. "Is something wrong?"

"This was waiting for me when I returned to my office." He holds up a letter. His name is scrawled across the envelope in indigo ink. It's from my imposter.

My stomach drops. "What does it say?"

"It's from the Shadow Queen. She accuses you of colluding with Kaidren Vale in murdering his father and conspiring to put Kaidren on the throne."

It's as if all the air has been knocked from my lungs and my legs are bolted to the floor. I can't breathe, can't move, can't force the cogs of my brain to come up with a coherent response. At long last, my brilliant reply is "What?"

"The Shadow Queen is accusing you of aiding the murder of Arliss Vale. According to her, we'll find the poison used to kill Arliss Vale in this room."

"You just found that in Kaidren Vale's room."

"This letter claims there was a second vial."

Someone is framing me—the same someone who killed Arliss and blackmailed Selva. Someone who *isn't* Kaidren. I have no doubt the decurio will find what they're looking for. "I didn't kill anyone."

"Murder or not, kishori is a poison. Simply having it in

your possession is a crime. If you're innocent, surely we can search your room to verify?"

There's no use protesting. I move aside and let them look. My room is too small for all of them, so the General searches alone, while the others wait in the hall, watching me as I try not to let my nerves show.

It's a quick search. He finds a vial of kishori beneath my mattress. It's almost comical. It's exactly where I had Sef hide the poison in Kaidren's room.

I try to look shocked.

"Remira, can you explain this?" General Fain asks.

"Someone must've planted it." It's a paltry defense and I know it.

Luc puts a hand on my shoulder. "General, with all due respect, this is absurd. My sister didn't kill anyone. Mira, just tell them where you were when Arliss was killed. If we confirm what she was doing, she's no longer a suspect, right?"

Reluctantly, General Fain nods. "Yes, sir. We determined that whoever poisoned Honorate Vale did so the night of the opening ceremony for the Tournament of Thrones. Where were you that night, Remira?"

I sift through my memory, to the night before I visited the Vale household and found him dead. That night, I . . .

Oh no.

I remember exactly where I was that night—but it's not something I can share.

I swallow. "Um—I'm not sure." A weak excuse. It's better than the truth.

General Fain addresses Luc. "Honored Praeceptor, did you see her that night?"

Luc opens his mouth to answer, but stops himself, frowning.

"Sir?" the General prompts.

Luc blinks slowly at General Fain, then at me. "Clear the room."

The soldiers give Luc identical looks of shock. Allowing him to speak privately with a suspect in the middle of an investigation goes against every protocol, but no one wants to defy the Praeceptor. With swift glances at one another, they obediently retreat into the hall.

Luc drops his voice once we're alone. "I remember that night. You told me you wanted to be alone. I came to your room with a snack later, but you weren't here."

"Maybe I was in the library," I say.

"You weren't. You weren't in the dining room either. I checked. And Sef left early that night."

Luc and Sef are the only people who would be willing to lie for me and say I was here, in Widow's Hall, the night of the murder. But Luc has selectmen with him at all times. They know he wasn't with me. And there are at least ten members of the staff who will attest they saw Sef leave—she always makes the rounds, saying her goodbyes before heading home.

Fear clogs my throat. I say nothing.

"Mira, I know you. You're not a killer."

"You're right. I'm not."

"Then tell me where you were. I'm trying to protect you. I can't do that if I don't know what I'm protecting you from."

I shake my head. "I can't."

"You can't tell *me*?" Luc's eyes shine with hurt. "I'm your brother. We tell each other everything."

Not everything. I purse my lips.

"What happened to 'every lie I'll ever tell'? Or was that just for me? I trust you without reservation, and you keep something from me?"

"You wouldn't understand."

"What secret could be so bad that not even I would understand? If this is something to do with the Shadow Queen—"

"It isn't."

He waits for me to say more. I don't.

Slowly, he shakes his head. "I can't lie for you. My guards know I wasn't with you that night. Surely, you wouldn't risk going to prison just to avoid telling me the truth?"

"The only truth that matters is I didn't kill Arliss Vale."

Luc looks so, so hurt. "I want to believe you, but I don't have your gift. If you don't give me something, they're going to arrest you."

"I know."

"I can't protect you from this, Mira."

It's not like he ever has anyway. "I know that too."

Luc's shoulders sag, and his expression is weary as he reopens the door.

General Fain looks first to Luc. "Sir? Has she revealed where she was on the night in question?"

Luc gives me a last, desperate look. Silently pleading with me to confide in him.

I have to look away. This is a truth he would never understand.

With a resigned sigh, Luc ducks his head. I think he's holding in tears. "No."

The world moves in slow motion as a decurio secures my arms behind my back with rope. "Remira Kyler, you are under arrest for the murder of Honorate Arliss Vale."

CHAPTER THIRTY-EIGHT

LESSONS ON REVENGE

The dungeons are darker and colder than I remember. Probably because it's my first time here as a prisoner. And probably because my cell is across from Kaidren Vale's.

He stands against the far wall of his cell, expression shifting between surprise and anger as the decurio lock me in. "What are *you* doing here?" He settles on anger. "Gloating?"

"Pretty sure gloating would be more effective from the other side of the bars," I say.

The soldier who locked my cell walks away, and Kaidren's brows rise as he realizes I'm as stuck in here as he is. "You were arrested? What for? Being a compulsive liar?"

"For helping you kill your father, actually."

His dark chuckle lacks humor. "It's rare to see irony strike so quickly."

He has every right to lash out at me, but I'm angry too. Getting arrested wasn't part of my plans for tonight. Neither was kissing the enemy or wrecking my brother's trust in me. Everything is spinning out of control, especially my emotions. "I found the same poison that killed Arliss in your room, and you freely admit you despised him. How was I to know I was framing you?"

"I didn't kill him."

"Not hearing you deny the poison was yours," I say.

Kaidren glowers at the floor. "I don't have to explain myself to you."

"You do if you want any hope of getting out of here."

He raises the force of his glare from the floor to me. There's so much fury swirling in his eyes, I take a half step back. "You think I want *your* help? Are you serious? I already tried reasoning with you. You threw it in my face. Now isn't the time to talk. That was hours ago, when I begged you to listen to me, and what did you do? Oh, right. *You framed me for murder.*"

"I didn't know I was framing you."

His expression twists into a sneer. "As if that would've changed anything. You wanted to get rid of me, so you did. Congratulations. I hope sitting across from me in prison is worth it."

"I have no intention of staying here. If we help each other—"

Kaidren cuts me off by throwing his head back and cackling. "You're joking."

"Rarely," I say flatly. "Come on. Wouldn't you rather hate me from outside prison? You want to get out of here, I want to clear my name. We can escape together, find Arliss's real killer, and both of us get what we want."

Kaidren purses his lips, considering. "No."

My jaw drops. "*No?*"

"That's what I said. In the past hour, I've resigned myself to sitting in here for a while. Now that you've joined me, I'd rather both of us rot in here than give you anything."

I fold my arms, trying to convey more confidence than I feel. "You know, I can just get myself out of here and leave you behind." It's an empty threat, and we both know it.

He shrugs, immediately calling my bluff. "Go ahead. I'm guessing your escape plan involves magic? I might be a liar, but the decurio will probably be more inclined to believe me if you disappear from a locked cell without a trace."

I hold in a groan. "You must have a price. What do you want?"

"Apologize." He says it instantly, as though he was just waiting for me to ask.

I want to object, but we need to get out of here, and—all right, *fine*—maybe I do owe him an apology. "I'm sorry for framing you," I say. "Really. Let me make it up to you by getting us out of here."

He studies my expression, searching for a hint of insincerity. He must not find one, because he sighs, looking more exhausted than angry. "Fine. Apology accepted. How do you plan to break us out of here?"

Escaping is the easy part. Aikkari are typically kept in separate cells from the rest of the public—tshira prisons are great for people without magic but useless for an aikkari with access to their source. The decurio don't know I'm aikkari, so Kaidren and I are in cells with tshira walls. "With magic. But before that, I need all the facts. Tell me everything you know about your father."

Kaidren looks doubtful. "We're on a mountain. We can't just leave—we need a place to go, and both our homes are out of the question."

"I've got that handled. Once we're out of here, I know the perfect place we can go where no one will find us."

"You expect me to trust you, after everything?"

"You definitely shouldn't trust me," I say. "Tell me about the poison. If you didn't kill Arliss, why did you have kishori?"

Kaidren's lips twist into a smirk. "I'm disappointed you haven't already worked that out. I didn't kill my father, but I've been poisoning him for two years."

Arliss first fell ill two years ago. No one knew what caused it, but suddenly, he was too sickly to attend Honorate meetings, and he was headed swiftly for death. My eyes widen with realization. "You're the reason he got sick."

"Like you said, I despised him."

"But not enough to kill him."

"Enough to know a quick, painless death was too easy. He cost my mother her life, and he didn't even care. I kept track of everything he ever did, read every Shadow Queen column that mentioned him. He had power and status people would kill for—and all he ever did was bed women and abuse his position for his own gain."

"You poisoned him to punish him?"

"Yes." Kaidren starts to pace, considering his own words. "Maybe. Part of it was to punish him, but mostly, I just wanted to force him to finally see me."

Arliss knew he had a child, and rather than acknowledge it, he fired Kaidren's mother, ensured she would never find employment in Virdei again, and ignored his son for years. Why shouldn't he have? Kaidren is Opheran, and as far as Arliss knew, he had the rest of his life to sire an heir he wasn't ashamed of.

He was a powerful man who valued legacy above all else. When someone like that thinks he's dying and has lost the chance to father more heirs, he becomes desperate. Desperate enough to seek out the bastard son he spent years pretending didn't exist.

"I spent every coin I had on kishori," Kaidren says. "A few times each week, I snuck into his house and slipped it into his food. Small doses. Never enough to kill. The same week I heard the news that the great Arliss Vale didn't attend the latest Honorate meeting, I received a summons to the Vale manor. He was sick in bed when I arrived. He looked so weak and fragile—and for the first time, he called me his son."

Finished with his story, Kaidren stops pacing and looks at me. His feet are hip width apart, his stance is self-assured, but there's a question in the quirk of his brow. He's wondering if I'm disgusted by his admission.

I probably should be. He just confessed to poisoning his own father, and all I can think is that I've never been more drawn to him.

"Was it worth it?" I ask.

"I planned to poison him for the rest of his life. Just enough so that he'd live on, sick and bedridden for years. And then I'd sit at his side on his dying day, and hold his hand while I told him what I'd done. Unfortunately, someone else killed him before I got the chance. My only regret is never getting to see the look in his eyes when I told him I was the reason he fell ill. The reason he never had a Virdeian son."

Cold words that inexplicably make me warm inside. Not because he's lying—he's *vicious* with his honesty—but because there must be something seriously wrong with me.

"Does that scare you?" Kaidren mistakes my silence for fear.

Slowly, I shake my head. "I'm not sure what it says about me that it doesn't."

"Probably the same thing it says about me." He comes to the front of the cell. "Now, I've told you everything. How are we getting out of here?"

"We're going to walk out. These"—I knock against the wall of the cell—"are made of tshira. All I need is a lie. I'll get a guard's attention, get him to lie about something, and—"

"I have a better idea." Kaidren gazes at me from between bars. His jaw is clenched with residual anger, but when our eyes meet, it softens. A corner of his mouth lifts in an almost smile. "I regret kissing you."

Heat ignites in the pit of my stomach.

His gaze holds me captive. He gives me a smile. A tender, real one. "Did it work?"

I nod, trying to find my voice. I don't know how to respond, or if he even expects a response. I press my hands to my cell bars and push magic out. They look the same, but magic has shifted their form to something malleable and easy to move through. I slip through and take hold of the bars over Kaidren's cell.

"Walk through."

He looks doubtful but steps forward anyway. We're outside our cells, but still in the dungeons. Already, I feel the magic waning.

I guide him down the hall, away from the entrance. Kaidren frowns as he follows me. "Why are we going this way? The door is in the opposite direction."

"The door isn't the most direct way out of here," I say. We're underground. The cells are carved into the tshira that makes up the mountain. When we reach the end of the tunnel, I touch my hand to the wall.

Magic hums within me, warm and soothing. I push it out. The tshira shudders, transforming into something like a membrane.

I tug Kaidren to stand next to me. "Come on." I try to pull him with me. Even though he just walked through solid bars, at the sight of the wall, he plants his feet. "Not sure if you noticed, but there's a wall in the way."

I resist the urge to roll my eyes, reminding myself that not everyone is familiar or comfortable with magic. I shove a hand through the wall, showing him it's no longer solid. "We need to hurry. It doesn't last forever, and I'm not sure how long I can hold it like this."

Kaidren takes a breath and holds it as we step into the wall. Passing through permeable tshira is a strange sensation. Like trudging through slush after a snowstorm. It's icy, thick, and unpleasant.

We're both out of breath when we tumble out on the other side. It's difficult to breathe when walking through solid objects.

It's not snowing, but it's freezing, and neither of us is dressed for it. We're still wearing our clothes from the masquerade—which means there's nothing to cover my shoulders, most of my back is bare, and Kaidren still wears his gray suit, sans shirt.

I hug myself, rubbing warmth into my arms, prickling with goose bumps. Kaidren slings an arm over my shoulder, huddling me against him for warmth. "We need to stop at your house. Quickly." I'm shivering so hard, it's difficult to speak as we shuffle forward. "We'll need food and warmer clothes to survive the night."

"Is that a good idea?" Despite his objections, Kaidren allows me to steer us toward the Vale manor. "That's the first place they'll look."

"They don't know we're missing yet. Soldiers patrol the dungeons, but their rotation is irregular overnight." A tidbit of information I picked up from my time with Flynn. "We have at least an hour and a half before anyone patrols our corner of the dungeons and finds us missing. We'll be long gone by then."

"Gone where? You never told me where we're going."

I tighten my arms around myself. "Back to Ophera."

CHAPTER THIRTY-NINE

THIEVES IN THE NIGHT

With the intricate laces up the back, it would've wasted more time and effort than it was worth to get me out of my ball gown, so I leave it on. I've blanketed it in a coat, cloak, and heavy sjaal from the Vale manor, and thrown an additional sweater and pants in a bag to change into when we reach our destination for the night.

Kaidren and I keep our heads ducked as we clamber into the sky cart. This time of night, there are only two that are operational, and this one's attendant is Tallus. Fortunately, he's rarely interested in making conversation.

True to form, he stands on one side of the cart, while Kaidren and I sit on the opposite end.

For most of the ride, we don't speak. I wait until we're about five minutes from the base of the mountain to spark up a conversation with Tallus. Over the years, I've come to learn his habits. I know exactly what I need to say to coax magic out of him. "Do you like working the sky cart?" I ask.

Kaidren frowns at me, no doubt confused why I'm choosing now to speak, after an hour of silence.

Tallus looks uneasy. "Yes. It's a great way to see the mountain."

I'm still cold. He means what he just said. Which I already

know—after all, we've had this conversation before. I nod as though this is new information. "Do you have family?"

"Yes, ma'am."

"What do they think of your job?"

His tone is gentler as he speaks of them. "They love it. They're jealous I get to see this view every day."

"They've never seen it for themselves?"

Tallus tenses. He always does. "Um . . . no. Of course not. They don't work in Virdei, so we're not allowed to have them in the sky carts." The heat of his lie is welcome in the night chill. He's right that allowing his family to use the transportation up and down the mountain for recreation isn't allowed. But, of course, he's done it. Who wouldn't?

I nod as if I believe him. The heat of his lie soaks through me, and I grab hold of the tshira sparrow trinket on my bracelet, pulsing magic into it for safekeeping.

Tallus eyes me warily, trying to see whether I believe him. He's tense for the rest of the journey.

When we reach Ophera, I pull up my hood. "Thank you." I slip off a glove and touch my bare hand to my tshira talisman, pulling the magic.

Kaidren exits the cart first and holds out a hand to help me down, but I don't follow him right away. First, I give Tallus a few coins.

He perks up, pocketing them quickly. "Thank you, ma—"

My fingertips are on his forehead before he can finish.

Heat flows from me to him. His eyes flicker closed as I tug at his memories like loose thread, unraveling his recollection of the past hour until there's nothing left.

He collapses to the floor, unconscious.

I grab Kaidren's hand and flee, pulling him after me.

Kaidren's jaw is lost somewhere on the snow-covered ground as we sprint away. "What the hell was that?"

"Magic." We slow our pace when we're a safe distance from the cart.

"I've never seen that before." He's out of breath and staring at me in horror. "What did you do to him?"

"Don't worry. He's fine. He'll wake up in a few minutes. All I did was manipulate my source."

Kaidren looks even more confused. "Meaning what?"

"I altered his perception of the truth. He won't remember we were in his cart. When the decurio realize we're missing, they'll ask him if he took anyone fitting our descriptions down the mountain. Now he won't remember doing it."

Kaidren is still gawking at me. "How often do you do that?"

"Not often," I say vaguely. "It's less precise than my other magic. Manipulating heat and tshira is easy enough. Memories are more complicated."

Kaidren clearly has more questions, but a particularly strong gust of wind whistles past us, blowing snow into our faces. We shudder and bundle deeper into our cloaks.

The Opheran streets are dark, but I could trace the path to our destination with my eyes closed and fast asleep. Light from the beacons of Widow's Hall only stretches so far. In Ophera, there are lanterns atop wooden posts at intervals, but they're poorly maintained. Many have flicked out, making most of the streets eerie, with long, oddly shaped shadows dancing over the ground.

I shiver. Without needing to ask, Kaidren presses closer and drapes part of his sjaal over the both of us. We stay nestled together as we trudge through the snow.

"You still haven't said where we're going." Kaidren raises his voice to be heard over the harsh wind.

"It's just up ahead." There's no point keeping this from him. In a matter of minutes, he'll know the truth for himself, but I've never confided this secret to anyone—not Luc, not Sef—and I'm not sure I even know how to say it.

No matter how often I return, my heartbeat is always a painful stutter as I approach. Despite my bone-deep chill, my palms start sweating as soon as I see the familiar front door.

I raise a fist and knock.

There's a long pause. It's late and she's probably sleeping. I'm more nervous than impatient, but the seconds we wait feel like hours before the door finally opens.

She's shorter than me by about half a head. Her skin is dark like umber with a warm undertone, and her hair is black as the night sky. Even though she's small and clearly exhausted, her dark eyes are bright and full of life.

There was a time I'd have given anything—everything—to keep that spark alive.

So I did.

Kaidren looks between the two of us in confusion. It's hard to miss the similarities in our features. In the shapes of our faces, the curves of our jaws, the slopes of our noses.

I can practically see his brain piecing it together.

She looks surprised to see me. I tend to keep to a regular visitation schedule. Once a month, late at night (never *this* late), and I never bring guests.

"Mira?" She rubs her eyes blearily.

I smile. With it, I try to convey the weight of all the things I can never say. "Hello, Aja."

CHAPTER FORTY

THE SEVEN-YEAR LIE

I was a child when I lost my mother. At ten years old, I arrived on the Kylers' doorstep, sobbing about how my mother was dead and I was all alone.

The tears I shed were true.

The story I told was a lie.

Ajalique Selane smiles as she directs me and Kaidren into her home. Just as she does every month when I come to visit. Just as she did the night Arliss Vale was killed.

Her tired eyes are warm, and her smile is genuine, but there's no tenderness in her gaze when she looks at me. Not anymore. Not since I erased all memory of my existence from her mind. Not since I've returned to Ophera, month after month, to ensure those memories remain lost.

Aja hurries to the fireplace, desperate to give us warmth. Not because I'm the daughter she loves, but because I'm a wealthy guest and she thinks she's supposed to.

The first time I returned, I told her I was Remira Kyler, daughter of her former lover Mathson, here to bestow small gifts and tokens of his affection. She flushed and trilled when I arrived at her door with a basket of food and expensive winter clothes, courtesy of "Mathson." She didn't question it. Aja has a childish kind of hope that died when she had me. Without me, it's back.

I keep my wrist covered when I see her, so she never knows I was born in Ophera—in this house, in fact. With its scuffed wooden furniture, windows with bars, and sparrows inked onto the walls. They're the only decoration. Sparrows are Aja's favorite, so she took a jar of ink, and together we painted them onto every drafty wall to make it feel like home.

"Please don't," I say as she reaches for her sparse collection of firewood. "We're fine. Save it for the next snowstorm."

"If you're sure," she says hesitantly. She always does.

"I hope you don't mind that I'm here so late, and that I brought a . . ." I glance at Kaidren, unsure what to call him. "A friend. Would it be all right if we stayed for the night?"

Aja looks surprised, but not unhappy. "Of course." She tilts her head to one side. "Did something happen? Is Mathson all right?"

Kaidren bristles at the question but doesn't say anything. He's smart enough to bridle his curiosity for now. It infuriates me that Aja's first instinct is to ask about the piece of scum who hasn't thought twice about her since her supposed death. I give a thin smile. "He's fine. We just need a place to gather our bearings for a few days. And you don't have to worry about feeding us. We have food."

Aja looks relieved. "Perfect."

"I'm sorry I don't have any gifts for you this time."

She waves me off. "Don't worry about that. Your company is gift enough."

She means that. It fills me with a warmth that has nothing to do with magic.

There are only two rooms in this house: the main room and the bedroom. When I lived here, the bedroom was mine. My mother had a mattress she sometimes dragged before the fireplace at night. Most nights, when she was between men, we shared my bed, because it was warmer to huddle together and I used to get nightmares. She would sing lullabies into my ear to soothe me. On nights when my dreams were especially terrifying, we'd go outside and watch the stars. She'd make up stories about them. How they were watching us right back and protecting me, even in my sleep.

Tonight, Aja takes the bedroom and leaves Kaidren and me in the main room with a spare blanket. I refused her offer of firewood, so I do what I did as a child—use magic to heat the embers in the hearth.

For a few minutes, Kaidren and I sit in silence, soaking in the warmth, before he heaves a dramatic sigh. "That woman is your mother, isn't she?"

"Yes." It comes out softer than I intended.

Kaidren waits, expecting me to explain. When I don't, he nudges his shoulder into mine. "Are you going to make me ask? I thought your mother was dead."

I hug my knees to my chest, refusing to look away from the hearth. "She doesn't remember me."

"Seemed like she remembers you just fine."

I shake my head. "She thinks we met for the first time seven years ago. She has no idea I'm her daughter."

Kaidren stills. "You took her memories. Like the cart attendant."

My body feels heavy as I nod. "Yes."

"Why?"

It's a good question. I've never had to articulate the answer before.

When I was a child, my mother lied to me constantly. She told me we weren't hanging precariously over the edge of financial ruin, that she was *sure* we had enough food to survive to the next week, that the men who came and left didn't break her.

I could always tell when the stories she wove were crafted from smoke and dreams rather than truth. For her sake, I accepted them. I pretended to believe her with a smile on my increasingly gaunt face. Until she lied about eating.

It started when I was nine. She worked two jobs, but her hours were irregular, I was growing out of my clothes faster than she could keep up with, the costs of food and our home were ever rising, and it all combined into the simple fact that there wasn't enough. Not for both of us. So, she'd feed me and lie about feeding herself.

"Don't worry, Mira. I already ate," she'd say as she set a piece of stale bread in front of me. It was hardly a meal, but I didn't complain because the heat in my belly told me it was more than she'd eaten in days.

The lies kept coming—*"I ate before you woke up"*—and I watched her wither away. Her skin stretched tighter and tighter over her bones, and her dark, glossy hair lost its shine.

My heart was breaking, and I was *fuming*. The man who'd made me, and cost my mother her stable employment in Virdei, was cozy and fed at the top of the mountain.

We needed a miracle, and the best miracles came from magic. I started collecting tshira before I had a plan. Took bits of it from wherever I could. Stole it from the stalls of charlatans and siphoned it from sledges returning from the mines.

It took months, but honestly, I was surprised how easy it was. Even then, I was a girl made of shadows. No one looked at me twice as I took what I needed. Finding the lies to fill the tshira was even easier. My mother lied all the time, with cruel men who lied right back, and to me.

I gathered up all the deception in my life and stockpiled

magic in the tshira. Then I used it to rid myself of the only person in the world who loved me.

Losing her took every scrap of tshira and all my waning energy. As she slept, I held my small, trembling hands to her forehead and sobbed myself dry.

I didn't have to fake the tears I wept at the threshold to the Kyler manor when I told them my mother was gone. When I told the father I despised that I was alone, desperate, and devastated.

For that first year, I lived in constant fear Mathson would figure it out. I shouldn't have bothered. Opherans starve and freeze and die. It's our lot in life, and Mathson easily accepted that the same fate befell my mother. I think he only regretted that I was spared.

"Remira." Kaidren's voice rouses me from my thoughts. "Why?"

"She was dying." I sound hoarse. "We were out of food and money. She could only afford to feed me. Whenever she told me she'd already eaten, I knew she was lying. She would have died if I hadn't left."

"It's been seven years. Are you going to keep the truth from her for the rest of her life?"

I don't have an answer, so I don't give one.

He sighs. "That wasn't an attack. I'm genuinely asking. One true thing?"

It's the first time he's asked me that and expected an answer to a direct question.

My voice is pathetic and feeble as I say, "Do you know what it feels like to have unequivocal proof that the person you love most would be better off if you never existed?"

Kaidren's mouth falls open, horrified. "That's not true."

"It is." I tighten my arms around my knees. "Memory

magic isn't permanent. I come here every month to make sure she never remembers. Maybe I'm horrible, but the first time I returned, I thought—I don't know—that maybe she'd be miserable. That she'd feel there was something missing." My throat tightens, and my vision blurs with tears I refuse to shed. "She was *happy*. Happier than I'd seen her in years."

Every day for seven years, I've told myself it was worth it. Mathson and Yelina hate me, my brother treats me like a servant, and the mountain I used to dream of is crueler than I ever imagined. But it's all worth it if Aja finally has enough.

She doesn't know to love me anymore. Seeing her smile at me with kindness and not affection cleaves my heart in two, but it's worth it—it *has* to be—because once upon a time, I was loved by someone who wanted nothing from me. Even if she doesn't remember, I'll hold on to those memories tight enough for the both of us.

"I'm sorry." Kaidren squeezes my hand. "Truly. But you have to tell her."

I don't think I could handle it. Letting her memories return, watching that flicker of recognition ignite, seeing how much she loves me—and then watching the reality of all the misery my existence causes her settle in.

I want her to be happy. But there's a small, awful part of me that wishes she was as miserable without me as I've been without her. As much as I miss her, the only thing worse than watching her life improve without me would be watching it worsen again with my return.

"We're not here to talk about Aja." I keep my secret fears to myself. "We need to discuss your father. Whoever killed him is the same person who framed me, and they blackmailed Selva Sixmen into resigning from the Honorate."

Kaidren wants to push the subject of my mother further,

but with a resigned nod, he accepts the new topic of conversation. "There's someone blackmailing the Honorate *besides* the Shadow Queen?"

I tell him about the imposter Shadow Queen and her threats surrounding Selva Sixmen's wife.

Kaidren's brows shoot up. "You thought that was *me?*"

"It made sense at the time," I say defensively.

"I'm flattered you think I'm so diabolical."

It's on the tip of my tongue to point out that he's spent the past two years poisoning his own father, but he continues before I can. "If you're right, that means Flynn isn't really Selva's son."

"I can't prove it. I don't even know for sure that Neveah had an affair, let alone who it was with."

Kaidren looks thoughtful. "What if it was *my* father? Think about it. The fake Shadow Queen killed Arliss and blackmailed Selva—but what's the connection between them?"

There isn't one, far as I can tell. The only thing that connects Selva and Arliss is that they both used to be Honorate.

Unless Neveah Sixmen had an affair with Arliss Vale and birthed his son—Flynn.

"When Arliss first got sick, he spent months trying to find himself an heir," says Kaidren. "He wanted anyone but the Opheran bastard he'd already fathered. Eventually, he was sick enough to settle for me, but he was known to sleep with a lot of women. Even married ones."

The logic is sound. But it's still just conjecture. "If Neveah had an affair with Arliss," I say slowly, "that would make Flynn . . ."

"My brother," Kaidren says. I can't tell from his tone how he feels about that.

"Even if we're right, it still doesn't answer the question of who killed Arliss."

"Selva?" Kaidren suggests. "If anyone found out Flynn wasn't his, then he wouldn't have an heir."

"Can't be," I say. "Arliss's killer was blackmailing Selva."

The real question is, who would care that Flynn was Arliss's son? Who would care enough to kill for it?

I study Kaidren. His brow is furrowed, lost in thought. "Maybe," I say slowly, "we can find Arliss's killer another way. I can't imagine there are too many places to buy kishori. Where did *you* get it?"

"Here in Ophera. One of those shops that sell the illegal goods my aunt Jules likes."

It raises another question that's been weighing on me. "I was wondering about that. Jules was adamant about hating Virdei. If she doesn't want to join the decurio, why does she collect magical artifacts?"

"There are more uses for magic than dying as a soldier," Kaidren says. "As I'm sure you're aware."

Fair enough. "Do you think you could find the shop that sold you the poison again?"

"I think so. But I doubt the shopkeep would tell us anything."

I grin. This part is easy. "I'm good at interrogating people. A lie is just as useful as the truth—so long as you ask the right questions."

CHAPTER FORTY-ONE

LIE TO ME

I shake out my sjaal to lie on, wrap myself in my cloak, and reach for the one blanket we've been given. I pause, hand poised over the thin wool, with a hesitant look at Kaidren.

He's already smirking at me. "I suppose you think you're getting that whole thing?"

"You're the one who claims to be a man of honor."

He chuckles. "As you're well aware, I was lying. Besides, it's large enough for both of us." He lifts an eyebrow in challenge. "Unless you think you'll struggle to keep your hands to yourself?"

My eyes narrow. "My self-control's just fine, thank you." Chin tipped up, I curl up on my sjaal next to the dying embers in the fireplace, back turned to Kaidren. He lies down behind me. He drapes the blanket first over me, then settles it around himself. We don't touch. There's less than half a pace separating us, but it might as well be a canyon. I'm painfully aware of every lick of distance that divides us.

For several heartbeats, we listen to each other breathe. Neither of us speaks, but the night is far from quiet. A snowstorm has started, and Aja's house is being battered from all sides. Wind and snow lash the windowpanes and sneak through the cracks in the walls. The house shudders, and the space is filled with a sharp, high-pitched whine.

Kaidren and I each shiver three times in the span of a few minutes, and neither of us is any closer to falling asleep.

"Damn this." Kaidren's gruff voice cuts through the sounds of the night. His arms curl around me, yanking me back to rest against him.

I don't fight it. It's cold, and his body heat is a comfort I can't deny. My head is tucked into the hollow beneath his chin, and his arms are banded securely around me.

With his heartbeat pounding in my ear, I allow myself a moment of honesty: I *like* this. Not just because it's cold, and not just because he's warm.

Kaidren Vale is vicious when he wants to be. But he's also thoughtful and caring. He looks at me as if I'm worthy of notice. He smells of pine trees and fire. And being near him kindles a kind of magic within me that's new and exciting.

He makes me nervous. Makes me feel as though the world is tilting and I'm sliding into the unknown. Wrapped up with him like this, I almost wonder if it would be worth it to let go, to lean into this feeling of powerlessness. But I can't—nothing scares me more than what I can't control.

I clear my throat. "You kissed me."

Kaidren hums in my ear. "Is this your way of telling me your lips are cold and you'd like me to warm them?" His breath on the back of my neck combined with his teasing tone makes me shiver.

I scoff to disguise my body's reaction to him. "It's my way of saying we need to be clear. I don't want things to be confused between us."

"Confused how?"

"This—what we're doing now—is to keep warm. Nothing more."

Kaidren doesn't speak for so long, I think he's silently accepted my assertion and is drifting off to sleep. Then, he gently rolls me over to face him. Embers from the hearth cast an orange glow over the sharp features of his face. "It could mean something. It could mean everything."

My heart leaps at the suggestion. My mind is less sure how to react.

"I meant what I said before," he says. "I can't get you out of my head. So, I've stopped trying. Even after everything, I don't regret kissing you."

My throat feels as if it's coated in a fine layer of dust. "Kaidren—"

He interrupts me, and I'm glad, because I don't know how I was planning on finishing that sentence. "I know you're aikkari, I know you're the Shadow Queen, I know about your mother. You know that I poisoned my father. We have all the ammunition we need to be each other's ruin. But I don't want that. I just want you."

This house is dim from the storm, but Kaidren is bright, and his face is beautiful. His eyes watch me with a hungry intensity that scares me almost as much as it excites me.

I'd be lying if I said I'm not tempted.

Good thing I'm an excellent liar.

I ignore the way my starheaded heart pangs in protest and shake my head. "You and me . . . we're a bad idea."

"Why?" His hand dips beneath my sjaal and glides along my waist until it rests on the bare skin of my back. "You kissed me back."

The heat of his skin against mine after spending so long avoiding his touch makes it impossible to think. "I—" My brain is already mush. It stops working altogether when he dips his head, pressing his lips to the side of my neck.

I shudder. The rest of my sentence becomes as scattered as sunshine in the mountains.

"You what?" His free hand tilts my head, baring more of my neck to him. He kisses the hollow at my throat, leaving me buzzing to the tips of my toes. My eyes slip closed, chest heaving from the effort of holding myself back.

One hand sears my back, the other tucks an errant kinky curl behind my ear as his nose glides up the column of my neck. "What were you going to say?" His breath tickles my ear. "You don't want me? Go ahead. Lie to me. I dare you."

My eyes flutter open. His lips hover just above mine, a tantalizing gasp away.

I pride myself on being a very good liar. But as I trip and fall headfirst into the depths of his eyes—dark and wild and treacherous—I stop lying. To myself and to him.

I seize his face between my icy hands and kiss him.

Ophera is freezing; Virdei is colder still. For seven years, I've kept my heart frozen solid. As I drag Kaidren's lips to mine, I'm set alight.

Flames consume me—where our lips meet, where his body melts into me, in my soul—and I can't get enough.

Kaidren holds nothing back. He kisses me as if he's starved. His lips pry mine apart, and he sighs into my open mouth. One hand cups the space where my neck curves into my jaw, the other draws lines up and down the slope of my spine. He tilts his head, giving him a better angle to coax my tongue to intertwine with his. I gasp at the newness of the sensation, and he swallows the sound.

Kaidren's breaths become my own. My arms coil around his neck as we move together. I match each shift of his head, every swipe of his tongue, with my own.

I'm lightheaded when he pulls away. My mind spins too quickly to have a single coherent thought. Kaidren is smiling widely and unevenly and, after a beat, I realize I am too.

His lips graze my temple. "If that was honesty, consider me a liar reformed."

I laugh. My cheeks are flushed and my hair is a mess, but with the way he's looking at me, I don't care.

His smile stretches wider, growing more lopsided. "I don't think I've ever heard you laugh before."

"That's because you're not funny." I can't stop grinning.

He chuckles. "I'm hilarious and charming." He takes my wrist and kisses the golden ink of my tattoo. "And you are all of the above, not to mention beautiful."

"You think I'm charming?"

"When you're not making me miserable. So, I suppose that only applies when you're not speaking."

I laugh again, and that slightly imperfect smile threatens to split his face open.

"I can't believe you don't think I'm funny. When we get back, I'll make you laugh every day."

My happy grin fades with his sobering words. Kissing him was a hazy distraction, but this—the way he's gazing tenderly at me, the idea that we have a future outside this firelit moment—isn't reality. It's just a moment in between.

Gently, I extricate my wrist from his hold and start to pull away.

Kaidren holds me still, smile replacing itself with a furrowed brow. "What's wrong?"

"I shouldn't have done that."

He jerks as though I've struck him. "You're saying you don't want this?"

"I'm not in the habit of wanting things I can't have."

"You can have me. I won't even put up a fight." He rolls us over, resting me beneath him and dropping his forehead to my own. "We'll find my father's killer and clear our names. When we return to Virdei, we'll win the Tournament. Together."

He thinks there are no longer any secrets between us. He thinks that if he wins the Tournament, I'll be content sitting at his side. He's wrong on both counts. I still have every intention of taking the throne for myself. A plan that only works if the person I'm stealing it from is my trusting and malleable brother. "Kaidren, I'm not going to help you win."

"Why not?"

I roll my eyes. "Why did you assume I would?"

"I thought you'd want to. I see the way Lucien treats you. You don't owe him your loyalty."

"So, instead I should give my loyalty to you? Because we kissed?"

Hurt flashes over his expression. He hides it quickly, but I feel guilty just the same. "I don't want to return to Virdei as your enemy," he says. "If you fight with me, we'll win. And then we can have it all."

He makes it all sound so simple. "If you win, *we* won't have anything. You will. I'll just be some girl dependent on your goodwill."

"I won't let that happen. You are clever and bold. Even if I didn't want you as I do, I'd want a mind like yours on my side. But I *do* want you. In all things. A conspirator in schemes and a partner in everything else."

"You want me for now, but eventually, I'll lose your interest. Affection fades, and truth changes. The things you mean today with imagined power will change if that power becomes realized."

The hurt expression he tried to disguise is back. "Not everyone is like the Honorate. People don't always change their minds or hearts so flippantly. Some people are loyal."

"People like us are loyal only to themselves. I'd stab you in the back to get ahead, and even if you won't admit it, so would you. But it doesn't matter either way. Even if you could promise me forever, I wouldn't want it. I'll never be happy as your shadow. I've been Luc's for years, and I'm tired."

"I'm nothing like Lucien."

"I told you I dreamed of being the most powerful person in the room," I say. "Second would never be enough for me."

"You mean *I* would never be enough for you."

My throat burns, but I refuse to cry. "Don't pretend you're any better. You can compete for a throne. I can't. You think if our roles were reversed, you'd settle for second?"

He doesn't answer—because he knows I'm right. His shoulders slump. "What would you have me do?"

"Nothing. When we return, you'll do what's best for you, and I'll do what's best for me."

His eyes skirt over my face, looking for any fissures, any way to change my mind. With a resigned sigh, he twists us so he's on his back and my head rests on his chest, ear to his heart. "I'm going to win."

"You're going to *try*," I say with a teasing grin, turning my head to look up at him.

His eyes are sad, but a corner of his mouth tips up wryly. "I believe I still owe you one true thing. What do you want to know?"

I don't even have to think about what to ask. "Why do you want to be Praeceptor? The truth this time."

He nods, as if he expected this question. "When my mom died, my world ended. It felt like I died with her. But my father . . . his life stayed exactly the same. I hated him for it. Not just because her death was his fault, but because he didn't even care. I wanted to do the same. Destroy something he loved, then force him to wake up every day knowing he was as worthless as he made us feel."

"You want to be Praeceptor to make him angry?"

"I wanted to force him to watch me win a position he could never hold. I wanted him to see the bastard son he hated more powerful than he ever was." Kaidren leans closer to my ear, as though whispering a secret. "You know what my first act as Praeceptor will be?"

"What?"

"Dismantling the Honorate." Kaidren's laugh is devoid of humor. "He cared so damn much about honor and legacy, but there's not a shred of honor among any of them. I wanted to watch as he saw his own name unmake a system he loved. I'd hoped he'd live to see it, but it doesn't matter. He believed in the stars and hell, and I believe that when I'm Praeceptor, he'll writhe in the afterlife, just as he deserves. When I join him down there, I'll have the final laugh."

A saner person might find his admission unsettling, but I burrow deeper into his chest, unable to hide a grin.

"That didn't scare you off?"

"I don't scare easily. You want to take over the world for revenge? I can't think of a better motive."

He laughs.

Before, when he described his plans as Praeceptor, when he spoke of improving the Honorate to improve Virdei, it was always a lie. Because he has no intentions of making the Honorate better. He means to destroy it completely.

"What are your plans for this new Virdei?" I ask.

"Everything I promised. But I won't use the Honorate to do it."

For a few beats, we say nothing.

"Tell me something," says Kaidren quietly. "Not as part of

an exchange. Not because you owe me anything. Just tell me something true about you."

I think about it. "My favorite food is goat stew. And I really like honey cakes."

"I didn't imagine you as someone who likes sweets."

"Why?" I tease. "Because I'm a conniving bitch?"

He laughs so hard he presses his face into my hair to muffle the sound. "Tell me something else."

"You were my first kiss."

His face lights up. "And your second."

I roll my eyes, but I'm smiling.

"More," he says demandingly.

"Now you're just being greedy."

He grins but doesn't say anything. Just waits expectantly for me to answer him.

I turn over my thoughts, trying to come up with something he might like to know. As I watch him, and he watches me, I realize there's only one thing I need him to hear before everything between us changes once again. "Whatever happens when we get back, I don't hate you."

His happiness dims with the bleak reminder that none of this is real. Just a moment in between. "I don't hate you either."

Neither of us says it, but we both know there's more: *I don't hate you. But if that's what it takes to win, I'll fight you as if I do.*

CHAPTER FORTY-TWO

PEDDLING POISON

Even though it's my home, I feel out of place as Kaidren and I walk the streets of Ophera. I'm wearing the sweater and pants I took from the Vale manor, and my hair is in simple braids, but I still attract curious looks.

It's my cloak. I might not be wearing a ball gown anymore, but this cloak is clearly expensive, and here, it stands out.

We're in the middle of the dark season, so the sky is grim and gray, even during the day. Kaidren and I keep our heads down and hoods drawn to avoid detection. We likely won't be recognized by civilians (most Opherans who frequent Virdei are already there for work by this hour), but we're headed for the more clustered areas. Anywhere with a high concentration of shops and peddlers tends to have decurio patrolling.

It's noisier as we exit Aja's residential neighborhood and near the town center. Here there are fewer houses and more chatter. We turn a corner, and the skies brighten. There's a glow ahead—a gathering of light posts in one central area, illuminating the five main streets littered with shops, stalls, and people.

The city at the base of the mountains is called Ivenna, the largest in Ophera. The usually snow-covered streets are clearer here, the buildings taller. The ground floors of most buildings are shops, the stories above are housing, and the narrow spaces between are crammed with wooden stalls for peddlers.

"Necklace for your lady?" A man at a wooden stall tries to entreat Kaidren and me over to him. "It will look so lovely against her neck. This one is special. It has magic." His eyes gleam as he thrusts a silver necklace with a crystal pendant toward Kaidren.

Kaidren jerks away from the brash salesman. "Not interested."

Each stall we pass perks to attention when they see us. Like the first man, they reach for their most expensive baubles to wave in our direction. They push all kinds of things, from jewelry to clothes to food. We ignore them all as Kaidren guides us through the streets to a shop.

Unlike the buildings around it, this one is a single story. A rickety sign hangs from a rusty chain in the front window. The shop is *very* small. End to end, it's only slightly larger than my room in Widow's Hall. The interior is dark, lit only by a few flickering candles. Every spare bit of space is filled with shelves covered in glass jars and sackcloth bags. Nothing is labeled, so I have no idea what kinds of things are sold here.

"Hello, hello. You look as if you have traveled far," an excited voice calls out to us. A thin aisle cuts from the front door to a counter. A man sits on a stool behind it. "Come, come." He beckons us forward, beaming. "I have exactly what you need."

There's no way for him to know that, but we dutifully make our way to him anyway. The aisle is so small, we have to turn sideways to squeeze through. The shopkeep's enthusiasm mounts the closer we get and the better look he gets at our clothes. "Well, what a lovely lady you have there, sir. I have many products for a young couple like yourselves. Maybe—"

"That's not why we're here," Kaidren interrupts him flatly. "You don't remember me?"

The shopkeep is staring at the velvet of my cloak. "Should I?"

"You sold me two vials of kishori."

The man's eyes go wide. He leaps from his stool, rushes to the front door, and slams it shut. Swiftly, he pulls a cord, and curtains descend over the window, hiding us from the outside. The shopkeep spins to glare at Kaidren. "Lower your voice," he hisses. "You can't go around flinging absurd accusations like that."

"It's not an accusation. It's a fact. I purchased two vials of kishori from you two years ago."

For a few moments, the shopkeep looks Kaidren over. After a pause, his brow clears with recognition. "*If* I did remember you—and I'm certainly not saying I do or that I sell what you claim I do—my shop has a very strict policy against returns."

Kaidren rolls his eyes. "I'm here for information. Have you sold kishori to anyone else recently?"

The man returns to the counter but doesn't sit. He appears on edge, leaning on the balls of his feet as though preparing to make a quick escape. "Who wants to know?"

"I do."

The man looks suspicious. "Do you work for the decurio?"

"No."

"I don't believe you. Even if I did, I don't sell what you claim you bought from me. I'm a good, honest merchant."

"Who peddles in poison," Kaidren says exasperatedly.

"I most certainly do not. Regardless, my clients value privacy. I don't keep track of everyone who buys from me."

"Surely you pay more attention to someone who purchases poison?"

"I don't sell poison," he says automatically.

This strategy is getting us nowhere.

The shopkeep has been spewing lies since we walked in,

and magic is an inferno in my gut. I lean over the counter, capturing his attention. "Are you sure you can't think of anyone you sold kishori to recently? My patience is wearing thin."

The shopkeep swells with indignation. "I don't sell—"

I don't feel like listening to him lie again, so I seize him by the arm. He tries to pull back, but I yank up his sleeve and grab hold of his bare skin.

He cries out as I push searing heat into his flesh. Not enough to leave a mark—at least, not yet—but enough to hurt like hell.

I drop his arm, and he stumbles back, slamming into a shelf behind him. Glass shatters to the floor, but he doesn't seem to care. He stares at me, eyes rounded with terror. "You're aikkari?"

"Yes. But don't worry. I'm not here because the decurio sent me; I'm just not very nice. Now answer the question: Have you sold kishori recently? Refuse to answer, or lie to me again, and I'll burn this whole place to the ground, just because I can and, as I said, I'm not very nice." I smile sweetly. "Do you believe me?"

He's shaking. "Y-yes."

"Excellent. Have you sold kishori recently?"

He flaps his head up and down. "Yes. I sold a vial a little over a month ago."

Just before the start of the Tournament. "To who?"

"A young man. I don't know his name, I swear. I never asked."

Unfortunately, that's the truth. "What do you remember about him?"

"He was like you," the shopkeep rushes to answer me. "Dressed real nice, like he was well off."

My interest is raised. "Was he Virdeian or Opheran? Did you see a tattoo?"

"I couldn't tell. He was wearing gloves. They were nice gloves. Nice boots and cloak too." His eyes shift wistfully to my outerwear. "Like yours."

Probably a Virdeian, and probably from above the Collar. "What did he look like?"

"He was taller than me, shorter than your young man."

The shopkeep is very short, and Kaidren is very tall. That does nothing to narrow it down. "Anything else?"

"This was months ago. I don't remember much. Of course, he had short hair, but—"

Of course? "Wait," I say. "What do you mean 'of course' he had short hair?"

The man looks confused. "It's like I said. He was like you, miss."

He said that before, but I assumed he meant his buyer was wealthy. Apparently, he's referring to something else. "What do you mean by that?"

"He was aikkari. A member of the decurio. He had that haircut they all have, but he wasn't dressed like one of them while he was here."

My blood runs cold. A young, wealthy member of the decurio who lives above the Collar . . . "Did you notice a mark on his face?"

The shopkeep's brow furrows. "Now that you mention it, yes. He had a little mole or something right near his mouth."

My eyes shoot to Kaidren to find him already looking at me. We both know exactly who the shopkeep just described. Flynn Sixmen.

CHAPTER FORTY-THREE

SCHEMING IN SHADOWS

Getting back up the mountain is simple enough. We keep our hoods pulled low and ride the sky cart early in the morning alongside several Opherans who work in Virdei. The cart is so full, no one pays us any mind.

The true challenge is getting into Widow's Hall undetected.

Getting in the way we left isn't an option. After our escape, the dungeons and stables underground are bound to be crawling with guards. Which leaves the doors.

When we reach the top of the mountain, the other passengers of the sky cart turn to make their way to the Honorate houses where they work, but Kaidren and I move to the arena.

It's locked now, before training, but the domed ceiling is made of tshira. Kaidren and I twist our way up the stairwell that clings to the outside of the arena and leads to the roof. We're both out of breath by the time we reach the top.

I place a hand on the tshira roof. Tendrils of heated magic spread through my body, making me feel light as a wispy cloud. I savor that feeling as, under the force of magic, the roof *melts*. It's still here, but its form is shifted from an impenetrable, solid barrier into a membrane, like with the cell walls when we fled prison.

Carefully, I climb through the tshira, slipping onto the ledge on the inside of the arena.

It's pitch-black in here.

Foreboding is a heavy sensation in my gut. I clutch Kaidren's hand—to keep track of him and so I don't fall—as we move down the benches in the stands. At the base, we enter an equipment room and steal two aikkari uniforms. They don't fit either of us perfectly, but they have masks that cover our faces, which is all we need.

We're concealed head to toe as we make our way to the servants' entrance to Widow's Hall.

A few servants glance at us as we enter, but we're soldiers, and they're trained to not ask questions. No one stops us as we slip inside.

The view from the balcony off Luc's office is the best in all of Virdei. But as I sit here with Kaidren, neither of us is enjoying the view. We're lying in wait, masks off, for Luc to return to his study and dismiss his guards.

In the meantime, Kaidren and I haven't exchanged a single word. I keep count of each painstaking second and avoid looking at him.

We're back in Virdei. We both know what that means, but so far, neither of us has said it out loud.

Four minutes of terse silence later, he turns to me. "Mira." He says my name softly, entreating me to look at him.

I do. And immediately regret it. There's more emotion pooling in his eyes than I know how to deal with right now.

"I just wanted to say that my offer stands. There's a place at my side, and it's reserved for you."

My heart thumps so hard it hurts. "I'm not going to back down."

"I know." He smiles, sad and wistful. "But I had to offer

again. Just in case. I've enjoyed this. Being at peace with you. Even if it was only for a moment."

"Me too."

Placing a hand on the side of my neck, he strokes my cheek with his thumb. After a pause, he kisses me. It's softer than his earlier kisses. It's sweet the way that I'm not, and full of longing. When he pulls away, he doesn't lower his hand. "I wish you and Lucien good luck in the Tournament."

I put my hand over his, not to push him away but because it's comforting. "No, you don't."

"You're right. I don't," he murmurs with a rueful grin. "But after this, everything between us changes. I think losing you will be easier if we lie to each other."

My heart is heavy. I wonder if I'm making the right decision, even as I know I won't change my mind. "In that case, good luck, Kaidren."

"Good luck, Remira."

We sit like that, not saying a word, until we hear the door to Luc's office open.

Only when I'm sure his guards have left, do I stand and push open the balcony door.

My brother sits at his desk, face buried in his hands, looking brutally exhausted, like he's going to collapse any second.

"Hey," I say softly.

He jumps. His head flies up, slumping eyes widening. Usually when I startle him, he relaxes when he sees it's me. This time, the tension doesn't fade. "Mira?" His tone is disbelieving. "Is it really you?"

"It's me."

He flicks through a dozen emotions before settling on relieved. He hurries around his desk to envelop me in a tight hug. "Stars in hell, Mira," he breathes into my hair. "You're *alive*. When no one found you, I worried you froze out on the mountain. Are you all right? Where have you been?"

"I'm all right."

Finally, his shoulders ease, and he squeezes me tighter. When he pulls away, he's frowning. "You have no idea how happy I am to see you, but it's not safe for you here. If someone catches you, they'll send you back to prison, and it won't be so easy to escape this time." Luc's eyes widen as he realizes something. Hurriedly, he releases me to lock his office door.

There's a chill behind me as the balcony door opens again, bringing with it a burst of cool air.

"You might want to sit," I say to Luc's back. "We have a lot to tell you."

"We?" Finished with the door, Luc turns to face me. His startled eyes jump to Kaidren, entering the study over my shoulder. "What the hell is going on?"

"We know who murdered Arliss Vale," I say. "It wasn't me, and it wasn't Kaidren."

"Then who was it?"

"Flynn Sixmen."

Luc stares at me.

Gently, I place my hands on his shoulders and steer him back to his chair, forcing him to sit. "Take a seat. Like I said, we have a lot to explain."

Arliss Vale. How many times can a single man die?

Killed by his son, then killed by an Opheran, now killed by an Honorate. At this rate, I have to wonder: Is there a single person left on this mountain who didn't want him dead?

The decurio claim they've finally caught the right man. This Queen of Shadows is less certain. Allow me to peel back the curtain and let you, the people, decide whether our newest suspect is guilty.

Let's hear the decurio's evidence against him, shall we?

First: A servant in Widow's Hall testifies to making a wax imprint and matching key to the bedchamber of the Honored Praeceptor's own sister.

Did our new suspect use this key to frame the unsuspecting Kyler? You decide.

Second: A shopkeep in Ophera claims our newest suspect purchased a bottle of the same poison used to kill Arliss Vale only a week before his death.

Third: There is not a soul who remembers seeing our current suspect on the night Arliss Vale was murdered.

Who is this latest accused suspect, you ask? None other than Flynn Sixmen.

Flynn Sixmen now sits behind the very bars that caged Bastard Vale for no longer than one day. An end to a legacy, and a start to an election. Choose wisely.

Bastard Vale, his name cleared—for now—once again competes to become the next Praeceptor of Virdei. Come bear witness to the third and final trial of the Tournament of Thrones. I have it on good authority, it will be the most exciting event yet.

Dear readers, wish Bastard Vale luck for me. I have a feeling he'll need it.

Fondly,
Shadow Queen

CHAPTER FORTY-FOUR

TRAITORS IN THE SNOW

At this point, I might as well just join the decurio outright, considering the number of times I've donned their armor in the past month.

The third trial hasn't even started yet, and I'm already out of breath. No matter how often I find myself in decurio armor, it never becomes any less nerve-wracking.

The field has been cordoned off into a square so that only the very center is available for use. Luc's team of six stands opposite Kaidren's as we wait for the event to start.

The arena feels tense. Possibly because this is the last trial—whoever wins this, wins the throne. Or possibly because it's General Tarek Fain running this event, and he lacks Flynn's natural charisma. He speaks in monotone as he goes over the parameters for the trial, and I find myself tuning him out.

Unconsciously, my eyes rake over Kaidren's team. I tell myself it's so I can assess them for weaknesses, but when my eyes pause on Kaidren, I know I'm only lying to myself.

He's already staring at me.

I'm completely obscured by my uniform, but he easily picks me from the row of decurio and holds my gaze through the mesh over my eyes.

There's a shift in Kaidren's countenance. His entire body

seems to exhale, as if he was holding his breath until he laid eyes on me.

There's an intensity to his stare. A glimpse of the ruthlessness lurking beneath his calm exterior. It's enticing. *Heated.* Even from a distance, he manages to scorch me from the inside out. I shudder and look away. He's a distraction I can't afford. One I've been actively avoiding since we said our goodbyes outside Luc's study.

Today isn't about him. It's about winning.

For this trial, the candidates are equipped with crossbows and given the task of shooting the opposing team's targets. The first candidate to reach fifty points wins.

The targets are wooden circles propped up on posts just behind each team's boundary line. There are three targets, each of a different size. The largest is worth ten points, the second largest is worth twenty, and the smallest—barely wider than a coin—is worth fifty.

We soldiers are responsible for guarding our targets, preventing the other team from gaining any points, and doing what we can to get our candidate close enough to the other side to aim effectively.

The most important rule for this game: only the candidates have crossbows. The rest of the soldiers can have weapons, but they're not allowed to fire the crossbow on behalf of the candidates.

For the past ten days—since Flynn was arrested, Kaidren and I were cleared of murder, and the Tournament was back on schedule—Luc and I have spent nearly all our time refamiliarizing him with the crossbow.

Target practice has been useful, but in my time *not* with Luc, I fashioned two bolts of my own. Wood on the outside, indistinguishable from the other bolts in his quiver, but on the inside, they have a tshira core.

We had no way of knowing which quiver was going to be Luc's ahead of time (at least, not without marking them in a way someone might notice), so Sef slipped one bolt in each bag before the start of the event.

Thanks to Luc's efforts at the masquerade ball (and no doubt the influence of his parents), his team is well equipped. Each soldier has a brand-new sword in a scabbard around our hips. Kaidren's team only has one.

This final event is as much a test of political prowess as it is a test of warfare. Aside from the crossbow, teams are only allowed to use weapons purchased by benefactors.

The rest of Luc's team cheered when General Fain delivered our swords. I didn't. To a trained soldier, it's a weapon. To me, it's just a heavy object I'll have to try not to stab myself with by accident.

I'm a ball of sweat as General Fain begins the countdown. The energy in the arena has been tempered by Flynn's absence, but as the General reaches "one," there are scattered cheers.

Blood roars in my ear.

Two soldiers—myself and a quick-footed decurio named Medin—stay behind to guard the targets and Luc. The remaining four run forward.

Luc loads his first bolt. There's no way to tell which is the modified one, at least not from the outside. I feel nothing from this one. It's solid wood.

He fires his first bolt, aiming for the largest target, worth ten points.

The bolt grazes the edge of the wooden circle but falls to the ground.

I swallow a curse. During target practice, he would have made that.

I scan Kaidren's team. He developed his strategy to make the best use of their single sword. One unarmed soldier stays near the targets, to guard them. The other five form a ring around Kaidren. The soldier at the front of the human shield wields the lone sword.

As Luc's team races across the narrowed arena, the circle around Kaidren parts.

He raises the crossbow, takes aim, and releases. He's immediately enveloped by his team.

The bolt launches in the direction of our twenty-point target.

Medin slashes it from the air with his sword. The splintered wood falls to the ground.

Luc shoots again. He makes another attempt at the ten-point target. His aim looks better this time, but Kaidren's soldier leaps, kicking it out of the way.

One of Luc's soldiers, Caspian, reaches the circle around Kaidren. Caspian begins a battle with the lone armed soldier on Kaidren's team.

Another one of Luc's team members reaches the circle and launches an attack of her own. In seconds, she draws blood from an unarmed decurio. She swipes her sword again and the unarmed soldier collapses, leaving a gap in the formation around Kaidren.

Caspian lunges through the opening, trying to rip Kaidren's crossbow from his hands—but before he can, the circle shifts, closing in around Kaidren again.

Luc takes another shot. This time, he aims for the twenty-point target. Again, he misses.

The audience groans. It wasn't even close.

I wince. We practiced these shots over and over. I didn't expect him to be an expert, but he's missing basic shots in a *very* public setting.

I tell myself it doesn't matter. As soon as he draws the modified bolt, I can steer it to victory. We just have to keep Kaidren from winning long enough to make it happen.

The mostly unarmed soldiers surrounding Kaidren do their best to defend him, but Luc's team all have swords. It isn't even close to a fair fight.

Another one of Kaidren's team crumbles in the next few minutes. I can't tell if they're dead, but they don't get back up, and the circle around Kaidren is forced to split apart.

Two unarmed soldiers fan out, drawing Luc's soldiers away from Kaidren, while the woman with the sword latches to his side.

Kaidren and Luc take aim at the same time.

Kaidren fires at the ten-point target; Luc shoots for the twenty.

Luc's veers wildly off track, but Kaidren's soars toward his intended target.

Medin blocks it easily.

Kaidren's expression darkens. He's rushed by a decurio, but his armed guard quickly fends off the attack. It gives Kaidren the window he needs to fire another bolt. This time, he doesn't shoot a target—he fires at Medin.

Medin isn't expecting it. The bolt grazes his thigh, and he doubles over.

As Medin slumps, Kaidren reloads swiftly and shoots again.

I raise my own sword in a vain attempt to block it, but I'm slow, and the blade is heavy in my inexperienced hands.

Kaidren's bolt sails true, and he hits the ten-point target.

The audience roars. The first score of the game.

"Sorry." Medin sounds strained, and his leg is bleeding, but he rights himself. "I won't let him score again."

Kaidren's guard is battling two of Luc's soldiers. She's quick. Even outnumbered, she outpaces them.

I loop my arm through Luc's. "I'm going to get you closer to the targets. From now on, only aim for fifty points."

He frowns. "I haven't made a single shot yet."

No one is immediately near us, but I drop my voice anyway. "I know. But one of the bolts in your quiver is modified. I'll make sure it hits, but you have to make it look believable. Don't worry about clean shots. Fire as quickly as possible."

Luc calls out to Caspian. Together, we flank Luc's sides, swords raised, as we lead him to the center of the field.

Kaidren did well selecting his lone armed soldier. She's disposed of one of Luc's soldiers and is still holding off two more, leaving Kaidren a wide berth.

Medin is charged by one of Kaidren's team.

Clearly, a sacrifice. They're unarmed, and Medin easily cuts him in the leg, sending him crashing to the ground. But the distraction gives Kaidren a window to take another shot.

He hits the twenty-point target.

My stomach drops. Kaidren has thirty points. Luc still has none.

Luc fires at the ten-point target. It grazes the side, but misses again.

He looks at me sheepishly. I hold in a slew of expletives and pretend I'm calm. "We need someone to guard with Medin," I say.

At Luc's command, a second decurio races to join Medin in protecting our targets. We can't afford a single mistake. All Kaidren needs is another twenty points to win the Tournament and the throne in one fell swoop.

Kaidren's armed guard races toward us. Caspian steps into her path, keeping her from reaching Luc.

They clash. Their feet move, weapons clang, in a dance. They're both quick, but she's outpacing him. She's light-footed and better at anticipating.

I catch Luc's arm. "Remember what I said. Take as many shots as you can."

He pauses in reloading his weapon to frown at me. "Where are you—"

Too late, he realizes my intention. Before he can do something foolish—like cry out to me or try to stop me—I release my brother and charge toward Kaidren.

He's reaching for another bolt from his quiver and doesn't notice me until I'm right in front of him.

I grab hold of his weapon, trying to rip it from his hands.

For a few moments, we grapple with it, but he's stronger than me. With a smirk, Kaidren yanks it from me.

Luc fires another bolt from behind me. Again, it's solid wood, and again, he misses.

I hold in a groan.

My only goal is to keep Kaidren distracted until I can cheat Luc's way to victory. My hands shake as I pull my weapon from its sheath around my hips. The sword feels clunky, but I swing it, trying to knock the crossbow from Kaidren's grip. He sidesteps me easily, looking more amused than threatened.

I grunt, trying to lift the heavy weapon again, but I stop as searing pain shoots up my calf.

It takes me a pause too long to realize it's Kaidren's armed soldier. She incapacitated Caspian, raced to me, and sliced the back of my calf.

I drip blood, and my leg is on fire. I grit my teeth to keep from crying out. My head spins, dizzy from trying not to keel over.

Luc fires again. Another wooden bolt, another miss.

Weakly, I turn to face my attacker. My arm wobbles as I try to lift my sword. Fear sits in my throat, like milk gone rancid. My opponent is tall and strong. Like me, she carries a sword. Unlike me, she actually knows how to wield it. She's already defeated just about all the trained soldiers on Luc's team. I don't stand a chance.

"*Wait!*" Kaidren speaks quickly, voice breathless. *Desperate*. "Let me. Go for the Praeceptor."

She pauses. She could kill me in seconds and then go to attack Luc, and she knows it. But it isn't her job to question her candidate, so she hands him her sword and runs over to Luc.

It's a foolish move on Kaidren's part, but I see it as the act of mercy it is. She was going to kill me, and despite himself—despite everything—he's protecting me.

My leg is still in pain as I raise my sword and he raises his. We circle each other, jabbing every few moments, but our movements are slow and unpracticed, so neither of us hits the other.

I lean all my weight on one leg, trying to ignore how the other one cries out in protest. It wants me to sit, but I don't have time for that.

"Are you all right?" Kaidren murmurs with a swift glance at my leg.

Luc shoots for the target and misses—again.

The crowd groans, and I'm temporarily distracted.

The next slice of his sword cuts my arm.

I drop my weapon as my hand instinctively rises to the bloody wound just above my elbow.

Kaidren freezes. He didn't mean to actually wound me.

He shouldn't care so much.

My heartbeat thuds as I consider him. From the moment he

arrived at Widow's Hall, I've been searching for Kaidren Vale's weakness. I realize now that it's been staring me in the face—*me*.

One of our team strikes down another of Kaidren's.

We can *win* this. We have every advantage. I just need to keep Kaidren preoccupied.

I make as if to lunge for Kaidren and shriek.

I'm only half faking as pain lances up my leg. My body wobbles before I crash to the ground.

If Kaidren wanted to, he could stab me from above, killing me. He'd have every right to in this game.

He doesn't. Instead, he takes a step toward me. Then stops himself. Conflict wages war on his face. "Are you all right?" he asks again, voice low.

I wince and cradle my leg to my chest. I release a hiss, trying to make myself look as pathetic as possible.

Kaidren crunches another step closer, brow softened in concern. The sword lowers to his side. "Mira?"

"I'm fine." I force the words out through my teeth. He's close enough now. "And I'm sorry." Before he can react, I leap to my feet.

It hurts like hell, my leg screams in protest, but it doesn't matter, because I wrench the crossbow from Kaidren, and before he knows what I'm doing, I throw it to the ground and stomp on it with my uninjured foot, cracking it in two.

The crowd is going wild.

Kaidren gawks at me. I've broken his crossbow. He has no way to hit the target, no way to win.

I start to limp away, but Kaidren tackles me to the ground.

I screech as I skid on my back, Kaidren on top of me.

We're both out of breath. He glares at me through the mesh of my mask. Fury and betrayal are twin storms in his harsh gaze. He speaks through gritted teeth. "That was cruel."

Guilt gnaws away at me. He let his guard down and I took advantage. If he hated me like he's supposed to—if he were able to treat me as an opponent, like he's supposed to—he would have won. I swallow, refusing to let my guilt reveal itself. Instead, I glare right back. "I thought that's what you liked best about me?"

He eyes his discarded sword as though contemplating running me through with it. I know he won't.

My heartbeat is a whir.

"Congrats on losing." My words would carry more bite if I wasn't bleeding from my arm and leg, and if he wasn't on top of me, keeping me from moving.

He chuckles darkly. "I haven't lost. Your brother hasn't hit a target all trial."

Kaidren's unfortunately right. Luc is a terrible shot. Even with all the time we spent practicing, in the final moment, when it actually counts, he can't do it.

Luc reloads again, and I feel for it with my mind. This one is different from the others. The modified bolt.

The only problem is Kaidren has me pinned and my hands are trapped.

Luc is about to fire. When he does, I need my hands free.

"I wouldn't be so sure about that," I say. Then I slam my head up, crashing against Kaidren's.

He jerks back with a groan.

I scramble out from under him. My leg is on fire, each step is agony, but I don't have time to focus on that.

Luc releases the final crossbow bolt, and I keep my hands low, palms directed at the bolt.

I feel for the tshira with my mind. It sails off course, but I nudge it over, right for the smallest target.

At my coaxing, the bolt flies true.

Fifty points.

The audience roars. Spectators jump to their feet. Several of them rush onto the field, leaping up and down.

Luc just won the Tournament.

The excitement is tangible. Almost infectious. I open my mouth to join their cheers, but pain from my leg wound finally catches up to me.

Instead of clapping, I collapse.

Across the field, Luc's parents hug him. Mathson has never looked prouder, and Yelina is so happy, she's sobbing. Meanwhile, I'm in so much pain, I can't even stand.

Footsteps approach from behind. I don't need to turn to know who it is, but I do anyway. Kaidren pauses at my side. He looks torn. His hand twitches to help me up. Then he looks between me—a pathetic, injured mess abandoned on the ground—and Luc—the inept Praeceptor once more—and his expression hardens. "What's wrong, Remira?" His voice is frosty. "Stand up. Take a bow."

My eyes sting. I don't regret winning. But I do wish there'd been a way to do it without hurting him. "I really am sorry."

He gives a dark chuckle, a heart-wrenching combination of bitter and defeated. "Don't be. You just got everything you ever wanted." The cheers in the arena swell, and his nostrils flare. "Soak it in. I hope it's worth it."

Kaidren leaves me there, bleeding in the snow, as the rest of the world celebrates Luc's victory.

CHAPTER FORTY-FIVE

GAME OF SMOKE AND MIRRORS

I rise early the morning of Luc's coronation.

I don my uniform and a silver medallion, then take the earliest sky cart available down the mountain. Over the past weeks, I've learned a lot from Flynn, about self-defense and, most relevant now: about security.

I've learned how the gateposts around the mountain's perimeter function. I know where each of them are, dotted around the boundary of the Republic. Which are the smallest, which have the most sentries, and which guards the most direct path up the mountain.

My hands shake as I shuffle toward the Sulen gatepost. It's a towerlike structure built of smooth stone. The walls are doused with water each morning and night, encasing the stone in a layer of ice. It's designed to make scaling the post a near impossibility.

A handful of sentries stand watch at each tower; the exact amount varies depending on how essential that particular post is. They're equipped with spyglasses to keep watch for approaching invaders and large torches to be lit in emergencies. Atop each post is a mirror, angled on a hinge, and a bell. In the event of an attack, sentries ring the bell and angle the mirror to reflect torchlight toward the next nearest gatepost. Each post echoes the call for help until it reaches Widow's Hall so they know to send reinforcements.

I arrive at the base of the tower and steel myself. A rope dangles from overhead. It's too thin and brittle to climb, but its purpose is to gain the attention of the sentries above.

I tug the rope once, then pause. Then twice and pause. Then a fourth time. It alerts those above to my presence and signals that I know the code—they can trust me.

My heart hammers with nerves, but I feel safer hidden beneath my armor. They can't read the terror in my expression.

A hollow tube drops down next. I take a breath and press my lips to the opening. "I come bearing orders from General Tarek Fain." My voice is as firm as I can manage. It echoes through the tube, carrying my message to the soldiers above.

There's a pause. It's likely only a few moments, but my twisting anxiety makes it feel as though hours have passed by the time a ladder descends.

My gloved hands tremble as I climb. As soon as I reach the top of the platform, I'm surrounded. Multiple decurio hold out weapons, ready to strike if I'm a threat.

I hold up my arms in a show of innocence. It feels fake, but the reality is, even though I come bearing a lie, I'm not a threat to any of them. "I'm here on orders from General Tarek Fain," I repeat.

They keep their weapons raised. It's unnerving, but they haven't killed me yet, so I keep speaking. "Today is the Praeceptor's coronation. He is reorganizing sentries for the day. Half of you will be stationed at the East Ledgwik, the other half will join the South Kai gatepost."

The aikkari standing nearest me frowns. "If we leave, then who will be stationed here?"

"More sentries are on their way as we speak." I practiced this lie so many times in the mirror, it rolls easily off my tongue. "In the wake of the many scandals within the Honorate,

General Fain was unsure who to trust. His strategy to ensure the safety and security of Virdei is to make the most direct pathway up the mountain into a fortress. No one, apart from the sentries assigned to this post, is to know who is stationed here today. General Fain is reordering the rotation in the final hour. Anyone who knew you were to be stationed here will no longer have any idea. It is the General's hope that this will effectively prevent collusion and sabotage on this important day." I reach around my neck. In an imitation of a motion General Fain made to Flynn weeks ago, I flash a silver necklace at them.

It's as if that one motion ignites a fire within the gatepost. All at once, soldiers begin moving, following directives, preparing to pack up and leave.

There are a few grumbles, but the medallion was enough for them to believe I've given them orders from the General. I stand near the ladder and watch as they gather up gloves, masks, and a few weapons before climbing out of the post.

As they depart, I pretend to make my way back up to Widow's Hall. I keep up the act until I no longer hear their trudging footsteps. Visibility on the mountain is awful—which works in my favor now as I climb right back up.

The station is abandoned now, leaving me free to set my stage. There are tshira spears bracketed to the walls. I take them down and scatter them across the floor. I do the same with the handful of swords left behind. I rip down the Virdeian banner on the wall and then tear it in two for good measure.

I drag my boots across the floor, leaving dark scuff marks. And, finally—the finishing touch—I smear a few streaks of dark red paint on the floor. A bit more on the walls. Coat it on the tips of a few spears.

When I'm finished, it tells the story I want: there's been a battle, and our defenses have been breached. When the sentries do their routine sweep of the gateposts, they'll find the most important one abandoned with signs of a struggle. Evidence that the guards stationed here fought valiantly and lost.

I wipe my hands against my pants and make my way to the sky cart to get back up the mountain to prepare. Today, Luc will be crowned Praeceptor of Virdei once more. All the pieces are perfectly aligned for me to take back all the power I've stolen for him. In this game of smoke and mirrors, I'm confident I'll win.

CHAPTER FORTY-SIX

CROWNING A FRAUD

My dress for the coronation is green, gold, and black. Sef picked it out for me. The emerald green makes me feel like I'm back in my Honorate robes, dressed for chamber. I feel powerful as I look at myself in the mirror. Regal. As if I am looking down on the rest of the world from a great height.

Sef knocks on my door. I run my hands over the front of my dress, smoothing it before going to greet her. She's here to do my hair before the start of the ceremony.

I grin as I open the door—but it isn't Sef on the other side.

My expression freezes.

It's a woman with dark eyes, dark hair, and my nose. A face I know as well as my own.

"A-Aja?" My voice trembles with shock. "What are you—" Realizing she's standing out in the hall where anyone could see her, I grab her arm and pull her inside. "What are you doing here?"

She doesn't answer right away. She looks me over, eyes swimming. She places one hand over her mouth, the other clenched over her chest.

I want to freeze this moment in time. The look on her face is one I haven't seen in seven years. A look I've longed for since I stole her memories and watched myself become a stranger to my own mother. Recognition. *Affection.*

My throat is suddenly clogged. I want to say something, but words are impossible, and all I do is stare at her.

Slowly, Aja reaches for my hand.

I let her take it with no resistance. She flips it over. A quivering finger glides over my tattoo. The first tear drips, landing on the golden sun. Her voice is hushed as she says, "You squeezed my hand so hard, I thought it was going to fall off." She looks up, meeting my gaze with a tenderness I've longed for. "But you didn't cry."

"You remember." I sound like I'm being strangled. I don't know when my own tears started, but my face is soaked, and I throw my arms around her. She's shorter than me now, but I sob into her chest as though I'm still that little girl who could fit in her lap.

"Mira." She whispers my name like a prayer. "My beautiful Mira."

My bottom lip trembles. I squeeze her tight, enjoying the lost sensation of being loved. "*Mom.*" I haven't called her that in seven years. It only makes me cry harder. "How are you here?"

She doesn't let me go. "After you left, I started having dreams. Today, I woke up and it all came back to me."

My most recent journey to Ophera was the first time I returned without clearing her memory. A foolish oversight. Seeing me again with no magic to temper her memories had consequences, but I have no regrets. I have a mother again.

Aja pulls away, only slightly, to run her hands over my face, my hair, my clothes. "You're so big," she says in awe. "And beautiful. You always were. But *look* at you in that dress. It's like that robe you used to wear. It was always too big for you."

I lean into her hand cupping my cheek. "You remember the robe?"

"I remember everything." Her watery smile slackens. "I missed you, Mira."

"You didn't know to miss me."

She shakes her head. "I *missed* you."

She's telling the truth, and it makes me sob harder.

There's a knock—Sef's signature rhythmic one. My eyes widen. I'd allowed myself to forget what today is, and all I have planned.

I swipe my eyes, trying to stop them from leaking. "Mom." I lower my voice to a whisper. "I need you to hide. Just for a moment."

She looks confused as I shuffle her toward the closet. I raise my voice to address Sef through the door. "Give me a second. Still getting into this dress."

"Do you need me to lace it up for you?"

"No. I got it." I open the closet and motion my mom inside. "It's just for a minute or two. Please stay quiet. I'll be right back."

She's so confused, she's stopped crying. Still, she nods in confirmation of my words as I shut the door.

I drag my hands over my face a final time, drying it as much as I can before letting Sef in.

She beams when she sees me. "It looks even better than I imagined. You are a vision. Ready for me to do your hair?"

"Thank you. I love it." I scramble for a way to get rid of her. "But I changed my mind about the hair. Do you think we could use those sparrow clips after all?"

Sef frowns. "You said you wanted—"

"I know, I know, but after seeing the dress on me, I really want those clips. If you don't mind. Please?"

Sef sighs. "Of course. I'll have to run and grab them. Give me five minutes?"

I hope my smile doesn't look as strained as it feels. "That's perfect. Thank you."

When she's gone, I let Aja out of the closet. "Sorry about that."

"It's all right. Are you going to introduce me to your friend?"

I wince. I want her here, with me, but today is Luc's coronation—the day the plan I've been putting in place for weeks culminates. I can't afford for anything to go wrong. Luc discovering I've been lying to him for years about my mother dying would ruin everything. "I love you, but no one can know you're here. Not yet. After today, I'll introduce you to everyone."

My mom's expression falls. "What are you saying? You want me to leave?"

"No. But I need you to. Just until after the coronation. Things are going to get complicated around here. But when it's over and the smoke clears, everything will be different. Better. I'll come for you then." When I've stolen the throne, Aja will come to live with me, here in Widow's Hall. Anyone who has a problem with it will have me to deal with.

The hurt expression on her face breaks my heart. "You don't need me anymore."

I hug her, squeezing with everything in me. "You have no idea how untrue that is." I give myself ten more seconds. Ten seconds of being loved unconditionally, before letting go. "I love you. More than anything. Just wait for me, all right? I'll see you tomorrow. Two days at the latest."

I usher my confused, brokenhearted mother out the door, sending her away with a silent prayer. I've barely finished sobbing when Sef returns. She's in a rush. "We're running late."

She sets her supplies on my vanity. "Now, let's get you ready to take over the world."

The chandelier in the ballroom sparkles white and gold today. It glances off the polished floors, the pearls around the coronation guests' throats, and the grease in Yelina's wig.

Chairs fill the space before the stage. Luc's parents sit in the first row. It's reserved for important guests, and the seats are cushioned in velvet. I made the seating chart myself. There's meant to be a third chair next to them, but it's filled.

I'm annoyed, and my stomach is already pooling with dread at having to deal with this, but I fix my expression to be impassive as I stand before them.

Yelina gives me her favorite sugary smile. "Sorry, dear. The organizers must have overfilled the front row by mistake." And then, because she loves nothing more than digging at me, she adds, "I'm so sorry. I was so looking forward to spending time with you." This is for her audience's benefit as much as it is mine.

I know she's lying. She knows I know she's lying. That's the fun of it for her.

Heat rises, from fury and magic alike. I force my temper to cool. Today, it's easier than ever to swallow my anger. For one thing, my real mother remembers me. For another, once my plans fall into motion, Yelina Kyler will eat her words. Choke on them, as I've had to do for years.

I give her my cheeriest smile. "Don't worry. My legs are a bit stiff, so I wanted to stand anyway. I only came over here to tell you that your wig is crooked."

She flinches, smile waning as she prepares a retort. I leave down the aisle before she thinks of one.

I watch the coronation from the back wall, amid other standing guests. Chattering quiets as Honorate Anleck steps onto the stage, followed by Luc.

In a typical Virdeian coronation, the reigning Praeceptor passes off a crown to his successor. It's a purely ceremonial gesture. The crown itself doesn't mean anything—we're not a monarchy like Petruvia—but we like to uphold traditions and call it decorum.

Since Luc is accepting the role of Praeceptor for a second term, Honorate Anleck is responsible for the passing of the crown.

Luc sinks into the green and gold cushioned seat on the stage—his throne. Anleck stands over him, holding the crown as he intones a series of platitudes about the importance of the role of the Praeceptor.

As he nears the end, he raises the crown higher. "Do you, Lucien Kyler, promise to uphold the values of this great Republic?"

Luc takes a breath. "I do."

"And do you, Lucien Kyler, promise to protect the people of Virdei from any and all threats, to the best of your abilities?"

"I do."

The ballroom is silent as Anleck begins to lower the crown. "With this, you are crowned the next Praeceptor of the great Republic of—"

The chamber plunges into darkness.

Anleck's words stall. The crowded ballroom erupts with startled whispers, but nobody moves.

It takes several moments for my eyes to adjust to sudden dim and gray. There are a few candles burning within the chandelier overhead, but the torches on the walls aren't lit, because the windows are wide and the turrets provide more than enough light in here.

At least, they did.

Now the beacons—the pillars that have lit this mountain for over a century—have been snuffed.

In the darkness, I can't see what's happening at the front of the room. As panic fills the ballroom, I dart into the aisle. I need to reach the stage—and Luc—before people begin to flee.

I'm halfway down the never-ending central walkway when the doors to the ballroom burst open.

A member of the decurio rushes inside. He holds a lamp, illuminating his frantic expression, and raises his voice, so it echoes around the chamber. "Widow's Hall is under attack."

CHAPTER FORTY-SEVEN

GIRL MADE OF SHADOWS

The audience is in an uproar. Whatever other announcement the soldier tries to make is lost to horrified shrieks. People leap from chairs and flood the walkway in their scramble for the ballroom doors.

I'm shoved in a dozen directions at once. There's a heavy thud as the doors slam shut, trapping us here. More people scream. The shoving in the aisle intensifies. The decurio lining the room try to herd people back to their seats, but no one listens.

I force myself through the throngs of terror, headed for the stage.

Unlike everyone else, my racing heart calmed with the decurio's announcement.

Virdei believes the Republic is under attack because they saw the remnants of the fake battle I staged at the Sulen gatepost.

I hadn't counted on the beacons going out, but this is merely the pieces of this game aligning themselves. Next I need to stoke the flames of panic and guide Luc to the trap awaiting him.

Manufacture a crisis, incapacitate Luc, force the Honorate in line.

Step one is complete.

By the time I fight my way to the front, my breaths have evened. I haul myself onto the platform and move behind the curtains.

Luc stands with Kaidren and the decurio who delivered the news. "What were you thinking?" Luc is uncharacteristically angry, yelling at the soldier. "Why would you announce something like that to the entire room? Were you trying to cause mass panic?"

"I'm sorry." The soldier ducks his head. "I thought the people had a right to know."

"Before the Praeceptor? Why was I not informed first? And why—"

He stops as the entire building rumbles.

"What was that?" Kaidren's head whips around, as though the source of the disturbance is in this room.

"Petruvia, sir," the soldier says.

At that, my steps freeze. I'm a few paces behind Luc, too stunned to move.

Luc gawks at the decurio. "What? Where is General Fain? Why is he not the one speaking with me?"

"General Fain is dealing with the invasion. Petruvia is *here*, sir. Right now. They attacked Widow's Hall and extinguished the beacons. The General is ensuring the entire building does not fall under siege. As of right now, we are officially at war."

I can't breathe. My throat is tight, and there's no air getting in. I'm the one who faked the attack to the Sulen gatepost—how the hell did Petruvia *actually* get here?

"If we're at war, we need to gather the Petruvians we have here at court." It takes everything in me for my voice to not tremble. "They're hostages now."

The soldier glances at me, then rolls his eyes, looking annoyed. "We can't do that."

"Why not?" I demand.

"Sir," he says to Luc, clearly intending to dismiss me. "Perhaps we can speak in private?"

Kaidren's expression darkens. "Answer her. *Now.*"

The soldier looks reluctant, but he can't ignore a direct order from an Honorate. "The Petruvians are missing. We checked their rooms as soon as this began. They and their bags are gone. They must have fled before the coronation."

It must've been those letters. Like the one I found in the Nights' fireplace. First the Opheran fields, now this. How many other war plans were discussed by mail that we missed?

"How did the Petruvian army even make it up the mountain? Don't we have security?" Kaidren asks.

"We're not sure how they got here without anyone knowing." The soldier looks nervous. "The Sulen gatepost was attacked. It guards the most direct path up the mountain. According to our sentry patrol, there were signs of a battle. Not that it should matter. As soon as they were attacked, those soldiers should have lit their torches, signaling that we were under attack. We're still not sure what went wrong."

I need details. "What signs of attack did the sentries find?"

The decurio answers my question but directs it at Luc without looking at me. "Weapons were discarded, there was blood everywhere, there were no signs of life, and there was a Petruvian flag hanging in the tower."

My heart clenches.

I didn't hang a Petruvian flag.

I convinced the guards to leave. I scattered weapons, spilled "blood," I even scuffed up the floor to make it look like there was a skirmish. But I never hung a flag.

Someone else swept through the gatepost I staged and actually gained access to the mountain.

I unwittingly created the perfect opportunity for sabotage. For our Republic to be sieged during the most important day of my life. Widow's Hall is actually under attack—and it's all my fault.

CHAPTER FORTY-EIGHT

ON MY HONOR

This is my fault, this is my fault, this is my fault . . .

The words rattle painfully around my skull, and I feel as if I'm drowning under the weight of guilt. My lungs are full, throat tightening from all the words I can't say.

"How are our defenses holding?" Luc asks. His voice sounds muffled, as if he's speaking from underwater, or from the other end of a tunnel.

It's my job to fix things, but I don't know how to fix this.

"We've sealed off entry into Widow's Hall, grounded all sky cart activities, and have teams of soldiers patrolling the rest of the mountain, but right now, it appears they're concentrating their attacks on Widow's Hall."

That's a relief, at least. So long as they're focused here, at the top of the mountain, civilians will be left unharmed. There's no way of knowing how long that will last.

My stomach flips violently as I think of my mother, headed back to Ophera less than an hour ago, and I have to swallow down bile. She made it back. She's okay. She has to be.

The curtains part, and Luc's parents enter the room. Mathson hurries over to us. "What the hell is going on?"

"Petruvia is attacking." Luc's voice shakes. "They're outside right now."

"*What?*" Yelina looks more shocked than I feel. "That's

impossible. How would they have gotten past our perimeter without us knowing? The Sulen gatepost is the most fortified on the mountain."

The decurio only shakes his head. "We don't know, ma'am. We've never experienced anything like this. Our focus now is making sure they don't gain access to Widow's Hall. We're in the process of gathering more soldiers to fight them off. But we're—"

"Wait." Alarm bells blare in the back of my mind as Yelina's words fully sink in. My thoughts are in frazzled disarray, but as I slowly turn to face her, a clearer image presents itself. "Yelina, how did you know they came in through the *Sulen* gatepost specifically? You just got here. No one told you that."

Luc frowns at me. "Mira, you aren't suggesting . . ." His sentence trails, and he laughs awkwardly. "Obviously, my mom had nothing to do with this."

"Then why isn't she answering the question?"

Luc opens his mouth, no doubt to defend her again, but his excuses on her behalf die with her prolonged silence. He eyes his mother with sudden wariness. "Mom? What is she talking about?"

For three seconds, Yelina stares at me, eyes slightly widened, lips slightly parted, before she scoffs. "It's the quickest way up the mountain, and Petruvia is to the east. Anyone with any knowledge of strategy would assume it's how they breached the perimeter."

I don't believe her for a second.

She hasn't lied—not technically—but her words are designed that way. Not speaking a direct mistruth, but still holding back from complete honesty. "Why do you know so much about battle strategy?"

"My son is the Praeceptor. My husband is a former Honorate."

Still not lying, but not directly answering my question either.

This situation is my fault, and I know it. I'm the one who ensured the Sulen gatepost was unguarded, but I suspect I'm not the only guilty party here.

I glance at the soldier who delivered the news. He's still here, looking uncomfortable. "Can you give us a moment?"

He's only too pleased to rush out of the room, not even pausing to ask Luc for instructions.

Kaidren makes to leave too, but I catch his sleeve, stopping him.

Shockingly, of everyone here, I trust him the most right now. But it's more than that. If there's to be war—if I'm to accuse my stepmother of starting it—I want him by my side.

Kaidren looks surprised, but with a nod, he stays where he is.

I look to Yelina. "That soldier said the Petruvians, who have been at our court for months, fled this morning. As if someone warned them."

"Or as if they knew the attack was coming. You're being absurd, Remira."

Still not directly denying my thinly veiled accusations. "What did you do? Did you tell Petruvia where to attack?" I can't believe Yelina would sabotage her son like this, especially on his coronation day. She's obsessed with Luc; she'd never do anything to jeopardize him or his reign.

Yelina's mouth flaps open and closed a few times, as if to answer me. Then, she purses her lips, saying nothing.

Her silence is the loudest possible action she could have taken.

Stars in hell, she really did it.

I'm not sure I've ever seen Mathson look so stunned. "Lina? This is ridiculous. Just say no."

"She can't," I say softly, still floored that I'm right. "It would be a lie."

Yelina's eyes flick to Kaidren.

"Don't worry about him," I say. "He already knows about me. Just answer the question: Did you tell Petruvia when and where to attack?"

Again, she says nothing.

Mathson and Luc look horrified. "Mom?" Luc says, panicked.

"You can easily prove me wrong," I say. "All you have to do is say you didn't do it. Just say no. One word, two letters."

Finally, she clears her throat. "How do I know *you* wouldn't lie? If I deny it, you'll tell them I'm lying and we'll just have to take your word for it."

I roll my eyes. There's an easy test for that. "Luc and I have been playing this game forever." I nudge Kaidren. "Will you get me an unlit torch? I'll ask her again. If she lies, I'll have magic to light it. If not, I won't be able to. Simple." I smirk at Yelina. "Unless you want to spare us the trouble now?"

She's glaring at me with more hatred than she ever has before. "Don't bother."

Luc staggers back as though she slapped him. "*You* led them here? On my coronation day? Why would you do that?"

I'm trying to figure that out myself. She loves Luc. Why would she want to ruin the biggest day of his life?

And *how?* They got through the Sulen gatepost because of me, but even before that, they needed to cross through Ophera without being detected by any Virdeian soldiers.

A feat only possible because Petruvia laid siege to the

eastern perimeter of Farvelle during the second trial, and because for the past few months, the Honorate has blocked any efforts to increase our presence on Ophera's border.

Suddenly, I feel so foolish I could scream.

The imposter Shadow Queen forced Selva Sixmen to block any order to increase security in Ophera. The imposter forced him to encourage *other* Honorate to block it as well. I assumed it was all Flynn's way of getting back at his father for murdering Neveah, but it was deeper than that.

"Flynn wasn't working alone," I say aloud. "You were his accomplice. You've been working for weeks to make sure Ophera wasn't guarded, and then you told Petruvia when and where to attack. You sabotaged your own son—"

"I didn't sabotage him," Yelina snaps. "Petruvia wasn't supposed to get this far."

"Why?" Luc demands.

"They were only supposed to breach our treaty. Sulen was supposed to be well guarded, so their soldiers would be easily apprehended. If they violated the treaty first and started a war, Virdei could draft a new one, with stricter limits."

"All this for the *treaty*?" Luc says.

"For war," Yelina corrects. "Every five years, we renegotiate that treaty to stave off war. But there are loopholes. We saw Petruvia exploit them—"

"Because of *you*," I say.

Yelina raises her voice, speaking over me. "There are flaws to treaties with terms that apply to a Praeceptor that changes every five years. Petruvia wants to negotiate with someone more stable—a king."

This was all for Luc. She wanted me framed for murder, and a crown for her son.

She was leading them into a trap, but they trusted her. She's

Petruvian, after all. Not to mention she'd already proved her loyalty by helping them take over Farvelle and weaken Ophera's borders.

"I already won the throne," says Luc.

"You won another five years in an impermanent role. Five years from now, you'll have to compete all over again. I'm talking about making you a king for *life*."

"Virdei is a Republic."

"We are a Republic in name only. We are basically already a monarchy with a rotating king."

Everything about her is vile, but in this one instance, she's right. The Republic only cares about appearances. Pretending the Honorate are good men; pretending the people's voices carry weight; pretending the role of Praeceptor is earned.

The truth is the Honorate are liars and thieves willing to do whatever it takes to keep their indiscretions out of the public eye. With the Honorate laws of succession, the people rarely ever vote for the men who represent them. And the Tournament doesn't ensure that the man on the throne is a worthy leader—just that he made a big enough spectacle to keep the people entertained.

"A new treaty, bound to a permanent king. One where we don't have to share control over Ophera or its resources. I was doing this for *you*." Yelina's voice is gentle, begging for Luc to listen. To understand.

"What about the part where you framed me for murder?" I snarl. "Was that for your son's benefit?"

Yelina stills. She doesn't deny it. She can't. She keeps her eyes on Luc, pleading with him to listen. "When I married your father, they told me he'd be Praeceptor one day and I'd be the wife of the most powerful man in the Republic. That never happened. I never got what I was promised, but my son will have everything."

"That wasn't my fault," I say.

But of course she'll never see it that way. Neveah Sixmen was Yelina's closest friend. Yelina wanted revenge on Selva for killing his wife, and revenge on me for existing. I'm the reason Mathson never became Praeceptor, as well as evidence that the husband she married as a trade agreement was unfaithful. She figured she'd take care of both her problems at once.

"You and Neveah were friends," I say. "You must've been furious when you realized she was murdered."

"Murdered?" Mathson glances between me and Yelina. "You're talking about Neveah Sixmen?"

"Yes." Yelina's back is rigid. "She was my best friend. Selva was an awful man and a cruel husband who made her miserable. Years ago, she had an affair with another Honorate."

I know who it is before she says it. "Arliss Vale."

"Yes. That was over twenty years ago. She always knew Flynn was his, but she never told anyone. Aside from me. She planned to protect that secret forever, but when Arliss got sick, she felt guilty for keeping his son from him. She was going to tell him." Yelina shudders. "But then she went missing. Selva learned the truth and killed her."

"When did you tell Flynn what happened?"

"I didn't. He figured it out on his own. He said he talked to some servant and put it together."

I draw in a sharp breath. Flynn must've spoken to Eduma. But why didn't she tell me?

She did. The realization is a smack in the face.

I use "Honorate Sixmen" and "Mister Sixmen" interchangeably—she didn't.

"Mister Sixmen came to see me last year. I thought I was finally getting out of here."

It wasn't Selva who came to see her. It was Flynn, his son,

who was slowly piecing it together. Like me, he questioned her about the day his mother disappeared and came to the same conclusion I did—that his father murdered his mother. Then he got to work getting even.

"Mom, you conspired to kill an Honorate?" says Luc.

Yelina shakes her head. "No."

I shove the magic toward her as soon as I feel it, scalding her. Yelina flinches and snaps a hand over her arm.

Luc's eyes fly to the red, raised skin. "You're lying."

She winces. "I didn't kill anyone. Flynn poisoned Arliss and forced Selva to resign from the Honorate. He planned to kill Selva too, but he wanted to destroy him first by taking him out of the Honorate."

"Why did he kill Arliss?"

Yelina's eyes narrow on Kaidren. "Because of him."

"Me?" Kaidren has been silently following the exchange with increasingly raised brows. "What does this have to do with me?"

"You're Opheran. After you announced yourself as Arliss's son, Flynn was worried Arliss would go hunting for another and figure out that he already had a Virdeian heir. If he had, he would have tried to claim Flynn instead of you."

"What does it matter? He's older than me. He's an Honorate either way."

"If everyone knew he was Arliss's son, he would be a bastard, he'd start his career on the back of a scandal, and he'd be the son of a lecherous adulterer. Where is the honor in that?"

I can't believe what I'm hearing. "All this to avoid a scandal?"

Yelina waves it off. "Arliss was already dying anyway."

I like Flynn. At least, I did. It's hard to think of him as someone so conniving and vain. But that's because I'm thinking of him as the brave soldier with the heart of gold. Like everyone else, I bought into the illusion. The truth is, he's an Honorate. As obsessed with honor and legacy as the rest of them.

Their plot might have worked. Except Yelina didn't count on me and Kaidren. If Kaidren hadn't found the shopkeep who proved Flynn guilty, her plan to frame me would've been successful. If I hadn't been plotting to steal a throne she wanted as a permanent fixture for Luc, Virdei would've easily countered Petruvia's attack.

I inadvertently ruined her plans, and she inadvertently ruined mine.

I take a heavy breath, trying to think. Petruvia is here, knocking on the doors to Widow's Hall, attempting to topple us. Unless we can find a way to end this war before it begins.

"What's Petruvia's goal, Yelina?" I ask.

She scowls at the floor, refusing to look at me. "To take over Virdei, obviously."

I nod slowly, processing our options. To do that, they'd want to kill as many members of the Honorate as they could. And the Praeceptor. They'll be desperate to find and kill Luc to bring Virdei to its knees.

I perk up as an idea comes to me. I know how we can stop this. "Someone get a member of the decurio."

"Why?" says Luc. "What are you thinking?"

"We need to convince the Petruvian army that you and all the Honorate are being secured in the arena."

"What will that do?"

"Lure them in so we can trap them inside," I say. "I have a plan. First, we're going to need tshira—a lot of it. Then we're going to need to gather as many people as we can in the ballroom."

CHAPTER FORTY-NINE

CARVED FROM ICE

The hall reverberates with the sound of harsh clangs. The chairs that once filled the ballroom have been shoved to the outskirts, making way for tables and servants.

Every staff member of Widow's Hall with hands to spare is here, pounding hunks of tshira with metal mallets into as fine a powder as we can manage.

My arm is already sore from the repetitive motion, but I can't stop.

Magic would make this easier. Most of the decurio are engaged in battle. But there are a few in here. A handful of aikkari with easy access to their sources are at a far table, reducing chunks of tshira to powder in seconds. But there aren't enough of them. Not for how much tshira we're going to need.

There's an unmissable air of panic in the hall, not helped by the war raging right outside our doors.

Every few minutes, Widow's Hall shudders with the force of Petruvian soldiers fighting to gain entrance.

The building shakes yet again.

People jump, and a few shout, but immediately after, there's a hush. We're all quiet, listening to see if they actually managed to get in this time.

My relief only lasts for a moment. With each blow to the exterior of Widow's Hall, Petruvia is more and more likely to break through. Sef works a few tables over with some of her friends from the staff. She's calm under pressure and despite the chaos and fear soaking the room, Sef's presence seems to soothe those around her.

Kaidren stands across from me. He's rolled up his sleeves to work, and I'd be lying if I said his exposed forearms weren't distracting. "It's a good plan." He brings down his mallet, smashing a chunk of tshira to bits. "It's going to work."

I swing my mallet faster. It's a good way to release frustration. "It has to."

As we speak, decurio ride out from the stables of Widow's Hall on greyback, pulling covered sledges. They're empty, but once they reach their destination, we will send a rumor through the Petruvian army that the Praeceptor and Honorate were taken into the arena for safety.

A decurio passes through, pushing a large wooden barrel. Kaidren and I scrape the tshira we've ground inside, and he moves to the next table.

I cast a quick glance around, ensuring there's no one within hearing distance. Even still, I lower my voice as I address Kaidren. "Aja was here."

His eyes widen. "You mean *here*, here? In Widow's Hall?"

"She came to see me before the coronation. She remembered everything."

He looks around. "Where is she?"

"I sent her back to Ophera." I swallow thickly. "There was too much going on today."

"When was this? Are you sure she—"

"She left almost half an hour before the start of the coronation, before Petruvia attacked. They didn't ground the sky carts until later. I'm going to check on her as soon as I can make it down the mountain," I say, and I try to will myself to feel as certain as I sound.

"When are you going to tell Luc?"

It's a good question. One I don't have an answer for just yet. I'm spared having to respond when I see my brother over Kaidren's shoulder. I purse my lips, saying nothing as he approaches.

Luc bends to whisper to me. "Good news. We've received word that several Petruvian soldiers are changing course for the arena. We're gathering all the tshira we have and taking it to the stables."

I glance around the room. Most everyone is still hard at work. "Are you going to make an announcement?"

"No. Let them keep at it. It's a good distraction. We'll tell everyone when it works."

If it works. None of us are brave enough to say it.

There are dozens of barrels of powdered tshira. While most of Widow's Hall stays in the ballroom, a group of us—Kaidren, Luc, members of the decurio, and myself—each take a barrel and carry them to the stables beneath Widow's Hall.

My limbs scream at me as I drag the heavy barrel, but I'm glad to have something to do other than sit in the ballroom, terrified we're going to lose.

General Fain is already in the stables, preparing transport for the tshira to the arena. Four greyhorns huff and stomp their feet, already attached to the sledge and raring to go. With a grunt, I lift my barrel onto the back of the vessel.

"Your only goal is getting this to the arena. By any means necessary," the General is telling three members of the decurio. "There are soldiers waiting on the roof. I don't care what's in your way—get this to them."

The building shudders again.

We freeze, breaths bated, waiting.

It doesn't sound like Petruvia has broken through.

Yet. It's a chilling thought. Made even more terrifying when I hear a shout from behind.

I spin around. Five soldiers enter the stables. They're wearing indigo, wielding swords, and their expressions are darkened with intent. They're Petruvian.

"Sir." The General shoves Luc behind him and the other decurio. "Get back to the ballroom." General Fain raises his weapon—a sharpened tshira blade. The three decurio with him draw their weapons as well.

My heart pounds as Kaidren and I press behind them. The Virdeians form a wall and launch themselves at the Petruvian soldiers.

Four Virdeians against five Petruvians. General Fain manages to fight two of them at once, but the Virdeians are outnumbered.

Their movements are so quick, I have trouble following. For every swing, there's a counter. For every move, a reaction.

A Petruvian feints right and swipes left—the decurio he's fighting isn't quick enough.

The decurio falls over. I'm not sure if he's dead, but he's immobile on the ground and can no longer fight.

Five Petruvians left, and only three Virdeians.

Fear creeps through my veins. I eye the sledge of tshira. It's already loaded, and the greyhorns are attached. It's ready to go.

"Sir—" General Fain grunts, addressing Luc as he sidesteps a blade from a Petruvian. "We've been breached. You need to get to safety. We can fend them off, but if anyone finds you, or worse, kills you . . ."

He doesn't finish, too busy fighting off soldiers, but he

doesn't need to. If the Petruvians kill Luc, the war will have ended, and Virdei will have lost.

That thought is horrifying enough on its own, but even more concerning—my insides are set alight. General Fain just lied. He doesn't believe Virdei can fight off these Petruvians.

My ears are ringing and my breaths are shallow with panic. I snatch Luc by the shoulders. "Go. Upstairs. Warn everyone in the ballroom that there's a breach in the stables, and get to safety. If you fall, Virdei falls."

Luc swallows but nods. He's trembling as he takes my hand, trying to pull me with him.

I plant my feet.

Luc stops. "What the hell are you doing?"

I look at the sledge again. Virdei is outnumbered. General Fain thinks we're going to lose, and the Petruvians in the arena aren't going to stay there forever. We won't have a second chance. If we miss this window of opportunity, all of this was for nothing, Virdei will be overrun by Petruvia, and it will be my fault.

"I'm going to transport the tshira to the arena," I say.

"*What?* No. Absolutely not."

I push the magic flowing through me from General Fain's lie into my bracelet. "I'm not asking."

Behind us, there's a grunt. A Petruvian just stabbed General Fain in the leg. He's still upright, but he's moving with a limp. We're running out of time.

"You're going to get yourself killed," Luc says.

"She won't," Kaidren says. "I'm going with her, and I'll make sure of it. I'm not going to let anything happen to her."

Luc ignores him. "I said no, Mira."

"We need to take care of Petruvia, and *you* need to not die. Those are the only things that matter right now. We don't have time to argue. Just trust me and get the hell out of here before you get yourself killed. Now, *go*." I shove him away and rush over to the sledge before he can stop me.

He shouts after me, demanding I turn around. Demanding I come with him to safety. I ignore him.

Kaidren reaches for a fallen sword. I don't think he has any idea how to use it, but it's the only weapon we've got.

I climb onto the bench behind the greyhorns, and Kaidren steps onto the front of the sledge.

My hands sweat beneath my gloves; more drips down my back. I take the reins, heart pounding so loudly, I hardly hear Kaidren call my name behind me.

"Yeah?" I put on my mask, trying to swallow my nerves and the overwhelming fear of failure.

"Please don't die."

"I'll do my best." My voice trembles. "And if *you* die, I'll find you in hell and make your afterlife miserable." With a deep breath, I tug on the reins and pat the side of the ox—and we're off, skidding out of the stables, headed for a battlefield of ice and an arena packed full of Petruvian soldiers.

CHAPTER FIFTY

PLAYING WITH FIRE

It is almost always the dark season in Virdei, so I'm used to gray skies and never seeing the sun. But without the beacons shining atop Widow's Hall, the mountain is dark and haunting.

Wind whines around us, rustling trees in the distance that I can't see. Wood creaks with the ever-shifting mountain breeze. And ringing above it all is the sound of stone clashing against metal as the kingdoms of Virdei and Petruvia go to war.

In the darkness, I can see only a few paces ahead, but I direct the oxen to move quickly.

Well, I try. They're stubborn and terrified, so they move at a slow trot, huffing anytime something appears suddenly in their path with the limited visibility.

There's a flash of metal ahead. I yank the reins to the left, urging the greyhorns to swerve.

They grunt as they reluctantly shift. The heavy sledge rumbles as we glide over the ice past a soldier. Now that we're passing her, I see she's in indigo—Petruvian.

Behind me, Kaidren cries out.

Metal slices the air, followed by a thud.

I tense, pulse picking up speed. "Kaidren?" My voice shakes as I call back to him.

"I'm fine." He's out of breath. As soon as he's spoken, the greyhorns stomp harder. The sledge shudders as we pass over something—another body.

I have no idea who we just trampled. Bile rises in my throat. I choke it down.

The arena isn't far from Widow's Hall, but the distance feels longer in the dark.

The greyhorns screech and stop. Just ahead is a cluster of soldiers. There are at least six—a blend of Petruvians and Virdeians—fighting. They swing weapons and shout, and I can't tell which side is winning.

A head twists toward us. A soldier in indigo charges in our direction.

The greyhorns are skittish. I pull at the reins, but they don't move.

Panic curdles my insides. I touch my skin to my tshira trinket, gathering magic. I kick at the sides of one of the oxen, and he jerks to the right.

The others follow suit.

We glide away, moving around the mass of soldiers.

I almost allow myself to be relieved. Until someone snatches my arm.

I scream.

"Mira!" Kaidren shouts my name.

The soldier who charged away from the battle has grabbed hold of my arm. He tugs, trying to rip me from the sledge.

I release a shriek as I slip from the bench.

I hear Kaidren on the sledge behind me, scrambling to get to me.

He's too late.

The greyhorns have slowed, and the Petruvian has me half pulled off the sledge. I dangle over the edge of the bench; one hand grips the reins as hard as I can, the other is being pulled by the stubborn Petruvian soldier alongside us.

I struggle to break free, but I'm stuck.

Kaidren appears on the edge of my periphery. He snatches my arm, trying to pull me back onto the bench. I feel as if I'm being ripped in half.

"Throw tshira at him!" I shout, voice strangled.

Kaidren hesitates. I see the indecision in his eyes. He'll have to let me go. I don't think I'm strong enough to stay upright on my own, but I don't see another option.

With a pained nod, Kaidren releases me.

My grip on the reins slips. For a terrible moment, I'm falling.

My fingers scrabble for anything to latch on to. They find purchase along the wooden bench. Splintered wood digs into my palms as I hold on as tight as I can. My arms strain.

I don't see the tshira flying through the air. Only hear as the Petruvian trying to yank me to my death sputters as he's hit with a face full of powdered tshira.

I shove every bit of magic in my chest toward him with a scream.

Flames ignite in front of me.

The soldier cries out, releasing me.

He falls into the snow.

I'm still fumbling, trying to get back onto the sledge.

Strong hands encase my waist, tugging me up until I'm resting on the sledge's bench, out of breath and slumped into Kaidren's side.

He's also panting. "You know, that's the second time I've saved your life."

"If we survive this, remind me to thank you."

I still haven't recovered my breath when the arena finally

comes into view. I exhale in relief as Kaidren and I leap off the sledge.

The massive double doors are half closed, revealing a glimpse of the chaos inside. A sea of soldiers in indigo, clamoring to get past a wall of decurio in white on the far end of the arena.

Though I can't see past them, I know they're guarding a covered sledge. It's empty, but the Petruvians don't know that. As long as they think there's something worth protecting inside, they're distracted.

A decurio waits at the base of the stairs outside the arena. She leaps to attention when she sees us. "Finally. Is this the tshira?"

"As much as we could get."

"We're taking this to the roof. Close the doors. Don't let anyone out." She reaches for a medallion around her neck and flashes it at us.

My breath mists the air as Kaidren and I step behind the arena doors. They stretch up nearly as high as the arena itself, made of thick wood and reinforced with steel.

I press my hands to my door and brace my feet in the snow. I meet Kaidren's eyes. In them, I see my same fear, my same doubt, my same determination. We nod.

Anxiety is a hole in my stomach, draining me of any and all feeling. I grunt as I shove the door.

The wood groans until, with a rumbling thud, they close.

Footsteps pound inside like low thunder. Hundreds of soldiers rush to the entrance, bashing against the wood, trying to see why the hell they're being barricaded inside.

We loop metal chains through the door handles and secure them with a padlock.

The doors are locked, and our enemies are trapped inside.

As the Petruvian soldiers hammer futilely, trying to burst out, the Virdeian decurio still inside are racing for the equipment rooms at the base of the stands to hide.

The windy night air fills with the drizzling sound of rainfall. It takes me a second to place what it is—tshira. Barrels and barrels of it falling from the skies, pouring on the soldiers in the arena.

I don't want to hear what comes next.

I take Kaidren by the arm and pull him toward the greyhorns. He doesn't fight me. We're climbing aboard the bench behind the oxen when it starts.

Screams.

Hundreds of bloodcurdling screams, loud and terrified, shaking me to my core.

It's the most horrifying thing I've ever heard. And it was my idea.

The contents of my stomach roil. My knees shake as I lean over and throw it all up.

A few weeks ago, I'd never seen someone die. Throughout the Tournament, I've watched several deaths. And now . . . I'm causing them. Hearing the agony I created.

Kaidren rubs circles into my back. "Are you all right?"

"No." I wipe my mouth with my sleeve and take the reins. I don't need comfort. I need to get out of here.

I can't bear to listen to this.

We don't speak as I begin to steer the sledge back to Widow's Hall. It's still so dark, I can barely see ahead of me.

Until the flames rise.

Orange firelight burns through the now-open dome of the arena.

In the newfound light, I see Widow's Hall, still standing; the scattered remnants of a battlefield; a few homes with shattered windows; and blood streaked across the snow.

The screams continue. The fire in the arena burns on, so brilliantly it's as if the beacons atop Widow's Hall are lit once again.

CHAPTER FIFTY-ONE

EVERY LIE I'VE EVER TOLD

There are no survivors.

Hours after the flames have subsided and the screams have died, decurio continue to sift through the wreckage. There are no signs of life.

The only Petruvian soldiers who made it out of the invasion with their lives were the ones not in the arena. They fled down the mountain once they heard the screams. We later received word that they took hostages as they ran—their only leverage in the war they just started.

It takes two days for the sky carts to work again. In that time, I help Luc with damage control. We assess the number of fallen Virdeian soldiers, take inventory of how much tshira we used in the invasion, and prepare medical units to tend to the wounded. All soldiers. So far, there have been no reported civilian injuries.

As soon as the sky carts are working again, Kaidren and I take one to the base of the mountain. To Aja.

Except when I knock on her front door, heart sitting in my throat, she doesn't answer.

A foreboding chill crawls up the back of my neck.

We try asking around, but those in neighboring houses all have the same story: They haven't seen Aja in three days. Since the invasion.

Kaidren tries to comfort me. He hugs me and murmurs meaningless assurances in my ear as we return to Widow's Hall. I ignore him.

I saw Aja the morning of the invasion. I sent her away. She was supposed to return to Ophera so I could find her later. She didn't. Kaidren means well, but I know what her absence means, even if he can't admit it.

She never made it down the mountain.

I storm into Luc's office.

"Mira." Luc gives me a disapproving frown. He sits across from General Fain. They both look up, shocked at the intrusion. "I'm in the middle of a meeting."

"It's an emergency. General, can I speak with you?"

They exchange looks.

For a moment, I think Luc's going to refuse, but when he meets my gaze and *really* looks at me, his expression shifts from irritated to concerned. He nods.

I shift my wild, frantic eyes to General Fain. "When were the sky carts grounded during the invasion?"

He tilts his head to the side, confused by the question. "Just before the coronation."

It takes about an hour to get down the mountain. Aja was in my room half an hour before the carts were grounded. "What about any carts already in the air?"

"I think they were brought back to Widow's Hall. The passengers were taken to safety here."

"You *think*?"

He raises his brows, no doubt not appreciating my harsh tone. "That's what they were instructed to do."

I want to be relieved, but I'm not. If Aja was in a sky cart and brought back to Widow's Hall, we would have found each other by now. "Did you hear anything about any Opherans during the invasion?"

"Just you, Miss Kyler," he says dryly. "You're the only Opheran who lives in Widow's Hall, and the only one invited to the coronation."

I already know this. "Were there any Opheran civilians found outside?"

"No. Any civilians outside above the Collar were brought into Widow's Hall for protection."

The panic I fought so hard to keep down rises now. Aja wasn't brought into Widow's Hall during the attack. Of this, I'm certain. "What if someone was caught outside Widow's Hall? What if they were never brought inside?"

"I'm not sure. It's possible they took refuge in a nearby home. Or perhaps were taken hostage. We haven't sorted out who is missing yet. Or . . ." The General stops.

"Or what?" But I already know what he's thinking.

"Or it's possible they were swept into the arena."

I heard those screams. I watched those flames.

The memory will forever haunt my nightmares. The thought of my mother's voice being among them is too horrifying to contemplate.

"Mira?" Luc is watching my expression. "What's wrong?"

"I need to speak with you," I say quietly. It's my only defense against the pressing urge to wail. "Privately."

This time, he doesn't hesitate. He politely excuses the General and motions for me to sit across from him.

I don't.

"The Opheran I was asking about is Aja."

"What?" Luc couldn't look more stunned if he tried. "Aja is dead."

"She's not." I can't look at him. "I lied."

"What the hell, Mira?" He's on his feet, coming closer to me. "Why would you lie about something like that?"

"We were dying." My throat burns, so my words are a croak. "She was going to starve."

"You didn't have to lie. Not to me."

I want to laugh at the absurdity, but he's not joking. "Do you honestly think your father would have even considered taking me in if he didn't think she was dead? Would *you*?"

"Of course I would." He speaks fiercely, but as soon as the words are out of his mouth, he winces. "I would have tried."

"Until your father inevitably refused and you rolled over and let it go. Like you always do." My eyes are stinging with angry, bitter tears. "You only agreed to take me in because you thought I had nothing. Anything more than that, and you'd have let me rot."

"Mira—"

"Don't. Don't pretend you care."

He comes closer. He wants to hug me, I can tell, but he resists. Instead, he puts a hand lightly on my shoulder. "You're my sister. Of course I care."

Maybe it's because I'm tired. Or maybe it's because I've cried so much in the past week, I'm bereft of tears, and all that's left is anger. Or maybe it's because I think my mother might be dead, and I think it might be my fault, and I've never hated anything as much as I do myself right now. Whatever the reason, for the first time, I let myself glare at my brother and speak my mind. "Oh, sure. You care. You care when you need something. You care when it suits you. But when I ask you for anything, I am *always* on my own."

Each word out of my mouth makes him flinch, but I've only just started.

"My entire life has revolved around *you*. Getting you whatever you need. Preparing you for whatever you can't handle on your own. But anything I ask of you that requires you to be uncomfortable, you refuse."

He looks more wounded than he has a right to. "I said I was sorry."

"Which time are you talking about? It happens *all the time*. You constantly leave me to fend for myself. What makes it worse is that I know you. You are *kind*. You're kind to strangers. You're kind when you need to be firm. But when it comes to me, there's never anything left."

Luc's hand slips from my shoulder, as if he can sense how useless and empty the gesture is. "It's not because I don't care. It's because you're strong. You've never needed me to defend you."

I laugh harshly.

It's what Aja said, right before she left. *"You don't need me anymore."*

It's not true. I've needed a mother like I've needed a brother. "You think I *like* fighting my own battles? I do it because I have to. Because you never did."

Luc's eyes shine with unshed tears. "I begged him to take you in. Before I even met you. As soon as I knew you existed, I wanted to be your family. Dad refused. You're right, I should've fought harder. I wish I did. But when I learned that you'd come here saying Aja had died, and he threw you out, I threatened him. I told him I'd tell anyone who listened about the bastard child he left to die in the streets, and it would cost him everything."

I've never heard this part of the story. I wish I cared. "Do you want me to thank you?"

Now he does hug me. "You don't have to thank me," he says into my hair. "Just talk to me. Tell me what you need."

I swallow. "Aja came to see me before the coronation. I sent her away. She would have been in a sky cart when the invasion started. She either burned in that arena, or she was taken hostage."

Luc looks uncomfortable. "There's a third option. You don't want to hear this, but—"

I stop him before he can finish the thought. "She's not dead."

"Mira." His voice is aggravatingly soft. He means it to be gentle, but all I hear is condescension. "There was a war. People died."

I move away from him. "There weren't any civilian deaths."

"Not yet. But we're still looking."

My eyes harden. "She's *not* dead. I'm going to find her."

Luc pauses for several seconds. I watch a thousand considerations flit through his mind. He wants to argue, but he must see the futility because finally, slowly, he nods. Doubt lingers in his expression, but it's joined by resolve. "Then let me help. You don't have to do this alone."

He's being earnest, but we've done this dance before. I fold my arms. "We'll search in Virdei first, but if that doesn't work, I'm looking farther. Even if she's in Petruvia," I say. "You either agree to help me no matter what, or you don't. But if you agree, I'm going to hold you to it. No half measures this time."

He wants to object. As of two days ago, we're at war with Petruvia. Finding Aja there will be nearly impossible without bloodshed. But he just told me I'm not in this alone, and he can't break his word so quickly. He swallows. Then nods, slowly. Reluctantly. "Whatever it takes."

"You promise me?"

"I swear. I won't let you down again." He must read the doubt in my expression because with a soft smile he says, "Do you trust me?"

It's the first time he's ever asked that of me. The truth is, I don't trust him, and he shouldn't trust me. He still doesn't know that I caused the invasion, or that his apologies have come too little, and far too late. Or that even now, I'm plotting ways to take the throne from him.

None of that matters. To find Aja, I'll need the unwavering support of the Praeceptor of Virdei. So, I smile and say, "With every lie I'll ever tell."

"Then we're golden. If she's alive, we're going to find her."

I hug him. All the while thinking of all the secrets I've yet to tell him. And all the ones I never will.

ACKNOWLEDGMENTS

Books aren't created in a vacuum. They require the support of a team, and I've been very fortunate to have so many amazing people in my corner. *To Steal a Throne* was a labor of love and I can't thank those who helped shape it into what it is enough. First, thank you to my parents for their unwavering love and support over the years throughout my publishing journey.

To every single person who played a role in this book's creation: thank you for everything! I owe so much gratitude to Naomi Davis and Camille Kellogg who played an integral role in this story's creation. Thank you both for truly *getting* this story, and for letting me flail around as I got this story idea off the ground. Thank you for every response to my frantic emails and for always being open to brainstorming with me. This book wouldn't be what it is without you.

Massive thanks to my agent, Maddalena Cavaciuti, for all your enthusiasm and support. Thank you to the entire team at Bloomsbury! I owe a special thanks to my editor, Meghan McCullough, who came into this project later in the process and hit the ground running with endless love for this story. It's been a dream working with you!

Thank you to editorial director Sarah Shumway, who helped me navigate change and cheered me on every step of the way. Thank you to my publisher, Mary Kate Castellani; Oona

Patrick, Laura Phillips, and Nicholas Church in production; Jeanette Levy in design; Briana Williams and Erica Barmash in marketing; Lex Higbee, who has been the most amazing publicist to me for three years; Alona Fryman in marketing design; Andrew Nguyen and Jennifer Choi on the rights team; Sarah Rucker, Allie Ludlow, Mary Joyce Perry, Valentina Rice, Valerie Esposito, Holly Ruck, Valerie Burke in sales, with an *extra* special thank-you to Michelle Zeng; Beth Eller in school and library; and Ashleigh James in audio. Thank you so much, everyone, for all that you do behind the scenes to make books!

I personally have no artistic vision whatsoever, so I'm eternally grateful to the incredibly talented Elena Masci who illustrated this absolutely stunning cover, and Sara Corbett who illustrated the map. Thank you both for bringing so many elements of this story to life.

To Steal a Throne is lucky enough to have support in the UK as well. Thank you so much to the team over at Rock the Boat for all that you do! Special thanks to my fabulous editor, Katie Jennings, whose enthusiasm for this book means the world to me. Thank you also to Dannie Price, Rowan Jackson, Rob Wilding, and Mark Rusher in marketing and publicity; Paul Nash and Laura McFarlane in production; Francesca Dawes and Julian Ball in sales; Hayley Warnham in design; and Kobe Grant on the editorial team. Thank you all!

One of the best parts of publishing is the friendships I've made along the way. I've met some of my favorite people in the world through publishing. Thank you to Emily Emmett, Eliza Luckey (and Lucy, who is an honorary team member), Amanda McBride, Joan Reardon, and Karen Sapiro.

Thank you to my friends in the Lit Squad for being absolute menaces. To Camille Baker, Bethany Baptiste, Sami Ellis, Elnora Gunter, Jas Hammonds, Allegra Hill, Deborah Kabwang,

Avione Lee, Britney Lewis, Shauna Robinson, and Melody Simpson: thank you for keeping me close to sane.

There are too many friends in the writing community to thank you all, but so many authors have touched my life and I'm grateful for all the support I've received over the years.

To Steal a Throne wouldn't exist without early assistance from lovely readers. Thank you to Rachel, Tasha, and Irina for reading *very* early versions of this book and giving feedback.

I was blessed with the most *amazing* street team for the release of my last book, *Drown Me with Dreams*. I still can't believe the enthusiasm and support y'all showed me leading up to the release of my sophomore book. Thank you so, so much to Maki, Nelly Alapnes, Brandie Bridges, Philly Chung, Phylicia Cooper, Liliana Foy, Sarah-Elizabeth Hughes, Loren Lawrence, Lucy Watson, and Jordyn Wilder. Words can't express how much I appreciate each of you. And an extra special thank-you to Amber Jefferson for truly going above and beyond!

Finally, a heartfelt thank-you goes out to my family. Especially my grandma Burton for handselling my books harder than anyone I know (hospital is a wild place to plug my books, but I'm grateful!). Thank you to my entire family for years of being my biggest supporters.